THE HOUSE ON SEVENTH STREET

KAREN VORBECK WILLIAMS

"Nancy, every place you go, it seems as if mysteries just pile up one after another."
—Carolyn Keene, *The Message in the Hollow Oak*

"The life of the dead is placed in the memory of the living."
—Marcus Tullius Cicero

Booktrope Editions
Seattle WA 2015

Cover Design by Rhianna Davies

This is a work of fiction. Names, characters, places, brands, media, and incidents are either the product of the author's imagination or are used fictitiously. Any resemblance to similarly named places or to persons living or deceased is unintentional.

Print ISBN 978-1-5137-0210-0

EPUB ISBN 978-1-5137-0252-0

Library of Congress Control Number: 2015911450

For Bette, my mother

Acknowledgments

A huge debt of gratitude goes to Marcia Ford. Writing a book is a solitary task until the manuscript is ready for an editor. You hope your editor will care about your work as much as you do. Marcia did, and for that alone, I can't thank her enough. To editor Angie Kiesling, thank you for your good-natured mad dash to the deadline for the BEA. Lee Rudolph, I truly appreciate that you mounted a white horse and came to my rescue. During the long life a book has on the road to publication, editor Laurel Busch appeared as a gift. I am grateful to her and my Booktrope team. Thanks also to my agent, Carolyn Jenks, who is brilliant and tends to lead with her heart. I happen to be lucky enough to have two highly talented family members who have also contributed to the success of this book. David Ragsdale and Meredith Rubin, you are and always have been the lights in my life and a real help to me. Architect Bruce Landenberger kindly agreed to draw the floorplans for the house. Thanks, Bruce. The Nancy Drew mysteries I enjoyed as a kid inspired this book. Carolyn Keene—with all "her" many faces—not my schoolteachers, taught me that reading could be fun.

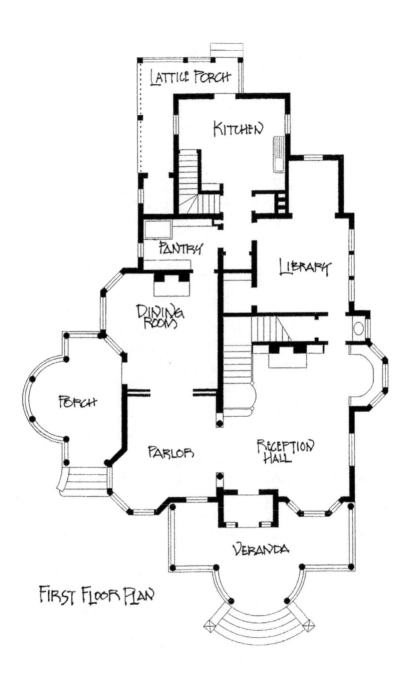

Lattice Porch

Kitchen

Pantry

Library

Dining Room

Porch

Parlor

Reception Hall

Veranda

First Floor Plan

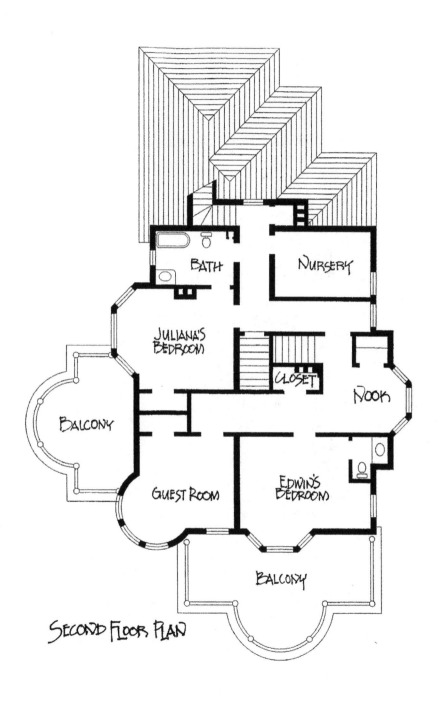

BATH

NURSERY

JULIANA'S BEDROOM

CLOSET

NOOK

BALCONY

GUEST ROOM

EDWIN'S BEDROOM

BALCONY

SECOND FLOOR PLAN

Prologue

October 1998

NEVER IN THE HISTORY of the old house on Seventh Street had anyone locked the kitchen door. A locked front door was caution enough in Grand Junction. One October morning, Henry Grumman opened the door, stepped out into the sunshine, and shuffled toward the '86 Cadillac in the driveway. It was Sunday, time for his weekly drive.

He opened the car door and settled in the driver's seat, then backed down the drive away from the old house where he was born. Heading south, he drove through a neighborhood that had not changed in fifty years. For Henry Grumman, sights in town had never lost their appeal. He welcomed the old streets leading to old parks, public buildings, stores, and his favorite, the railroad station with its fine brick depot built when he was a boy. Of the people he had known over his lifetime, most were now dead or had moved away. In Henry's memory, they still lived in the houses and worked at the stores. These days he was just a little forgetful, just a little more comfortable in the past than the present.

This Sunday he wanted to visit Unaweep Canyon and drove south out of town into the desert. Whitewater and the mouth of the canyon were only fifteen miles away. He remembered the stories his father had told about the early days, when there was nothing here but desert—just brown tracks through the dry white lakebeds. Back then, timbers were left alongside the way for stranded travelers to lay over a flooded wash or a sink of mud. Folks depended upon that and the blanket and water they carried in the trunk. If there was trouble, a car might have to wait for hours before another car came along. There was no need for that now. He felt pride in the progress made, grateful for the ease with which he now traveled.

Henry turned right at State Road 141 and soon entered the canyon. He slowed and rolled down his windows. How fresh and green the air smelled! He looked up at red canyon walls to his right and across the divide to the other side, the colors muted and misty through highflying dust in the air.

Over the years, he had come to Unaweep Canyon with his first wife, Nora. She had loved the canyon. Nora was an artist, the mother of his daughters, a beautiful woman he had married in 1937. They had twenty-three years together before her fatal heart attack. She always brought a lunch and a sketchpad along. He brought his camera and they would stay all day walking trails or just sitting and taking in the view, hardly talking. He had kept all her paintings and drawings and still thought about her every day.

Alongside State Road 141, the colors of fall had come on. Shrub oak and skunk brush glowed red, tall grasses flamed gold against low spreads of straw colored cheat grass, weathered sagebrush stood gray and dusty green. In spring, the canyon floor held green meadows and patches of wild blue lupine. In time for Henry's visit, the aspen and cottonwood trees had turned yellow below the dark shaded cliffs—and above everything a piercing blue sky. He came here because he felt like he was part of the cliffs and distant views—like the way he felt he was part of the town. He was more at home here than he had ever been in the rooms on Seventh Street, and not since his wife, Nora, had he felt part of another human being.

Once, Nora had told him what the Indian word "unaweep" meant. He tried to remember.

Though he had wanted sons, Nora had two daughters. He had not known how to be a father to them. He would have known with sons. He would have taught them the business, taken them fishing, and to ball games—maybe even played catch in the driveway. His daughters were both very pretty girls. He was glad of that, but he hadn't known how to talk with them, or what went on in their heads. He didn't know what to teach them—except for correcting their childish English and making them put their napkins in their laps. Later he taught them how to waltz and foxtrot.

Looking back on the past to his failures made him uncomfortable, but sometimes those things rudely pushed into his mind and before he knew it, he would linger there for a time. Henry knew he had not been much of a father to those girls. He regretted that.

He turned left on a dirt road heading toward cliffs formed of granite and large Dakota sandstone blocks. The road would take him up to the overlook—the place he liked to sit and watch the clouds roll in. From that spot, he could see illimitable space stretching west to Utah and onward.

The old Cadillac bumped along the dusty road following the curves of the foothills and the crevices in the canyon walls. From a distance, the cliffs appeared as a solid face, but up close there were openings, gorges carved through the ages by streams and wind. The road took him there.

Canyon with two mouths, he remembered. That's what "unaweep" means.

The road narrowed, becoming steeper and more twisted as he pushed his old car over imbedded stones and deep ruts. She groaned and whined, her wheels spun in loose gravel, and he gave her more gas. He had sat in the driver's seat since he was twelve. Henry knew how to maneuver a car over rutted roads. The car responded to him. Master of this day's adventure, Henry rolled up his window to keep out the dust and the road wound higher, above a deep ravine.

Henry was beginning to think he had taken the wrong road. He did not remember driving so long on such a rough road to his favorite overlook. He could see a dry creek bed far below and the road was so bumpy that he wanted to turn around and go back. This was not the road he knew.

Henry pushed the car on, looking for a place wide enough to turn around, but if anything, the road narrowed. Pushing on, he felt the undercarriage hit hard against a stone in the road. He bounced in his seat, his head almost hitting the ceiling. Still no turnaround. He gave it the gas and felt something rip from below. The car gasped and came to a stop. Smoke came from under the hood and soon flames.

Henry quickly opened the door and looked straight down at a deep ravine. There was no place to put his feet on solid ground. Something was on fire. He could smell it. Struggling to breathe, his heart pounding, he scrambled over to the passenger door. Fire licked up the hood. Flames darted toward the windshield.

Henry tumbled out to the road. The intense heat forced him to his knees. Aware that he had better get as far away from the car as he could, he grabbed onto a sapling growing between the rocks above his head and struggled to his feet.

No longer fast on his feet, Henry felt his heart beat, his lungs clamp down as he tried to run up the road. Fighting for each breath, his legs like water, he hoped he would not fall. The very moment that hope came to mind, he felt his right ankle twist and he stumbled. His hands reached out to break his fall. His wrists crumbled from the weight of his body and he fell on his face, crushing his glasses.

Raw fear propelled him to his knees. He pulled up and looked back over his shoulder. The whole car was in flames. Henry tried to stand, but his ankle would not hold him. He crawled until his knees were bloody and he could no longer feel the heat of the fire. He turned for a look in time to see and hear the explosion.

As if he had come to the end of a long race, Henry pulled himself up on a flat rock at the edge of the ravine. Still struggling to catch his breath, he looked toward what was left of the burning car. Sparks flew and bits of flaming debris floated down to the parched streambed.

He looked out over the canyon to the distant cliffs and off to the west, to the endless mesas and mountain rises, and a sky of drifting clouds. Henry knew he could not walk out of there. There was little chance that he would be found. This was the place where he would die.

He thought of his daughters, remembering that he had left them a fortune. They would want for nothing.

Henry looked out over the view he loved so well knowing that tonight he would see the sun set and fall away, leaving him alone in the dark.

1

June 1999

WINNA JESSUP PARKED outside the old house on Seventh Street and slowly got out of the car. She turned to look past the circular drive to the lawns and how the house rested in what was left of the gardens. Wondering if there had ever been a time when the sight of her grandparents' house did not excite her, she stopped a moment to study the eighty-seven-year-old frame structure, its tall windows, its turret with the bell dome, and the carved garlands under the eaves. Except for the remaining curls of white paint, the trim lay nearly bare; the house's once gray-green paint had faded to chalk and was peeling. Winna thought it looked like Dickens' vision of Miss Havisham's moldy wedding cake.

She turned to the broad street and the sidewalk. Winna and her sister had played hopscotch and jacks on the neighborhood's smooth sidewalks. Now, more than fifty years later the pavement was cracked and heaved up by tree roots, a sight that made Winna feel old. Wondering if little girls still played sidewalk games, she thought back to her daughter's childhood. Had Emily? She couldn't remember.

Shaded by towering trees, Seventh Street was home to imposing old houses settled in like becalmed ships in a green sea of
well-nourished lawns. Most of the houses, in random architectural
styles, were built within the first twenty-five years of the twentieth
century. Seventh Street had always been the right address.

First Winna wanted to look at the gardens where so many happy
childhood memories took root. Stepping through ankle deep lawn,
she approached her grandmother's rose garden, once the most
formal part of the landscape. The ornate cast-iron birdbath still
stood at the center of the cross-path. How strange, she thought,
someone has recently edged the beds.

When she was a child, the garden's neat grass paths running
along the mounded beds of roses had been her favorite place to
play. Standing there in its ruins, Winna remembered how important that garden had been to her. With their dolls, she and her sister
Chloe had pretended that the paths were rooms. She and Chloe had
hidden behind fragrant rose walls during a game of hide and seek
with neighborhood friends. Most days they played alone, spending
all day in the garden. When their grandmother called, they would
run to the summerhouse where lunch waited.

Winna's grandmother and the rose garden had declined together
and after her death, it fell into ruin. Her father, Henry, who had
lived in the house the last twenty years of his life, wasn't a gardener.
All but the red rose still climbing over the summerhouse had long
since disappeared.

The birdbath had not changed, held as it was by a slender lady
whose iron arms cradled it at her waist. It was empty, the bowl
encrusted with the dust of dried algae. A sudden breath of wind
rustled the leaves in the trees across the lawn, bringing Winna a
memory. Her grandmother had given her the job of keeping the
birdbath filled with water.

Dropping her handbag on the lawn, she made her way to the
hose coiled neatly by the house and returned to wash out the dirt.
The water rose in the basin and the sun danced in its ripples, evok-
ing her little sister's fingers splashing and stirring the water.

"Please let me do it," Chloe said.

"No, you can't. Gramma said you can't because you left the hose running. You wasted water." Even then, she knew that Chloe wished she was old enough to do all the more grownup things Winna could do.

Winna turned for a look at the old house again. Two summers ago, she had made her last visit to see her father. At the time, the house seemed to need a paint job, but now it appeared in terrible decline. She returned the hose to its coil and walked to the front of the house, looking toward the pillared verandah, up to the second story topped by a large attic with prominent dormer windows. In one, a shadow seemed to beckon. She smiled to herself and thought again of her grandmother Juliana.

Bordered by tall etched-glass panels, the grand front door loomed above the steps to the verandah. *How gloomy the old place looks. They are all gone.* Winna was stopped for a moment by the thought that her generation would be the next to die.

Digging into her handbag, she climbed the stairs, laid her hand on a long ornate key, and slipped it easily into the keyhole. The door gave way to a gentle push and Winna stepped into a narrow vestibule leading to the large reception hall.

The moment she opened the door, a blast of heat overcame her. The reception hall and the parlor looked lifeless and smelled of decay. Bracing herself, her face brushed by a spider's web. Faded walls seemed to sigh, exhaling dust as she hurried to open the windows. Harsh sunlight slanted in through the hall and parlor, casting shadows across the floors, igniting the dust particles she stirred as she moved through the overheated rooms. In that light, everything looked callously abandoned and lonely. What had once seemed opulent and antique now looked shabby, neglected. Winna fought tears as she struggled to throw open the windows, but they had been nailed shut. Again she thought of her father, wondering what had possessed him.

Her father had disappeared the previous fall. For six terrible months, she and Chloe had wondered what had happened to him.

From New Hampshire, her frequent calls to her sister were fruitless. Chloe had no news. With the snowmelt had come the spring hikers, one of whom found Henry's body—food for mountain lions. After his funeral and burial in the family plot, Winna returned to her home in New Hampshire. It took several weeks to rearrange her schedule, pack up her car, and drive over two thousand miles back to Grand Junction to finalize his estate and put the Grumman family home on the market. Everyone said she should fly, but Winna was in no hurry. She had accepted a job photographing the Dakotas, a history piece in *American Roads*. A fine art photographer, she had not done photojournalism in a long time and jumped at the chance. Eager to return to her home and her work in the East, she planned to stay in Colorado only as long as it took to settle her father's affairs.

Winna was not prepared for what she found in the old house that day. In May, when she had flown in to arrange for her father's funeral, she had stayed with an old school friend. The overpowering smell and heat of long pent-up rooms, the specter of draped spiders' webs everywhere, the refrigerator now a morgue for leftovers, drove Winna out of doors, back to her car.

The house has been shut up for eight months. What on earth did I expect?

Exhausted and surprised by the sudden realization that she could not spend a single night in that house, Winna turned up the air-conditioning in her car and drove to a downtown motel. She picked up the phone in her room and called her daughter, Emily, to tell her she was in town. "I'll see you tomorrow," she promised.

Right now, she needed a bath, a light dinner, and a bed.

Heading for the shower, she wondered why she suddenly felt afraid of what had always been her favorite house. Why, after looking forward to coming back to the town where she was born, did she want to go home? Yes, there was grueling work ahead, but something about the house unsettled her.

2

STOPPING WORK FOR A MOMENT, Emily turned from the jumbled closet for a look at the reception hall, its spacious alcove decorated with an ornate mosaic tile floor, the antique cast-iron fireplace set with painted tiles, and the window nook overlooking the rose garden. Here, the tall windows filled the room with light through a pattern of clear leaded-glass panels bordered with stained-glass medallions near the top. The whole effect was one of gentle opulence.

Wondering what it would cost to build a house like this today, Emily walked to the middle of the alcove where rose and green patterns of light filtering in through the stained glass washed over her. Quite aware that she felt like playing, dancing in the colored light like she had as a child, she laughed at herself and went to the window for a look. The rose garden's newly edged beds stood starkly defined against the unmown lawn. Someone had been working there.

"Mom," she called, "come here."

"Just a second."

"Who's been working in the rose garden?"

Winna appeared at her side. "I don't know. I noticed that when I first arrived. With all the work that needs doing around here I guess I won't complain."

With her mother's return to the house, Emily hoped that she might want to stay in Grand Junction. She had so many memories of the old house and her grandfather, not all of them pleasant. Almost every morning since her mother's arrival, she had driven into town from the foothills of Pinyon Mesa to help with the sorting, packing, cleaning—whatever was on the list. Her mother's open affection, and obvious delight in her six-month-old daughter, Isabelle, pleased her. Ever since her husband, Hugh, had accepted the managing editor's job at the *Daily Sentinel* and they had moved to Grand Junction, she had fantasized that her mother would come back to live in the town where she was born.

Following her arrival at the house on Seventh Street, Winna's first project had been working windows. Once that was accomplished, she had to face some major cleaning and the troubled feelings she had about the place. At first, she dreaded coming to the house and didn't understand why. It wasn't just the dirt and hard work, but an underlying feeling that something was terribly wrong—like some risk of danger waiting for her inside these walls. The house seemed haunted in a way she could not explain even to herself—no ghosts popping in for a visit, but a lingering feeling that someone watched. Sometimes she would look up from whatever she was doing, expecting to see someone enter the room. When no one did, she felt relieved but uneasy, like somebody was waiting on the other side of the wall. She comforted herself with the thought that as a child the house had been a charmed yet disturbing place for her. It was entirely natural that fragments of those impressions would remain.

For years, Winna had visited the house in her dreams. There, grandmother Juliana was still alive and disappointed with Winna for not visiting more often. There, Juliana would sit in the shade of her garden crying, saying how much she missed Edwina, asking where she had been and what she had been doing. From these encounters with Juliana's lonely ghost, Winna would wake shaken and guilt-ridden. She had to admit that her grandmother had been a strong influence on her and so had the house. When she thought about it in the light of day, she realized that her mother was also still alive in her dreams. She had not yet dreamed of her father, but in Winna's dream world, her mother and grandmother were still very much among the living.

Winna, with her daughter's help, had spent the last two weeks making piles off to the side of the main staircase, labeling them SALVATION ARMY, YARD SALE, KEEP, and EMILY'S. That morning, after sorting through the large reception hall closet and filling a tall barrel with trash, Winna noticed that Emily had come to the last box.

"Almost finished here," Emily said, reaching into the box. She hesitated a moment. "Look what I found."

Winna stopped sorting old coats and boots to come for a look at the framed studio portrait Emily held in her hands.

"Who was she?"

Winna looked at the picture and smiled. "That's Juliana—your great-grandmother—with your Poppa Henry."

Inside the tarnished gold frame, Juliana sat three-quarter view holding the child close in her lap, her left cheek obscured by little Henry's bald head, her full lips parted slightly. Henry's big dark eyes were open and bright, two of his fingers thrust into a grinning mouth.

"She looks very sweet," Emily said.

Winna chuckled. "Sweet? That's not a word I would use to describe your great-grandmother."

Winna watched her daughter move into the light from a window. She had already lost most of the weight she had gained during her pregnancy and looked trim and long-legged in khaki shorts and a white tee. From toddlerhood onward, Emily had been contented, cheerful, and perceptive, a delight to her mother. Winna liked to joke that she had learned more from her daughter than she had taught her. She wasn't a bit surprised when she won a scholarship to study environmental science at Boston University. Now she wrote a popular weekly newspaper column on sustainable desert living with tips on gardening, home building, and maintenance.

Fixed on the photograph, Emily walked to the sofa and sat down. "I need a break."

Winna joined her. "Gramma was smart—the smartest person in the family. When she was 'sweet' it was because she wanted something."

"What year was this?"

Winna thought a moment. "It had to have been 1916—the year Daddy was born. Gramma died in the mid-sixties—when you were a baby."

"I don't know why I'm so drawn to this," Emily said. "Maybe because the more I look at her eyes the more sadness I see. I wonder why. It's not the face you'd expect from a proud new mom."

"I'm sure Gramma wasn't your everyday new mom," Winna said, rolling her eyes. She took the frame and looked again, realizing she had never known her grandmother as pictured there—young and fragile, sweetly silent. She had never seen the pale luxuriant curls that ringed Juliana's disarming face, or her large dark eyes shining with sadness. The grandmother she knew had short-cropped gray hair and dressed in well-tailored afternoon dresses and business suits. Yet here the finely woven pale lace of the pictured bodice draped her small frame gracefully as she held her child against her breast. In contrast with his mother's somber expression, baby Henry's face radiated an exuberant smile and bright dark eyes. It looked to Winna that at six months he was eager to begin his exciting life.

"I'd like to offer an educated guess. This was shot at a studio by a professional, but the picture isn't what I'd expect from the period. It's interesting that Juliana picked this one out of all the proofs. It captures something very intimate. Maybe that's why you are drawn to it. It's an outstanding portrait—one I would be proud to say I shot myself."

Winna thought back to her grandmother's last illness. "She died months after a massive brain hemorrhage. The last time I saw her she was lying in the nursing home—emaciated and demented—I didn't recognize her and I know she didn't recognize me. She was only in her mid-seventies." Having stepped two years into her seventh decade, Winna no longer thought seventy was so very old.

"I have to laugh every time I think of the last word she said before she died. Dad was there and he told me she'd looked around the dreary room she shared with several other dying patients and said, 'Ridiculous!' I can hear that voice. Having to die like an ordinary human being was probably out of the question."

Emily smiled and looked at the portrait again. "Look at Poppa Henry's face. Mom, we'll never know for sure how he died."

"It's hard for me to look at that joyful little face and know his end." Winna kissed her finger and touched it to her father's baby face. With the back of her hand, she wiped the sweat from her forehead again.

"Is it hotter than hell or is it just me?" Before they began work in the house that morning, Winna had opened all the windows, but even under the shade of old trees the heat had crept in.

"It's hotter than hell," Emily said, "unless I'm having hot flashes too."

"Just you wait." Winna stood up and walked to the hall closet, now empty except for a familiar wooden cigar box. She picked it up and opened the lid. "Look, Emily, our marbles."

With her daughter at her side, Winna hurried the box into the light, sitting down in the middle of the parlor rug. "Here's my big fat agate—and my favorite flint."

Emily reached for the marbles in Winna's hand. "Come on, Mom, let's play. Now that you're over the hill I bet I can beat you."

"I'm sure you can." Winna ran her hands through the brightly colored glass, snagging something that was neither round nor smooth. She lifted what appeared to be a vintage ring into the light. "It looks like a yellow diamond."

Emily took it from her hand. "It's huge. It can't be real. I've never seen a stone this large. I *want* it!"

"How about if I let you try it on?"

Emily smiled at her mother as she tried slipping it onto her ring finger. It didn't fit there but slid easily onto her pinky where it looked too large, almost comical. She handed it back. "You'd better take that to the jewelry store and see what they think it is."

"It's probably nothing or it wouldn't be hanging out with the marbles." Winna looked at it again. "Sure looks real," she said, slipping the ring into her pocket as she stood up. She took two steps forward into a bright shaft of light and stopped, retrieving the ring for another look. Dazzlingly beautiful, it looked very real to Winna. Why was it with the marbles?

3

FOLLOWING LUNCH AT an air-conditioned cafe, Winna and Emily drove home in the air-conditioned car. Winna dragged two old fans out of the cellar and set them up in the parlor where they found a drawer full of old black-and-white snapshots. Winna quickly sorted through them, stopping to look at a very old picture of the house.

"Look, the trees were just planted. The house was painted a dark color back then—with white trim."

Emily looked over her mother's shoulder. "It looks kind of spooky."

"The story I heard was that my grandfather Edwin built the house when he was looking for a wife. He found just the girl—her father was a state senator and a big deal lawyer. Off and on, he was elected district attorney here in town. Your great-great-grand-father's name was Andrew D. Smythe—are you going to remember all this?" Winna jabbed her daughter with her elbow and chuckled.

"He was Juliana's father," Emily said, getting it straight. "But don't count on me remembering his name."

"In those days, the Grummans owned the only department store in town. In the beginning, it was a dry goods store founded by your great-great-grandfather Grumman—back when Main Street was about a block long and still had tumbleweeds blowing in from the desert."

"I remember the store, Mom. You took me there when I was little." Emily handed her mother a snapshot. "Here's a recent picture of Poppa. Do you want to keep it?"

Winna glanced at it, and took it in hand.

"He's wearing his favorite tweed sports coat, a white shirt, and that bolo tie—his uniform. I think he wore that every day. Last time I saw him he looked a little dusty and unkempt. I remember the days when he dressed stylishly in a suit with a vest and tie. He was so handsome. I wanted to marry him when I was four."

Emily laughed and reached for the picture. "He looks almost frail here."

"You know, he was born to wealth. Through his work, he added to the family wealth, but he never lived like a wealthy man. He seemed not to care when people joked and accused him of being frugal."

"That's a symptom left over from the Depression," Emily said.

Winna smiled. "He used to say, 'you can only spend a dollar once.'"

The parlor phone rang. Winna stepped over a rolled-up rug, side-stepped several packing boxes, and, catching her breath, reached for the receiver.

"Hello."

"Hello, Winna?"

She knew the light ethereal voice. "Chloe," she said, flashing a grimace at Emily. "I thought you weren't speaking to me 'ever again'—at least not in this life."

"I called to apologize. I don't know what forces influenced me last week. Actually, I do now. Juno did my chart yesterday."

"Ah, I see. The planets in juxtaposition to the moon as it crossed over your roof made you paranoid—and rude."

"Look, Winna, I called to apologize," Chloe said. "You are my sister and Daddy's in his grave. We have problems to solve."

"I have problems to solve, you mean. I'm the one who flew out here in May and had to arrange the funeral and the reception without any help from you." Winna couldn't resist the jab. "You didn't even bother to attend, Chloe."

"Are you going to bring up the funeral every time we talk?"

"I'm the one who's been in this house working her butt off in the boiling heat, sorting the mess left by two generations of pack rats."

"I've been disinherited, Winna. You know Daddy hates me."

"Daddy's gone. He isn't here to hate you. He gave absolutely no one a hard time at the funeral. But everyone in town noticed that one of Henry Grumman's two children was missing."

"How do you know he wasn't there? I'm sure he was. I feel him everywhere I go."

Winna rolled her eyes at Emily and shook her head in disbelief.

"Actually, I called to tell you about a conversation we had the day Juno updated my chart."

"Chloe, I can never understand your conversations with Juno."

"No, the conversation I had with Daddy."

Winna didn't even bother to let sarcasm creep into her voice, "Oh?"

"He came to me in a vision. I saw him on that mountain where he died—beautiful—I don't have words to describe it—maybe I can paint it. He looked transformed, the light of the universe shone through him, altering his aura—you know that muddy brown his aura always showed."

"Chloe, I've never seen an aura."

"That's because you are spiritually stunted and your mind is closed," she said. "Anyway, in the vision Daddy was bathed in a clear white-gold light. He spoke such loving words to me that the pain at the back of my left shoulder instantly melted. You know, the pain that dogs me if I don't get my weekly massage. He's at peace, at last," she said, her voice coming dramatically over the line. "Do you want to know what he said?"

Winna said "sure" as she shrugged *not really*.

"He forgave me!"

"Forgave you?"

"He said he was sorry he cut me out of the will."

"How wonderful—how convenient." Winna began to pace.

"Don't be sarcastic, Winna! It's impossible to communicate with you. You have such a tiny little closed-up mind. You're always judging me. You don't know what it's like having someone sit in judgment of you all your life."

"Chloe, we've had this conversation about judging each other," she said as she spun on her heels. "What do you want from me? Dad wrote you out of his will for his own reasons. I'm discussing Dad's estate right now with Reed. I'm not exactly a money-grubbing monster, you know. But there are problems—I have concerns and you haven't been around for me to discuss them with you."

"Daddy said he'd try to contact you—to let you know that he's changed his mind. How can he reach you? *You*, of all people, won't be open to receive him."

Winna could hear her fifty-seven-year-old sister sobbing. For years she had watched her sister slip further and further into a world Winna did not understand—a world full of sadistic and benevolent planets, talkative spirits, and mind readers.

Winna knew that no one would guess they were related, let alone sisters. Compared to Chloe—who was strikingly beautiful, tall, and willowy—Winna could see that she was pretty enough—short and curvy, her light-brown hair streaked with silver. Chloe hid her gray away at the beauty parlor. Winna, an Anglo-Catholic, actually went to church. Her sister found that baffling and had said so. Chloe was a metaphysical seeker with a budding interest in shamanism. The last of the Grummans, they blended like oil and water.

"I'm listening," Winna said, "I know the dead don't hold grudges. Dad was tough. He hurt us both." Chloe's pitiable little gasps and sobs accused her over the line. "There's something I want from you."

In a voice rank with self-pity, Chloe said, "What?"

"Why don't you come over and help me go through this house? Maybe that will help both of us feel better."

"I—I—that would be hard right now. I'll have to see."

"It's important, Chloe. There are things here that I want you to have and we need to talk."

"I don't know, Winna. Juno warned me—and Todd is just settling in."

"Todd is a part of your new life. Wouldn't you like to settle history before you face the future?"

"I don't know. I'll ask Juno what she thinks. I'll stop by on the weekend. Gotta go."

Click.

"Goodbye, Chloe."

Winna put the phone down and looked around as if to remind herself where she was. She stood beneath the arched ceiling in the parlor of her family's old house. Beyond the windows the view held the pillared side porch, and under the old trees the dead shade garden, punctuated by two tall cast-iron urns, sitting among the weeds. When Winna was a child Gramma Juliana had kept the urns filled with dragon wing begonias and trailing ivy. Now they sprouted thirsty weeds.

Winna thought back to after Juliana's death, when the house stood empty for a number of years. Then not long before his second marriage failed, her father had taken up residence there with Ruth. It had been a terrible marriage. Ruth was demanding and ran up bills without consulting Henry—Chloe had told her that much. Finally, Ruth deserted him and moved to Phoenix, leaving him high and dry, expecting a big check in the mail every month. She lived with him less than a year and got nothing in the divorce. Winna wondered if she was dead.

How can it be that Dad has left no mark—no impression that he had ever lived in these rooms? Except for Ruth's contributions—the avocado wall-to-wall carpet in the kitchen and the carpets covering the tiled floors in the bathrooms—nothing of his remained. Winna had found pill bottles in the bathroom cabinet, his clothes in the master bedroom upstairs, a stack of newspapers and some unpaid bills on the kitchen table, but everything else had belonged to her grandparents. Her father had just moved in with his wife. Why? Any normal person would have had a yard sale and gotten rid of the junk, auctioned the treasures they didn't want, ripped off the wallpaper and painted, hung their own pictures, and brought in some comfortable modern furniture.

The parlor, now cluttered with packing boxes, had once been a sumptuous room. Winna had spent her first days in the house shooting pictures in the moody old rooms, the light wonderfully eerie as it fell through lace and stained glass over the deep long windows. The old mahogany sofa upholstered in faded coral brocade was still richly draped with paisley throws and silk pillows. A dancer twirled atop a high twisted green marble pedestal near paintings hung in elaborate gold frames—dark oils of classical landscapes and tall ships on stormy seas. Even the empty jardinières where ferns and begonias once grew were fascinating to her camera's lens.

The place seemed timeless to Winna, the house and the desert valley. She knew that her father had lived in the house and the town in the past more than the present. Like the visible strata in the cliff face where an ancient ocean had lapped against its shores, the place seemed to hold past, present, and future together as one timeless whole.

Winna burst into tears. The Grumman house was a treasure trove and all hers, yet she felt sadly alone, abandoned.

Emily came to her and gave her a hug. "Poor Mom. I don't know how you put up with her."

"It isn't Chloe," she cried, "it's—it's everything."

"Dad?" Emily's brown eyes searched Winna's face.

Through tangled emotions, Winna tried to make sense of her sadness. For the past three years, she had lived alone after her husband of thirty-five years had left her—left her with the wrinkles around her eyes, her ten extra pounds, her silvery hair. *I'm old, yesterday's news*, she had believed at the time. As far as she could tell, Walt was old too. But that did not seem to matter to his new young wife. She was a lawyer—so was Walt. How sweet, she had thought bitterly at the time, they have something in common.

Winna collapsed on the sofa. "I don't know. I guess so. I really haven't gotten over it—what happened with your father. I've been obsessed with the hurt. I've spent the last three years trying to convince myself that my career was enough, that my exhibits in Boston and New York are fulfilling, that having important clients means I'm loved, that being an even bigger success would make me happy.

When Dad died, and the will was read, I knew I had to come here to settle everything. I felt relieved to leave New Castle for a while—to get away from all the work. I thought I'd feel better here, but I'm just hotter."

The sound of Isabelle's waking echoed down the hall as Emily sat down beside her mother. "You will feel better here, Mom. You and Dad were together a long time." Emily took her mother's hand. "I want you to move here—to be near me."

Since Emily had been in diapers, she had known how to comfort. "No, honey, I can't leave my life, my work, or my friends any more than you could leave yours. You mustn't think I could ever live in Grand Junction again.

"Oh, Lord." Winna wiped the tears from her cheeks with the back of one hand. "Let's go stare at the baby."

4

1910

JULIANA GRACE SMYTHE was in love. He was her first love, but she knew she would never love anyone else. She and Adolph Whitaker—she called him Dolph—had gone to school together since the first grade, but it wasn't until she was fifteen that she fell in love with him.

It began at the high school on a spring day, just warm enough to go outside for lunch. After her classics class, Juliana set out to meet her best friend, Daisy, on the side lawn. Reflecting on a passage of Cicero they had studied—"It is from nature that the sentiment of loving and the affection that springs from kindly feeling are born"—she reached their usual meeting place. To better ask Daisy about it, Juliana wanted to put Cicero's wisdom into her own words. True friendship is everlasting because it is human nature to love and nature cannot be changed. With all her heart she believed that. She planned to ask her best friend if she agreed. In the fall term, they had studied Virgil and Juliana was most thankful that they had moved on.

Daisy wasn't there. Juliana sat down with her lunch pail and her copy of *Laelius de Amicitia* to wait under a young elm whose buds were just about to burst. She anxiously looked for her friend, then diverted her eyes across the sunny lawn up the face of the two-story stone building to the octagonal bell tower. How exciting it would be if she could climb to the top and see the view—maybe she could get permission to ring the bell one morning. She lowered her eyes to the lawn again and searched the sidewalk now lined with students finding places to sit on the stone benches and the lawn. Daisy was not among them.

Just then, Adolph Whitaker walked by with his lunch pail. He smiled warmly and said, "Waiting for Daisy?"

She could feel her face light up just as it always did when a boy spoke to her. "Hello, Dolph. Have you seen her?"

"I usually see her first thing—on my way to class—but not this morning. Maybe she's home sick."

"Oh bother," Juliana said, scanning the lawn once again. She hated eating alone but was not going to get up and search for one of her other friends. "Well, it's not as if they give us all day to eat our lunch," she said, opening her lunch pail.

"An hour never seems long enough," he said. "If you'd like company, I'll spend that hour with you, fair Juliana."

Juliana smiled and patted the grass. "You always sound like a poem."

"A poet should, should he not?" He sat down cross-legged and opened his lunch pail. Dolph was slight, only a few inches taller than Juliana. His dark curly hair parted in the middle with rows of waves heavily oiled into place. His fair skin set off the large blue-green eyes as they studied Juliana.

"I should like to read one of your poems, Dolph," she said, unwrapping her sandwich. As she took a bite, a little dab of mayonnaise remained at the corner of her mouth and she licked it off. "Do you write stories too?" She held her hand up, hiding the fact that her mouth was full.

His face assumed an air of mystery. "At the moment my pen is doing a turn on a new account of the affair between the lovers of Camelot."

"Guinevere and Lancelot in modern dress? I'd like to do a modern version of *Pygmalion and Galatea*. Only I'd make him a surgeon and her a mermaid."

Dolph laughed. "You wicked little thing. It sounds like you've read *Frankenstein*."

"Yes, and I adored it—never cried so hard in my life."

He glanced at the book lying upside down in the folds of her skirt. "What's that you're reading now?"

"Cicero. I just worship him. Virgil's *Aeneid*—we read that last term—was interesting to be sure, but it took every ounce of my strength to get an A in that class."

"I read both last year and had the opposite impression. It must be the difference in our sex." He left his eyes on her face too long and she looked away.

"You are the smallest girl in your class. I'd guess you are also the youngest?"

"Yes. Fifth grade was too easy and they moved me to sixth," she said.

"Juliana—such a bright little creature. If I were to describe you in a poem, I'd say your skin is white as cream and your eyes a dark amber honey.

Juliana felt herself blush. "That sounds like a compliment—cream and honey?"

Dolph was two years older, a top student, and he had just complimented her.

He laughed. "Cicero said, 'A friend is, as it were, a second self.'"

She grinned, rolled her eyes, and matched his quote with another: "Every man can tell how many goats or sheep he possesses, but not how many friends."

He was up to the challenge. "I like this one: 'Trust no one unless you have eaten much salt with him.' Ah ha, pass the salt, Juliana."

So went their first real conversation. When the bell rang, Dolph reached for her hand. "Now we must part, fair Juliana, but methinks I've found a kindred spirit."

Adolph Graham Whitaker would become a great writer, Juliana was sure of it. She liked the idea of marrying a writer. He was the last thing she thought of that night before she fell asleep. He is just my sort of person. I think he is handsome. His eyes—do they smolder? No, they pierce. No, I think they devour. His mouth? The lips are full and there is a little twist to his smile, as if there is something on his mind that he is not willing to reveal. I like that. He's mysterious? No, girls should be mysterious. Boys are mystifying. I think he is just my sort. Soon Dolph called on her at home. Her mother would allow them to sit alone in the parlor for an hour, on nice days outside on the porch. They had lunch together every day at school. Juliana asked Daisy to please understand her sudden abandonment—she was in love.

"Someday, when you are in love, you will know exactly how I feel, Daisy. Then you will forgive me."

The time came when she had to face the certainty that Dolph would take his full scholarship and go off to a fine school in the East. He would leave her behind in Grand Junction, in her mind a perfectly backward cow town where her father was district attorney. He dealt with all kinds of unseemly things: Indian troubles, squabbles about water rights, murders. He talked about his work every night at the dinner table. Juliana found his conversation to be either fascinatingly sordid or endlessly boring.

Grand Junction had grown out of the desert. The hard sun-baked soil, the color of ash, nurtured little but tumbleweeds and sage on the dry plain where once Utes had hunted. In 1881, the government drove the Indians away to reservations in southern Colorado and Utah. The US cavalry escorted a long line of Ute braves on horseback—women and children on foot—out of the west end of the valley. They were barely out of sight as scores of white men on horses hastened in from the southeast to stake out the choicest land for farms. Wagons full of land-seeking families rode into the valley eager to claim acreage for a ranch or a house site in town. Two rivers, the Gunnison from the mountains to the southeast and the Colorado from the northeast, coursed into the valley. The newcomers diverted river water into ditches and later canals, turning Grand Junction into a farming paradise. Water was all that light colored soil had needed to nurture orchards and fields.

Indians from the reservation still came into town, spreading their blankets on Main Street's sidewalks, selling beadwork, pottery, jewelry, and blankets. The Indian school took Ute children from the reservation and boarded them outside of town, dressing the girls in white dresses and the boys in pants, jackets, and shirts. Hoping they would assimilate, they taught them a trade, English, and Christianity.

Orchards and fields surrounded that rough-edged civilization with its nineteenth-century Main Street bordered by blocks of small bungalows and modest frame houses. On or near Main Street stately buildings rose above the valley floor: the Mesa County Courthouse, the towered bank building, the railroad station. The residents were proud of Seventh Street, one of the few choice streets where the well-to-do were building handsome houses, and ashamed of the southernmost street near the railroad tracks where nice women never walked. Everywhere—in vacant lots, along roadsides, or on the outskirts of town—swaths of alkali and the tumbleweeds reminded the residents that this was a dry, inhospitable land.

Two things Juliana would never forget happened in the spring of 1910. Her parents took her to see the one and only Grand Junction performance of Buffalo Bill's Wild West Show. Colonel William Cody, she had learned, got the name Buffalo Bill for having killed thousands of buffalo over a period of eighteen months—more than anybody else. Juliana had already dismissed that particular achievement of his as dubious. But when she saw him under his cowboy hat, wearing buckskins and riding a palomino, she could not help her feelings of awe. Even though he was an old man by the time she saw him, never in her life, or in the life she hoped to have, would there be a more striking figure. The Rough Riders of the World reenacted the Great Train Robbery and the Battle of Summit Springs. She thrilled at the sight of the mounted warriors of the world in martial array: Russian Cossacks, German cuirassiers, Bedouin Arabs, South

American gauchos, English lancers, and Irish dragoons fresh from four years of European triumph. Her only disappointment? Annie Oakley was not in the show.

The second thing she would never forget came the following Saturday. Juliana was certain she would never again have such a remarkable, eventful week. She and Dolph had run off alone, away from the Peach Blossom Festival. Hand in hand they had sneaked down a narrow lane, through someone's vegetable garden. Breathless, excited by their daring, they dodged into a small orchard unseen. Dolph kissed her and pulled her down in the tall grass. The sky was azure, the grass green and fresh. She lay there under pink blossoms letting him kiss her all he wanted. She knew she shouldn't, but he tasted delicious and her heart beat with delight at his touch. Neither spoke, but they looked deeply into one another's eyes. His hand grazed her breast, then he lifted her skirt. Before she came to her senses, she let his warm hand move gently up the inside of her thigh. She let out a little embarrassed cry and sat up, smoothing her skirt, afraid to look Dolph in the eye.

"It's all right, Juliana," he said. "I'm sorry, but I'm overcome with love for you."

She looked at him with tears in her eyes. "I don't want to talk about it now," she said. "You mustn't tell."

"No, I would never—" he said, kissing her again.

She did not want to talk about what he had done or what she had felt, but she would think about it again and again, until she could think of nothing else.

They were not away from the festival for long and no one had missed them, but Juliana and Dolph had traveled a million miles together. As far as Juliana knew, no other girl had ever done things like that or felt the way he had made her feel. She was almost right about that. Girls from good families did not have such adventures. She knew that. Juliana had always been precocious.

That summer Dolph worked at the grocery store where he would filch a pint of strawberries for Mrs. Smythe or a chocolate for Juliana. He would sneak them outside behind the store to his bicycle and hide them in the basket under the jacket his mother made him carry. After work, he took the treats to the Smythes.

Juliana expected him as she waited in the gazebo. Through the lattice and the vines she saw him ride up on his bicycle, lean it against the fence, and walk up the front steps. Almost like a game of hide and seek, she wanted him to find her in that leafy bower. Now Dolph was out of view. She wanted to run to him, but knew enough about romance to not appear over-eager. Right now, she guessed, he was ringing the doorbell and her mother was answering. Mrs. Smythe would welcome him with a smile, and when she saw what he brought—a jar of jam, maybe, or oranges shipped all the way from California—she would thank him.

How he could afford to buy these lovely things, Juliana did not know. He couldn't and the fact that he did proved how very much he loved her and wanted her mother's approval.

Dolph came down the front steps and hurried to the garden path toward the gazebo. She knew her mother had told him where she was. He carried something in his hand—something for her.

Juliana spent that late afternoon side by side with Dolph on the gazebo's wooden bench. He had presented her with a chocolate and she could tell that he delighted in watching her slowly nibble it away.

"Would you like a bite?" she teased.

"No, it's just for you. Tomorrow I will bring you a lollipop so I can watch you devour it with that dear little tongue."

Juliana was quite aware that her mother kept watch on them from the kitchen window. Sometimes she could see her standing there or at the window of an upstairs bedroom. She could, in fact, appear at any one of the windows on that side of the house. Juliana knew that her mother could not spend all day on alert and, when the coast was clear, she would grab Dolph by the hand and take him next door, behind Mr. Osgood's tool shed where they found a secluded spot perfect for a kiss and a long embrace.

Mrs. Smythe stood at the dining room window. From there she usually saw her daughter with her beau studiously huddled together reading a book or a manuscript. Sometimes they scribbled in their notebooks. She wondered what on earth they had to talk about. Their conversations never seemed to end. Today the gazebo was empty and she hurried out to the porch to see if they had decided to favor the porch swing. They weren't there.

I must tell that child again that if she wants to be free to entertain her beau at home, she is required to stay in sight.

Mrs. Smythe hurriedly crossed the porch, wiping her hands on her apron. She looked across the street to see if Mrs. Partridge was in her garden. Thankful that she was not—ashamed to have her neighbors see her so humbly attired—she untied her apron and dropped it on the porch swing before she put a foot on the front steps. Taking the path to the other side of the house where the cutting garden grew, she found them there, walking among the flowers like two innocent children full of summer wonder. She marveled at how her daughter was growing up, so small and lovely in her afternoon dress with the puffed sleeves. The upswept hair and chignon made her look grown-up, but a pale blue ribbon tied in her strawberry blonde hair reminded that she was still a child. Mrs. Smythe had not won the argument about whether or not Juliana was old enough to wear a chignon.

Before the summer was over Juliana felt very grown-up, but she had worries. She was quite aware that her young lover was poor as a church mouse. Yes, he had a full scholarship to a fine university and a promising talent, but she knew that poets and teachers were not wealthy. She tried to think of suggestions for Dolph—how he might make his fortune. So far, she had not thought of anything—like a banker or industrialist—that he was eager to adopt as his life's calling. She did not think about the ways she could be wealthy on her own. She knew that girls got married and with all her heart she wanted to marry Dolph. Then her nights would be filled with his kisses, but she most certainly did not want to be poor.

Usually when Juliana helped her mother with the dishes, she would entertain herself by singing or reciting poetry. One afternoon, as her mother filled the dishpan with hot water, Juliana said, "Father grew up poor, but I think he's well enough off now." By Grand Junction standards, her father had done well. Juliana was quite aware that their house and her clothes were nicer than many of her friends'.

"Right now, dear, your father is down in the market because of the—dare I say—damn trust busters." The Standard Oil Company faced antitrust regulations and her husband had large holdings.

"Are we going to be poor?" Juliana felt more petulant than fearful.

Mrs. Smythe dipped a dinner plate into the rinse pan and handed it to her daughter. "No. You mustn't worry."

"Is that why Millie only comes on Tuesdays and Thursdays now?" she said, wiping the plate dry with a linen tea towel.

"Yes, dear, but your father has assured me that he is just going through a rough spot."

Juliana put the plate in the cupboard. "Are there any writers who are rich?"

"I suppose so. Mark Twain was once a wealthy man, but I hear he frittered away much of his money. You know, he just passed away and his poor daughter may go wanting for an inheritance," she said, passing her daughter another clean plate. "Famous as he was, he had trouble with bill collectors."

"I'd like a husband who is richer than Father," Juliana said.

"We must be thankful for all we have, child."

Juliana wondered who her mother was reminding to be grateful—herself or her daughter. "I am. Surely I am," she said, furiously drying the plate with a linen towel. "But is it wrong to want more?"

"That depends. You never want to benefit from ill-gotten gains. That is how a number of men get rich. Now, I know, I should not forget that your father's interest in Standard Oil could be seen as ill-gotten gains, but he's a relatively small holder. Dash it! I missed this glass," she said, reaching for a tall drinking glass. "Now the wash water is ruined with grease.

"That reminds me. How can your young man afford to bring me strawberries and those lovely scallions from yesterday? It is utterly charming of him, of course, but he should not be spending his money like that. Please tell him to be wise and save it for school."

"If he was rich you wouldn't have to think like that," Juliana said. "Aren't wealthy men smarter and more powerful?"

Juliana's mother held the just rinsed glass up to the light for inspection. "That's what one might think, but not all wealthy men are happy men."

Juliana did not believe that for a minute.

On his prospects for wealth, Dolph had said that he expected to do well. Becoming a writer takes time, he had said. When they married, they would have to live on a teacher's salary for a while. Juliana was determined to change his mind.

5

1999

THE BACK PORCH, off the kitchen, looked over a spacious lawn to a bank of trees and shrubs forming a dense protective screen. The rustic Adirondack swing, its paint peeling, still hung at the end of the porch behind the lattice where the sky blue flowers Winna knew as morning glories—her grandmother called them "love in vain"—used to open on summer mornings. Under a small horseshoe hanging from a blacksmith's nail, the old rocking chairs sat along the inside wall with the weather-beaten wicker loveseat and matching tables.

Winna looked out across the lawn to the summerhouse where on summer afternoons she and Chloe used to draw and play with their paper dolls. It was a small one-room house with lattice work on either side of the door. Door-length windows looked out on the big house and gardens.

Out of the corner of her eye, she saw movement like the last traces of a figure in flight. Ever since she'd been working in the house she'd experienced these fleeting encounters with her imagination: a shadow hurrying off at the end of the upstairs hall, the sound of footsteps on the attic stairs. Was it her imagination or had she come upon a lost memory trying to surface? She dismissed it as foolishness and forced herself to get back to work—making decisions about the old porch furniture. She gave the whole lot a second look and decided to put it in the yard sale. It was still serviceable.

A local jeweler had identified the ring they had found among the marbles as a four-carat yellow diamond—like nothing he'd ever seen in Grand Junction. He suggested she get it appraised in Denver. That left her with yet another unsettled feeling. Why on earth would a valuable ring be left with a collection of children's marbles? It didn't make sense. Was that someone's idea of a clever hiding place? Winna had never seen the ring before. She would have remembered such a thing had it been in her grandmother's jewelry box. Had it belonged to her wicked stepmother Ruth? Was Ruth playing marbles and the ring interfered with her game? That guess made Winna laugh. The logical guess was that it had somehow belonged to Juliana.

The weekend had come and gone with no sign of Chloe. Winna sat down with her father's heap of unopened mail. At the kitchen table, she sorted the letters into categories. Most envelopes contained things for the wastebasket, but there were unpaid bills, some of them past due when Henry was still alive. Finally she came to an unopened envelope addressed by a familiar hand—hers. She looked at the postmark. She'd sent the card on his last birthday.

Realizing what she held in her hand, Winna felt a sharp stab to her heart. He hadn't even opened it. She decided she would. The card featured a drawing of a father holding his little girl above his head. They were playing, lovingly delighted with one another. Printed at the bottom it read, "To the BEST DAD in the whole world." Winna was stunned. She didn't remember the card or what had possessed her to send those words—she hoped it wasn't sarcasm. She opened it to see what she had written:

Wishing you a Happy Birthday, Daddy. Hope your day is special. All is well here at my little house by the sea—wish you would come for a visit and see for yourself. Still adjusting to the single life. Any tips? Business is good. Lots of love, Winna

Winna began to sob. Her whole body shook. Her hands trembled so wildly that she could not hold the card in her hand. He hadn't remembered her birthday in forty years, but even worse, she hadn't expected he would. He didn't care. Winna let the tears flow.

When calm, she looked around her. An overwhelming feeling of neglect filled the house. It was apparent that her father had been neglected too. The housekeeper was a joke and his daughters had all but deserted him. She hadn't known, she told herself. She lived thousands of miles away. What's more, he never called, was never in when she called, never answered her letters. Worst of all he didn't care. He didn't care. As far as Winna could tell, he didn't even notice. It was as if his job was over. He had fed, clothed, and educated his daughter, got her married off, and sent her on her way.

Both he and the house seemed just fine when she'd visited two summers ago. She had to admit that she had not looked through cupboards and drawers. On that last visit she stayed with her friend Kate. Winna never felt lonelier than when she was with her father. As a remedy, she spent as much time as she could with friends. Now, missing her friend, she promised herself to get back in touch when Kate got home. She was in Denver helping her daughter, who had just had another baby.

There was a reason for her neglect. She reminded herself of his drinking days. One of the times she had flown in for a visit, the two had sat together in silence in the old parlor after dinner one night. Trying to erase the uncomfortable feeling of that silence, she had struck up a conversation she no longer remembered. *I probably told him about my child, my husband, my work—my life.* In midsentence—hers—Henry had thrown back his head and let out a long high-pitched howl like a lonely wolf baying at the moon.

At the end of that horrifying howl he cried, "I am so bored!"

She hadn't known what to do, what to say, but she wanted to cry. She told herself that he was drunk, that she should not take his outburst personally. She picked up something to read. She couldn't concentrate and, feigning her own end-of-the-day tiredness, went off to the guest room, to cry herself to sleep.

Her father had been a stranger who seemed not to notice she was alive. She had never really known him and he had never made the effort to know her. Does that give a daughter the right to neglect her aging father? She couldn't think about that—not now—not after what had happened to him.

Though Chloe had moved back to Grand Junction seven years before their father's death, she saw very little of Henry. Winna remembered complaining phone calls from her sister, who told her about their encounters, and his politics. The big Ross Perot sign stuck in the front lawn through two election cycles embarrassed Chloe. Henry had tried his best to keep Bill Clinton out of the White House. He hated the president, but Chloe supported him. She had even tried to explain to her father why the President's affair with Monica Lewinsky had come about. Why there was almost nothing wrong with it. The only thing Chloe disapproved of was that they'd never actually had "sexual relations." According to Chloe, poor Monica had done all the work and had none of the pleasure.

Then there were her father's old-fashioned ideas on women's roles and race. When Chloe told her about their political arguments, Winna shook her head and said, "At least he talks to you."

She wanted to feel justified in her neglect, but she couldn't. She had regrets, and she found it cruel and ironic that his death had made her sympathetic toward him in a way that made her feel guilty. She was never going to have a relationship with her father. It was too late.

A cup of tea in hand, she decided to take a moment to rest and sat down on the porch swing. *I am going to do my best to remember something pleasant, something tangible that passed between Dad and me.* She wanted some happy memory, a moment when she knew he loved her. Her eyes fell on the horseshoe hanging over the rocking chairs. She smiled and wondered if her father had tacked it there. Had it belonged to Peaches?

WINNA AND CHLOE were still in grade school when a traveling carnival came to town for just one night—a school night. It wasn't Winna's first carnival, but it was Chloe's. The carnies had set up on a vacant lot somewhere on the outskirts of town. By the time the Grummans arrived, a large crowd had gathered and there were lines waiting for the merry-go-round. They passed through the midway where human freaks waited inside a large tent. They stopped to look at large colorful posters, cartoons of the fat lady and the thin man, the bearded woman, the Siamese twins, and the man whose skin was covered in tattoos. Winna begged to go inside, but Henry had said it was not kind or polite to stare at people with deformities.

Hawkers inside colorful booths cried out for them to take a chance, win a prize, shoot at ducks, throw darts at balloons. Winna watched hopefully as Henry did his best to win prizes for both of them. Having failed, he bought them cotton candy and they headed off to the Ferris wheel.

For the first time, Winna was disappointed by the carnival. She could see how poor and broken down the carnies looked, the shabbiness of the tents, the chipped paint on the Ferris wheel. Worst of all, she suddenly felt ashamed that she had asked her father if she could go in to see the freaks. She thought of how sad they must be and wondered why they would sit there and let themselves be embarrassed.

Still, this was Winna's special night out with her father. She and Chloe had been allowed to go to the carnival on a school night. They'd had cotton candy and rides on the Ferris wheel. They'd lined up with the crowd around a pen where a pretty red roan pony was up for raffle. After they had jumped up and down, and tugged on his sleeve begging, their father had agreed to buy a raffle ticket.

Late that night, after everyone had gone to sleep, Winna heard the telephone ring. Her father answered it. She fell back to sleep before he hung up, but in the morning there was a surprise waiting for them—a glossy roan pony with soulful brown eyes staring at them from the middle of the living room floor. Luckily, a remodeling project was underway and the rugs and furniture had been removed.

Her mother suggested that Henry take his delirious children and the pony outside on the lawn for a ride while she fixed breakfast. Before the girls left for school, their father showed them how to saddle and bridle him. They took turns riding him around the back lawn.

"Isn't he a peach?" Her father stroked the pony's sleek rump. "He's just perfect for you girls to ride," he said, lifting Chloe onto his back.

By the time they ran off to catch the school bus, they had named their new pony "Peaches."

That evening during dinner, Henry told them the whole story, beginning with the phone call. He described it in detail—being jarred awake, stumbling in the dark to the phone on the hall table, the strange voice coming over the line. The girls laughed at his impression of the man on the phone.

"Mr. Grumman, y'all won that there pony. If y'all want 'im, you better come git 'im rat now."

Half asleep, Henry drove his car to the vacant lot where carnival workers packed up under the lights. He bridled the pony and put the fancy black-and-silver-studded saddle into the trunk of his car. With help from two other men, he stuffed the pony into the back seat and drove all the way out to Peach Tree Ridge with the pony's head over his shoulder.

"When I got home I realized I had a big problem—where to put a pony for the night. It was too dark to see my way to the pasture—besides, there's a break in the fence. The little shed was full of rusty milk cans and I couldn't keep a confused pony in the car overnight and hope to have a back seat by morning. There was nothing to do but bring him into the house. The rugs had been taken up and I figured your mother wouldn't be mad at me. So I put a knot in the bridle's end, and closed a living room window on the strap to secure it."

The next day Henry took the day off from work. Winna watched him fix the fence. She helped him clean out the old shed just off the pasture. It was the perfect size for a pony. They let Peaches loose in the pasture where an irrigation ditch ran down a gentle slope toward neighboring fields. All that green grass and running water would provide a good home for Peaches.

Daddy loved animals, Winna reminded herself. He could relate to them. Then she remembered Garfie, the dog, and the story her mother had told her.

The way she told it, Nora had been distraught over the death of film star John Garfield. She took it pretty hard. She'd seen every one of his movies and regarded him as one of the greats. When Winna asked why, she had said it was because he knew how to play the common man with honesty and dignity. Just a year earlier, he had stood up to the House Un-American Activities Committee, denying that he was a communist and refusing to name others. Winna remembered how much her mother hated Joseph McCarthy and how she had explained his "witch-hunt." It was the first time Winna had heard that expression.

"I heard about his death—at thirty-nine from a heart attack—on the radio that morning," Nora said. "And for the first time I learned that he was not John Garfield, after all. He was born Jacob Julius Garfinkle, a Jew."

Alone with the housework and feeling sad, Nora had grabbed her grocery list and headed for the car. Just outside the kitchen door, she found a strange dog standing there, a scruffy, whining wretch, with round brown eyes peering out from under a mop of curly white and red-spotted hair. The dog stood knee-high with a long fringed tail carried between his legs. She said she had never seen another dog like him.

Nora gave him a bowl of water. He gulped it down thirstily and she gave him another. While the poor wretch waited beside the kitchen door, she hopped into the car and drove to the store. Just in case the dog was still there when she got home, she bought some dog food.

The dog had waited for her to return. Nora was glad. She fed him and after he had wolfed down the whole can, she invited him in.

When the girls came home from school they begged their mother to let them keep him.

"You'd have to help feed him."

"We will!"

"It would be your job to keep his water bowl full. If you promise me you'll help — we can give him a home."

She seemed already attached herself, and insisted on naming him Garfinkle. Winna liked the name because it sounded funny.

The rest of the afternoon, they fussed over Garfinkle, making a bed for him and showing him around the house. They bathed him and combed the tangles out of his coat. Garfinkle looked at them with big brown eyes full of sad stories he could not tell and seemed to feel right at home.

The moment their father walked through the door, Garfinkle got in a terrible panic. He ran and hid under the kitchen table, cowering and whining with his face to the wall, terrified of Henry.

Nora figured that where he'd come from, a male in the household had been cruel to him, had probably dumped him off in the country. That's why he was afraid.

Henry got down on his haunches to talk to Garfinkle.

"Look here, fella, come on out from under that table," he coaxed. "I won't hurt you. It's okay, pooch, you look like a real peach to me." After a few days of pleading, Winna's father had sweet-talked the dog out from under the table and into his arms.

It wasn't long before Garfinkle was completely at home. He dozed in his cool spot under the hedge, his eyes traveling from Henry to the lawnmower. When Henry had to mend a fence or haul trash to the dump, the dog followed him like a toddler.

Puffing slowly on his pipe, Henry would pump up a bicycle tire, or clip the hedge, or look for a tool in the garage. Then he'd draw smoke into his lungs and talk to his best friend.

"Where'd you put that hammer, Garfie?" he said, scratching his head. "It belongs right here on this nail. Okay, fella, fess up. Where'd you hide it?" They had become inseparable.

WINNA HAD FINISHED her tea and her memories. Dad had never been angry with Garfie, never scolded him, never hit him. He loved that dog. Winna tried to dismiss a twinge of envy.

6

BY SUNDAY, AFTER SHE missed church again, exhaustion grabbed Winna and flung her into bed at the La Court Motel, where she had stayed since her arrival. She needed a nap and a shower before joining old friends for cocktails.

Lying in bed in the air-conditioned room, she thought of the old La Court Hotel. They had torn it down—a tragedy in her mind. What grew into a 125-room hotel started small in 1904 with only 22 rooms. Enlarged in the late twenties, the building had always gleamed white under its red roof at the west end of Main Street, a beacon of refinement, the grandest building the town had to offer. A comfortable lobby with cozy fireplaces welcomed guests to the best dining room in town—the only place in Grand Junction where Gramma Juliana enjoyed dining.

Winna remembered the hotel best during the 1950s when she was a teenager. Her grandmother took her there for birthday luncheons followed by a shopping trip to Grumman's. On these occasions, Winna would dress carefully—always in her best dress with a hat and gloves. Juliana wore fashionable suits, usually dark, a mink stole of whole pelts (by May it was too warm for one of her fur coats), a brightly colored hat with a short net veil, and gloves.

Together they would ascend the front steps hand in hand, grand-mother gently reminding granddaughter to watch her manners. She needn't have bothered. Winna stood in perfect awe of that vener-able hotel, with its elegant dining room, and hoped to make her grandmother proud.

On her fifteenth birthday, the day she wanted to remember, Winna saw herself sitting with her grandmother in the hotel dining room at a table draped in white linen. A waitress in a dove gray uniform with a ruffled white apron and starched white triangle at the top of her head approached and handed them the menu. Winna had a hard time deciding what she wanted to eat. She knew the rules for dining out. Never order the most expensive thing on the menu and never com-plain about the food in the presence of your host or hostess.

Gramma always asked for a table near the windows overlooking the porch. From there she could keep her eye on the movement of diners and businessmen as they came and went. Winna figured she knew everyone in town.

Her grandmother stiffened, then nudged Winna's arm. "That's Lillian Collier and her daughter—see the woman in the red hat?"

Winna nodded yes as a matronly woman walked arm in arm with a girl up the front steps toward the door.

"That poor woman. Her daughter—not the young one you see—but the elder. While she was away at college, she married someone Lillian had never met. She didn't even tell her parents until after the wedding—now she expects everyone in the family to welcome the man like nothing had happened—like they hadn't been forgotten on the most important day of their daughter's life."

Winna tried to sympathize with Lillian Collier's terrible misfor-tune. She'd heard of things like that happening before and knew it was frowned upon—by her grandmother at least. But she did not connect the comment with the fact that Juliana's son, Winna's father, had done the same thing—got married out of town without his par-ents' blessing or presence.

The Shirley Temple and the martini arrived; her grandmother pulled off her gloves and reached for her drink. She took a sip and sighed. "Your father and mother did much the same to me, but I've forgiven them."

"Maybe Mrs. Collier will forgive her daughter too," Winna said.

With the martini half gone, her grandmother wanted to reminisce about the day Vice President Richard Nixon came to town. It was during Eisenhower's first electoral campaign. In her role as president of the Colorado Federation of Women's Republican Clubs, she had been responsible for welcoming him and had enlisted her eldest granddaughter's help.

"Remember the day Dick and Pat came to town?" she opened.

"Dick and Pat?"

"Yes, the Nixons. I was so proud of you—my beautiful granddaughter in that lovely dress. Surely you remember meeting them at the airport with a bouquet of roses for Mrs. Nixon. Don't you remember your picture on the front page of the *Sentinel*, precious?"

Winna smiled at her grandmother's obvious pride and blushed. "I was so scared. I practiced what I was going to say over and over again. 'Welcome to Grand Junction, Senator and Mrs. Nixon.' I can still say it in my sleep."

The appetizers arrived, fresh grapefruit sections minted and swimming in ginger ale served in long-stem dessert glasses. Winna asked if she might sprinkle it with sugar. Her grandmother grimaced but nodded "yes."

"The best part was having lunch at your house with you and the governor's wife. I still remember what you served—chicken salad."

Juliana laughed. "And Jessie blackened it with the pepper grinder." She looked at her granddaughter and smiled. "You were very naughty, Winna. I still remember what you said to my distinguished guest. 'My goodness, you sure do like pepper,'" she said, imitating her granddaughter's faux pas.

They both laughed. "Does she still speak to you?" Winna asked.

"Of course. Politics are strong cement."

Winna's memory included Chloe's tears. She had not been asked to meet the Nixons at the airport or to lunch with the governor's wife. Both Winna and her mother had tried to comfort her. Winna had felt so bad about it that she had spoken to her grandmother, asking if Chloe could come too. But her grandmother explained that Mrs. Haffenreffer, the vice president of the Republican Women's Club, wanted her granddaughter to hand Mrs. Nixon a Grand Junction peach and that they couldn't have a whole gaggle of grandchildren trailing after the Nixons at the airport.

After the election, the invitation to President Eisenhower's inaugural ball arrived. Winna had watched with excitement as her mother, a talented seamstress, made the ball gown. She used a Vogue pattern and the antique lace her grandmother insisted on wearing. Nora had cut the gown out of black satin—a long circle skirt and bodice with wrist-length sleeves, topped by the lace cape collar. It was a dignified yet glamorous evening dress for a woman of a certain age.

Winna shivered in her air-conditioned room at the motel and pulled the covers close, trying to calculate if it really was her fifteenth birthday when her grandmother bought the ring. She thought so.

After lunch at the hotel, she had taken her time at Grumman's. Her grandmother said she could have any one thing she wanted and not to worry about the price. When she was younger, they stopped in the toy department and it took her about ten minutes to find a china tea set or a beautiful new doll in a pink dress. But by the time she was fifteen it took time to decide which one thing on all three floors at Grumman's she wanted more than any other.

They stopped at the jewelry counter, then the shoe department, then back to the jewelry counter. Then Winna remembered the dress department. They ended up at the jewelry counter again where she was urged to select "something real." Her grandmother did not believe in costume jewelry.

"Never waste money on junk," her grandmother said, pointing to a ring with a smooth oval emerald set in yellow gold and studded with diamond baguettes. Both Juliana and Winna had May birthdays and the emerald was their birthstone.

Her grandmother burst into verse. "Who first beholds the light of day in spring's sweet flowery month of May and wears an emerald all her life, shall be a loved and happy wife."

How could Winna resist? She decided on the ring because it symbolized a bond between them—born in the same month, they belonged to the same club. The emerald was their insignia. Ultimately, the emerald proved to be a foolish purchase. She had lost it.

Winna felt the delicious warmth of the blanket in the chilly room and closed her eyes. Following Gramma Juliana and young Winna as they strolled hand in hand down the wide aisles at Grumman's, she fell asleep.

STILL MARRIED AFTER forty years, Kate and Jim Cross had been high school sweethearts. They lived comfortably in a spacious adobe home north of town. Their living room—crowded with about two dozen other guests, none of whom Winna recognized—had a magnificent view of Kate's remarkable flower garden planted against an adobe wall with the red rocks of Pinyon Mesa in the background.

Across the living room, the windows looked out on the Book Cliffs rising abruptly from the flat arid land, sealing off the valley to the north, a ragged, barren study in weathered rock and plunging shale, the colors of alkali, ash, and terracotta. To Winna, the Book Cliffs resembled an earthbound moonscape. She wanted to photograph it at sunrise or during a snowstorm—a blizzard would be best. She laughed at herself.

She had dressed for the occasion in a brown silk blouse with a matching broomstick skirt, her mother's squash blossom necklace, and turquoise earrings. All dressed up, sipping white wine, she was more interested in the play of violet shadows on Mount Garfield than she was in anyone in the room.

She heard Kate call her name and turned away from the window. With a naughty sparkle in her eyes, Kate held the hand of a man with white hair and a beard. She pulled him toward her. "I'll bet you can't guess who this handsome hunk used to be."

Winna smiled as she studied his face. "Wow, I'm stumped." But just as the words left her mouth, she recognized the blue eyes and felt her face flush with embarrassment. "It's been such a long time, Johnny."

"Over forty years," he said, reaching for her hand. "Look, Kate, I'm at an advantage here. Winna hasn't changed a bit."

"It only took me a second," she insisted. "I could never forget Johnny Hodell. The last time I saw you, you had brown hair and didn't have a beard, in—when was it—1956?"

He pulled her in for a hug. "You were and are gorgeous." Then turning to their hostess, he said, "Please excuse us, Katie, we are going to retire to the patio."

Suddenly Winna found herself in the soft light of a fading day standing on the Crosses' patio with John Hodell. He had been her steady during their junior and senior years in high school. Back then, he was a handsome member of the baseball and ski teams. He drove a highly polished red 1954 Chevy convertible with leather seats. Their whole relationship had developed in that car. Those were the fun memories, but there were others. Winna looked at him and pushed them from her mind. *Surely he had changed—grown up.*

Suddenly tiny beads of sweat moistened the backs of her hands and trickled down the curve of her spine. "It's awfully hot—or is it just me?"

"It's nice out here," he said, looking cool and relaxed, his smiling eyes fixed on Winna's burning face.

As the reflected light of an approaching sunset splashed Mount Garfield pink and silver, she took the hand John offered. He led her to the porch chairs facing the view. With forty-some years to account for, they fell easily into conversation. She went first, bringing him up to date with a quick review of her life: college, marriage, child, career, divorce. Drawn to him as if their separation had been forty minutes, she wondered why she felt frozen in time, why she was still holding his hand. Gently, she slipped her hand from his grasp and picked up her drink.

His voice was soft, deep, musical. He looked at her the same way he had when they were sixteen. Then, she had loved him. He smoothed his moustache with two fingers and ran his hand through what was left of his hair. Had he always done that, stroked his hair?

"Nothing much has happened to me." He appeared almost apologetic. "After you and Maggie, I never found another love. But I've had fun looking." His eyes twinkled as he gave Winna an achingly familiar smile. "No children—of that I'm certain. I spent three years in Vietnam. I was luckier than most, I had a job with my dad when I got home. Now it's all work all the time—very boring."

For a second it had slipped Winna's mind that during college he had married their schoolmate Maggie Hart, one of Winna's best friends. Maggie was a natural athlete, a striking blonde with naturally curly hair, one of the prettiest, most popular girls at school. During the last two years of high school, Maggie and Winna had been best friends with Kate. The three of them did everything together. After high school, Winna had lost touch with Maggie. She tried to remember why. She had gone off to college and Maggie had not. Winna had written, but her friend hadn't answered her letters. She remembered her disappointment. Maggie had died young, while Winna was living on the East Coast. She searched her mind for the forgotten details.

"Actually, I don't want you to think I'm boring," he said, resting his drink on the little paunch hidden under his loose-fitting shirt. "I still ski and play tennis. I like to read—history mostly—and I collect Indian art."

Winna laughed. "Then you are not boring."

Suddenly his eyes wandered and he caught himself. "I see your sister, Chloe, here and there. She's been married a few times, I understand."

"Twice—working on a third," she said, wishing she had worded it differently.

"I've seen her with Todd Cody. Is he her guy?"

She brightened. "That's his name. I haven't met him yet. He's fifteen years younger than Chloe. Of course, she looks twenty years younger than she is—so they're probably a great looking match."

"I didn't know he was engaged."

Winna smiled. "Well, I doubt it's formal."

"Actually, he's one of my foremen."

"Really?" She was eager for a personal reference.

"Todd's a great guy—reliable, hardworking, fun to bend an elbow with."

Winna breathed an audible sigh of relief. "I've been concerned. Chloe's been through a lot. Dad was beastly toward her. He left everything to me, including the house."

"Wow, that's tough."

"The house—it's a mess." Uncomfortable, she wondered if she had been too open about her sister. Winna rolled her eyes. "You must come see my mess. I'm up to my neck in antiques at the house on Seventh."

"Your grandparents' house?"

"Dad lived there too. He sold the house on Peach Tree Ridge and moved there in the seventies."

"Sorry to hear about your father. The TV and newspapers were full of it." John seemed to look at her with caution. "First the disappearance was big news, the search, and finally the discovery—by a hiker?" He shifted himself into a more comfortable position. "I thought of you often—during all that."

Winna hadn't seen the press coverage. "Chloe wanted me to come and help her search for him, but I couldn't. She even hired a psychic. It didn't pay off—I believed it wouldn't. But it did give us reason for an argument.

"Hiking around the mountains and coming upon my father's dead body was the last thing in the world I wanted to do. I stayed home, lit candles, and prayed. Besides," she said, pausing to remember, "I had imagined a happy ending for my father."

John looked surprised and she gave up a little laugh. "I thought maybe he'd gone for a drive in the mountains, parked the car, and took a walk on a trail where he'd come upon a little house. Inside the house lived a woman about his age. Dad had always needed a woman in his life. He'd been alone for years—since Ruth left. And I imagined that he and this little old lady were glad for each other's company and he stayed there with her playing cards, enjoying the sunsets from their high mountain perch."

"That's a nice story, Winna," he smiled again, patting her knee, then seemed to retreat for a beat into his own thoughts.

"Unaweep Canyon," he said, pulling on his neatly trimmed white beard. "What was he doing there?"

"We don't know. Dad really loved the place and it's so close to town. Police suspect he became disoriented. The stress of being lost may have brought on a stroke or a heart attack that caused his fall."

"According to the papers, the car had burned and was found at the top of the canyon and your father at the bottom. Why did it take so long to find his body?"

"Actually, his body was found before the car. The police said none of that was unusual. His body didn't fall right below the car, so it wasn't a matter of getting out of the car and falling. You know how complex mountain terrain can be. Searchers can walk right past a body and not see it. All kinds of search parties looked right after Dad disappeared but they never looked in the right place. Chloe even hired a helicopter. No luck. Then the snows came. I had a phone conversation with the man who found him and he has promised to take me to the place—you know—where he was."

John gave her a quizzical look and smiled. "It's rather surprising to me that Chloe did so much to find him—after all, she'd been disinherited."

"She didn't know then—not until the will was read."

"I'm sorry, Winna. I can see this is upsetting to you." He looked away, into his glass. "Why don't I freshen our drinks, and then you can tell me about the house?"

"Thanks. I'm okay. I don't want another drink."

"Still a cheap date." He smiled, his eyes crinkling at the corners. "I won't either."

They grew silent for a moment, watching Mount Garfield vanish into the darkness, as the last long narrow splash of red dropped behind a cottonwood grove.

"John, I'm sorry, but I'm struggling to remember what happened to Maggie. I know she died around the time we took Dad to Denver to dry out."

"She died in '82—in Aspen—ski accident." He looked at the ice in his empty glass and Winna guessed he wished it were full.

"I'm sorry. She was such a great friend and a wonderful skier. I'll never forget skiing with her. We had so much fun." Winna paused a moment as a memory came to mind. "Did she ever tell you about the time we were spring skiing at Aspen? We were hot and took off our sweaters, tied them around our waists, and skied in our bras. That got us hoots from the boys on the chairlift."

"No, she didn't," he said with a forced smile. Winna remembered that young John would have frowned on such gay abandon, unless he had been the one to remove her sweater.

The last time Winna saw John was before they went off to college. She was ready to say goodbye and get on with her life, but he was not happy with their separation. Feeling on edge with the memory, she paused and returned to the subject of the house.

"I don't know how I'm going to get that old house cleaned out and ready to sell. My daughter Emily has been a great help, but things are going slowly. My home and my work are waiting for me in New Hampshire. I've got to hire some help."

He leaned in as if to come to her aid. "What kind of help are you looking for?"

"Handyman and garden jobs—someone strong—there are heavy pieces of furniture to move, painting to do, trash removal, the yard—you name it." She suddenly felt overwhelmed.

"I know a guy. Can't think of his name right now. Todd knows him too," he said. "Why don't you call me at my office and I'll look him up for you. Sometimes I have work for him."

"Great. I will." She paused, then glanced at John. "It's funny being here with you—in this town. The place is so haunted for me—"

He laughed. "I know what you mean. I feel like—well—let's just say my memories of you at sixteen are vivid."

Winna blushed and looked down at her hands, afraid to admit that in his presence she felt completely vulnerable, unsure that she still had sixty-one years under her belt.

"Now, pretty lady, I've kept you to myself long enough. Let's go inside." He grabbed Winna's hand, pulled her up from the chair, and led her back inside the house.

"Look at them." Holding her gaze, John inclined his head toward the roomful of guests. "You went to school with almost half of them. You did so well identifying me. Let's mingle a little, and see if you can identify the remains of your former schoolmates."

7

1938

NORA GRUMMAN OPENED her eyes and looked at the clock on the bedside table. It was eight—only four hours of sleep. Henry's place in bed was cold. He had gone to work. She felt sorry for him and pulled his pillow into her arms for a long hug and a kiss. She rolled over to her back and stared at the ceiling. Still dancing, the music lingered in her head.

What a night it had been—the music, the crowded ballroom, the lavish Christmas decorations, the women's gowns, the men in tuxes, her partners' delighted faces. Again, she felt Henry holding her close, waltzing her around the room, whispering in her ear. He was a wonderful dancer. She had never been so happy—a happiness so intense she felt she would burst if she didn't share it.

Wide awake, she got out of bed, reached for her robe, and headed for the coffee pot. With the coffee made and a cup to sip, she sat down in their barely furnished living room, a couple of *Life* magazines in her lap. Their apartment did not have a desk or even a table and she couldn't find a pen or stationery. On the back of an envelope, with a pencil, she began a letter to her mother.

> Oh, Mother!
> We did have such a wonderful time last night at the
> La Court—the night of the big party in our honor.
> I'll send you a clipping from the newspaper so you
> will know who all was there—everyone said they
> wished you hadn't moved away and asked me to
> send you their love.

Nora described the decorations, the flowers, what everyone
wore. She explained that Juliana had wanted to give the party in
honor of the bride and groom while Nora could still wear a formal.
She wrote that she could feel the baby she was carrying just a little,
but she didn't show yet. She had worn the gown her mother had
made—the blue one that matched her eyes. She thanked her, saying:

> Everyone went mad over it—and me—if I do say
> so. I am not conceited, you know that, but it was so
> much fun to have everyone so fond of and proud of
> me. Mrs. Chandler said I looked like a 'Dresden Doll.'

Nora described the men in their tuxes and how Henry had
looked like a prince, the band Juliana had hired, the delightful
music. She said that she hardly had a chance to dance with her husband because all the men had wanted to dance with her. How, at
last in his arms, he had said that the more he looked around at other
girls, the more he loved his Nora.

> It's so much fun being so happy. Henry and I decided
> last night that we just couldn't be unhappy—we just
> don't know how. I think I'll go back to sleep. I just
> had to tell you what a wonderful time we had and I
> couldn't hold it any longer. Mother, I can't begin to
> tell you—I wish you could be here. All our love, Nora

THE DAY AFTER Winna was born by caesarian section, Nora counted sixteen bouquets of flowers from family and friends delivered to her hospital room: roses, carnations, lilies, and lilacs crowded onto table tops, windowsills, even into the corners of the room. The Watsons, who owned one of the two flower shops in town, sent a large purple orchid; in Grand Junction orchids were seldom seen and much prized. Because St. Mary's Hospital was famous for terrible food, Nora's best friend brought delicious meals. There were gifts: a satin baby pillow, a pretty compact and nightgown for the new mother, and lots of cards and telegrams filled with good wishes. All this, even though the child was a girl named Edwina for her grandfather. She was supposed to have been another Edwin. Nora was glad it was a girl and laughed off the memory of her father-in-law's offer to pay her three-hundred dollars if she would give him a grandson.

Lying in bed surrounded by the sweet scent of flowers, Nora could see Grand Mesa out her window, a blue flattop mountain bordering the east side of the valley. All her life she had watched clouds move over the valley dropping blankets of shade over the mountains.

Now and then, she still pinched herself. She had come back to Grand Junction. The very town she was excited to leave when her father was promoted and transferred to LA in 1935. She grew to love Hollywood and the City of Angels with its theatres, art museums, and nearby beaches. She liked the cool foggy mornings, the afternoon sunshine, the almost constant presence of flowers in the garden. Sometimes—with a sense of liberation—she thought back to the unimportant little town where she was born, glad to be living so far away.

Then one day, as Nora was helping her mother shell peas in the kitchen, Henry Grumman—and Grand Junction—came to her door. She welcomed him inside the house and into her heart. They had been friends in high school, had dated once or twice. He had changed. No longer boyish, he stood there a full-grown man with love in his eyes. Their reunion led to a brief, passionate courtship followed by a wedding at Carmel by the Sea. Nora's pregnancy was also a surprise, an event that pulled them back to Colorado where Henry had been promised a partnership in the family business. Home again, they struggled to live on the small salary Edwin Grumman paid his son. Henry did not complain and encouraged Nora to be patient. His father would increase his wage as he took on more responsibility and ascended to full partnership.

Nora lay in her hospital bed learning how to nurse her baby girl. Even though her friends swore by an infant formula, she wanted to breast-feed her baby. Dr. Sloane seemed not to have an opinion one way or another and neither did Henry. Magazine ads made using the baby formula sound preferable, easier, even more nutritious. Nora thought differently—Mother Nature could not be improved upon. At first, nursing was painful. Nora worried, but as the days passed it became easier and the baby gained weight.

Every time her mind wandered off to all she had left behind, Nora told herself to forget California. She loved her husband and the tiny daughter in her arms. She would make her life here. Two very dear friends still lived in town and the mountains and countryside beckoned to her. She wanted to spend time there with her drawing materials, to draw the mesas and the rows of peach trees in the orchards, and to paint the skies with oils.

After eight days of hospital confinement, Nora was helped into Edwin Grumman's shiny black Cadillac Fleetwood, baby Edwina was placed in her arms, and they were transported to the house on Seventh Street where her mother-in-law, Juliana, would nurse her back to health. A caesarian section required a long period of bed rest.

Carried upstairs by two hospital orderlies, Nora was put to bed in the guest room. She had not wanted to be isolated upstairs all day and had hoped they could make her a bed in the library. Juliana insisted that she be in a proper bedroom where she could rest away from the household bustle. The baby was taken to the nursery down the hall from her room—Henry's old bedroom. Nora was told that confined to bed in a quiet room, she would heal faster and regain her strength. She knew it was useless to complain and surrendered herself to Juliana's will and care.

THE GRUMMANS HAD two servants, a married couple who lived on the third floor at the back of the house. Maria kept house and cooked, and Roberto did maintenance and the lawn and gardens. After Nora and the baby arrived, Juliana told Maria to carry on with her usual chores, she would take care of the mother and child. With her patient captive upstairs, Juliana put on a cotton housedress and apron and bustled through her chores, never complaining about extra work—diapers and baths for baby, clean bandages for mother.

At the time of Winna's birth, Juliana was too old to have any more children of her own. She knew she appeared matronly, her waist thickened, her once lustrous hair bobbed and streaked gray, her honey brown eyes glistening behind thick glasses.

Overwhelmed by the fierce love she felt for her first grandchild, she made time to sit down and write a flowery poem about little Edwina's rosebud mouth, petal soft skin, deep-as-the-midnight-sky eyes, and her own rose-colored glasses. She liked to write poetry, long, long letters to her friends, and short stories. She submitted her poems and stories to newspapers and magazines—sometimes with success.

Within two days of Nora's release from the hospital, Juliana held a dinner party, inviting her three best friends and their husbands. Juliana was a good cook and enjoyed planning and helping Maria prepare the meal.

When Nora insisted that she felt well enough to come down for dinner, Juliana sent Henry upstairs to quash that idea. "She may very well be able to walk down the stairs, but walking back up would pose a threat to her. The doctor said no stairs! I insist you talk sense into your wife."

Juliana wanted to be the center of attention that evening. She asked Henry to bring baby Edwina downstairs for a showing and she was passed around and ogled. One by one, the ladies excused themselves and went upstairs to say hello to Nora. After courtesies were paid, Juliana asked Maria to take dinner up to her daughter-in-law. She had insisted that her son dine with her guests. Nora dined alone.

It was obvious to Nora that having a baby in the house filled the new grandmother with a burst of fresh energy. *She probably misses the days when she had babies of her own.* No one ever talked about the Grummans' daughter, Grace, who was born when Henry was three. The child had died of influenza at the age of five, leaving Juliana to grieve—unreasonably long, according to old Dr. Northrop. Henry had said that the doctor suggested to Edwin that as an aid to his wife's recovery, the child's name go unmentioned. Nora followed that advice and was careful not to pry.

After their arrival at the house on Seventh Street, when baby Edwina was brought in to nurse, she did not seem hungry. Urging her baby to the breast, Nora felt comforted by the infant's eyes focused intently on her face.

"Who are you, little one?" she whispered, wishing for her own mother. *It is true babies are little strangers. She looks at me like I'm a stranger with a face she must memorize.*

Nora's mother had wanted to come for the birth. It had been planned, but Hope Neely was recovering from a recent bout of pneumonia. Nora missed her.

Puzzled by her mother-in-law, she wondered when they would bond. Nora was willing. She admired Juliana, saw her as intelligent and accomplished, but her affection seemed to run hot and cold. Every time Nora began to fear that Juliana disliked her or wonder if she had somehow offended, her mother-in-law would tell her how lovely she was or say something about how much she hoped they would be good friends. Once, Juliana told her how deeply she had loved her own mother-in-law, how she hoped Nora would love her just as much.

When Juliana weighed her granddaughter every day, she happily reported her progress to Nora. Even though the baby seemed to spend very little time at the breast, she was gaining weight nicely. Soon Nora's breasts were engorged and Juliana called the doctor.

Faced with his patient's bleeding nipples and agonizingly inflamed breasts, Dr. Sloane forbade her to continue breastfeeding. He bound her tightly in strips of an old sheet and prescribed large doses of aspirin. The aspirin made her head spin and her ears ring but never quite touched her pain. All she could do was close her eyes and try to sleep the nightmare away.

The doctor insisted that they give the baby formula, but he had nothing to prescribe for Nora's disappointment, her feelings of failure. As clean bed linens snuggled her to sleep, she could not help but compare Juliana's lovely guest room—the rose covered wallpaper and white curtains, the pretty twin beds covered with pale green coverlets—with the tiny, barely furnished apartment she shared with Henry.

She longed for those four small rooms: to sleep curled around Henry's back, to get back to her first cookbook and the mastery of a new art. She wanted to sew curtains for the living room. Handsome new material was waiting for her at home. Nora wanted to go home, even to the ironing board they used for a kitchen table.

JULIANA REIGNED VICTORIOUS. The doctor insisted that the baby be bottle-fed and her daughter-in-law was drying up in the guest room. She was certain it was for the best. Unknown to everyone, she had been feeding the baby with formula. She went on with her usual preparation, no longer hiding like a sneak thief mixing it up out of sight.

Juliana had been unable to nurse her own babies and believed the infant formula superior. In fact, she believed she had done Nora a favor. The silly girl was old-fashioned in her thinking and would soon get over her disappointment. Besides, she wanted to feed her granddaughter herself, to hold the bottle and rock the precious child in her arms.

She had not recovered from her son's decision to marry without her blessing, or the fact that the wedding had taken place in California. She wondered why Nora, who had come from a fine family, hadn't known better.

Juliana had to admit that Henry had chosen well. He married the daughter of a formerly prominent family in Grand Junction. It was, in her opinion, good fortune that Nora's immediate pregnancy had brought her wandering son home. Ever since he had dropped out of college, he had fruitlessly looked for a job—first in New Orleans and then San Francisco—his two favorite cities. The Depression had made it impossible for him.

His first two years, Henry had attended Mesa College. His grades were good and he applied to Columbia University's School of Journalism. When his letter of acceptance arrived, Juliana could not wait to hear the news. She steamed open the envelope. Then came the bitter disappointment. He left Columbia after only one semester, having failed every class. Henry did not want to be a journalist after all. Saying that "a life of hard work and adventure" would suit him better, he wanted to ship out to South America on one of United Fruit Company's banana boats.

She doubted that. His remark was designed to horrify her. She had to tell her friends something. "Henry has gone out into the world to find himself." At the very least, that sounded poetic and not so shameful. Though she could hardly let herself think it, she feared that her son wanted to get as far away from her as possible. The unions came to her rescue when they forced United Fruit to stop hiring non-union men. For the first time in her life, she thanked a union.

Nora and Henry had joked about getting pregnant on their wedding night, but Juliana wondered. Whether or not Nora was pregnant before the marriage, the scheduled caesarian delivery of the baby exactly nine months to the day after their marriage date had worked perfectly.

ONE AFTERNOON NORA looked up from her book to see her mother-in-law standing in the guest room doorway with the baby wrapped in a blanket, fondly contemplating her grandchild's face. Without a word, Juliana raised her narrowing eyes and looked at Nora with a cynical smile on her face.

"Nora, my dear," she said coolly, "you know I could take this child away from you if I wanted."

Nora caught her breath and closed her book. "What? What are you saying?" As if she felt a chill, she grasped the opening to her bed jacket and pulled it close. "Why in the world would you want to do that?"

Juliana spoke bluntly, her eyes unwavering. "I don't—but I could if I had a reason." Then with a shrug, as if to say, "Well, like it or not, now you know," she turned and disappeared into the hall with Nora's baby in her arms.

8

1999

EXCEPT FOR THE RELATIVELY new double-door refrigerator, Winna liked to joke that the large kitchen on Seventh Street should be preserved in a museum. A vintage 1950s electric stove—still in working condition—squatted beside the original four-legged wood-burning stove still shining like a well-blackened shoe. A cast-iron sink and drain board on tall fat legs stood under a large sunny window, the built-in breakfast nook waited below a row of stained-glass windows with square green medallions set among stylized leaves. The windows opened to a view of the garden as if through a leafy portal.

No wonder Ruth left Dad, Winna thought. He was famously frugal and probably wouldn't part with the money to modernize the kitchen or anything else.

She couldn't enter the room without her mind reeling backward in time. More than any other room, the kitchen remained a monument to Juliana's peculiar brand of logic. Though she had money to spend, she could not part with anything that still worked. She never owned a dishwasher. On occasion, she insisted on washing the dishes herself. When she did, she sang or recited poetry aloud from memory—the way she had as a child drying dishes for her mother.

Winna had to believe that her grandmother must have made sense to herself. Not much interested in politics herself, Winna saw her grandmother as a rabid Republican with early feminist leanings. Most of the women in the country had to wait until 1920 for full women's suffrage, but in 1893 Colorado women got the vote. Colorado men had crossed the mountains, settling the territory side by side with their hearty, steadfast wives. They knew their women were as smart and capable as men and allowed them the vote. As a young woman, Juliana helped in voter registration campaigns and talked to women's groups about the importance of the vote. She conceived of and funded the first mobile library in Grand Junction, bringing books to farming families and the poor who lived in town. She left the church because she believed in evolution and thought the church was "pig headed" in insisting that the Bible was a science book. Although she treated her Mexican housekeeper like a creature well beneath her, she refused an opportunity to join the DAR. She thought they were a pack of snooty racists. Juliana was Juliana.

Having a grandmother deeply involved in politics had made a strong impression on young Winna. In the fall of 1948, while playing jacks on the sidewalk outside the school, Winna and her girlfriends started talking about the coming presidential election. She was the only kid who wanted the Republican, Thomas Dewey. All the others wanted Democrat Harry Truman.

One of her friends loudly announced that her daddy thought Dewey looked like a shyster.

Wondering *what's a shyster?* Winna shot back. "No, siree."

Her friend had another talking point. "Dewey's just for the rich people. Truman's for the common folks."

"So's Dewey!" Winna argued, not sure if she was exactly right about common folks. In reaction to the Democrats' frequent mentioning of "common people," she had heard her grandmother say that she would hit anyone over the head with her pocketbook who called her common. Winna knew that Juliana passionately disliked

Harry Truman because she had heard her call him "that haber-
dasher!" It sounded just awful.

When Truman won by a hair, Winna's elders thought the world
had come to an end. For too many years already they had suffered
Roosevelt's New Deal. With her face screwed up like she had
smelled something rancid, Juliana pronounced it "Rue-zee-velt."
She thought his First Lady was both scandalously leftist and arro-
gantly patrician. Eleanor Roosevelt, alone, inspired her to work for
the Republican Party. By 1949, Juliana had become president of the
Colorado Federation of Women's Republican Clubs.

WINNA HAD FIGURED out how to make coffee using the ancient
aluminum drip coffee maker she found in the kitchen. At the table,
mottled with light coming through the trees, Emily sipped her cup
as she fed the baby rice cereal.

Winna had some news. "You know the ring we found with the
marbles? The jeweler said it's a real canary yellow diamond—probably worth eighty-thousand dollars."

"What!" Isabelle jumped at Emily's spirited response. She
stopped eating and looked wide-eyed at her mother.

"He said that if I didn't believe him, I could get an appraisal in
Denver, if I wanted to take it there."   '

"Where's the ring now?" she asked. Isabelle kicked her feet impatiently, waiting for the spoon Emily had poised in midair.

Her brand new Nikon D1 in hand, Winna focused on Isabelle's
enormous brown eyes, with dark lashes casting feathery shadows
over her ivory skin. She got the shot and put down her camera.

"I opened a safe deposit box at the bank." Winna refilled her cup,
then nuzzled her granddaughter's plump cheek. She smelled deli-
ciously sweet, even with cereal all over her face. She could hardly
wait to hold her.

"That's good. Why in the world was a ring like that put away
with the marbles?"

"Your guess is as good as mine," Winna said, ready to change
the subject. "I love seeing Isabelle here—in this room—the fifth

generation. It's my favorite room. Not because of its beauty—it has none—but the memories. At this very table I ate at least a million of Gramma's waffles with chunks of cold butter and warm maple syrup. She called me Edwina and corrected people who erred by calling me Winna." Smiling at the memory, she placed her camera on the table and sat down. "It's strange; even though Dad lived here for years, you wouldn't know it. All I see is Juliana—her amazing taste, her elegance, her strange personality."

"Why didn't Ruth make Poppa throw out all the junk? She just moved in and lived with it?" Emily asked, opening a jar of applesauce.

"Not for long. As I remember, she didn't like the house on Peach Tree Ridge so Daddy said they could sell it and live here. She probably thought she'd become the lady of the manor but got a horrible surprise when he refused to part with anything that had belonged to his mother. I think she gave up and left for California not too long after that—maybe a year."

"Why wouldn't he want the place cleaned out? Keep the treasures and dump the rest?" she asked, her spoon headed for Isabelle's open mouth.

"Your trash is my treasure—that kind of thing. Daddy was his mother's devoted acolyte. He was always dragging out some old thing from a closet and bringing it to me for show and tell."

"Sounds weird to me," Emily said, smiling at her daughter's messy face. "My favorite room is the master bedroom—all that light. Mom, if you want to give me anything, I want that bed—the whole bedroom set, really."

"Sure, if Chloe doesn't want it. I'm surprised you like it so much—it's so heavy and masculine."

"I like masculine—remember I live with a man."

"I like Juliana's room better—all that cool light, the quiet colors."

"It's interesting that she took the room at the back, as far as she could get from her husband."

"You're right. It would've been logical for her to take the room next door to his—it's a far grander room." Winna paused for a thought. "Often when I go into her room, I remember a story she told me—the most romantic story I've ever heard. She was ill then and resting in bed. She thought she was dying, I suppose—otherwise I don't think she would've told me."

Emily wet a face cloth at the kitchen sink. "You were her favorite."

"Yes. She never said so, but everybody else pointed it out to me. Especially Mother and Chloe. It seemed odd to me that she wouldn't call me Winna. If I was her favorite why would she call me 'Edwina' when she knew I hated my name? Probably because I knew I was supposed to have been 'Edwin.'" Winna paused, sipping the strong hot coffee. She had never felt comfortable as the favorite. It had been impossible to believe she deserved lt.

"I went to visit her when she was sick and Gramma told me a fantastic story. One that's almost hard to believe. She said that she had fallen in love for the first time in high school, but he went away to college, to work, to war—I don't remember where he went—but he went away for several years leaving her behind—as she put it—to pine for him. When he finally returned to Grand Junction, Gramma had already married Poppa Ed."

"He was a catch," Emily said, dabbing at the baby's mouth and chin.

"One of the richest men on the Western Slope. Anyway, sometime later Gramma and her old sweetheart became reacquainted. She gave me no details, saying only that she'd decided to leave Poppa and my father—who was a baby at the time—and run away with her lover."

"My God, weren't you shocked?"

"Actually, I didn't think about it like that until later. I was a romantic teenager with stars in my eyes—you know. Gramma said she packed her bags. She went to the train station to meet him, but at the last minute she couldn't get on the train. When it came down to the moment, she realized that she couldn't leave her baby son. She said she kissed her lover goodbye and watched the train pull out of the station. Later, she learned that he had died on that trip."

9

1932–1946

LOOKING DOWNCAST, her hair a touch out of place as if she had been slaving somewhere in the house, Juliana approached her husband in the library. Edwin was relaxed in his favorite leather easy chair with the evening paper, a cloud of cigar smoke around his head. His wife came quietly and sat at his feet, leaning against the ottoman. He lowered the paper and gazed down on her.

"Edwin, my dear," she said. "You are a dear and generous husband, but soon I must face the Spring Ball and have nothing to wear."

"When's the dance?" Having just remembered that he had wanted an old book from one of the top shelves, he was distracted. His eyes fixed high up on the wall as he tried to zero in on the large volume—brown, he thought. He promised himself that the moment he was free of her he would find it.

"April twenty-fifth—only a month away."

He appraised his wife and had to admit that at the moment she looked a bit tatty.

"Surely you want me to make a good impression, to look like the wife of a prominent man."

Edwin's eyes narrowed. He rubbed his chin and nodded, hoping to show some empathy.

"I looked through my closet, dear," she said, looking hopeful that her plea would reach him, "and found that I would have to present myself wearing last year's fashions. You can be sure that my friends will have shopped in Denver for the very latest."

"If they are your friends," he said, "why don't they shop at Grumman's?"

"Well, dear, I can't answer that." She removed the comb from her hair and, gathering stray strands together, repinned them. "You are a man, and don't understand the consequences of these things, but I tell you, Edwin, it's important to keep up."

Edwin squashed the newspaper in his lap and puffed harder on his cigar. "My dear," he said, "you know all you have to do is ask and the doors at Grumman's are opened for you. I'll tell Wilcox to expect you in the ladies' department day after tomorrow—will that be time enough?" He knew she would rather take the train to Denver for a few days of shopping, but was relieved to see her nod weakly.

She had let him know that he was her second choice for a husband and he got back at her quietly through his pocket book and by withdrawing his affection and attention. Edwin hadn't analyzed his feelings for her. He didn't know why he had adopted what he saw as his refusal to argue with his wife. Juliana had suffered a nervous collapse in 1918, early in their marriage when Henry was still a toddler. He remembered how hopeless she had been, how miserably unhappy, her rages at him and their son. Since then, he had given her wide berth.

"I have one more request, dear," she said. "The Conrads and the Hendersons are coming to dinner Friday night and I want to serve something special—from the butcher. You know Mr. Ricci runs a cash-and-carry business. He does not accept checks nor will he let me charge."

"You can charge at the market," he said as he lifted the newspaper. "Why do you insist on patronizing that dago place anyway?" He frowned at her over the paper.

She winced. "I wish you wouldn't use that awful word, Edwin. Mr. Ricci has the very best meat in town."

Edwin shook his head. "Very well." He reached deep into his pants pocket. From the wad of bills in his hand, he peeled off two dollars. "Will that be enough?"

"I'm serving roast beef. I wanted to make you proud by serving a lovely meal."

"Well, then here," he said, dipping inside his pocket for more. He produced a handful of coins, selected three quarters, and placed them in her eager palm. "Here's enough to provide a feast."

EDWIN GRUMMAN WAS born outside Kansas City where both of his grandfathers farmed. His parents migrated to Grand Junction in 1882 where his father, Edwin Sr., founded the original Grumman's department store. No matter how successful he was as a businessman, Edwin Jr. remained a man of unsophisticated tastes and little education. He had quit high school to go into the family business. His manners were rusty at best and though he was tall and handsome, with gentle blue-gray eyes and fine-chiseled features, he came across as unpolished.

Juliana had no money of her own, not until her parents died just after the war. The devoted couple passed away within weeks of one another, her father following her mother. Juliana believed her father had been unwilling to go on without his beloved wife. By the time her father passed, he had amassed a small fortune, leaving Juliana free from her husband's control.

Edwin was quite aware that except when she needed his favor, Juliana never let him forget her superior education and breeding. She had come from educated people and money—though not as much money as he had amassed. He supposed that when she corrected his English and manners in front of family and friends, she did not want people to think she didn't know the difference.

"Get to the point, dear," she would suggest, interrupting his meandering stories.

Edwin never snapped back at her. He obeyed her commands or ignored her. He took comfort in his favorite easy chair behind a newspaper or one of his railroading histories, smoking his Cuban cigars, as if her jabs had not hit their mark.

JULIANA RESENTED EDWIN'S stoicism, his womanish ways, his lack of interest in her, his careless social graces, his barely passable manners, and most of all, what she saw as his sluggish intellect. His habits irritated her. Even in summer, after he washed his hair, he was so afraid of catching a cold that he wore a knitted cap on his head for half the day until his hair had dried. She hated driving with him in the car. He insisted on going just under the speed limit while preaching about the rudeness of the honking drivers held captive behind him. The more they honked the more he self-righteously hogged the road. Edwin would gladly hold up traffic until a train of cars behind him covered half a mile. She was so angry with him one morning that she told him she did not mind one bit if he did not come home to dinner.

"Stay at the store forever. I can't bear looking at you!" she had raged.

Juliana herself was appalled by her rages. She dreaded her memory of the time when little Henry was about two years old, and she had flown into a rage at some little thing he'd done. When she had calmed down, she saw how much she had frightened him, how he shook with terror, how his crying made him vomit his lunch. She cried for days after that.

Edwin had to shorten his hours at the store. She could no longer be left alone with the servants or take care of her child. The doctor said she needed a rest cure.

Before Juliana left for California and her best friend Laura's loving care, she wrote a long letter to her husband outlining exactly how she wanted her son raised if she should die, then made a list of her belongings and to whom each possession should go upon her death. She slipped the list into an envelope, sealed it, and wrote, "To be opened only after my death, Juliana S. Grumman."

She left little Henry with her mother in Grand Junction and took the train west. In Santa Monica she stayed in a guest cottage on the beach at her friend's estate. For two months she walked the beach, slept under an umbrella stuck in the sand, and thought how different her life would have been if she had waited for her first love, if she hadn't been so impatient and sure that wealth would make her happy.

Edwin's letters from home proclaimed his love. He promised to be more thoughtful and begged her to return. While her mother took care of her child, she watched seagulls dip over the rolling waves. At night, she was lulled to sleep by the gentle moon-rays coming in through the window and the sound of the sea.

WHEN HER GRANDCHILDREN were young, Juliana was always delighted to receive Winna and Chloe. The girls spent many days and nights at the house on Seventh Street. They slept in the guest room at the front of the house—the one with the turret bay windows and a door to the north balcony. From there, they could look down on their grandmother's shade garden.

Juliana taught them the names of the plants there: Colorado columbine, lady's mantle with its soft-as-velvet leaves, apple green sweet woodruff, tiny nodding coral bells at the border's edge and, in spring, crocuses and jonquils. It was a great luxury to have a cool green place to sit in the dappled shade of trees on a hot summer day and she had made sure the children understood that.

As they sat together in the garden, Juliana would tell stories, and one time she taught them a nursery rhyme: "Mistress Mary quite contrary, how does your garden grow? With silver bells and cockle-shells. Sing cuckolds all in a row."

ONE SUMMER, FOLLOWING days of scorching heat, the girls came to stay for a couple of days. From the summerhouse, Winna watched as violent thunderheads moved into the valley. After splashing the sky with lighting and beating the clouds with thunder, down came a torrential rain. Like little natives whose prayers had been answered at the end of a rain dance, Winna and Chloe ran out into the rose garden.

Once the thunder had passed, the children found the rain showers to be a kind of magical play. They danced in the rain and the flickering light of the sun as it peeked in and out of the clouds. They were South Sea island maidens bathing under a waterfall, or fairies frolicking beneath rain-drenched shrubs. They shrieked with joy when a rainbow arched out of the clouds. Their skin soaked in warm drizzle, they watched droplets of rain, like shining diamonds, roll into the pollen dusted hearts of red and pink velvet roses.

Into this bliss Poppa Edwin came. His galoshes protected polished black wing tips as he picked his way carefully through the wet grass under a big black umbrella.

"Come on out of the rain, Edwina," he called, a worried look on his face. "Get your little sister and come on in." Her grandfather looked as uncomfortable in the rain as a fish out of water.

"Mother lets us play in the rain."

"Your grandmother sent me on out here to get you. You know how she is afraid of storms." He shivered as if the sight of two little girls in soaking clothes would catch him his death.

"Aw, Poppa," she begged. "It's okay—we aren't cold—are we, Chloe?"

"It's nice in the rain," Chloe chimed. "Can we play with your umbrella?"

"Certainly not. You'll get struck dead by lightning," he said, taking Chloe by the hand. "Your grandmother wants you inside—so inside you go." He dragged her up the grass path. "Come, Edwina."

Winna followed, calling ahead, "But Poppa, the lightning is over." She wondered why her grandparents did not know how to enjoy life, why they were always bickering among themselves or worrying about this and that, especially about how their mother raised them.

"That mother of yours lets you run wild," Edwin announced as they approached the house.

"She does not," Chloe yelled, pulling free of his clutch. "She's the best mother in the whole world and you are mean to say that!"

"Hush up or I'll take you home," he groused, yanking her arm.

Chloe began to cry and Winna put on her best sulk as Juliana, armed with fluffy white towels, hurried the girls onto the verandah and stripped them naked.

"Now you wrap up in these towels while Maria dries your clothes," she snapped before she disappeared into the safety of the house.

Young Winna wondered why her grandparents did not love each other. As far as she knew, married people did. She did not understand. But in time, her nightmares about the house revealed that there was something terribly wrong on Seventh Street.

10

1999

WINNA WAITED UNTIL the heat wave had passed before she ventured into the attic early one morning. The stairs to that dark inferno lay behind a door at the end of the second floor hall, just outside Juliana's bedroom. The attic stretched the width of the front of the house. In the back, old rooms once used by servants were accessible only by the backstairs. As she came to the top of the stairs, cold light from the dormer window at the north end fell like a searchlight across a shambles of old furniture: a landscape of tangled wooden and metal shapes, a haphazard growth of abandoned objects once central to life. Over her shoulder, like a tall dark figure in hiding, a brick chimney rose out of the attic floor up through the nail-pierced roof.

She shivered with eerie recognition as she pushed past an old-fashioned wooden high chair sitting erect beside a metal flour cabinet. At her feet, discarded kitchen implements lay in a half-empty cardboard box. They looked old enough to have come from her father's childhood.

Kneeling beside the box, she carefully picked her way past tarnished silver and rusty knives to the apple peeler lying at the bottom.

She brought the ingenious device into the light, remembering when her grandmother had let her turn the gear that made the iron implement swiftly pierce, core, and peel the fruit for her apple pies.

ON SATURDAY MORNINGS when Winna was thirteen, she went to the house on Seventh Street for lessons in French and housekeeping. She was aware that her grandmother saw these Saturday mornings as an opportunity to remedy what was lacking in Winna's education at home.

She could still hear her grandmother's voice: "Edwina"—she didn't believe in nick-names—"it's apparent to me that your mother has no intention of teaching you the things a well-bred young woman should know. Your mother is so busy painting those ridiculous pictures, she doesn't have the time to bother—but I do. You do want to be a good wife. I can't begin to understand how you'll get along in life unless I teach you myself."

Her grandmother had explained that Winna should do her best to marry a wealthy man. "After the first couple of years, it's easier to love a rich man than a poor man," Gramma cautioned. "I do not care one bit for George Bernard Shaw, but he did say, 'The lack of money is the root of all evil' and I know from experience that he's right about that. Still, my dear, you should hope to love the man you marry—he should be someone very like you, with the same interests and, more importantly, the same background."

Gramma had said that if she didn't marry a wealthy man like her grandfather, Winna would need to know how to keep up appearances and, using her own wits, fit into society. Juliana taught her how to polish silver, write thank-you notes, keep accounts, write checks, sit like a lady, hold a cigarette like a lady, and all the rules for accessorizing her clothes in every season.

On child rearing she had said how important it was to keep a child in a playpen most of the day where it was safe and that the best way to amuse a toddler was to put him in a highchair, dip his fingers in honey, and hand him a feather. On getting her way with an obstinate husband she had said, "You must use your womanly wiles. A man cannot bear to see a woman weep. Most will give in if you start crying."

Young Winna was repelled yet fascinated by her grandmother's lessons, for along with the particulars seemed to come a scandalous philosophy for impressing others and getting one's way.

Eager to explore the rest of the attic, Winna rose to her feet taking the apple peeler with her. It held such happy memories for her. Cleaned up, it might be usable again. It was, after all, a handy tool—a much better implement than any modern convenience that had followed.

Winna had come to the attic on a mission she had almost forgotten. After the party and her reunion with John Hodell and other old classmates at Kate's party, she wanted to find her high school yearbooks. She vaguely remembered that her father had mentioned putting them in the attic—or she assumed he had—along with a box of other things that belonged to her.

On the far wall, she noticed a stack of tall metal shelves loaded with boxes and books. The attic was hard to navigate, but she made her way to the shelves weighed down with old account books, boxes of canceled checks, and check registers. Another crate held dozens of 78 phonograph records and some complete operas in their own boxes.

Admonishing herself for stopping to look and remember her childhood with every object she touched, Winna pulled away from the dusty shelves. She turned toward the large dormer window and made her way to the light end of the attic. In the midst of the clutter, she found a curiously large open place where a familiar braided rug sprawled over the floorboards. Someone had positioned furniture around it.

As light from the dormers seemed to shift then dim, and the smell of old things, of decay, weighed the air, she stared at the scene in disbelief. Winna put her hand over her nose and mouth. Stunned, she realized exactly what lay before her—the reproduction of a room she remembered very well. Shrouded in thick, slanted light, two small wicker beds with matching night tables, twin brass lamps with pink, fringed lampshades, an ornately carved oak dresser with an adjustable mirror, and a child-sized walnut rocker surrounded a handmade cedar chest stacked with old dolls. Winna closed her eyes, fully expecting that the vision would be gone when she opened them again.

Decades had passed, yet she found herself standing at the edge of the bedroom she had shared with her sister, the furniture arranged as it had been when she and Chloe were very young. Pale blue plisse spreads covered the beds. Layers of dust grayed the chest and the dresser as cobwebs made their way between the mirror and the coat rack hung with a child's woolen coat and hat. Winna saw her reflection in the cloudy mirror. In the dim light, the dark roof boards pierced with sharp fang-like nails hovered like an open mouth close over her head.

She trembled as she reached out to touch one of the dolls in the toy box—a baby doll dressed in a white dress and cap lay there with her eyes closed. Winna picked her up. The doll's colorless eyes snapped open as her small voice cried "ma-ma." There was something diabolical in that faded face with the button nose and open red mouth baring two pearly-white teeth. Winna shivered and let her fall like a hot coal.

Who had made this tableau? The act of stepping on the rug brought her to her knees. It had to be Dad. She burst into tears as her memory climbed the stairs to that very room in the old house on Ouray Avenue where they had lived before they moved to the country. There, she had played with Chloe on this rug. There, she had slept in her bed under the window facing the street.

She knelt to open the bottom dresser drawer. A memory came so fresh it frightened her. Winna had been bad and her mother sent her to her room, this room. She had run there to hide from her father. Her mind racing, she tried to come up with an excuse to tell him. Why had she taken little Chloe by the hand and led her out of the yard for a walk down Twelfth Street where they were not allowed to go? They were both barefoot and Chloe had cut her foot. Dr. Sloane had to come to the house and stitch up her wound.

Then her mother had called her father to come home from the store and spank Winna.

She heard the screen door slam shut and her father's voice call her mother's name. Little Winna couldn't think of any good excuse for what she had done. There were voices—her mother and father talking—then his footsteps came up the stairs. She got up off the rug and ran into the closet to hide. Footsteps tramped up the stairs and from her position behind a hanging bathrobe, she wished someone's arms were around her.

"Come get your spanking." He knew where she was. He opened the closet door, his forehead contorted with rage. Winna looked up at him and saw his neatly pressed suit and vest, his spotless starched shirt, and the red stripes on his blue tie. He glared down on her, his dark eyes sparked with rage, then turned to sit on one of the beds. Winna had been so bad that he had to come home from work.

He had been spanking her for as long as she could remember and she knew what to do. She had to be very brave—braver than when her mother took her to the dentist. She had to will herself to pull down her panties and lay bottoms up over his lap, then wait for him to spank her with his big hand.

He hit her for what seemed like an eternity. At first, she did her best not to cry, but it hurt so much that she couldn't help it. When he'd had enough, he let her slip off his knees to the floor. He told her to go to bed and that she could not come down for dinner.

As if she could memorize every thread, the child stared at the rug of rose-and-moss-colored wool. She couldn't look at his angry face and was glad when he left her alone.

Exhausting herself with tears, she lay in bed under the open window hoping for a breeze, listening to the voices that came up through the floor. She looked out the window, at the blue sky and the street below. Her father got into his car and drove away. She stayed by the window a long time, watching the street, the people passing by—mothers pushing baby carriages and good children riding their bikes. None of them knew what she had done or what had just happened. They didn't know that the worst girl in the world lived on their street or that she was looking at them, wishing she were good too.

As the afternoon light deepened, the delightful smell of dinner simmering on the stove downstairs made Winna hungry. She was hot in the upstairs room and could hear Chloe and her mother talking. Out the window, she watched the fathers come home from work and park their cars in their driveways. The whole neighborhood went about the business of the early evening. After a while, her father came home again. As the sun sank low behind the trees, she finally felt a hint of cool air breathe in through the window. It took forever to get dark and cool down.

Winna's mother had taught her that when she was afraid or sad, she could make herself think about something happy. She knew how to fill her mind with pretty pictures and remember her favorite places and things—like how it felt to taste ice cream or smell roses.

The next morning the room was cool. Before she got dressed, she used a hand mirror to look at the red marks her father had seared on her bottom. As if those marks were a perverse kind of trophy, she put on a fresh pair of white cotton panties and ran downstairs to show her mother.

Nora scrambled eggs for breakfast and reminded her daughter that spankings are what you get when you don't mind. "Your father and I hope that someday you'll learn to listen."

Winna hoped so too.

Desperate to chase away the gloom, to make her mother and sister smile, she danced around the kitchen in her panties mugging in the mirror. She sang as she danced, making up a silly song about big red handprints on a little white butt. Stretching her elastic waistband, she gave the mirror a peek at her bottom. Chloe laughed so hard she fell off her chair.

When her dance was over, Chloe asked to see the handprints up close.

"First let me see your cut," Winna said, lifting her sister's little foot for a look at the gash and the black threads holding it together.

Chloe must have seen the shame on Winna's face, because she reached out to pat her sister on the cheek. "You're sorry, Winna," she said, her eyes warm and sad as she kissed her. "I heard Daddy spank you upstairs. It made me cry."

RAYS OF SUN, coming in through the dirty attic window, splashed the old rug with soft light. Reassuring herself, Winna looked around making sure she knew where she was. Feeling exhausted, she got up off the rug and wiped away the tears.

Look what this house has done to me. She could not spend time going down memory lane with every object she saw or she would never get home. Feeling like Dorothy stranded in Oz, she looked again at the room with no walls. It seemed eerily sad. She did not want to stay there another moment. Her stomach wrenched with hunger and she guessed it must be time for lunch. As she stood to go, she realized that she no longer had the apple peeler in her possession. Thinking that she must have put it down somewhere, she decided to return to the shelves.

Just then, she noticed a second wall of shelves on the south side of the attic. As she approached, something caught her attention. An old wooden trunk sat alone in an uncluttered spot just behind the chimney. She stepped over several boxes, pushed aside an aged easy chair, and reached out to touch it. She had been looking for one of these for years.

Lifting the brass latch, she opened the lid. The trunk opened up like a dresser full of drawers. Winna delved into one empty drawer and then another. The third contained a thick package wrapped in sea-green satin, tied with a tarnished gold cord. It looked like a stack of letters. Because of the darkness behind the chimney and her growing hunger, she closed the trunk and carried the package down to the kitchen.

11

BEFORE WINNA COULD cook and eat at the house on Seventh Street, the cupboards had to be cleaned and the refrigerator scoured and stocked. Realizing she might be in Grand Junction for weeks, she readied her grandmother's old bedroom at the back, away from the street, and moved in.

As she made a salad, she reminded herself to ask Seth—the handyman referred by John Hodell—to help her rip up the ugly avocado green rug on the kitchen floor. Winna remembered the handsome tile floor underneath and hoped it was still in good condition.

As if in answer to a prayer, Seth had arrived at the kitchen door the day after she called him. He parked his Ford pickup truck—*Seth's Yard Service* painted on the doors—in the drive and introduced himself as an admirer of the old house and a sometime employee of John's. He showed interest in helping out, saying he had done a lot of painting and could repair just about anything. He gave her references, and offered the use of his truck to haul trash to the dump.

Smiling as if it was a joke, Seth Armstrong Taylor had given Winna his full name. He looked about her age and reminded her of someone. She could not put her finger on where or if she had seen him before. Clean shaven, Seth wore his graying hair long, tied in a ponytail at the nape of his neck, one earlobe pierced by a small diamond stud. Winna had seen men wearing small loops in their ears but never adorned with something that sparkled. She assumed he was gay and tried to remember which ear she'd heard gay men pierced—left or right. Though dressed in jeans and a leather vest over his tee, there was something ascetic about his appearance, maybe his thin angular face or the startling pale gray eyes. He spoke like an educated person, perhaps an artist, and immediately seemed at ease.

He went to work on the overgrown shrubs about to block the kitchen entrance and painted Juliana's bedroom so that Winna could move in. By the end of his first week, Winna had to restrain herself from giving him a hug and telling him he had changed her life. Seth seemed to know, almost before she did, what needed doing.

With her salad almost complete, she heard a voice at the front door echoing through the house.

"Winna!" Chloe called musically. "Winna, where art thou?"

Her sister had shown up at last. "I'm in the kitchen."

Chloe Elizabeth Grumman Ayers Thorpe—now back to Grumman—breezed into the room looking radiant. "I parked in front—decided to use the front door for a change. I was going to ring the doorbell. Did you know it's unlocked?"

Winna let her eyes fill with the vision of her sister who had inherited their mother's long legs and the grace and presence of a dancer. Chloe never dieted or worked out. She had milk chocolate brown eyes wide-set in a heart-shaped face. Her lips painted cherry red, she wore her ash blonde hair long, cut and curled like Farrah Fawcett, falling just between her shoulder blades. Her bare feet in sandals, the nails painted red, peeked from under a long flowing skirt, teal blue printed in metallic gold. Her matching shirt yoke, fashioned from the skirt fabric, made the whole outfit scream cowgirl.

"My goodness, Chloe," Winna said, holding a salad spoon aloft, "you are full of surprises." They hugged. "It's good to see you." She didn't add the "at last" that lingered at the back of her tongue.

Chloe pecked Winna's cheek. "I meant to get here before now."

"Never mind that. Do you want lunch? I've made a salad."

Chloe cast a doubtful look at the salad bowl. "Sure. Do you have enough?"

"I'll beef it up. Sit down."

Her expression thoughtful, Chloe sat down at the oak table and almost immediately began tracing the outline of the grain with her long polished thumbnail. Except for the vermillion nails, Winna was reminded of her sister as a child, her hesitance, the way she waited for Winna to engage her.

Winna went to work. "How are the boys?" she asked of Chloe's two teenaged sons.

"Right now they are in California with Austin. He wants them to go to school out there next year."

"How do you feel about that?" she asked, tearing more lettuce into the bowl. She bit her tongue and did not add that Chloe would surely miss them. On the other hand, maybe she would be glad to have them off her hands. In that case, her sister would take Winna's words as a judgment against her. Talking with Chloe could be tricky.

"Well, I am considering it. It's a great school and a great chance for them to spend more time with their father—boys need their fathers." Chloe paused, then looked at her sister, "How are you doing?"

Winna sighed. "This house has made me into a time traveler. I'm no longer living in the last year of the twentieth century. I'm no longer sixty-one. I'm twelve and you're eight."

They had lived in the country then, on seven acres of land, in an old farmhouse. Winna's happiest memory of their days together in the country flashed to mind.

"Do you remember that summer evening on Peach Tree Ridge when you and I sat holding hands on the side of the hill watching the sun set over Pinyon Mesa?"

Chloe's face lit up. "I remember it perfectly—the sky ablaze with a violent orange and purple fire," she said, using the words of a painter. "We were close then." Chloe paused as if she was considering that loss. "Why do you suppose both of us remember that sunset?"

"Because we saw God. Wouldn't you say?"

"Yes, but I wouldn't say it that way. You know I don't believe in a bearded man in the sky."

"I know. Neither do I," Winna said as she peeled another hard-boiled egg, cut up more lettuce and tomato, and added the rest of a can of tuna. She turned to look at Chloe and caught her staring, her expression filled with questions as she lowered her eyes. "What are you thinking?"

"Oh, just about those days."

"It's fun to know someone with the same memories," Winna said.

Chloe got up and went to the silverware drawer for a fork and knife. "Todd moved in the last of his things this weekend—that's why I didn't make it," she said, looking at Winna. "I'm sorry. I can't stay long today, but I promise to come back tomorrow—all day if you need me."

"I do need you. I hoped you'd go through the library and decide which books you'd like and which should be sent for appraisal. There's so much to tell you—we have to talk. Guess what Emily and I found—a gigantic canary yellow diamond ring worth big bucks, the jeweler says."

"Here—in this house?" Chloe sat down.

"Yes, we found it in the front hall closet in our old box of marbles. Can you beat that?"

"Are you are just trying to entice me into giving you a hand?"

Winna laughed. "I should have thought of that weeks ago."

Spotting the satin wrapped package Winna had dropped on the table, Chloe seemed thankful for a distraction. "What's this?"

"I'm not sure. I just found it in the attic. I'd guess there are letters inside," she said, dressing the salad and dividing it between two plates. "Open it."

Chloe untied the cord and carefully folded back the cloth that covered a stack of yellowed letters, bound by yet another tarnished gold cord.

"The letters are addressed to Miss Juliana Smythe, Gunnison Avenue, Grand Junction—this one is from Providence, Rhode Island. It's postmarked September 5, 1910." She quickly flipped through the whole stack, "They're all from the same person. And according to the postmarks, it looks like Gramma kept them in chronological order."

Winna handed Chloe a plate and took the first letter from Chloe's hand. The return address on the envelope read "A.G. Whitaker, 472 Benefit Street, Providence, Rhode Island." She slipped the folded letter out of the envelope and, as if it had been read a million times before, it fell open in her hands. It was dated August 24. She read it aloud.

> My Dear Juliana,
>
> You know my heart. I don't have to tell you how hard it was for me to say goodbye to you today. I write this as the train speeds through De Beque Canyon. I can see its shadow in the still reaches of the river, a long dark train moving east, trailing a plume of smoke. Sometimes I see your tear-streaked face reflected in the window glass. Now you are a phantom. No longer flesh and blood, begging me not to leave you.
>
> I hate to bring pain into your life, my darling, but I must follow my destiny. I cannot count the times you have said that you want success for me, for me to take my place among the great writers both living and dead. We've talked about how I cannot thrive in Grand Junction. I should wither there. The only bright light in my place of birth is you, Juliana.
>
> You are my inspiration. Do not begrudge me the four years it will take to graduate from college. You have another year of high school and college to look forward to. In the end, we will be together as man and wife. This we have promised.
>
> Until then, I remain your faithful kindred spirit,
> Dolph

"Wow," Chloe said, smiling broadly. "So formal yet so mushy. I love it."

"This must be the lover Gramma told me about," Winna said, laying the letter aside and opening another.

"She had a lover?"

"I've told you the story—the guy who died on the train—of a broken heart."

"Oh, yeah," Chloe said, leaning back in her chair. "She was so plain and so mean. How could any man have died for the love of her?"

"Look at the pictures of her when she was young—she looked like the girl next door," Winna said, in defense of Juliana. "You remember her when she was an unhappy old lady."

Chloe suddenly jumped in her seat, then fanned herself with one hand. "There's someone standing outside the kitchen door."

Alarmed by Chloe's apparent fear, Winna went tentatively to the door, pulling aside the lace panel that covered the window. With a hint of a smile on his lips, Seth stood on the steps.

Surprised to see him, she opened the door. "Come in, Seth. I didn't expect you."

"You told me to stop back when I was free. Is this a bad time?" He seemed hesitant.

"No. No. Help never comes at a bad time," she said, inviting him in.

She turned toward her sister. "Seth, this is Chloe, my sister."

"How-de-do, Seth."

Winna could not believe that Chloe actually batted her eyes at him. He grinned and returned her greeting.

"Seth is my new discovery," Winna said. "He works around the house for me."

Gesturing toward the kitchen carpet, she asked, "Would you like to rip up the carpet in this room and haul it to the dump? Then we'll talk about whether or not the floor underneath needs repair."

"Sounds fun," he said with a trace of good-natured sarcasm. "I'll get my tools."

Seth headed back to his truck as the sisters escaped from the kitchen with their salads and the stack of letters. They settled into the old furniture on the porch overlooking the lawn where they could eat in peace and read Adolph Whitaker's love letters.

12

"*SOLAMENTE UNA VEZ...*" Connie Francis's voice sobbed above the hum of voices in the crowded restaurant. *Only one time.* Long ago, that voice had come to Winna under the stars, through the magic of Johnny Hodell's car radio. Now, a candle flickered on a restaurant table and Winna handed the waitress the menu.

John had been out of town and weeks had passed since Winna had seen him at the party. He'd come by that morning to take a look at the foundation and general wellbeing of the house on Seventh Street. He assessed the condition of the electrical service and pronounced the old furnace terminally ill. After the basement tour, she showed him some of the house's treasures. He complimented Seth's handiwork—the newly restored kitchen floor.

The waitress brought their drinks and a fresh basket of warm tortilla chips and salsa.

"Winna, I have a cheeky question," John said, looking at her a tad sheepishly.

"Shoot."

"Don't take this the wrong way. It's only a question," he said as he looked into the depths of his margarita. "How's Chloe doing financially?"

"She gets by, I guess. She picked up a lot of cash from her last divorce—enough to buy a house. I thought Austin was such a nice man—he loved her madly. Anyway, she's certainly not well-off and she's not starving."

He had another question. "How long has Chloe known that your father disinherited her?"

"She learned the same time I did, I believe—after Dad died. We were all sitting in Reed's office. It was an awful moment—'everything to my daughter Edwina. To my daughter Chloe, the sum of one dollar.' Just awful."

"You realize your father's accident could have been arranged— that's if one is prone to conspiracy theories, which I'm not."

"It sounds like you are." Winna doused her indignation with a big sip of her margarita. "My God, John, there's no way Chloe would ever do such a thing. Frankly, I find it offensive that you would even suggest it."

"I'm sorry, Winna," he said, pulling back. "I know it's none of my business." He paused a moment in silence, took another sip, and said, "Are you saying you never even thought of the possibility?"

"Never."

"Everyone in town wondered why he went over the cliff when his car didn't—it was such a weird accident. Did the police check out the car?"

"I don't know—it was an accident." Winna stirred her drink with the straw. "I told you what I thought happened—what the police believed."

"But how? Did they do an autopsy?"

"Yes, of all that was left. They found nothing suspicious, John."

The food arrived. John was silent while the waitress bustled nearby.

"Enjoy!" she said and disappeared.

Enjoy? Ten million grams of fat. Winna stared into a platter full of chicken enchiladas under bubbling chili verde and melted cheese slathered with sour cream and sliced avocado, trying to decide which upset her more: her lack of discretion in ordering, or the man across the table.

"Looks good," John said, digging into his enchiladas.

Winna said nothing as she cut into her food. She lifted a healthy bite of chicken smothered in tangy chili and cream into her mouth. "I'd like another margarita."

"Now I know I've upset you," John said. "Are you going to get drunk?"

"No, you're right, John. I won't have another but I am upset. Surely you don't blame me," she said, tasting a bite of succulent chili relleno stuffed with melted cheese.

Their silence lasted until the warm food and tequila did their magic and Winna felt herself let go. "Okay, I admit I have had dark thoughts about Dad's accident."

"Of course, it's only natural with all the stuff that goes on these days. The TV and newspapers are full of it."

"Let me tell you *my* dark thoughts." She rested her fork on her plate. "I'm afraid of Todd Cody, Chloe's lover. I don't know the man—but I do know Chloe. She's not capable of murder," she said, picking up her glass for a sip of melted ice. "Todd, on the other hand, might be capable of arranging things so that he marries into money."

John looked skeptical. "Is there that much—worth the bother?"

"Yes, it would be 'worth the bother.'"

"And you think that's why he's going to marry your sister? See, I'm not so twisted after all," he said with a wink.

THE NEXT MORNING as Winna and Emily sorted through shelves loaded with three different china patterns, Winna could not get her conversation with John the night before off her mind.

"John thinks that something sinister happened in Unaweep Canyon—that Chloe had something to do with Dad's death."

"Really? I doubt we need to worry about that. But, Mom, I've been feeling guilty for not visiting Poppa Henry more often."

"I'm to blame, honey," Winna said, separating the Willow Tree plates from the Spode. "He was tough to visit—didn't know how to make you feel welcome. I didn't understand him so I couldn't help you understand him either." She sat down and looked at her daughter. "Let me tell you a story about him—about the day he took me to Unaweep Canyon. Come sit down a minute."

Emily took a chair as Winna's memory returned to the early eighties. "Once, when I came back home to see Daddy, he drove me there for a picnic. He knew all the side roads, how to get to the top of the cliffs. Those were still his drinking days and as we headed out of town toward Whitewater, I was glad there was no traffic. I couldn't tell if he was sober or not, but I'd seen him tuck a silver flask into his back pocket.

"We made it into the canyon just fine. It must have been late spring because the wet meadows were green and filled with wild blue lupines. The sky was another shade of blue with bright white clouds drifting south—you should see my pictures. Dad didn't mind stopping every time I shouted, 'Photo op!' He'd pull over, I'd get out and wander around with my camera as long as I wanted. Each time I went back to the car, it seemed like he was a little drunker.

"At some point he turned off the highway and we drove up a dirt road that took us to the top of the canyon wall. He knew the way—exactly where he wanted to go. When we reached a turnoff, he parked the car and got out. He asked me to bring the picnic basket and follow. He headed down a footpath toward a cluster of pinyon pines. Walking toward a group of flat rocks shaded by junipers, we stopped at a spot very near the edge of the cliff with a view of the wide canyon below. From there, the road running through the canyon looked like a narrow gray line drawn on a map. I could feel the pull of gravity and was glad for the twisted tree limb that came between me and the sheer drop below—almost like the bar on a Ferris wheel seat.

"We sat down to eat in silence. Then Dad told me a story. It's the only story I remember him ever telling me. As he spoke, I realized what the canyon meant to him and that he had been there often. It is the only memory I have that helps me deal with the way he died.

"He said no one knows for sure how the canyon was formed— some say it was the rivers that came through there millions of years ago and others say glaciers created the canyon. Neither theory can be proven.

"Showing my geological ignorance, I suggested to him that the canyon had been there from the beginning of time. Who says it had to be formed by anything? Maybe that's just the way it is—the way it's always been."

Winna paused and looked at her daughter. "And, Emily, here's what interests me—the old question. Is it nature or nurture? Was Daddy, am I, are you who you are because of how your parents raised you, or because you were born with a certain nature? The canyon made me wonder about that and it still does."

"It's nature," Emily said. "That's why people raised in the same family can be so different—like you and Chloe."

"I don't know. The family treated Chloe and me very differently. Anyway, Daddy and I didn't talk about that. You couldn't talk about things like that with him."

"Did you ever try?"

"Sure. If you asked a personal question, he'd drift away. Like once I asked why he dropped out of college and he said, 'I wasn't much of a student.' He said it in a way that closed me off. It didn't help that he turned his back and left the room."

"Maybe he had something to hide."

"Maybe, but let me finish telling you about that day. He had more to tell me. The mystery of the canyon's formation wasn't the only unusual thing. He was drinking from his flask while we talked and the more he drank the longer his silences grew. I had always hated the silence between us and had a habit of rushing to fill it with words.

"He said that the canyon is open at both ends—that's unusual. There isn't a river there, but there are two streams. One runs in one direction and the other in another direction. He seemed to think that was mysterious and asked how two streams could run in opposite directions out of opposite ends of the same canyon.

"I didn't know and I doubted that what he said could possibly be true. He was slurring his words and his eyelids had dropped, making him look sleepy. By then I wanted to go, but he wasn't ready.

"I can still see his eyes moving slowly down the canyon and up to the blue horizon. He looked as if he had gone into a trance. He reached up and out with one hand like he wanted to show me whatever it was he saw. 'This place—' He didn't say any more, but his face seemed alive—like it does in his baby picture—as if he were lost in a beautiful vision. For the first time in his life he was trying to share something with me."

Winna suddenly stood up and returned to the stacks of plates on the dining room table. She looked at Emily and quickly wiped the tears off her cheek. "I was afraid, Emily. He was experiencing a beautiful moment, and I was afraid. All I could think was how I was going to get him back to the car and would he let me drive home."

Emily hesitated and looked away from her mother.

"He scared me too, Mom. I don't know why. He was just so distant, so vacant—like nobody was home."

13

WINNA ARRIVED AT the Crystal Café for her lunch date with Kate. She picked a table with a view of Main Street. The street had changed since the fifties when she and Johnny had dragged Main in his convertible. Now it was more like a downtown mall with planters full of trees, shrubs, and flowers. Bronze sculptures decorated the sidewalks. Traffic had to slow as the street curved and snaked its way past all the plantings. *The trees are a nice addition*, Winna thought. They filtered the hard-edged light, giving a pleasant cooling shade to the sidewalks and parked cars. But Main Street no longer looked like the nineteenth-century Western street she first knew.

She looked up just as Kate came through the door. She looked like she'd just left the beauty parlor. Spotting Winna right away, she brightened and scurried through the line of people now waiting for tables.

"Hi, Winna," she called. "Always on time."

Winna gave her a hug and they sat down. Kate reached for Winna's hand, patting it like the hand of a child. "You are a wonder. I've always wanted to ask why you've never done anything with your hair."

Winna assumed she meant why she had not colored away the gray. "I guess I like it. Have you colored yours?" she asked, giving Kate's flawlessly even dark-brown hair a quick glance.

"You bet." Kate smiled and winked, fluffing her "do" with one hand. "I don't have your courage."

Remembering Kate's tendency to speak her mind, Winna laughed. "I'll take that as a compliment."

"You should," Kate said. "You know me better than anyone."

Winna had to admit she probably did. "We practically lived together for how many years?"

"Well, I moved to Peach Tree Ridge when I was in eighth grade—I think you were a freshman. We were together almost every day—especially in summer."

"Sometimes I wonder if we had way too much freedom—riding off on our horses, swimming in the canal. When I think about the wild things we did—the trouble we could have gotten into—I'm amazed we're still alive."

After ordering lunch, Winna confessed that she had always been jealous of Kate's clothes. "You were so sweet to let me borrow them."

"I thought yours were better—believe me! If I hadn't, I wouldn't have traded with you so often. Remember how we used to call each other the night before school, plan what we were going to wear the next day, and meet under the pear trees to swap?"

"Remember the ghost ranch? I was thinking about that the other day—what fun it was for us to pack up and ride all that way out to the foothills with our sleeping bags and something to cook for dinner and breakfast."

"These days people can't let their kids have adventures like that—it's a shame. We knew how to take care of ourselves, make a fire, cook something to eat, and sleep out under the stars."

To this day, Winna could not remember any other adventure from her youth that compared to riding off with Kate through the countryside to an abandoned farmstead in the shadow of the Book Cliffs several miles from home. Arriving late in the afternoon, they had unloaded their sleeping bags and rations near the house and let the horses go in the old pasture, certain that the ramshackle fence would fool them into thinking they could not escape. Searching for firewood, laying a fire—they were masters of the task at hand.

Like a traveler coming home after a long journey, Winna had stepped onto the old porch full of anticipation. They knew nothing about the house's former owners or why they had deserted the place, and would lie around the campfire at night making up love stories with tragic endings.

"Every summer when we visited the house, it had changed— seemed more haunted," Winna said. "One by one, the windows were shot out and the furniture stolen."

Kate's face lit up. "Remember the night we tried to sleep indoors?"

"Of course. I count that as my one and only encounter with ghosts. I'll have to encourage Chloe with that story. She thinks I'm hopelessly skeptical about the unseen."

"What imaginations we had!"

"After that one terrifying night, we never tried that again."

Winna remembered making camp outside—in back of the house—lighting the campfire, roasting wienies on a stick, and eating baked beans from the fire-warmed blackened can. The sun set over Pinyon Mesa, lighting the sky pink and violet, and more wood was thrown on the fire. Fully dressed except for boots, they had burrowed into their sleeping bags. The moon rose high and Winna could see the horses still grazing the dry pasture. When she turned her eyes up to the sky, it seemed that the stars were close enough to touch.

The women turned the conversation to the present, catching up with recent events. Kate was busy golfing at the country club three mornings a week, playing tennis once a week with her husband and another couple. She and Jim also belonged to a folk dance group that met once a month for a hoedown.

No wonder she's so slim, Winna thought. Kate still had horses and invited her to ride. A standing invitation Winna planned to accept. When their lunch arrived, a cheeseburger for her and a salad for

Kate, Winna told Kate all about Adolph Whitaker's letters and the jumble of treasures and trash packed into the old house. Kate wanted to know about Winna's plans for the future, especially what she was thinking about John.

"We saw each other for dinner. We're getting reacquainted. That's all," she said.

Kate picked through her salad, avoiding the tomatoes and red onion. Winna guessed she wasn't very hungry. "You remember he married Maggie?" Kate said.

Winna nodded yes. "Did you see much of her after high school?"

Kate looked thoughtful. "Now that you mention it, I'd say not. Why do you ask?"

"I wrote her a couple of times and she never responded. I felt a little disappointed—hurt, actually." Winna regretted the waver in her voice following that admission.

"Once she got involved with John, she moved to Boulder and took a job of some kind there," Kate said. "She may not have gotten your letters. He was in school. I think they got married there. I got the impression that it was all very hush-hush."

"Maybe she was pregnant?"

"I don't know. They never had children," Kate seemed to drift for a second before she went on. "When they came back to town— before he went to Vietnam—I didn't hear from her. Bumped into her here and there. She was friendly enough, but didn't seem inter- ested in resuming our relationship."

"Tell me about her death." Even though John had recently told her what had happened, Winna wondered what Kate knew.

Kate shook her head as if she still couldn't believe it. "I was so shocked—she was a fine skier. John was with her when it happened. She ran into a tree and broke her neck."

"Did he see it happen?"

"I think so. You know she was so good that he actually liked skiing with her. Jim won't ski with me."

"Johnny never skied with me," Winna admitted, "but Maggie would— and you. I think I was the poorest skier of the lot—a real gaper."

"No you weren't. I remember having lots of fun with you—especially on trails. God, we had fun," Kate reached for Winna's hand.

Winna smiled and opened her mouth to add her assent, but she wasn't fast enough.

"After the war, John came home lost and troubled—he was doing drugs. He and my Jim have always been best friends—like brothers, really. At one point Jim sat him down for a heart-to-heart. John was stealing money from his father to pay for drugs and gambling debts."

"Really? That's hard to believe. He told Jim that?" Winna said, feeling stunned, troubled.

"Yes—like a confession of sorts. He hated himself. Mr. Hodell was quite old then and had trusted his son to take over the business. John was devastated when he died and started going to Gamblers Anonymous. He wanted to pull himself and his father's business back into shape and asked Jim to help him."

"How could Jim trust him? I mean, after stealing from his father?"

"Jim loves him like a brother and believed in him—he still does. He didn't go into business with him until John got his act together—then Jim became the financial brains." Kate looked sure, as if she was confident that John had reformed.

Thinking Kate's husband might well be a saint, Winna asked, "How has that worked out?"

"Very well. Jim is a good manager and John is a good contractor. They don't get mixed up in each other's territory and, if I may say so, they operate the leading firm in the area. Once John cleaned up his act, he stayed cleaned up. We are kind of proud of him for that."

Kate had told Winna more about John's past than he had. Winna sipped a second cup of tea as they talked and laughed and told stories from the past. When she looked at her watch, it was nearly three o'clock. They had forgotten the time.

"Oh, Lordy, it's late," Kate said as they prepared to go. "Promise that you'll go riding with me soon."

They hugged, pecked each other's cheeks, and said goodbye.

That night, lying in bed in Juliana's bedroom, Winna remembered Kate as a girl—her dark hair and snapping green eyes, her body straight as a stick. Winna's body had developed sooner than Kate's and her friend had teased her about having big boobs. Winna chuckled to herself. The night of the sweetheart formal she had helped Kate stuff her strapless bra with Kleenex. She wondered if Kate would remember that. The memory delighted her but she fell asleep thinking of beautiful Maggie, her eyes like a doll's eyes, smiling blue, fringed with thick black lashes. And now she was dead.

14

1954

WINNA WAS ALLOWED to read movie magazines and *Seventeen*, but she kept the romance magazines she had borrowed from Kate—who had borrowed them from Maggie—a secret from her mother by smuggling them in and out of the house inside her coat and hiding them under her mattress. She believed the stories in *True Story* were written by young women just about her age, that these romantic confessions, which included "going all the way" and always ended in disaster and remorse, were real. In every plot, young girls were abandoned by the young men they had loved and trusted, or if they got pregnant, were disowned and banished from their families. The moral of these tales was that girls had sex at their own peril, but they did it anyway because it was impossible to resist.

At a slumber party one night, Winna and her friends washed and rinsed color into their hair. Winna hennaed her brown hair to look like Rhonda Fleming. Blonde Maggie became raven-haired Linda Darnell. The house filled up with ecstatic redheads and dark-haired sirens giggling, twirling pin curls, anxious to see themselves transformed by morning. At another party, Maggie brought makeup and the girls made each other up to look like movie stars. They curled their eyelashes, piled on the mascara, plucked each other's eyebrows, and painted their lips ruby red. Into the wee hours, Winna and her friends swooned to songs on the radio where hearts cried, sighed, and died for them.

By eighth grade, Maggie Hart had taken over Winna's world. She lived downtown not far from the junior high school and sometimes Winna's mother allowed her to walk home with Maggie after school. Sometimes on weekends, Maggie came for a visit to the country. Maggie was a good student and popular at school—a favorite of all the girls. At sleepovers they listened to "The Night Owl" on radio KEXO. The disc jockey played songs all night long, reading dedications from mailed-in postcards. Side by side in Maggie's double bed, they listened for hours. Under her hot pink chenille bedspread, the soft glow of her frilly white lampshade overhead, the disc jockey's low voice saturated the dusky room. The drums would beat or the violins would swell and their hearts responded, but Maggie and Winna didn't move, or else the bobby pins would fall out of their pin curls.

His voice low, seductive, the disc jockey said, "Tommy's got a message for Maggie."

"That's you!" Winna cried as they both popped straight up in bed. "That's gotta be you!"

The girls hugged, then Mario Lanza's voice crooned, *Be my love...*

How romantic, Winna swooned—wishing, hoping, longing someday to have a boyfriend like Tommy, a football player, who stood strong and muscular behind his little boy smile. She had a boyfriend, but she didn't love him like Maggie loved Tommy. Someday, she thought deep into the night, finally falling asleep to Guy Mitchell's tuneful sobs.

During the summer between eighth and ninth grades, Maggie and Winna spent hours practicing for the day they would be allowed to go out on their first date. With a portable radio as their constant companion, they danced on Mrs. Hart's big old kitchen floor. First Maggie would lead and Winna would follow, then they would switch parts. They held each other close, pretending that they danced in the arms of a boy.

That fall, Maggie and Winna had a sleepover in the Harts' attic. As strong moonlight poured in through the bare window, the girls sat on the old mattress they had made up into a bed. Brushing their hair, they talked about how they couldn't wait to have boyfriends with cars.

"Only one more month to Tommy's birthday," Maggie sighed, a thought so divine that her hairbrush slipped dreamily from her hand. "His father already lets him drive around out back in the vacant lot. When he's sixteen we can go everywhere together."

On her way to pinning three rows of curls that would transform her already curly hair into a fluffy golden halo, Maggie used her front teeth to open a bobby pin.

"Are you going to park with him?" Winna asked, pinning her last curl into place.

"Jeez, I guess so. Yes," she said, twirling her fingers around a free lock.

Winna settled carefully on her pillow. "Are you going to let him pet?" She was trying to be funny.

"No!" Maggie protested, flopping on her back. "I'd be all shy. I wouldn't want him to see me," she said, unbuttoning her pajama top. "Look at them, do you think my boobs look all right?"

Maggie lay flat on her back in moonlight streaming through the window, her breasts small hills, her eyes closed.

"They're pretty," Winna said.

Maggie shone white in the moonlight, like she'd been carved from marble, her breasts smooth and round as a pearl. Knowing how it felt to touch her own, Winna reached out with one finger and slowly, lightly traced smaller and smaller circles around Maggie's breast, stopping to rest at its peak. The dark attic seemed to vibrate with a blurry light, as Maggie caught her breath and turned to face Winna.

Winna stopped breathing. Embarrassed, she tucked her hand under the covers.

Maggie looked away as if she had just seen something move across the room and closed her pajama top over her breasts.

"I have a guardian angel," she murmured. "He protects me— watches over me," she sighed. Her drowsy blue eyes, half hidden under the lids, fixed on the moon in the window.

"How do you know?" Winna wondered if Maggie had ever seen him and if he spoke to her.

"He's over there," she whispered, languidly nodding her head, indicating that Winna should look behind her toward the foot of the mattress. "He's watching us now."

Frightened by the possibility that Maggie was right, that they weren't alone in the attic, she looked anxiously in that direction.

"Don't be afraid, he'll keep us safe," Maggie yawned, rolling onto her stomach.

A tall, shimmering, El Greco-lean figure stood in the shadows, just outside the range of the moonlight. Instead of white, the color of angels, it radiated violet and blue, but looked exactly like an angel to Winna. It gave her just a tiny glimpse of itself before it vanished— just enough to leave Winna wondering if she had really seen it.

"I think I saw him," she said, unafraid and suddenly very sleepy. She yawned, and as if angels had the power to put spells on young girls, closed her eyes. "Why don't I have a guardian angel?"

"You do—everybody does. Watch for him," Maggie mumbled, her voice trailing off to sleep.

15

1955

BY THE TIME she was a sophomore in high school, Winna was already interested in photography. She had grown up drawing and painting alongside her mother and sister, but the camera fascinated her. She liked the discipline and following the rules. The camera would yield only as much as Winna's mastery would allow. Then there were the happy accidents and trying to understand them. She received great pleasure from working with a machine, manipulating it for effect as she tried to make sense of it. Winna volunteered her services as a photographer to the school newspaper.

She was a good student in every subject but biology and would have been better if she had not been as pretty, not so busy dreaming about what she was going to wear to the weekend dances and parties.

School dances, held in the high school gym, sometimes had live music in the form of a small student band called the Starlighters. At the first dance that fall, a disc jockey played records—songs from the hit parade past and present. The kids danced to Frankie Laine, Bill Haley and his Comets, Patti Page, and Frank Sinatra among others. They were not immune to the great dance music of the forties and jitterbugged to Benny Goodman, Glen Miller, Count Basie, and Tommy Dorsey.

Winna had gone to the dance with Greg. They had been dating for about two weeks, since the night of Maggie's birthday party where they had noticed each other for the first time.

As music poured out of the big speakers, Greg asked her to dance. After their second dance, Winna was worried. She had tried her best to follow, but Greg liked to talk. Every time the conversation got going, he would forget his feet and just stand there and sway. Once, he stopped all motion except for the gestures he made with his hands while trying to explain how he had fixed his little sister's bicycle. When he was silent and the music took over, he tried his best to dance, but more often than not, his indecision led him to change direction midstep. His apologetic sighs confirmed her belief that dancing was not his gift. Looking miserable, Greg asked if they could stand out the next dance and they wandered off to chat with one of Greg's friends and his date.

Johnny Hodell must have spotted Winna on the sidelines looking left out, her eyes focused enviously on the dance floor. Greg had turned away to talk to a group of boys. The piano beat out the first slow strains of "Unforgettable" as Nat King Cole's voice made her dizzy with longing.

A big smile on his face, Johnny approached in time to the music. He took her hand and swung her out on the dance floor, then pulled her close. They floated together like two feathers on a millpond. By the time the violins swelled, Winna was in love and they had not said a word.

He changed his moves to a slow swing, bringing her in for long close embraces, ending the dance with a low dip. When he pulled her up into his arms again, she was his. He returned her to Greg, thanked her for the dance, and hurried off to dance with Maggie.

The evening wore on and Greg did his duty. Finally, using his skill for words, he opened up to Winna about his need for dancing lessons. Winna suggested they get together after school to practice, but Greg declined. He seemed ready to accept his fate as a non-dancing man. As the evening wore on—for Winna "wore" was the right word—they stood on the sidelines during the fast dances watching other kids jitterbug and boogie and they bumped around together to the slow music. Winna liked the boy but she wished the evening would end—she wished Johnny would ask her to dance once more.

It was getting late when drums sounded the urgent opening rhythm of Benny Goodman's "Sing, Sing, Sing." Greg dragged Winna to the sidelines. Within seconds, Johnny was at her side. He said nothing, just grabbed her hand and swung her out onto the dance floor.

"Don't you ever *ask* a girl to dance?" she shouted above the music.

He shook his head "no" and, smooth as butter from his spot on the floor, whipped her around his tall agile body, spinning her into kicks, pushes, and underarm passes. The music and his moves worked hard on her and she let herself go. Whirling, swaying, her head, shoulders, and hips swung to the music. She could feel herself fly. All the other dancers had circled around to watch. Her face shone with the joy of it all. At the end of the dance, Johnny swung her out and pulled her back into his arms; breathless, she collapsed into the heat of his body and the whole crowd clapped and cheered.

WINNA ASKED JOHNNY to the Sadie Hawkins Day Dance. She dressed up as Daisy Mae in short cut-off jeans. She had sewn colorful patches to the seat and made a peasant blouse from a piece of dark blue cotton with large white polka dots. Johnny dressed up as Li'l Abner with a straw hat, white T-shirt, jeans, and big work boots. After the kids voted for the couple that looked most like the comic strip characters, Johnny and Winna were crowned king and queen.

After the dance, they parked outside the Grummans' house on Peach Tree Ridge. Following a torrent of passionate kisses, he leaned back in his seat. "You are trouble," he sighed, then looked into her eyes. "I love that about you."

"I love you, Johnny." Winna meant every word.

"Let's go steady," he said.

Winna did not have to think about his offer, she had dreamed about it. She reached out to touch his cheek "yes." He kissed her and, when they parted, tugged the class ring off his finger.

"It's too big for you."

"I'll wear it around my neck on a chain."

He took her right hand in his and gazed at her emerald ring, turning it in the light, making it sparkle. "Are you going to give me your ring?"

Winna did not want to give him the ring, her grandmother's gift. He had just given her a ring and she felt embarrassed by his question. "Girls don't give rings to their steadies."

He did not appear offended and coaxed with a smile. "We could start a new tradition."

Winna laughed. "My grandmother would kill me."

Even though her mother had said that she would not be allowed to go steady, her parents did not protest. Her father and Johnny's father were brother Kiwanians and friends. Winna was fond of Mrs. Hodell, a tiny French woman who owned her own dress shop and seemed genuinely interested in her son's new girlfriend. Mr. Hodell looked at Winna with a twinkle in his eye, as though he wished he were sixteen again.

Johnny called her every night. At school, they walked from class to class holding hands. He drove her home from school every day and asked her out to the picture show. Suddenly he was everywhere she was. It felt good when he kissed her—like he wished they would never part. She liked being his girl. No one had ever adored her the way he did.

16

1999

THE OAK-PANELED LIBRARY at the house on Seventh Street held hundreds of books on floor-to-ceiling bookshelves tucked under Moorish arches. The library table with the tall cloisonné vase still stood in the middle of the room. Juliana had kept the vase full of flowers—often from the rose garden. A collection of small antique oriental rugs were scattered on the parquet floor. For light, marble torchieres had been placed at intervals. Brass reading lamps hovered over leather club chairs. The only other seating was a small French tufted loveseat set between the two tall windows overlooking what had once been a beautiful lawn and the rose garden—once, Juliana's collection of Boston ferns had flourished in the light there.

Winna had settled in with a cup of tea and a small book she had discovered in the library the day before, *The Awakening* by Kate Chopin. She had picked it up almost absentmindedly and turned to the opening sentence. She didn't stop until she had read the entire first chapter. That night she read a few chapters before she fell asleep. Published in 1899, this well-worn edition of the novel smelled musty from all those forgotten years. Someone had marked the passages devoted to the married heroine's desire for freedom and the love of a young man. It was the story of a woman trapped in a respectable yet predictable marriage with a husband who was unfailingly good to her. He did not rouse her passions, neither intellectual nor carnal. Servants and friends cared for her children, leaving her idle. Winna guessed it was her grandmother who had marked the pages and that she had returned to them again and again.

Winna didn't have long to sit and read. Chloe and Todd had actually offered to help and might arrive at any minute. She turned the page and found a thin, yellowed newspaper clipping tucked close to the binding. It was a poem titled *The Silent City of San Rafael* by Juliana Smythe Grumman. She put the book down and read her grandmother's poem. In blank verse, Juliana described a San Rafael Mountain scene in late afternoon light—its "rooftops, turrets, and minarets" outlined in misty light as if the ruins of an ancient city lay under the setting sun. The verse went on to say a painter, try as he might, could never capture what she saw or what God had created there. Winna read the poem twice and was considering this new glimpse of her grandmother when she heard a huge racket coming up the driveway—the bass from a car radio made the old windows rattle.

A shiny black pickup truck with dual wheels pulled up to the back door. The thundering stopped and a tall blond man wearing a cowboy hat on the back of his head got out of the driver's seat. As she wondered who it could possibly be, she saw her sister hop down from the passenger seat. Winna shook her head and laughed to herself. So, that's Chloe's Todd and the truck is his very manly vehicle. Before she could move, she heard the kitchen door open and their voices.

"I'm in the library," she called.

With the energy of an eight-year-old, Chloe burst through the door dragging the handsome young man with a six-pack of Coors in his hand. Her introduction was offhand.

"You both know who you are?" she asked, flopping into one of the leather chairs.

"Howdy there, Winnie," Todd grinned, showing a row of perfect white teeth. "I'm pleased to meet you." He extended his hand. "Chloe here's told me all about her big sis."

Winna laughed, dazzled by his smile. "Her mean old sister?" she asked, going to greet him.

His eyes invited her to like him. "Ah, now Winnie, she's said nothin' but good things—'bout how you was a life-saver when you gals was kids and all."

With a Travolta cleft in his chin, Todd's face was as open as the front page of the newspaper, his baby blue eyes as innocent as the morning sky. Just then, Winna felt quite willing to overlook his grammar, his accent, and the fact that he'd called her Winnie. He stood over six feet tall in his eye-catching python and black leather cowboy boots, a shock of curly blond hair peeking out from under his hat. Was it bleached? His face and muscular neck and arms were tanned from working in the sun. His black Levi's looked as though they would keep his shape even on a hanger.

"My goodness, Chloe," Winna said, dragging her out of the chair for a hug, "look at you two—as handsome a couple as I've ever seen." And they were both radiating with—was it lust?—for one another.

"He's as sweet as he is pretty," Chloe said, punching his hard belly playfully, "and the best thing about him is everything."

Todd blushed. "Listen, ladies, I come on over here to work, and I plan to stay as long as you need me. I'll put the beer in the icebox— for later. Now where do I commence?"

"I like your attitude, Todd. Let's start in here," Winna said. She couldn't place his accent. "Where are you from?"

"Texas—moved out here 'bout five years ago."

"Well there's at least a week's work in here alone," Winna said. "Chloe, if you'd like, you can help me go through the books. I've got plenty of packing boxes. And Todd, see that old secretary over there? I don't know why, but it's blocking the door to a closet. Would you pull it out so we can get in there?"

Chloe approached the bookshelves as if she was searching for treasure. "When I was a kid, I never even looked in Gramma's library." She pulled out a book and read the title. "*Strong Poison* by Dorothy L. Sayers. That sounds ominous."

"Gramma loved mysteries. Wow, look at this big beauty." Winna pulled out an oversized picture book, *A Thousand Years of Jewelry*. She sighed and shoved the book back on the shelf. "I'm at it again. Every time I pick up anything in this house, I want to sit down and spend time with it. This is my curse."

"Hey, you gals," Todd called from across the room. "I can't budge this here desk. Give me a hand? This thing's taller than Shaquille O'Neal and wider."

Winna and Chloe came to his aid and helped push the old secretary desk away from the door. Winna stood just outside of a closet full of things she remembered very well: old puzzles, family games like checkers, Parcheesi, and Scrabble, shelves full of outdated cameras and camera cases, old flash units, a slide projector, an 8mm movie projector, and several pairs of binoculars. Juliana's postcard collection, scrapbooks, and Poppa Ed's coin and stamp collections lay on the shelves just as they always had. The old chess set sat within easy reach.

Chloe took it down for a look. "Lordy," she said, holding a white knight aloft. "He's beautiful."

"Would you like to have the chess set?" Winna asked.

"Yes! I'll teach you to play, Todd." She winked at him.

"I'm a seven card stud kinda guy, Clo."

"Don't tell me," Chloe said, "real men don't play chess?"

Todd winked and stuck his head inside the closet. "You gals, there's this old wood box—full of papers, and some of them looks like they might could be stocks."

Chloe looked at Winna with a huge grin. "This is more fun than Christmas morning!"

Todd pulled the carved chest into the light. The sisters knelt as Todd handed Winna a stack of stock certificates. Some were silver and gold mining stocks, others public utilities and assorted company stocks.

"I wonder if these are good anymore?"

Todd read the name written on the face of one. "This one belongs to Edwin Werner Grumman—your dad?"

"Our grandfather," Chloe said.

Rummaging through a small box she had found in the chest, Winna unearthed a creamy white envelope inscribed with the following words: *To be opened only after my death, Juliana S. Grumman.* Under the envelope, she found a packet of letters, poems, and a notebook with what appeared to be a story written in Juliana's hand.

Someone had opened the envelope. The letter was dated December 12, 1918. Winna read it aloud.

> Dearest Edwin,
>
> I hope you will let Mother and Daddy raise the baby until you marry again. Dear, you must try to understand my parents better than you ever have before. Remember that they love me and adore the baby and will love you if you give them half a chance.
>
> Dear, you must marry again. You must not go through life without a woman's companionship. I only ask three things—that you will take your time about doing it, three or four years even—that you will choose your new wife with one thought uppermost in your mind, that she will make a good mother for Henry. Last, you must not let her entirely supplant me in the life and affections of yourself and our son. Please don't let the baby forget me, dear. It seems as though I could not bear that. And won't you please study and think how to be a better father to little Henry?
>
> Be wise and patient, dear, in governing him. Don't make the mistake of thinking the rod the only method of punishment. Try to teach him cleanliness of body and mind. Try, yourself, to cultivate some of the little attributes of a gentleman so that you

can be an example to him. It has been a grief to me, dear, that you have considered good grooming, proper table manners, and the little attentions to women of so little importance. Those things are important—they are a stranger's only means of judging you. They are a human being's marks of good breeding, not unsimilar to the distinguishing marks of a pedigreed animal.

Let our son choose his own vocation, following his natural bent. I would like him to have a college education. Encourage him in letters. I shall not live to become the writer I was meant to be. Let him know I want him to be a writer. Bring him up with a love of good books, paintings, and music. I need not speak of the outdoors, I know. You will expose him to nature's beauties and lessons.

Let him live in our home. I've made your house into a home of beauty and refinement. I've not been as good a wife to you as you deserved. Our up-bringing, cultural backgrounds, differing values, and desires, all seemed to foster antagonism rather than harmony and unity. So it has not always been easy for me, dear. You have been good to me, though, and patient and generous, and there have been happy moments.

Love me always, won't you, dear, and keep my memory green in our son's mind. I wish I might have lived to cuddle my grandchildren.

I love you both, oh, so much.

Your own wife,
Juliana

Her handwritten last will and testament, a list of her possessions, and how she wanted them disbursed, followed. The will closed with, "Please do carry out my wishes in these matters with all good feeling. Juliana S. Grumman."

Surprised by her grandmother's wishes, Winna read the simple list remembering her husband, son, aunts, uncles, brother, mother and father, and someone named Daisy. "Please give Daisy my wrist watch. She hasn't been a good friend to me and she has hurt me dozens of times, but I'm fond of her anyway. When the watch is given to her, I want her to know that she hurt me."

Winna did a mental calculation. "She was in her twenties when she wrote this. Why would one so young expect to die?"

"Trying to control everyone—even beyond the grave," Chloe said as she took the letter from her sister's hand. "I love the part where she asks Poppa to let his son follow his natural bent and then she turns around and says, 'I want him to be a writer.'" Chloe was pacing, fuming at the letter in her hand. "God, are these tear splashes in the ink? At least she showed some emotion, even if it wasn't genuine."

Looking utterly baffled, Todd asked, "You didn't like your grandma?"

Chloe turned on her heels. "The real question is why my grandmother didn't like me."

SOMETHING HAD TO be done about Chloe. Winna felt that her sister had suffered too much. She had no idea why she was the favored grandchild and, in the end, her father's favored child. When she was young, she had imagined her grandmother's preference had something to do with birth order. She was the first. All that undeserved adoration had always felt like a curse.

After Chloe and Todd left, she opened a can of soup and ate it in the kitchen, then hiked up the stairs to Juliana's bedroom, bringing with her the notebook she'd found with the will. Exhausted, she quickly dressed for bed, pulled back the pale satin coverlet, and climbed into Juliana's tall walnut bed. Winna always felt like a queen as she snuggled in under the high headboard with its raised panels, crown-like flourishes, finials, and dentils. Intending to read the short story written in Juliana's hand, she turned on the bedside lamp and put on her glasses.

She had already wasted much of her time reading *The Awakening* and the letters Juliana had saved from people like her father and brother and Laura, a best friend who had moved to California. Winna had looked through everyone's marriage certificates, some going back to the 1820s.

The story, in an old notebook filled with yellowing paper, was written in pencil and had no title. Remembering that her grand-mother had wanted to be a writer, she lifted the notebook into the lamplight.

17

Juliana's Story

CHARLOTTE BLACKLEASH sits alone in the morning room with the draperies drawn. It is her favorite room, the place where she keeps her desk and writes letters, where she sits in the big easy chair with her dainty feet up on the ottoman and reads the paper every evening (by the fire in winter). She scours the library for the books she wants to read and brings them here where she can curl up on the sofa, pull the soft blue afghan up around her shoulders, and read all day if she wants. It has been her favorite room ever since she moved into the small mansion her husband had built shortly before their marriage. Ruefully, she thinks back to those days—when she had been treasured. Then, she had looked forward to life with the wealthy man who adored her. In less than three years he had grown detached, otherwise engaged, always busy at his law office. Now she sees no sign that he even thinks of her, she hears no endearing words from his lips. He has to be reminded of her birthday and their anniversary. The first bloom is long gone from their romance.

Well, well, Winna thought. This sounds a lot like Juliana and Edwin's marriage. She felt her face catch fire, pulled off the covers, and read on.

The sound of rain pelting the windows brings Charlotte a shiver. The windows look out on the rose garden, but Charlotte is deathly afraid of rain and has left the drapes drawn. It's the thunder and lightning that terrifies her, but the sight of rain brings her feelings of sadness and dread. She remembers the violent storms from her childhood that wracked the skies above Grand River Crossing. How they had driven her to hide under the bed where her mother would find her fixed with terror.

Last night Lawrence was late for supper and she is still angry with him. He likes his roast beef medium rare and has been known to throw a fit if it is served otherwise. She had looked at the clock at seven-thirty and told the cook to hold the roast. By eight she was hungry and made herself a cocktail. It was most unlike Lawrence to be late. When he had not come home by nine she ate alone in the dining room.

Her husband is always on time. He is as dependable, as predictable as the grandfather clock in the hall—one of the many things about him that bored her.

Finally, Lawrence appeared in the dining room just as she had finished her coffee. Charlotte rang the bell for his supper.

"I'm sorry to be late, my dear," he said as he went to the sideboard and poured himself a glass of wine.

"I suppose you had a good reason." She spoke icily without looking at him.

He spent at least an hour unloading one of his long, tedious stories about the day—something about a merger between two small local companies and their insistence that he accept a position on their board. She can't remember the details this morning because she didn't listen. She was too wrapped up in what she wanted to say if he ever took a breath. Things like: You know, Lawrence, they have invented the telephone, and last time I looked, we had one in the hall. You might have called and let me know that I should not hold dinner.

The sound of rain outside makes her feel all the more forlorn. The roses are in full bloom and she can't bear to look out at a garden full of sodden, drooping flowers. The rain will ruin them. She wipes a tear from her eye, then looks at her diamond encrusted watch. It is already ten and she wishes the rain would cease.

Suddenly, Kaitlyn bustles into the room humming a jolly tune whose very sound seems unspeakably rude. Her plump Irish maid stops abruptly, throwing back her head at the sight of her mistress sitting there in the gloom.

"I dare say, Madam, 'tis no good you sittin' alone like this." Flinging wide the draperies, she lets in the morning light and stops to gaze out the window. "Why, sure enough, it looks like the storm is passin' on."

Feeling molested and compelled to leave at once, Charlotte says nothing to her servant. She walks out of the morning room and ascends the staircase to the second floor toward her bedroom and then, as if forced by an omniscient power, turns toward the stairs to the attic, compelled once again to enter the top reaches of the house. Like a slave to something unholy, she climbs the stairs hating herself, terrified that against her will, she is forced to revisit that place.

She's building a little suspense here. What's in the attic and who compels her? Winna asked herself as she popped out of bed for a quick trip downstairs to get a splash of scotch. Back in bed, she pulled the covers up, plumped her pillows, took a sip, and read on.

The large, nearly empty attic space filled with cold light from the window still smells of new-cut pine. The rain has ceased and the sun is breaking through the dormer. Charlotte remembers the old house where she grew up. There, the attic was full of dusty old things. New houses, she thinks, have idle lifeless attics, no memories lurk here, nothing nostalgic or romantic and dusty, only my shame.

With a leaden weight in her heart, she is drawn to the high dormer window for a view of Broderick Place Boulevard. She looks down to see a farmer on his way to market passing below. He drives a horse-drawn wagon burdened with fresh produce. Across the street, old Mrs. Curlew folds her umbrella and herds her four grandchildren and two dogs toward Grant Park. Charlotte wonders what it feels like to be Mrs. Curlew or that farmer whose lives are filled with drudgery and guesses that both are happier than she. She longs for a child but has not yet been blessed.

Withdrawing from the window, she succumbs to her desire to open the trunk again. She had asked the gardener to drag it up the attic stairs and place it behind the chimney where it would be hidden from sight. She hurries to the dark corner and lifts the trunk's top, revealing a set of wooden drawers. Charlotte pulls out one of the drawers and reaches inside, removing a heavy piece of jewelry.

Hastening to the window, she holds the jewels up to the sun letting its light gambol over six strands of perfectly round lustrous white pearls attached to a large canary yellow diamond, the centerpiece of a priceless choker. Charlotte turns the great yellow diamond in the light and watches set rows of small white diamonds dance a glistening circle around it. Weeping uncontrollably, she pulls away from the window and fastens the choker around her throat.

Then slipping behind the chimney to revisit the trunk, she opens another drawer and scoops out its contents. Then another drawer, and yet another, yields up precious gems. Her hands full, she hurries back to the window where she sits down on the floor in a splash of sunlight and drops the treasure into her lap.

The plain pale linen of her morning dress looks shabby as a backdrop for jewels of this magnitude. She should be wearing satin or silk taffeta. She lifts a cornflower-blue star sapphire ring set in platinum, circled by rubies and diamonds, and slips it on her finger. With a wavering hand, she turns a pendant necklace with a magnificent emerald at the center to the light. Curiously cut with intricate designs, the emerald looks very old and its markings primitive, almost out of place hanging under strands of pear-shaped pearls and pale green and blue beads. Are they topaz? Charlotte knows very little about jewels, but she knows that she holds a king's ransom.

Trembling with ecstasy, she fondles the fiery gems set in icy precious metals remembering his kiss, the pressure of his body against her back, the excitement as he fastened the choker around her throat.

"Oh, Gramma, please not 'trembles with ecstasy, fondles icy metals, fiery gems.' Don't make me have to read your description of them having sex."

In an instant, her joy turns to painful yearning. She can wear none of these pieces in public. Indeed, no one must ever know she possesses them. Quickly, she returns the jewels to their hiding place, climbs down the stairs, and enters the morning room, closing the door behind her. Sitting at her desk, she lifts a sheet of writing paper from a drawer, opens her fountain pen, and begins to write.

My darling Andrew,
My heart is breaking. Since you left me, I have realized that I cannot live without you. Respectability, the thing I thought I needed more than love, means nothing without you.

I made a terrible mistake when I let you go. Lawrence has no feelings for me. It's as if I live alone. I'm something he wears on his arm like a wristlet.

Now all I have are precious things hidden away—my memories and things you gave me, things I dare not mention. I visit them, I hold them and long for you. Please come for me. I will meet you anywhere you say. I cannot live without your love. Charlotte

Slowly, she puts down her pen, blots the ink, folds the paper twice, and slips it into an envelope. She addresses the envelope and takes it to the front hall where bright sunlight startles through etched-glass panels on either side of the door. Intending to go to the post office right away, she puts on her hat and coat and opens the door.

Suddenly stunned, she gives up a little cry. The post office will have to wait. Quickly, she slips the envelope into her pocket and puts on a forced smile.

"Lawrence! Why are you home so early? It's barely noon," she gasps as her husband approaches the door, leaving his brand new Winton touring car in the drive.

Lawrence smiles at her. "I want to make up for last night—being late. We haven't been out for a drive in ages and it's going to be a beautiful day. We can have lunch at the County House."

Winna put down the notebook and lifted her drink for a sip. She wondered where she'd put her slippers. She felt compelled like Charlotte to hurry up to the attic and look through the trunk again. After a brief talk with herself about waiting until morning, she took another sip of scotch and read on—the unfaithful Charlotte changed her clothes and agreed to go for a ride with her boring husband.

"The air, my darling, will do us both good," he says, opening the door for his wife. She climbs into the passenger seat. He had put the top down, but she is sheltered under a wide-brimmed hat tied on with a swath of fine white tulle. She feels a bit unnerved wondering what is on her husband's mind.

As the car climbs the road to Satan's Needle, the day fairly glows with pink sunlight radiating off red sandstone. In this land of strange red rock formations, twisted junipers grow starkly beautiful under the bright cerulean sky. Charlotte does not care about the landscape, all she can think of is the last time she had been on this road with Andrew. Thoughts of her lover bring the hidden jewels to mind.

Though born and bred in this little town, the son of a humble stonemason, Andrew possesses a brilliant mind. In school, he had excelled in every subject. His professors persuaded him to go to college. Now he is a world-famous architect with homes in New York and London. Charlotte feels sure of her contribution to his success, she had encouraged him, believed in him. She had provided the inspiration, had given him his desire for success and wealth, but she had been a fool, unable to wait the long years it had taken him to make his fortune. She had married Lawrence instead—Lawrence was a bird in the hand…"

Winna raced through the next part of the story gritting her teeth as her grandmother described the guilt she felt as a faithless wife, her self-hatred, and wounded awareness that Lawrence had not proposed the drive into the country so that he could spend time with her. No, he was quite plainly in love with his fancy new car.

Every day Charlotte waits for the postman, for Andrew's answer to her letter. But no letter comes. Late one afternoon, as the golden light of the day fades to dusky shadows, the evening paper arrives. Charlotte pours herself a sherry and settles into her favorite chair with the paper. She scours the front page. The war is raging in the Isonzo River Valley between Italy and Austria-Hungary. All of Europe has gone mad. She sighs and decides to look for the society column. As she thumbs through the paper, she notices a headline near the top of page four.

Death Claims Former Resident

Andrew M. Pierce of New York City and London, formerly of Grand River Crossing, died in early June as he traveled east by train after visiting his mother, Mrs. Hetty Pierce, of Grand River Crossing. A renowned architect, Mr. Pierce made frequent visits home to this city. Mrs. Pierce reported to the *Daily Telegraph* that she received word from the Denver and Rio Grande Railroad that the cause of her son's death is yet unknown.

As if she had fallen from the roof of a skyscraper, Charlotte feels the breath leave her body, then sobs in agonizing waves. She slips to the floor, toppling onto the carpet in a faint. When she comes to her senses, she calls for Kaitlyn who helps her to her room and into bed.

The story had come to a sudden end. Winna dropped the old notebook on the bedside table. If Grand River Crossing was used as a pseudonym for Grand Junction, was Andrew Pierce Adolph Whitaker? If so, Charlotte Blackleash was Juliana Grumman. Did Juliana have a good imagination for storytelling—expanding her own romantic story of tragic loss to include a lover with great wealth, the gifts of priceless jewelry? Why did she stop there?

Winna got out of bed, went down the hall, and opened the door to the attic stairs. She felt around for the light switch. A light bulb went on somewhere in the attic. As her bare feet picked their way carefully up the stairs, she told herself she should wait until morning, but she knew she would not be able to sleep until she had searched the trunk again.

The attic, haunted in the light of one bare low-wattage bulb, looked like the garret in Winna's recurring nightmare—a dream about her grandmother's house that she had carried to bed with her for years. Though the dreams had stopped, she had not forgotten the terrible dark attic where a dead body lay hidden in a rolled up rug. She looked across the tangled array of stored objects and shivered. Everything seemed covered with frost.

She reminded herself that it was only dust.

The floorboards were rough and splintery as she picked her way carefully toward the chimney, wishing she had stopped to find her slippers. Passing the eerie bedroom tableau, she soon found herself kneeling beside the old wooden trunk.

Words from Juliana's story came to mind, "Then another drawer, and yet another, yields up precious gems."

She knew the first and second drawers were empty and that the third had held Adolph Whitaker's letters. She opened the fourth drawer and found nothing. There were three other drawers. Winna pulled them out and let them fall to the floor.

Could there be a hidden panel somewhere? She ran her hand over the back of the trunk. Nothing. Then she saw it on the very bottom, a hidden compartment. She opened it. But it too was empty.

After her foray into the attic, sleep did not come easily. She lay awake thinking about Juliana, convinced that the story she wrote was pure fiction. There were no jewels, but there was an affair. She had told Winna about it. Who *was* Juliana?

Winna thought of her granddaughter, little Isabelle. She will never know the child, the girl, the woman I've been or the truth about my life. I barely know myself. Some of the things I've done are a complete mystery to me.

Gramma told me that she had wanted to leave her husband and baby son and run away with Whitaker. She had been capable of that much, at least, but what about Charlotte Blackleash? There was no son in the story, she had needed respectability, stability, money—then the excitement of being with her lover, not the love of a little boy.

Winna rolled over and pulled a second pillow close against her body, aware that allowing her mind to race would not bring sleep. But she could not rest.

18

ON THE WEEKEND, Chloe and Todd came to dinner at the house. Realizing too late that she hadn't thought to serve a steak or something Todd might like to eat, Winna scooped chicken salad into avocado halves and placed them on a bed of field greens tossed with a fresh lemon and olive oil dressing. She sliced some French bread and, for dessert, served her quick raspberry charlotte. Todd seemed unfazed and accepted his beer in a glass. He called the plate "pretty" and appeared to enjoy the meal. Chloe, clad as if she had been invited to the White House for dinner, wore a strapless green silk dress with a gathered bodice that emphasized her lovely breasts. Chloe sipped white wine and nibbled while she talked.

"Back then—the seventies—I was in therapy and my shrink said I should write a letter to Daddy. She wanted me to vent—let him know what a lousy father he'd been. She wanted me to be specific—like the details—and express how I felt inside."

Todd leaned back in his chair looking doubtful and said, "Did you write it?"

"Yes—I sure did," she said, tossing her head of honeyed curls as if it had been her victory. "I knew at the time that Mercury was in retrograde, but I did it anyway."

"But you didn't mail it, I hope," Winna said.

Chloe downed the last of her drink and looked at Winna. "I did."

"Wow!" was all Winna could say.

"Ruth read it too. I got a phone call. She didn't breathe a word about having read the letter but invited me to meet her for lunch downtown. She chose a public place for her scolding. I 'crushed him,' she said. He was 'hurt and angry.' She was angry too, and you know what she said? 'Don't be surprised if he disinherits you.'"

"So you knew he disinherited you?"

"He wouldn't see me after that—not for a couple of years."

"Really," Winna said, "and I thought it had been a terrible surprise for you at the reading of the will."

"I'm just figuring it out now, Winna. I didn't know—I didn't think he would actually do it," Chloe said. "It was a terrible surprise—and then to hear those words—one dollar."

"It might have been a good idea to write the letter for therapy's sake and just file it away for safe keeping," Winna said.

"No kidding. I should have made a ritual fire of it—sent it skyward as incense. Not having the sense to do that, I should have sued the shrink for—how much is my share of the estate—a couple of million dollars? By the way, nobody has ever given me that dollar."

"Do you think Ruth suggested to Dad that he disinherit you?"

"Who knows. She was clever at manipulating him. When she walked out on him, she got a separation agreement that included alimony. Knowing he was usually drunk and not that attentive to his checkbook, she would call from California and claim that he hadn't sent a check."

"Chloe, remember when you heard her voice message on the answering machine—all pitiful and hurt? 'You didn't send my check, Henry.'" That bitter memory drove Winna to stand up in anger, then quickly sit down again. "But, Todd, when Chloe looked at Dad's checkbook, he had sent it."

"Yeah, and she'd done that more than once. I found a couple of months where he sent her two checks."

Winna brightened. "Remember the letter we wrote her?"

"How could I forget?" Chloe rolled her eyes. "Todd, we guessed that she wasn't reporting the support checks, so we wrote this letter to her threatening to reveal her trick to the IRS if she didn't give him a divorce."

"And it worked. He'd been trying to get rid of her for three years at least," Winna said. "We did good, sis."

Todd had listened all evening without saying much. He went back and forth to the refrigerator for beer, offering little but facial expressions—frowns, a deep thoughtfulness to his eyes, and occasional disbelief. Winna figured that he was scandalized by the family dysfunction.

"Sorry, Todd, there's nothing worse than listening to people talk about their memories—memories you don't share. You look a bit shocked. What was your family like?"

"Oh, I don't know," Todd's face softened. "Just nice folks down on the farm. My mom made the best fried chicken in two counties and baked apple pies that let you know there's something right with the world. She kept a big garden in tomatoes and sold them by the roadside. I helped her with the canning."

Charmed, she asked, "And your dad?"

Todd smiled. "He was a great dad. Made me a fishin' pole, took me fishin', taught me to shoot. We'd sit on the porch or by the fire and he'd read to me from the Bible."

"Are they still living?"

"Dad is. Mom went to her maker some years back."

"See, Winna, some people have normal families," Chloe jabbed.

After the dishes were done, they went out on the porch to catch the night air and talked until late. Through watching Todd with Chloe and listening to his conversation, Winna began to think well of him. He seemed sweet and just as spacey as Chloe. After they left, Winna could not get Chloe off her mind.

Before moving back to town after her divorce, Winna's sister had lived in LA. Chloe had never gone long without a man to love her. She had followed her own brand of spirituality and her causes: the environment, animal welfare, and the support of local merchants under pressure from big-box stores run by huge corporations.

Unlike me, Winna thought, Chloe has approached her life fearlessly, breaking the rules, making a big adventure out of it. She wondered if Chloe saw herself in that light. She knew how her sister thought of her—someone afraid to let go and have adventures, someone closed-minded and disapproving.

Winna knew how different they were and wondered how that could be. They had been so close as children. She had watched over Chloe like a little mother. Then, Winna had loved her sister more than anyone else on earth and now she had to love her from a distance. Her father's cruel denial of Chloe's birthright came suddenly to mind and spun her into circles of anger, then tears. How could he—over something that happened twenty years ago? And me? He's made me an object of envy and given me the appearance of greed. Winna knew that she could not let her father's wishes stand and promised herself that tomorrow she would make an appointment with Reed Thompson, her father's lawyer.

19

Late 1940s

EVEN THOUGH YEARS had passed, Winna had not forgotten the day she first saw their new home in the country: a sprawling farmhouse with a big front porch. Almost everyone on Peach Tree Ridge had enough land to keep a horse, a milk cow, and a vegetable garden. Wild asparagus grew along the ditch banks, and nearby the Grand Valley Canal snaked past a cherry orchard, a small vineyard, and farms growing melons and hay.

The first summer there, Winna explored the remains of old orchards growing in unexpected places: a row of pear trees along the lane, apricot trees beside the ditch bank, a wild pear thicket in the field to the west, and gnarled old apple trees in two spotty rows just below the rise of the hill. Even though no one pruned or sprayed the trees, there were plenty of only slightly wormy apples to eat—the apricots were spotless, perfect. In spring, the fruit trees blossomed pink and white all across the land and in summer the girls climbed them.

When the apricots were sweet and juicy, the rosy color of the setting sun, Winna climbed one of the large trees growing over the irrigation ditch. Chloe followed, and like hungry birds, they rested high in the tree and ate their fill. From the treetop Winna could look over the tall privet hedge to the house and beyond to Pinyon Mesa bathed in red sunlight and blue shadows.

Out of the corner of her eye, Winna saw Chloe slip, then fall, letting out a little yelp as her body crashed through leaves and branches. She landed face-up in the shallow ditch below. On her way into the water, she hit her head on the plank they used as a foot-bridge. From the top of the tree, Winna could see her lying under water, her eyes closed, her arms at her sides in the ditch as narrow as a coffin. Her blonde hair looked like seaweed as it floated with the current away from her peaceful face. Winna screamed for their mother to come.

The tree rained apricots as she raced from limb to limb down to the ground. Reaching the ditch bank, Winna grabbed her sister by one arm, pulled her to a sitting position, and dragged her up through the weeds into her arms. She watched Chloe struggle to catch her breath and cough up water from her lungs. By the time Nora got down the hill, Chloe was crying and Winna had stopped shaking.

Dr. Sloane drove out from town to examine Chloe. They had had a scare but Chloe would be fine. Winna felt proud that she had been swift and strong enough to pull her little sister out of the water in time.

This was not the first time Chloe had taken a dangerous dive. After seeing *Peter Pan*, she must have thought she could fly. Without the benefit of pixie dust, she jumped off the second story porch and got the wind knocked out of her for a frightening few minutes. In time, Chloe learned to climb down the chimney at night and escape undetected. She showed Winna how to do it, but Winna wasn't that brave.

When she was six, Chloe wanted to be a boy. Her father's and grandfather's frequent mention of their bad luck—the absence of a male heir—must have inspired her. That summer she got hold of Nora's sewing shears and chopped off her hair.

Nora took one look at her nearly scalped child and dragged a stool outside on the lawn, draped a towel around Chloe's neck, and with a lot of advice from Winna, recut her hair. When she had done her best to smooth out the rough spots, she stood back for a look.

"It looks better," she sighed.

"Do I still look like a girl?" Chloe asked, squinting back the bright sunshine.

Winna thought her sister was hopeless.

Chloe's favorite outfit was a pair of jeans, a white shirt, her fancy red cowboy boots, and a kid-sized Stetson. Before Nora took her daughters into town to shop or to the picture show, Winna bathed and slipped into a dress, but Chloe refused. Nora would give in and let her youngest daughter wear jeans on the streets of downtown Grand Junction.

Winna was horrified. "I'm not going to walk anywhere near her in public."

That fall Chloe would enter first grade. But all summer long she went around shirtless like the boys, walking with a swagger, talking out of the side of her mouth like the toughs she'd imagined or seen in the movies. She would not answer to her name. Everyone had to call her Bill.

"Do something about Chloe," Winna begged, but her mother ignored her.

On Labor Day weekend, Chloe showed up in the shallow end at Moyer swimming pool wearing boys' swim trunks. Winna watched all the kids tease her.

"Look at Chloe. She's dressed like a boy!"

"Your titties are showing! Your titties are showing!"

She knew her little sister hated a teasing even more than she hated being a girl.

Trying to save face, Chloe pulled up nose-to-nose to one of her tormentors and yelled, "I can swim and you can't."

"Liar! You can't swim!" he taunted.

"Yes, I can," she yelled. She had sounded so positive that she must have believed it herself. "I'll show you," she said, climbing out of the pool and marching herself down to the deep end.

Winna ran after her. She knew her sister well enough to know that she had convinced herself that if she really wanted to swim, she could. Winna was too late. Chloe had jumped in and sunk to the bottom. When she came up flailing and gasping for air, the life-guard dove in and saved her.

Nora was ready to dry off her daughters and take them home. As the sisters climbed into the car, Chloe burst into tears. "I don't like girls' swimsuits."

It was easy for Winna to see her mother's heartbreak. Sheltering her nonconformist daughter in her arms, she whispered, "Don't cry, Chloe. Don't cry."

Winna leaned over the back seat to pet her.

"You don't have to wear dresses unless you want to," Nora said, kissing her on the forehead as Winna prepared to contradict.

"Of course she has to wear dresses."

"At school," Chloe cried, hanging her head in shame. "The kids will tease me if I don't—I have to wear dresses to school—I do," she sobbed.

"Yes," Winna said. "They won't let you in." Hoping to comfort and at the same time convert her, she said, "It's not so bad. You look pretty in a dress, and Mother will buy you new dresses for school. Won't you, Mother?"

Chloe rubbed the tears off her cheeks. Though she looked defeated, she sat up straight and, with the shaky voice of a soldier accepting a dangerous mission, said, "Let's go shopping for girls' shoes."

WHILE CHLOE WAS trying to fly, Winna was busy building an altar in her room. She had been converted to Catholicism by the film *The Bells of Saint Mary's*, starring Bing Crosby as a priest and Ingrid Bergman as a teaching nun.

Winna had seen nuns on the streets of Grand Junction, sweep-ing down sidewalks in black habits, their faces washed clean of make-up. She had stared in fascination. Then came the questions. No, they don't get married. Yes, they shave their heads. Some said that they were stern, even mean to children. But Bergman floated in

her long black habit, the white of her headdress framing her beautiful face, her eyes glowing with love. Her saintly character lived in
service to the children of the convent school.

After seeing the movie, Winna decided she wanted to be a nun.
She cleaned up her room and moved the furniture. She added an
altar—a large box lovingly draped with one of her mother's bridge
cloths—and adorned it with a candle and flowers. She cut the
oval picture of the Good Shepherd Christ from a Congregational
Sunday school certificate, and placed him at the center, leaning
against the vase.

Alone in her room, she would light the candle and kneel.
Breathing in the scent of the match, the burning wick, and wax, she
pressed her hands flat against one another under her chin, just like
Ingrid Bergman. She closed her eyes and prayed, "Our Father, who
art in heaven, hallowed be thy name…," just like Ingrid Bergman.

Winna was convinced that God liked her so much better that
way—like the nun in the movie. After she said "Amen," she gazed
at the picture of the Gentle Shepherd and he gazed lovingly back
at her. His peaceful blue eyes filled her with a longing she did not
understand. She wished she could crawl into his arms and rest her
head on his shoulder.

20

1999

WINNA PULLED UP in front of Chloe's little bungalow on Teller Avenue. The house was a fairly recent purchase, a work in progress. A ladder leaned against the screened-in porch. The front had just been repainted a soft putty color. The porch, trimmed in plum, glowed with a fresh coat of rose. The blue-green gate in the picket fence swung easily as Winna lifted the latch. Rose, teal, and plum were the colors Chloe wore.

Chloe's garden, growing on either side of the walk, welcomed her with a chorus of wind chimes in the globe willows. Beyond two small patches of lawn, gone dormant from lack of water, flowerbeds burst with sunflowers, pink coreopsis, rosy yarrow, and magenta love-lies-bleeding. Behind the tangle of flowers stood a nearly life-sized wooden goddess dressed in flowing green robes emblazoned with gilt planets and moons, her gaze heavenward. Startled birds rushed from the feeder and pedestal bath as Winna approached.

Instead of a doorbell, Chloe had installed a triangle. Knowing her visit would be a surprise, Winna created just enough racket to wake the dead and waited for Chloe to come to the door.

Dressed in a flowing robe similar to the one adorning her garden goddess, Chloe looked as if she had just gotten up.

"Winna, what a surprise." She appeared pleased. "Come in—I just made coffee."

"Is Todd at work?" Winna hoped he was. "I'm sorry to come by so early."

"He left about seven—I slept late."

She led her sister through the front room, stunning in deep plum, with long blue-green curtains dragging on the hardwood floor around two large light-filled windows. She had hung two of Nora's abstract paintings, one over the sofa and the other just above a green table. Winna enjoyed seeing them again.

"Mother's paintings never looked at home in my New England house," she said. "Here, they're perfectly wonderful."

The sofa, a nearly white, deeply tufted leather sectional, was strewn with colorful pillows. Several had toppled to the floor. The large round glass-top coffee table held two wine glasses, a couple of empty wine bottles, an ashtray overflowing with butts, and a dozen candle holders with candle stubs dripping wax.

"Sorry for the mess," she said, steering Winna toward the kitchen.

"I like what you've done. The garden is lovely."

"Thanks—I wish it wasn't so dry."

Chloe pointed to one of the yellow vinyl and chrome dinette chairs that surrounded the matching kitchen table. "Have a seat."

Winna obeyed and sat down. "Chloe, yesterday I went to see Reed," Winna said, revealing the reason for her visit.

"Oh," she said. "How's Reed?"

Winna accepted a bright pink mug from her sister's hand. "I told him I want you reinherited, so to speak."

Chloe seemed to stop breathing. She sat down and gazed into her cup.

"Unfortunately, in gifting you, the taxes would be horrendous—about half of everything to the government. It appears that Dad's estate is over four million, not counting the house and its contents."

Suddenly, Chloe stood and walked to the kitchen sink. "How much will I get?" she asked with her back to her sister.

"Let me finish explaining," Winna said, wondering why Chloe seemed so jumpy. "Reed suggests I set up a discretionary trust for you, in my name. The trust will revert to you upon my death when you or your heirs will become the successor trustees. As I understand it, during my lifetime there will be a third-party trustee for you to deal with—you won't have to come to me. A percentage of the earnings will be yours and you and that third party will decide what other disbursements are fitting. We aren't sure of the amount yet, but the earnings will be considerable—a comfortable living. I know, Chloe, that this is a lot to take in and, if you want, Reed could explain it to you in more detail."

Chloe turned to face her sister. Tears flooded her eyes and she began to tremble so violently that hot coffee splashed down the front of her robe. "Oh, shit," she cried in pain. "I'm such a goddamn fool." Furiously, she rubbed the spill with a kitchen towel. "Why do I feel guilty? Like I don't deserve this."

"It's not about deserving," Winna said, wishing she felt free to embrace her. "I don't deserve it either—it's just our birthright. Remember, the fortune was built by three generations and added to by Gramma's inheritance. Dad grew the fortune and maintained it after her death. For all his invisibility, Daddy was a great manager and business man."

Chloe sighed. "I was born into wealth but never felt wealthy, not even as a kid. It's like real financial abundance has eluded me all my life—Juno says there is abundance in my chart, but I've been in a long cycle—I know you don't care about this—but this past year, by transit, when Saturn came forward and opposed the Sun…" Chloe trailed off and slumped into a kitchen chair. "I won't go on except to say that it hasn't been easy, Winna."

"None of this has been easy. Dad's awful death and that awful will. We can't expect major tragedy to be easy," she said. "Notwithstanding the position of the stars, life gets thorny." Winna stopped. Her words lit no sign of affirmation in Chloe's eyes. She didn't know how to talk to her anymore.

"I just couldn't let the will stand. It was so unfair and I couldn't enjoy having wealth, knowing you were left out."

Chloe rushed into Winna's arms. "Thank you. Now I'm the happiest I've been in a long time. Thank you."

"You're welcome. I'm just sorry you had to go through that."

"I'm happy," she said. "I'm actually happy." She beamed at Winna and hugged herself. "I've finally learned that I won't find all-encompassing happiness through a man." Chloe stood, clutching the back of her chair. "Neptune has a square, hard ninety-degree angle to Venus in my chart. This makes me yearn for the ideal. It's different now, because I'm wise to it, but in the past when I met a man, my eagerness made me project the ideal onto him. Then there always came that moment of betrayal when I realized that the man I had married was just ordinary, or worse. Of course, I blamed him."

"I did the same with Walt. I think the expression goes, 'The honeymoon's over.'"

"No, it's not that simple, Winna. It's deeper than that old cliché." Chloe was pacing, her voice rising with excitement. "If you live long enough, you learn. Really learn! Now I know that happiness is found only inside one's self—the transcendence that comes from inside, from one's own creativity."

"I'm glad you're happy," Winna said, biting her tongue. She did not want to say what she thought. To her, transcendence meant moving beyond the self toward God.

"And this money is great, Winna. It'll free me up to garden, paint, and do my real work," Chloe said, refilling her cup. "I want to make an impact on the environment—the way this stupid country does business." She paused, her face suddenly troubled. "Explain why I can't just have half the money?"

Winna took a deep breath. Readjusting to her sister's sudden change of tone, she said, "The taxes. Dad's estate is much larger than anyone expected, and once we sell the house and antiques, it will be more. If I simply hand over half to you, we'd have to pay tons of gift taxes."

"That's okay," she said, bouncing into the chair. "How much is there?"

"We aren't sure yet, but Reed thinks that with the sale of the house and its contents, it will top five million—maybe more."

"Really? Money has never been that important to me, but it would be fun to have a big chunk all at once. I've never had that."

"You have two sons. What about your boys?" Winna said. "You'd have nothing to leave them if you had 'fun' with a million or two. Think of the fun they'd miss."

Winna watched Chloe check herself before she replied.

"I guess you're right. That makes sense, actually," she said, thoughtfully. "But how much will I have to live on?"

"Reed figures it will be anywhere between eighty and ninety thousand a year, depending on how it's invested."

"Good Lord, that's way more than I make now." Chloe gave Winna a hug.

"Look, Chloe, we don't really know what's in that house. Remember the ring I found? Who knows what else we might find."

"Let's hope we find the Hope Diamond," Chloe said, kissing her sister's cheek.

Winna laughed. "No thanks. I think the Hope Diamond is cursed. Now, why don't you show me your paintings?" she said, returning the kiss.

"Do you really want to see them?"

"Sure I do. Then I want to tell you about Gramma's short story—I think we have a mystery on our hands."

Chloe led Winna from the kitchen to the glassed-in back porch. "Look, I even have a northern exposure—it's perfect."

Finished canvases leaned along the walls. Two easels with oil paintings in progress sat in the center of the room. The first canvas depicted the Book Cliffs under a stormy sky. In the foreground, a shaft of sunlight lit a peach orchard in full rosy bloom. The second canvas looked like Ute Canyon with twisted pinyon trees, a stand of yuccas in full bloom, and a hawk circling the evening sky.

"Chloe," she gasped, delighted. "I had no idea. These are impressive."

Emboldened, Chloe showed her everything.

"My little sister has become an accomplished painter." Winna was awed. The paintings were highly disciplined, uniquely styled, and finely crafted—by no means the work of a dilettante.

The sisters spent the day together, talking about their lives as children. Chloe had not done well in school and confessed that for years she thought she was retarded. That was after one of her teachers forced her to read in front of the class. Chloe struggled with the words and her teacher embarrassed her by saying, "How on earth did *you* qualify for second grade?"

"I had a hard start with reading too," Winna said. "One night Daddy offered to help me with a new book. The words came slowly and I could feel his impatience. 'I don't have time to sit here while you horse around,' he said. 'Now straighten up and look at this sentence.'"

"You can guess what happened next. I didn't do well and he called me a 'dummy,' got up from the davenport, and walked off, leaving me in tears. I was sure I was the dumbest kid alive."

"I remember how you used to get in trouble," Chloe said. "Actually, I hated the way Dad treated you. The way he looked at you put me on guard. Remember the time you were wearing a nice new dress to go and visit Gramma and Poppa—the day Lucky jumped up on you and put his muddy feet on your dress?"

"Yes, and I kicked him," Winna said. "Dad saw me and yelled, 'I'll teach you how not to treat a dog.' Then he kicked me across the driveway."

"He was horrible to you when we were little. I was always trying to be as good as I could possibly be because of all the spankings you got. Then I got closer to Dad—loved hanging out with him at the store—he taught me to shoot—to drive. I guess that's one of the reasons it hurt so much when he disinherited me. I knew Gramma favored you and hoped that Daddy favored me."

Winna forced a laugh. "Right now I'm going to forget all about that and try to remember something wonderful about our childhood. Help me."

Chloe's face brightened. "How about the flume? I think that was my favorite thing."

On hot summer days, the sisters had played in the flume, a long metal trough designed to move water from the canal to the fields and orchards. It stood high over the ground, just big enough for Winna, Chloe, and the water bugs. No grownups could reach them, only voices calling them home. Feeling far away, the sisters laid back and let cool bronze water pass over their bodies. Up high, where the wind rustled the leaves in the trees, they watched the cars whiz by on the distant road and made up a guessing game: where had each car been and where was it going?

Often in their play, they pretended to be orphans, but in the flume, they were orphan fairies having a bath. They made believe that they had been born under nodding blue flowers, lived on nectar, and dressed in white frocks spun from cottonwood silk.

21

IN THE SMALL adobe house high on Little Park Road, "Mood Indigo" played full blast on an old record player. The day had been reasonably warm, instead of unbearably hot, and Winna had driven into the foothills for dinner with her daughter's family.

Emily filled a wine glass with Chardonnay and handed it to her mother. "Let's join Hugh on the deck."

"Aren't you old-fashioned this evening," Winna said, glancing at the Duke Ellington album cover lying beside the vintage phonograph. "I love it."

"That would be my husband's choice of music." Emily opened the slider to a hanging deck built into the rocks. Below and perpendicular to the house, the couple had made a garden of native plants. Cactus and yucca were the only ones Winna recognized. The garden birdfeeder was busy with doves and quail.

They found Hugh waiting for the sunset with Isabelle in his arms. From that height, one could see most of the Grand Valley.

"It's like the view from an airplane and I never get over it," Hugh sighed.

When standing, Hugh was six feet tall, had a muscular build, and wore his blond hair and moustache in a style that made Winna think of pictures she'd seen of General Custer. He had to wear a jacket and tie at work, but when he relaxed, he wore jeans, plaid shirts, tees, and sneakers. Hugh never affected cowboy dress with hats or boots—he knew he had come from Boston.

"Hi, Granny Winna, have a seat," he said, rising to greet his mother-in-law.

"Don't get up, Hugh. You look too comfortable, but let me have the baby."

"No, it's my turn." He chuckled. "I'll let you hold her when she starts to fuss."

Winna smiled at her son-in-law. Her affection for Hugh Rogers, the youngest son of pop-novelist David Tellison Rogers, was sincere. She knew that as managing editor of the *Daily Sentinel*, he held an important job, but most of all she loved reading his weekly column on Grand Valley history. Hugh wrote with humor and style. Emily had met him in college where they both studied journalism. Not long after their marriage, and by pure coincidence, Hugh was offered a job at the *Sentinel*. He told Winna that he'd had an interest in paleontology and had always wanted to live in the West where he could spend his weekends scouting for fossils. She was astonished when Emily and Hugh had moved to the town where she was born.

He smiled at Winna, as if he understood how eager she was to hold Isabelle. "Here, Granny, take your favorite grandchild," he said, handing her the baby.

She received the child, who responded with a sunny grin, babbling and pulling at Winna's earrings. "Are you going to join us, Emily?" she called.

"Here I am," she said, exiting the kitchen with a platter of cheese, olives, and crackers. "It's hard to tear myself away from my masterpieces."

"I'm hungry," Winna said.

Emily's face lit up. "I can't wait to read the story—you did bring it?"

Winna reached for her bag and pulled the old notebook from the side pocket. "It'll only take a few minutes—then I want Hugh to read it."

While Emily read Juliana's story, Winna gently bounced Isabelle on her knee and told Hugh the story her grandmother had told her years ago about her first love and his death on the train. At her story's end, Winna grew silent as an old sadness crept inside and the landscape disappeared in purple shadows. She'd been having flashbacks to her first love and not all the memories were happy. She remembered how controlling and possessive Johnny had been, how his words had sometimes descended to abuse.

"I think my old boyfriend John Hodell lives up here somewhere," she said, watching the last gleam of the sun slip behind the mesa. "You know John, don't you?"

"Yes, we are very neighborly up here in the boonies," Hugh said, pointing several hundreds of yards below and to the left. "That's John's house down there."

Nearly the same color as the boulders around it, John's adobe house blended with the earth itself, red as sandstone. In the last dim light, the house took the shape of a large rock formation. As they sipped their wine and nibbled, they watched the sky darken and a full moon rise over Grand Mesa. The stars twinkled above, the city lights twinkled below, and a young coyote crept near the bird feeder in the garden.

"Let's put Isabelle to bed," Hugh said.

They left Emily alone, reading by the light of a hurricane lamp. When they returned, Emily had finished the story. She had leaned her head against the back of the chair. With her eyes closed, the notebook lay open in her lap.

"Well?" Winna asked. "What do you think?"

"I don't know," Emily sighed. "She barely disguised her characters and settings with made-up names. My instincts tell me she wrote her very purple prose from experience."

"That's what Chloe thinks. What do you think of the fact that she didn't finish it?"

"She couldn't bring herself to make it real. Maybe she didn't want to spend her time confessing her adultery and mercenary tendencies."

"I think that she simply had a good imagination and embellished her love story," Winna said. The thought of her grandmother having an illicit affair as described in the story about Charlotte Blackleash was hard for her to welcome. "Gramma had wanted to be a writer and might have thought a sizzling romance novel would be commercially successful. I've found lots of old nineteenth and early twentieth-century romantic novels on her library shelves."

"You're probably right. But what if Poppa Henry was Adolph Whitaker's son?" Emily added.

"Emily!" Winna cried, then reconsidered. "I guess it's possible."

"Well, who did Poppa Henry look like?"

"He looked like his mother."

"Her hair wasn't dark. Poppa's was almost black. What about your grandfather? His hair wasn't dark, at least not in the photos I've seen. Neither of them had Poppa's coloring."

"No, but—that's impossible. She already had a child in the story she told me."

Winna reclaimed the notebook and handed it to Hugh. "Please read this. We need your opinion."

"Let's go inside," Hugh said. "It's getting buggy."

Emily had set up a buffet with salads and bread. Winna helped herself to a green salad, a delicious-looking Niçoise cold pasta, and settled down on the sofa facing the picture windows and the view of the valley. Hugh took the notebook and his dinner to a chair on the other side of the fireplace where it would be quiet.

As they ate, Winna tried to make sense of things. "First we found the letter from Whitaker—written on the train and mailed from Rhode Island—which proves the story she told me long ago was true." Winna took a sip of wine. "Then I found the letter from Juliana to Edwin, saying goodbye, as though she expected to die— her handwritten will enclosed."

Emily looked as if she couldn't wait for her mother to finish her sentence. "That letter may have been written when she decided to leave her husband and go away with Whitaker. Maybe she wanted him to think she was dead."

"My Lord," Winna said, realizing that if Edwin thought Juliana was dead, she wouldn't have to worry that she'd be remembered as a faithless wife and mother. "Wait a minute. In the goodbye letter with the will, Juliana already has a baby. That jibes with the story she told me about not being able to leave her child and kills your theory that Whitaker could be his father."

"Why did Juliana keep the letter and the will—and who opened it?" Emily wanted to know.

"As far as I can tell, she saved everything—I don't suppose she forgot about it."

"It's too confusing," Emily said. "I think we need to write all this down."

"If you really want to be confused, let me tell you what the Denver jeweler said about the ring we found. It's a clear yellow diamond, about four carats and worth over $120,000."

"How did it get to Denver?"

"I mailed it."

"You're kidding. Where is it now?"

"In the safe deposit box at the bank."

"Good. Don't ever mail a $120,000 anything again," Emily said, looking distracted. "Is it a coincidence that a yellow diamond appears in the choker in Juliana's story?"

"Good question."

"Hugh?" Emily called, interrupting her husband who was engrossed in Juliana's story. "How can Mom find out if Adolph Whitaker really died on the train?"

"It probably got picked up by the paper. Do you know what year?"

"Gramma told me he came back to town when Dad was about a year old. That would make it 1917."

"All you have to do is go down to the library and look through old editions—they're on microfilm." Hugh thumbed back a few pages. "Charlotte's letter to Andrew is dated June 15—no year. But I wouldn't count on the letters or anything else in the story being true. It reads like fiction to me."

When Hugh had finished Juliana's story, he joined the women. "The young architect in the story could not have become rich enough to afford the jewels described—architects do okay but not that kind of money."

"I hadn't thought of that," Winna admitted. "Maybe that's why she stopped writing—her plot was faulty."

"In any case," he said, "in the archives it won't be hard to look through a whole year and even the years before and after. You can scan the headlines rather quickly."

"I'll do it tomorrow," she said, suddenly willing to abandon rooms full of work waiting impatiently on Seventh Street.

Emily looked at her mother and smiled. "Okay, Mom, now why don't you tell us about your old boyfriend, J-O-H-N-N-Y?"

Winna laughed. "What do you want to know?"

"Well, was he a good kisser?"

Winna rolled her eyes. "On a scale of zero to ten, he was a—ten."

"Is he still?"

"That's for me to know and you to find out," Winna joked as her mind flashed on scandalous scenes from her past when she and Johnny Hodell steamed up his car's windows and matted the tall grass in the apple orchard. Stirred by her memories, Winna sighed and wondered if ... no. Not now, she told herself.

22

1956

ALL IT TOOK was for Winna to load up her old Mercury with
a bunch of girlfriends for a night at the picture show and a drag
down Main for Johnny to feel threatened. Then they would fight.
She would accuse him of never taking her anywhere anymore,
never wanting anything from her but sex, and he would say that
was about all she was good for. Ashamed that she had become no
more to him than a toy and furious with him for bringing that to her
attention, she would break up with him again.

But always after their fights, he swept her away by the sweetness of
his apologies, the earnestness of his promises, the urgency of his kisses.
She would go back to him, only to wonder in a very few days why
she had been so stupid. Why she could not part with him. They didn't
talk anymore, not even about their plans for college because, to Johnny,
that meant separation from her. All she knew was that he thought he
would study history or business and that he wanted to be rich.

One night, they parked on a dirt road that ran alongside a farmer's field. The stars and a sliver of moon gave off enough light for
them to make out the silhouette of a hay wagon parked in the middle

of a newly mown field. Johnny did not reach across the seat for her, but got out of the car and walked around to the passenger door.

"Come on, baby," he said, opening the door for her. "Let's go for a walk."

The evening was warm and dry as a bone. She crossed the field in ballerina flats and a cotton sleeveless blouse, her full skirt catching a sudden gust of breeze. Enveloped in dark night air and quiet, they walked toward the hay wagon. No words were necessary. Winna knew where they were going and what they were going to do when they got there.

They climbed up on the hay. He first, his hand extended for her. He removed his cotton shirt, spread it out on the hay for her to lie down on, then crawled into her arms. She wrapped her arms around his strong bare back and looked up at the stars, shining like bright pinpoints in the sky. She loved him—loved how they came together, how he made her feel.

Alone in the dark, deeply lost in one another, they suddenly found themselves at the center of a bright light. Winna screamed. Voices spoiled the night silence—hoots, whistles, laughter—mocking, suggestive male noises she'd always hated. Johnny took Winna's hand and helped her up. They jumped off the wagon and ran. Terrified that someone would recognize her, Winna lifted her skirt over her face as they raced for his convertible. Petrified for her reputation, she hurled herself on the floor of the front seat and sobbed. Johnny sped away chuckling. He thought it was funny. She hated him.

ONE AFTERNOON, AFTER they had parked a while on the canal road, Johnny looked her up and down and said, "Did you know you're getting fat?"

"I'm not. That's not true—nobody else has said that." She wanted to cry and rage at him. At the back of her mind, she knew she had not been picked for cheerleading last spring or homecoming royalty that fall and her pedal pushers did seem tight. Swallowing a huge lump in her throat, she looked at the emerald ring her grandmother had bought her, twisting it in the sunlight to make it sparkle.

"Everyone wonders why I date you," he said coolly.

Winna couldn't speak. She believed him and that scared her.

"You are lucky that I date you at all."

She wanted to run. "You're mean!" she yelled.

"No one is going to marry you because you aren't a virgin," he said. He was quiet a moment. Both stared straight ahead past the canal as his words took hold of her. "I probably shouldn't marry you either," he said flatly, as if he were discussing the weather.

She knew he was right. Chances were no one would marry her. That was the fear expressed by every bad girl in every *True Story* magazine story she had ever read. To save face, she would not dissolve into tears. That was what he wanted—her all soft and begging for mercy. Instead, she struggled to remove his class ring from the chain around her neck.

"I hate your guts!" she yelled, throwing the ring in his face. It stung him hard as it bounced off his forehead and hit the dashboard. She knew what to say next, the worst thing she could possibly say to him.

"I never want to see you again." She hoped her words would cut his heart out. "Take me home."

"Get out and walk," he said.

She got out of the car. He turned the car around and headed back to First Street.

Feeling utterly alone, she walked beside the canal as it drifted lazily past reeds and cattails. Dragonflies flitted by. A horsefly buzzed around her head, landed on her arm, and bit her. Rubbing out the pain, she ran past a cornfield and a farmhouse huddled in the shade of a cottonwood grove. She wondered if she should jump in the canal and drown herself. But after years of swimming in the canal, she didn't think she knew how to drown there. She needed a flash flood to sweep her away, a mire of quicksand to swallow her. Tears came. Johnny was right about everything.

By the time she saw his car driving back along on the canal road, she believed he was right; she *was* lucky that he dated her. She felt grateful to him for coming back.

"Come on," he said, opening the passenger door as the car rolled slowly along beside her. "Get in. I'll take you home."

Marching alongside the open door in silence, not looking at him, not speaking, she wanted to look like she still had some pride.

Johnny began to chuckle. "You look pretty damn silly stomping down the road in tears," he said as if they had not had a horrible fight—as if he had never even thought all those terrible things. "Ah, come on, Winna. Get in. Let's not fight."

"I'm not crying," she said, hoping for some dignity. She climbed into the passenger seat and sat close to the door. He turned the car around and headed toward First Street once more. She wanted to crawl into his arms and hear him say that he loved her.

By the time they stopped in front of her house, Johnny had apologized to her. He assured her that he had not meant a word he'd said, that he had just been upset because on Saturday she went shopping with Kate and had not helped him wash his car.

That night, she could not sleep. She lay there promising herself that tomorrow she would break up with him for good. To be true to herself, she must make the break. But by morning, things did not seem so bad. She told herself that she could not live without him. He was all she had. She went on her first diet, cutting back at every meal and going hungry in between. Then she discovered the buttermilk and banana diet and ate nothing else until she was thin.

FOR WEEKS, WINNA worried that she was pregnant. When she finally told Johnny, he knew what to do. He had a married friend who was willing to take her urine specimen to his wife's doctor. Winna was to pee in a bottle and he would see to all the rest. After a few torturous days, Johnny informed her that the rabbit had died— she was pregnant. Winna thought the world had come to an end, but he seemed strong. Suddenly thoughtful and concerned, he said he would marry her. Neither of them breathed a word to anyone.

All day long at school, Winna had nothing else on her mind. At night, she could not sleep. She lay awake looking out the window at the moon through the cottonwood tree, whispering a prayer.

"Oh, God, help me. Make it not happen. Make it go away. If you make me not pregnant, I'll never have sex again—I'll never even let myself *want* to have sex again." She held her breath for a long time, dissolving into the sheets, trying to make her heart stop. If I want to, she thought, I can will myself to die. She lay there, asking life to drift out of her body, dizzy from the desire to be no more. The last thing I'll see is the moon. The moon doesn't care what happens to me.

The day came when Winna had to talk to her mother. She walked downtown after school and climbed the stairs to her studio. Nora had set herself up in an empty office on the top floor at Grumman's. She'd had the carpets pulled up, the drapes pulled down, and the windows exposed to the light. The studio gave off the familiar smell of oil paint, turpentine, and mineral spirits. Canvases cluttered the walls in no apparent order. Framed pictures leaned against the walls in corners. Two easels were set up in front of the window. The moment she entered the room, Winna fell into the only easy chair. Before her mother could properly greet her, she gave up a sob and began to cry.

"I'm pregnant, Mother," she said, terrified.

Nora appeared strangely calm. "Oh—I see. How do you know?" Her clothes covered with a paint-smeared smock, she came to sit on the arm of Winna's chair and placed a hand on her daughter's shoulder.

"There was a urine test—the doctor said so."

"I've worried—you know—with you and Johnny being together so much." She stood and pulled Winna up and into her arms. "My poor girl," she whispered.

EXCEPT FOR THAT day, Nora did not mention Winna's problem again. Instead, an uncomfortable silence came between them. Winna couldn't talk to Kate or Maggie and was afraid to ask questions, to even think about what was happening to her body.

Without a word about her problem, her mother arranged for their annual shopping trip to Denver. On the train, as they passed through high canyon walls above the Colorado River, Nora told Winna the truth about their trip.

"Dr. Sloane found a doctor for you. When you come back to Grand Junction, you won't be pregnant anymore," she said, taking her daughter's hand.

Winna did not ask questions, she understood. She squeezed her mother's hand, then put her head on her shoulder. "I love you, Mother," she whispered.

They arrived in Denver that afternoon and checked into the Brown Palace Hotel. At nine o'clock that night, they took a taxi to a modest residential neighborhood where Nora had been instructed to get out of the taxi at the corner of Walker Street and Geronimo Way. After they paid the taxi and it was well out of sight, they walked to an address two blocks down on Geronimo. Nora rang the bell of a large Victorian house in need of fresh paint.

A woman answered the door. Nora gave her four hundred dollars in cash, and was asked to wait in the front room. She sat down and Winna was ushered through a door into a room that looked like it had once been a kitchen.

NORA SAT ALONE in the dimly lit room across from a lumpy gray davenport, her feet on a Navajo rug. She thought of her poor frightened child on the other side of the wall, of her uninformed husband waiting for them at home. For Winna's sake, Nora was glad that she was not like her mother. It had been less than a year since her mother's death. She had been a kind woman, very loving to her child, but she was strict and judgmental about moral failure. Glad that she could help her daughter, Nora tried to imagine herself being in Winna's place. Her mother would have berated and judged her, then sent her away to hide until the baby was born. Suddenly, her eyes ran with tears and her mind opened to the thought that she could be wrong. She'd hidden everything, never confided in that dear woman, never gave her mother the chance Winna had given her.

It wasn't long before the doctor reappeared at the door. He told Nora to take Winna back to the hotel and put her to bed. If she complained of pain, Nora was not to give her aspirin. A hot water bottle on her back would help. She would need bed rest until at least noon tomorrow.

"My wife called a taxi for you," he said as he ushered her into the kitchen.

Nora saw her daughter sitting quietly across the small room, head bent, hands folded in her lap, her eyes glued to the floor. She looked like she was trying not to cry. She could feel her child's loneliness and was eager to take her away. She wanted to hold her, to rock her like a baby.

"The taxi is waiting for you in the alley," the doctor said.

On the drive downtown to the hotel, Nora held Winna's hand. She kept silent for a while, watching the house and car lights flicker past in the dark. "Everything is going to be all right now," Nora heard herself say. She put her arm around Winna's shoulders and pulled her close, letting her rest her head on her breast.

THE DAY FOLLOWING their return to Grand Junction, Winna told Johnny that he didn't have to marry her. "I'm not pregnant anymore," she said.

He wanted to know what had happened and she told him the truth: the trip to Denver, the doctor in the kitchen, her fear. He looked at her in stunned silence. Winna was glad there were no tears in his eyes. "Everything is all right now," she said. "You can go off to school. I haven't ruined your life."

He was silent a moment. "I wanted to marry you." Winna had never seen him look so sad.

"It wouldn't have worked. We don't know how to be married, Johnny."

He put his arms around her and held her. "We could have made it work," he whispered. "Someday..." He hesitated, pulling back for a look at her face. "Promise me that someday, no matter where we are or who we marry, you'll let me find you again."

Winna slipped his class ring off the chain around her neck and put it in his hand. "I promise," she said.

23

1999

THE FULL MOON seemed to follow Winna down the mountain as she drove her trusty old Lincoln Town Car on the winding road back to Grand Junction. Walt had purchased the car in 1993. She had driven it a hundred and two thousand miles, and still made it all the way from New Castle to Grand Junction. She had always wanted to make that trip—a vagabond, free as a bird, traveling across the country with her camera—even though she ended up being on assignment for *American Roads,* she felt the freedom she had longed for. It was fun being a photojournalist for a change.

At a sharp curve on a steep decline, she shifted into second to slow her speed. Thinking happily about her evening with Emily and Hugh, she felt certain that her daughter had made a good marriage and was happy with her husband and child. There were no other cars on the mountain road. Winna kept her headlights on high-beam. In the moonlight, nothing in the landscape looked familiar, but her headlights flashed on a mailbox with "J. L. HODELL" neatly painted in white letters. For an instant, she thought of stopping, but the house was dark. It didn't look like John was home.

John Hodell had been on her mind since she last saw him. She had invited him to dinner, offering to cook the trout he'd caught on a weekend fishing trip. As he watched her pan-sear the fish, she felt something happen between them. She couldn't exactly name it, but his eyes were lit with pleasure and she felt the happiness of a young girl enjoying attention that was also affection. The feeling lingered with her long after he had left and was with her still as she drove down the mountain.

That ease and contentment kept them at the table late into the night. For the first time, he talked about his life after the war—about the gambling that led to financial ruin, about Jim Cross coming to the rescue, helping him see that he had to get help. He told her about his long climb back to what he called "sanity." Once John was "clean," Jim had become his business partner. John talked about Jim's loyalty. How his faith in him had changed his life. Winna had not asked and there was no mention of his taking money from the business to pay gambling debts. They had embraced tenderly when they said good night and had kissed.

Driving downhill, she applied her brakes on a curve and admonished herself to slow down. A fitting image, she thought, of my life as Johnny's girl. Back then, before women's lib, she was both young and clueless. A thrilling thing—Johnny's love—but clearly a downhill ride for me. "What a mess we made, John," she said aloud as her tires whined around another curve.

After their trout dinner, he had called the next morning to discuss the possibility of replacing the furnace. Before he said goodbye, he asked her to dinner at his house. She had accepted.

Winna turned into a residential neighborhood at the base of the foothills. I'm not going to be a fool about John. I'm too old to be a fool. Don't kid yourself, Winna. Resolutions and promises to herself accompanied Winna the rest of the way home.

AS WINNA PULLED into the driveway at the house on Seventh Street, she noticed the attic light was lit. Had it been burning since she searched the trunk? In her excitement, she must have forgotten to turn it off. She parked in front of the garage and entered through the kitchen door. It was not terribly late, but Winna was tired and climbed the stairs to the second floor, stopping to flip off the light at the bottom of the attic stairs.

She readied herself for bed and pulled the chain on the bedside table lamp, plunging herself into darkness—the perfect setting to discharge the accumulation of the day. Juliana, Edwin, Dolph, and baby Henry materialized in her mind until the memory of John's kiss chased them away. Turning on her side, she snuggled into her pillows remembering how John had made love to her when she was sixteen.

She closed her eyes as the words of her childhood prayer came to mind for the first time in fifty years. "Now I lay me down to sleep…." Look at what an old house full of memories does to you, she thought as tears wet her pillow.

The bewildering sound of carefully placed footsteps on the attic stairs stopped her tears. Terrified, she lifted her head as the attic door opened with a click. Winna held her breath as the dark figure of a tall man crept past her open door. She froze as his footsteps quietly descended the back stairs. She was not dreaming. He was in the kitchen. She heard the sound of the kitchen door open and quickly got to her feet. Racing across the hall to the old nursery's window, she saw the intruder run down the driveway, turn on Chipeta Avenue, and disappear into the night.

STILL SHAKEN FROM the events of the night before, Winna poured her first cup of coffee, stirring in both sugar and cream. She remembered that until Walt had left her for another woman, she had always taken her coffee black. Was that the way she hoped to sweeten her bitter cup?

She sat down in the library to mull over last night's visit from the police. She had been terrified and, for the first time in her life, dialed 911. From window to window, she ran in the dark, making sure he was gone. She thought of the doors and hurried to check every one—all but the kitchen door were locked. Within minutes of

her call, the police had arrived at the front door. Scared to be alone
in the house for another minute, Winna had to restrain herself from
rushing into their arms.

She couldn't remember their names—only that one was young,
blond, freckle-faced, and about to burst out of his uniform and the
other tall, dark, and handsome. She had taken them upstairs to the
attic where they did their best to look around in all the clutter.

"Is anything missing?" the blond one asked as he cast his eyes
over the tangle of dark objects jutting from the attic floor.

"I have no idea. Look at this mess," she said, throwing her arms wide.

"Who has keys to the house?" the other officer asked as he shined
a long flashlight into the dark corners of the attic. "You should
change the locks."

"The kitchen door wasn't locked," Winna said. "We've never
locked the kitchen door—not in over eighty years."

He gave her a sheepish grin, then shook his head and said, "I'll
bet you'll lock it now."

He flashed his light to the floor. "Nice and dusty. Come look at
these footprints."

Winna doubted their value. "They might be mine. I can't count
how many times I've been back and forth across this floor."

The blond officer got down to his haunches for a look. "These
tracks are pretty confused and if he picked up dust on his shoes and
made a track in the hall, we probably destroyed it on our way in."

After the attic, she had shown them her room and described how
she lay in bed holding her breath, hoping the intruder would think
she was asleep and wouldn't have to come in and kill her.

They dusted for fingerprints around the attic door, then checked
the front door and the door to the side porch to make sure they
were locked.

"Ok, Mrs. Jessup, we're through here. Before we leave, though, I
want to see the key to the kitchen door," the dark-haired one said.

Feeling like a foolish child, Winna disappeared into the library
to look for the key. The officers waited for her in the reception hall
while she rummaged through some drawers and finally found it.

The moment she appeared in the hall, the older officer held out his hand, palm open, and she placed the key there.

He looked at it and smiled. "Get the lock changed and keep your door locked. This is the oldest key I've seen in a long time."

"We'll write this up, but don't expect much in the way of an investigation—especially since nothing is missing. House break-ins are very common and hard to solve unless you catch the burglar in the act, or if stolen goods resurface somewhere later. Now lock yourself in and don't answer the door again tonight."

"THEY MUST HAVE thought I was an idiot," she said to herself on her way to the kitchen for another cup of coffee. Wondering who on earth had been in her attic last night, she comforted herself with the thought that she'd have new locks on the doors by the end of the day.

Putting the terrors of the night before out of mind, she reached for the last of Adolph Whitaker's letters. Winna had already read a few. The earlier letters were written while Adolph was a student at Brown University. He wrote to Juliana during her senior year in high school and the two years she attended college in Denver. Had Dolph written only twenty-eight letters in a span of five years? It seemed likely that Juliana had only saved her favorites.

He described his classes—mostly classics and English literature—wrote his thoughts, and little poems.

> If college bred
> Means a four-year loaf,
> O tell me where the flour is found,
> By one who needs the dough.

Winna wondered if his literary skills included something that corny or if it was a popular saying with the college crowd at that time.

Dolph seemed to thrive in his studies. His career at Brown went smoothly except for bouts of homesickness and his interminable yearning for Juliana. Autumn letters spoke of the pain of separation.

He used metaphors for their separation like "cruel abandonment of summer," his heart "fleeing the cold winds of autumn." The bereavement of a tree as it sheds its leaves, "its very life force." Late winter and spring letters welled with "ardent longing" and the "soon to be fulfilled promise of new life," of his "swift flight to Colorado," and the "joy awaiting him in her embrace."

In Grand Junction every summer, Dolph's "dear selfless mother" labored as a cleaning woman while he worked his old job at the grocery. He recalled his days off when he and Juliana blissfully strolled in local parks, fished by the river, or picnicked at Whitman Park. He wrote his memories: picking peaches with Juliana at harvest time and taking a horse-drawn wagon into the country to visit friends. Yet August always came and when Dolph boarded the eastbound train, they were torn apart. "Our every parting is a little death," he wrote.

During his senior year at Brown, something new came into his life.

Dearest Juliana,

Content is the man whose happy labors are rewarded. Just loving you has made me the happiest man in the world, my dearest. I do not deserve the great good luck that has befallen me now. Today I received a letter from Mrs. William Ailesbury of Ailesbury Court in Newport.

Newport is a seaside haven for the very rich and powerful who live in palaces on Narragansett Bay, not so far south of Providence. Every summer, captains of industry and their families and friends come for the salubrious ocean breezes. They refer to their mansions beside the sea as summer cottages. I find that quite laughable.

I shall not keep you in suspense another moment, my sweet. How I wish you were here to share my joy! I am told that Mrs. A. is one of Newport's finest, most illustrious hostesses, famous for her patronage of the arts and her divertissements. Put these two fine attributes of womanhood together and you have a monumental piece of good luck for artists. This paragon of good taste and intellectual curiosity finds great joy in introducing her favorite artists and entertaining her wealthy friends, both of whom she, no doubt, seeks to impress.

She has invited me to read at her first-of-the-season soiree, luckily in early June. I won't miss more than a week of the summer with you.

Be happy for me, my darling. I am beside myself with trepidation and joy. My distinguished hostess has commissioned me to write an ode to the roses of summer. An interesting choice, for her name is Rose. It shall be the first lucre I have earned as a writer. Now I must add generosity to the list of her many virtues.

Do not be heartbroken if you receive few letters in the weeks to come. With Mrs. A's commission and my final studies, I will hardly have time to sleep.

Everything I do, my darling, is for you—that I may soon afford to marry. I remain your faithful kindred spirit,

Dolph

P.S. Mrs. A. says she first read my work in the chapbook of poems Brown printed last year. How that poor little thing fell into her hands, I do not know.

After he graduated from college, Dolph took a job as an English teacher at Moses Brown, a private school in Providence. Before his early summer appearances at Ailesbury Court, he had appeared at several other mansions in Newport. Obviously, Dolph was in demand. His letters reassured Juliana that they would be married the following year, but that that summer he could not afford the time it would take to go home.

His next letter came a mere week later. Winna was most interested in the following paragraphs.

> You cannot be more disappointed than I am,
> Juliana. I would be there by your side this summer
> if I could. I am trying to make my way in the world
> and your sudden proclamation that you no longer
> believe that I will be able to support you has left me
> astounded, not to mention heartbroken.
>
> You promised to wait for me. We both knew
> it would not be easy. We both promised that our
> letters would sustain us.

In the following letter, Dolph seemed somewhat relieved by
Juliana's reply.

> A misunderstanding is something I never want
> to have with you, my darling. As you wisely
> said, I am sensitive, maybe overly so, about the
> differences in our background—at least where
> wealth is concerned. You deserve to have a happy
> life. I cannot give up writing, but I can give up
> teaching for something more lucrative and I will
> seriously think about how to proceed to that end.

A letter written the winter of 1915 was the last one she saved.

> Dearest Juliana,
> My guilty hand takes pen in hand at last. I
> am sorry for not writing, my dearest. You cannot
> imagine the demands of my schedule. I have not
> heard from you in an age. Are you ill?
>
> I know my absence from Grand Junction last
> summer disappointed you terribly. By fall, your
> letters were scarce and unforgiving. I have apologized

repeatedly in my heart, if not enough to you. At this late date, I do not know what to say to reassure you. I know I have not written very often. Are you unable to forgive me, or have you met someone else?

Both lack of forgiveness and faithlessness are disastrous vices in a woman, Juliana.

In your last letter, you speak of nothing but your father's business affairs, Daisy's latest slight, the stories you plan to write, and the gifts you received for your birthday. You show no interest in my welfare and ask no questions about my work. You say nothing of our love. It might as well have been a letter to a brother.

Are you punishing me? If so, I am all but mortally wounded by your silence, your cold refusal to speak of our love.

Rose has generously introduced me to a representative at Alfred A. Knopf, a just established New York publisher who is interested in my novel. For you alone, Juliana, I informed her that I cannot stay on for the season this year and must return to my fiancée in July. We have a wedding to plan.

My hope is that you will return to Providence with me in August, just as we have always promised. You will love the world I inhabit here—a world of wealth, beauty, and high art. A world where you belong. Rose has arranged several appearances for me in both New York and Newport in April and May.

In truth, all I look forward to is being with you, Juliana. Please write and salve my wounds. Don't be cruel, my own dear kindred spirit.

Dolph

How had Juliana interpreted this last letter? In Winna's mind, Dolph seemed full of ambition for both art and love. The letter seemed to reveal a decline in their bond and she found herself sympathizing with Dolph. Those were vastly different times. She reread the paragraph beginning with "Rose." It was the first letter where he had called her by her given name. Was there a romantic involvement with Mrs. A., his Rose? How had Juliana responded to this? Without Juliana's letters, her view was incomplete, but one fact was plain.

The rhythm of Dolph's visits to Grand Junction saw him arriving in early to mid-summer and returning to Providence in late August. Winna decided she would scan the library's microfilm for editions printed in August 1915-1917 to see if they mentioned the death of a man on an eastbound train.

Before she left the house for the library, she called John to tell him about the light in the attic and what had happened the night before.

After listening quietly to the whole story, John said, "I don't like this. I'm concerned about you being alone in that house. Have you told Emily and Hugh?"

"No. That's why I'm telling you. I didn't want to worry them or Chloe. But I guess someone should know."

"You thought I wouldn't worry?"

"Well—"

"Have you called the police?"

"Yes, last night," she said, feeling as if he was grilling her. "I guess I thought you might have some kind of level-headed idea. Like who the hell was in my attic at ten-thirty last night, or what I should do now?"

"You might start by locking your kitchen door," he said without a trace of humor in his voice. "Do you think that by locking the front and side doors you've fooled someone bent on getting in?"

"We've never locked the kitchen door," she said, sounding lame even to herself.

"Thank God you didn't try to be a hero and approach him. You could be dead this morning."

24

THE NEWSPAPERS FROM late July 1916 were full of stories about the aftermath of the World War I Battle of the Somme, where British troops suffered sixty thousand casualties at the onset of their attack. German saboteurs blew up a munitions plant on Black Tom Island, New Jersey. Winna shook her head in disbelief. German saboteurs in New Jersey? In the days that followed, Romania declared war on Austria-Hungary and Germany declared war on Romania—nothing about a death on a train in Colorado in July, August, or September 1916.

Winna returned to the file drawer and looked for July and August of 1915. On July 28, US forces invaded Haiti. She was shocked by how little she knew of this period in history. Europe was at war and President Woodrow Wilson feared that Germany might invade Haiti in order to establish a military base there. German settlers in Haiti were begging Germany to invade and restore order to the chaos there. In sleepy little Grand Junction, the new dam on the Colorado River at De Beque Canyon made the news, as did the successful fruit harvest aided by the first water that had been routed into the Grand Valley canals. Miss Gustafson was teaching ladies how to make their own hats, but no mention of Adolph Whitaker's death appeared in any of the late summer editions.

Next, she tried 1917. On July 28, ten thousand Negroes marched on Fifth Avenue in New York in silent protest to the race riot in East St. Louis, Illinois, where thousands of blacks were forced to flee the city when their homes were burned. The silent marchers walked behind a row of drummers and carried banners calling for equal rights and justice, the only sound the beat of muffled drums. In August, the *Daily Sentinel* printed a story about the Russian newspaper *Pravda* calling on all citizens to kill capitalists and priests. Later in the month, ten suffragists were arrested as they picketed the White House.

"The world was just as screwy back then as it is now," she said to herself. Discouraged, bleary-eyed, and fatigued from hunger, Winna wondered if she had missed something. Would she have to retrace her steps? Just to be sure, she decided she would and found herself enjoying the journey back in time as she wandered off into pleasure reading stories like the early motoring adventurers who had decided to drive nine cars from Grand Junction to Salt Lake City on a road that disappeared in places, then picked up again as wagon tracks.

Admonishing herself for getting off track, she wheeled back to August 1915. Nothing. If Dolph died in August, it may not have been reported for several weeks. Armed with a candy bar, she moved forward in time and found what she was looking for in the September 5 edition of the *Daily Sentinel*.

Railroad Reports Former Resident Dead

GRAND JUNCTION: Mrs. Laura M. Whitaker of 357 First Street, Grand Junction, has received news from authorities at the Denver and Rio Grande Railroad that her son, Adolph G. Whitaker, 26, of Providence, Rhode Island, died en route to his home after a visit to Grand Junction this summer.

No details about the circumstances of death, which occurred on August 27 after Mr. Whitaker boarded the eastbound train, are yet available to this newspaper. Mr. Whitaker was a graduate of

Grand Junction High School and Brown University in Providence, Rhode Island. He was employed as an English teacher at Moses Brown School in that same city. He is survived by his mother, widow of the late Edgar D. Whitaker. Funeral arrangements are pending.

Sugar and adrenaline combined, Winna felt giddy. Especially interested in Whitaker's address, she reread and copied the tiny article. "I want to see that house," she mumbled to herself.

Adolph Whitaker suddenly seemed very real. A peculiar sadness crept inside, as she wondered how Juliana had felt when she saw the article. It must have been a terrible shock. Or had she known about the death before the story appeared? Perhaps Dolph's mother had sent word to her? But she was a married woman. It was likely that the lovers had concealed their love affair from Mrs. Whitaker just as they had from Juliana's husband.

She remembered the day her grandmother had told her about her lover's death on the train and how terribly sad she had looked.

"He died of a broken heart," Winna had said as she reached for her grandmother's hand.

Juliana closed her eyes and tears spilled onto her cheeks. "And I've lived with one, precious." She asked for a Kleenex and Winna handed her the box. She blew her nose, then smiled at her grand-daughter. "One day, when you are a woman, you'll not be so surprised by my story. You'll be glad your grandmother was trea-sured by—" She stopped without saying his name.

Winna bent to kiss her cheek. "I'm glad now, Gramma. I'm glad you had a special love."

Juliana smiled as if she had a secret she could not reveal—the same expression Winna had seen on her grandmother's face on the day she stole a look at Juliana hiding Christmas presents in a closet.

ARRIVING HOME FROM the library shortly after four o'clock, Winna had to rummage in her handbag for the key to the kitchen door. She unlocked it and stepped inside, deciding to lock the door behind her. Bone tired from her day at the library, she headed upstairs to Juliana's bathroom, hoping that a loll in the bath would both cool and revive her.

As tepid water filled the big tub, she undressed, leaving her clothes in a puddle on the floor. She relaxed into the water trying to put the newspaper article out of mind—evidence of a major tragedy in her grandmother's life. The whole puzzle exhausted her and she forced herself to think of something else—the room itself.

Of late, she had found herself looking critically at all the rooms, imagining how she would get rid of the wallpaper and repaint, refinish the hardwood floors and restore the magnificent tiles, and whether or not she would invest in a new furnace. Seth had looked disappointed when she had hired a company to paint the exterior, but reassured when she told him that he was too valuable to waste on such a long project. A display of drapery fabric in the window of a store downtown had nearly pulled her inside. In truth, she had noticed herself behaving as if she planned to stay—to make the house her home.

Remembering the upstairs hall closet she wanted to look through, she promised herself to get to it soon. Only with her grandmother's permission and supervision had young Winna been allowed to look at the gowns Juliana had saved. Some looked very old, like she had worn them as a girl. All were special occasion dresses, the kind you wear once or twice to a ball or wedding. All were made from rich fabrics: laces, satins, and silks. Some sparkled with sequins and faceted beads, just the thing to dazzle a child.

Relaxing against the cool slanted back of the claw-foot tub, Winna looked around the room. Juliana had thought of everything, even a bidet. She may have lived with a broken heart, but she knew how to do it in style. Above the white tile wainscoting, the walls had been painted a soft, almost imperceptible green. The floor, decorated in a pattern of tiles shaped like ginkgo leaves in the same but more saturated green, lay over a white ground. The etched-glass windows glowed with a gentle light giving the room a feeling of peace and cleanliness. Even the old fixtures were in good condition. *There is nothing I'd change here. It's perfect,* she thought, closing her eyes, letting herself sink farther into the luscious cool water.

Suddenly, Winna felt the hand of reality touch her for the first time. *Gramma lied to me. Daddy was not a toddler when Dolph died—he wasn't born until 1916, the year after Whitaker died.* It was possible that he was Whitaker's son.

25

1945

AT NIGHT, FOR A BRIEF time during the war, people in Grand Junction dimmed their lights and covered their windows with shades or heavy curtains. Children went to bed hoping that no careless child had left a lamp shining in the window. Folks worried that if German aircraft flew overhead, they could see the lights of towns, of lonely farms, of a single car making its way down a country road, of a match struck in the dark.

At the picture show, Juliana saw newsreels with scenes from the war in Europe—whole villages full of lost and bewildered people on the move. Big-eyed children wrapped in heavy coats, boots, and shawls, walking down country roads pushing carts full of their belongings because the hated Germans were coming. In the newsreels, Juliana heard the screaming air-raid sirens and saw people run through the streets of London looking for shelter. After the bombs, everything fell silent as the camera panned over the rubble, the destruction of historic buildings, precious art, precious lives.

Evenings, Juliana and Edwin drank nightcaps in the parlor beside the radio. As he spoke to the British people, Churchill's reasoned, refined voice comforted the English-speaking world. She even welcomed the voice of FDR. Without her vote, he had recently been reelected to a fourth term. Juliana conceded that the middle of a world war was probably a bad time to change the government.

It was a necessary war. She knew that. Almost everyone but pacifists, socialists, and isolationists agreed. Newscaster Edward R. Murrow brought them the day's news from the front. He spoke of battles won and lost and how the Allies were now winning. He spoke of meetings between world leaders, of Princess Elizabeth joining the British Army as a driver. In January, three months before his suicide, the Führer's terrifying voice entered her well-furnished and decorated parlor. He was speaking to the German people, admitting that, at the moment, things weren't going well for the Fatherland. He had not lost hope and wanted them to know that, in time, they would rule the world if they kept up their spirits and fought hard. Juliana did not understand German, but as in all his rants, she understood the evil passions he stirred. She, like most people, was mesmerized and could not turn off the radio.

In Grand Junction, Juliana suffered few war-related hardships, but sugar, gasoline, butter, coffee, and meat were rationed. She fussed over the fact that she couldn't get silk or the new nylon stockings. Both fibers were needed for parachutes. Some women used leg paint and learned how to draw straight, dark lines up the backs of their legs to simulate stocking seams, but Juliana would not stoop to that. Housewives saved tin cans for use in armaments and their bacon grease—collected door to door in Grand Junction—for use in ammunition. The war with Japan raged on and in May, Pvt. Henry S. Grumman, #36289471, waited for his orders at Fort Leavenworth, Kansas. From the beginning, they had not drafted fathers, but hundreds of thousands of American soldiers had died and with the war in the Pacific still raging, they finally had to draft Juliana's son.

Crazy with worry, Juliana saw Nora's brave front for the sake of her children as certain evidence that she didn't care what happened to Henry. Edwin firmly expected divine providence to protect his son. Juliana kept her worries from the children. Winna and Chloe were too young to even imagine anything bad happening to their father. With a brave face, she told her granddaughters that when the war was over, their daddy would come home and they believed her.

Not long after Henry was drafted, atomic bombs were dropped on Hiroshima and Nagasaki. When Juliana saw the mushroom clouds in the newsreels, she vowed never to go to the pictures again. She kept that vow. Just nine days after the bombs fell, it was announced on the radio that the Japanese had surrendered and the war was over. Henry Grumman did not have to go into battle. He would not have that adventure, but he didn't come home for a long time. They sent him from Fort Leavenworth to Fort Hood, and then to Camp San Luis Obispo for his postwar duties.

By late 1946, Juliana could not get out of bed in the morning, sometimes rising as late as noon. Often, she was unable to eat until dinnertime. After dinner, she drank bourbon to help her fall asleep. She began to lose weight, lose interest in her house, in everything. She stopped calling on friends. She wanted to be alone.

By fall, when Henry had not yet come home from the army, she found herself spending most of her days rocking herself in the gold damask rocker that had belonged to her grandmother. If anyone had noticed and asked her why, she would not have known what to tell them. It had become hard for her to concentrate on anything, even her own thoughts, which seemed jumbled and senseless.

ONE EVENING, EDWIN came home from work and found Juliana sitting in the middle of the library floor, the world globe in her lap, sobbing uncontrollably.

"Dear, dear girl," he said, going to her. "What's troubling you?" He bent to offer his hand, but she looked as if she did not hear him. "Juliana," he said, kneeling beside her. His wife's head drooped as if her neck was broken, her hair in tangles, her tears dripping off Europe like a river running south toward the pole.

"Juliana! What's going on here?" He tried to take her father's old globe from her hands and return it to its floor stand, but she only hugged it tighter and moaned.

Edwin straightened up and tried another tactic. "Get up off the floor this minute. I'll not stand for this kind of behavior from a grown woman!" He demanded. "I'll not be frightened like this by women's tears." He used the toe of his wingtips to nudge at her back. "You look like a crazy woman."

Suddenly, she turned and looked up at him. No new tears wet her cheeks, her eyes were vacant. "Yes, I'm afraid I am—crazy."

When she stood, the globe slipped from her lap and thundered across the floor, stopping under the Boston ferns. She reached for her husband and the crying came again in horrible anguished gasps. He led her into the alcove and made her sit down on the window seat.

"Don't move, Juliana. I'll get us both a drink."

When he returned, they sipped their bourbon and water in silence. Juliana propped up on needlepoint pillows with Edwin beside her, his elbows resting on his knees. Soon, both felt better.

Juliana wanted to talk. "I'm sorry. I don't know what came over me—some terrible sadness—I've been—"

"Don't try to explain, dear. Just put it out of your mind. You mustn't dwell on it. You are fine now." Edwin was uncomfortable with all that emotion. He was embarrassed for his wife, ashamed. He was sure the servants had heard.

"Now you rest here and I'll see what Maria has for dinner," he said and left her for the kitchen.

THE TIME CAME when Edwin knew his wife was not fine and he called the doctor to the house. He found Juliana in a stupor, staring at the wall, unwilling or unable to look at anyone or speak. The doctor encouraged Edwin to take her to Minnesota for treatment at the Mayo Clinic.

Edwin had hoped it wouldn't come to this. He wondered why, with her less than stable history, he hadn't seen it coming. He'd just read a newspaper story about the war's contribution to the public's decline in mental health. People everywhere were suffering from anxiety and depression. The ramping up of the Cold War didn't help. The US was testing atomic bombs in the Pacific. The Russians had been at work developing a bomb. The arms race was on. The mushroom clouds over Japan were enough to undo a woman of Juliana's delicate temperament. Edwin knew that much. Most people believed that the bombs dropped on Japan had saved lives, that they had ended the war. Still, people felt the horror of it. Like a killer after a murder, Edwin thought, they return in their dreams to the scene of the crime.

At the Mayo Clinic, Juliana underwent a course of both talk therapy and electro-shock therapy. She stayed for three months and returned to Grand Junction greatly improved. Not long after her return her parents died. Edwin was afraid that would send Juliana into another downward spiral, but she grieved reasonably and kept busy tending to her sizeable inheritance. Her beloved son had finally come home.

26

1999

ON A WOODEN DECK hanging from a sandstone cliff three steps down from his living room sliders, John Hodell balanced a tray of hors d'oeuvres on one hand and with the other offered Winna a martini studded with four olives.

She laughed. "I can't drink these anymore," she said, accepting the drink anyway.

"Sure you can." He smiled, bending low, offering her a choice of hors d'oeuvres. "Here we have several old favorites, prepared by my own loving hands, delicious tidbits from the past. Little repasts wrapped in fond memories—like this onion dip with chips *pomme de terre*, these bologna cornucopias filled with julienne of carrots and sweet pickles, or this—my favorite—crunchy celery stuffed with real cheese food."

Laughing, she reached for one of the little cornucopias and sipped gingerly from the rim of the martini glass, surprised by how much she enjoyed the sting of gin on her lips and tongue.

"You are talented, John. You've gone to a great deal of trouble to take us back to the fifties." She nibbled on the cold bologna spiced with hot dog mustard. With the martini, it tasted surprisingly delicious. "How did you ever find the time?"

"I took the afternoon off to do these—and sweep the dirt under the carpets," he said, resting the tray in front of her on the patio table. "Unfortunately, there's lots left to do." He sat down beside her. "But a good host must stop and visit during cocktails."

"Yes he must," she said, patting his hand. "I'll help you in the kitchen after cocktails—if I can still stand."

The evening was warm and Winna settled back in her chair to relax, glad that she had worn comfortable sandals and a white linen tunic and slacks. Sips of martini went down easily.

"Your view is just as lovely as Emily's and Hugh's," she said. "My goodness, this view two nights in a row. Lucky me." She felt warm and tingly and decided to put the martini down. "Just look at that sun setting—and the lights of the city coming on."

"Did you lock your kitchen door, Winna?"

"Yes, John. Twice—no three times—even while I took a bath. I figured I should lock myself in."

"What did you find at the library?"

"Oh, my goodness, I almost forgot," she said, surprised that she had neglected to mention her exciting discovery. John's presence, the martini, and the funny hors d'oeuvres had been a distraction. "Gramma's lover died on that train trip on August 27, 1915, which means that she lied to me. She didn't have a son to abandon until late April of the next year. I may be the granddaughter of a poet not a department store magnate."

John leaned back in his chair, letting his muscular legs stretch full length across the deck floor. "Have you counted the months?" he asked as he ticked off the fingers on both hands. "Fascinating. So maybe Whitaker knocked up Grandma."

Winna laughed at the image John had created in her mind. She changed the subject. "The old newspapers were totally fascinating. What with World War I and Grand Junction still a cow town with Indian troubles of sorts."

John's eyes narrowed in the light of the setting sun. "I've been thinking about your unexpected visitor, Winna," he said, crunching on a stalk of celery. "Who's read the story about the jewels hidden in the trunk?"

"Just family, Emily and Hugh. I told Chloe the gist of it, but she hasn't read it yet. They all know I found nothing when I searched the trunk. I told you what I found while Emily and I were looking through an old box of marbles—the ring. And it's valuable. I sent it to be appraised in Denver and it's a real canary yellow diamond."

"Someone else must know about the trunk in the attic."

"Just you."

"I don't count," he said. Then, sounding like he wanted to get to the bottom of this business, he said, "Tell me again about the recreation of your childhood bedroom in the attic."

"I already told you all there is to tell, John. It's not something I want to talk about now—here on this lovely evening," she said, feeling her throat tighten and a hot flash coming on. "The more I think about it—there's something very scary about that."

"All right, lady. I can tell when it's time to feed you," he said, taking her hand, helping her up from her chair. "You said you'd help me fix dinner."

"Yes," she said, relieved. "I'd like that. Where's the kitchen?"

Winna made a tossed salad while John fired up the grill and fried up an iron skillet full of onions, chili peppers, potatoes, and chorizo that he seasoned with cumin. She was starving by the time the steaks were ready and they sat down to eat outside at the patio table.

As flames from two hurricane candles flickered softly, John looked at Winna and raised a glass of wine for a toast. "Here's to Winna, the girl I couldn't forget."

"I'll drink to that," she said, blushing, trying to make light of his touching compliment, of the affection that shone in his eyes.

After dinner, they moved inside. John sipped from a snifter of cognac, she from a cup of hot herbal tea. They sat side by side in two handsome leather club chairs separated by a low wooden table, its warm patina lit by an ornate tin lamp studded with brightly colored bits of glass. Furnished largely in the mission style, the rest of the living room held several interesting antiques; a modern Kulim rug covered the terra cotta tile floor. One of the white walls, lined with glass shelves, held John's collection of Indian pottery, glowing colorfully under the track lighting. The north-facing wall, built entirely of glass, glittered with the lights of the city below.

For a long time they talked easily and laughed about the old days. "You know, Winna," John said, shaking his head in disbelief, "in those days, as often as I saw your father, I never guessed he was an alcoholic."

"That didn't register with me either—until after Ruth left. Of course, he got worse then. Anyway, once I realized his problem, I had to admit that all the signs had been there for years. He was always respectable, hard working. He never let us down that way."

"Tell me about him," John said, his expression sympathetic, even ponderous. "What was he like as a father?"

"Oh, John, I don't know," she said, not anxious to stir up bitter memories. "In the late eighties he did get sober—went to AA meetings for years. We were proud of him for that."

As if it were a crystal ball, John turned his gaze to his drink, a pool of warm cognac. "You know, Winna, I had no idea you were so private—I remember you being just the opposite."

He turned to look her way and their eyes met. "Do you really want to hear all about how frightened I was of my father? How, as a child, he scolded and hit me. How, as an adult, he distanced himself from me and showed no interest in my life. You know, when Walt left me and I called to tell Dad that my marriage was over, his only reply was, 'How's the weather out there?'"

John sat up straight in his chair. "What?" He reached out to touch her shoulder.

"Thanks," she said, taking his hand in hers. "Maybe that's why I'm so interested in Juliana's marriage. I'd like to know what happened when Dad was a child. What were his parents like? There's a picture of him with his mother holding him when he was a baby. His face is so happy—alight with joy. What happened between the time that picture was taken and when I was a girl? I never saw joy on that face, only alcohol-fueled mania or a withdrawn quiet. What did they do to him?"

John shook his head. "You know, it isn't always the parents—"

The door chime interrupted. John went to answer and Winna wondered who it could be so late. She heard laughter and loud voices coming from the front hall, then Chloe and Todd appeared through the shadows with John at their side.

"We've come to celebrate!" Chloe called from across the room. "We have good news." She was flushed with excitement and looked a bit tipsy.

Surprised, Winna got to her feet. "How did you find me?"

From the way they were dressed, their good news seemed obvious. Chloe wore tight white satin jeans hitched around her tiny waist with a silver concho belt, a white satin and lace blouse. A tulle train fell to her waist from a white felt cowboy hat studded at the crown with sequins and pearls.

"I called Emily," Chloe said, rushing to throw her arms around her big sister. "We got married this afternoon!"

"Congratulations, Buddy," John said, clasping Todd's shoulders. The groom wore an astonishing wedding shirt with a black-banded collar and a white front-pleated bib.

"Don't look so shocked, Winna," Chloe said, her smile bright as a neon sign. "We have to celebrate." She spun around holding a huge bottle of champagne aloft. "We had an amazing dinner at La Petite Rue—but you, above all others, must celebrate with us—the night is still young."

"My goodness, Chloe," Winna said, bewildered. Trying to look happy, she kissed her cheek and reached for Todd's hand. "Todd, you are full of surprises."

"Chloe wants your blessing," Todd said.

John took Winna's hand. "The time for a blessing is before a wedding, Chloe."

Winna felt tears rush to her eyes. "I wish I could have been there—it would have meant so much to me."

"You know us, Winna," Chloe said, hugging Todd around the waist, "We're kinda private. It's not that we got married on a whim, or anything. Last week Juno told me this afternoon would be the perfect time—so we just did it."

John and Winna looked at one another. He stepped behind her and gently pulled her close against him. "Winna's ok. Aren't you, kid?"

"Of course, just surprised," she said, warmed by his embrace. "You know how I am—a sap for engraved invitations, the church, the loving family gathered around."

Over champagne and toasts into the wee hours of the morning, Chloe gushed and sighed with happiness. Todd did his "aw shucks" kind of blushes. John played the host and Winna suffered hot flashes.

Chloe and Todd said their goodbyes at about one thirty and were gone. Winna grabbed her purse and turned to say good night to John. As Todd's headlights went on in the driveway, John took her hand and pulled her into his arms.

"After all that champagne—I don't want you to drive home alone."

"I'm fine, John. I hardly had a drop." His lips held her like a magnet and they stood a long time in the foyer locked together.

"Don't go," he whispered between kisses.

She lifted his face in both hands. "I'm tempted," she said, "but I'm going."

She gave him a peck on the cheek and, heaving a big sigh, opened the door.

"You don't know what you're missing," John said.

"Yes I do," she called as she hurried to her car.

Winna was halfway down the mountain with no memory of the drive down the first leg of Little Park Road. Her head swam with visions of John: his face, his eyes, his sweet grin. After Walt, she had not expected this. "That part of my life is over," she had told herself. "Now is the time to focus on my career."

John is so different from Walt. He actually talks with me not at me. He hasn't put on the TV once in my presence. He was a jerk in high school, but he's changed. Is this too good to be true?

As she neared the foothills, she caught a last glimpse of city lights and wondered if John had gone to bed. Was he sitting alone beside the window? Did he walk out to the deck and watch her car lights move down off the mesa? That's what she would do. Do men do things like that, moon over a woman? She doubted it.

Approaching a sharp, steep curve, she applied her brakes. Nothing happened. She pumped the brakes again. Still nothing. Terrified, she thought of shifting into second. The car swerved violently and she knew she was going too fast to down shift. She grabbed at the emergency brake and gave it a tug.

In shadows cast by a bright full moon, she could not see what lay below the road. Knowing there were several deep ravines along the way, she pumped the brakes hoping they would respond this time. Her headlights splashed on another tight curve just ahead. She turned the wheel sharply, pulling at the emergency brake again. The weight of the car tipped to the outside. As the car careened around the curve, the tires squealed. Winna gave up a terrified scream. Keeping control, her high beams flashed on the landscape. She was nearing the bottom of the foothills where the road flattened out. Her heart pounded violently as the car began to slow. She shifted into second, then first gear. The car staggered and she pulled the emergency break, bringing the car to a stop. Breathless, her whole body trembling, she sat a moment in the dark, trying to calm her shaking and the rapid beating of her heart.

27

AFTER A CAUTIOUS early morning drive—emergency break in hand—with Emily following, Winna dropped her car off for repair. With Isabelle strapped in her car seat behind them, they headed down North Avenue toward First Street intent on a look at Adolph Whitaker's boyhood home.

What a pretty woman, Winna thought, looking at Emily in a rayon print skirt and a bright red sleeveless blouse tied in a knot at the waist. A row of silver bracelets jangled on her arm as she turned the wheel.

"When will your car be ready?" Emily asked, tucking a stray strand of dark hair behind one ear.

"He thought this afternoon—said he'd leave a message on my answering machine." Winna laughed. "You know, maybe I should look into getting one of those mobile phones."

"You can't have one until I get one. But you can afford a new car, Mom," she scolded. "How old is that car anyway?"

"Only six years—I love 'that car.'"

"What on earth for?" She gave her the look. "Why don't you let Hugh help you find a new car. After last night—"

"It was only the brakes."

Emily heaved a sigh of defeat and rolled her eyes.

North Avenue evoked memories for Winna: Johnny's red hot convertible, nights parked under the flashing neon lights at the Top Hat Drive In, Johnny's face cast in alternating blue and pink light as uniformed car-hops slid trays of burgers, fries, and frosty mugs of root beer through the window.

She looked at Emily, fresh and cool at the wheel of her air-conditioned car. She wanted to tell her about those days, how different things were. But would she be interested? She doubted it.

Emily suggested they stop for coffee and pulled into the parking lot of a diner. They got out, retrieved the baby from her car seat, and went inside. Almost immediately after they sat down in an empty booth, Isabelle began to fuss and Emily opened her blouse to nurse. They ordered coffee.

"Well, Mom?" Emily said, giving her mother a sideways glance. "You haven't said a word about your dinner with John."

"I haven't?"

"No."

"Then I must have a reason." She patted her daughter's hand to soften the blow. "Did Chloe tell you she planned to crash our party?"

"Chloe told me nothing—just wanted to know where you were."

"Then you don't know," she said. "They got married yesterday by a justice of the peace."

"No kidding. You two are so different—polar opposites. She's so off the cuff, so New Age, and you're so traditional. I have to say that you are much more tolerant of her weird beliefs than she is of your weird beliefs."

"I am? What do you mean?"

"Well, you politely listen to stuff about Juno, but she can't stand to hear a word about Jesus."

"Juno and Jesus—do I go around talking about Jesus?"

"No, but—"

"Look, honey, I'm not that tolerant."

"I think you're both nuts," Emily said with a smile.

"Just wait till you are old and life has done a number on you. You'll want a place of peace, a belief in something larger than you and your little life."

Emily shrugged, removed the sleeping baby from her breast, and rebuttoned her blouse. With Isabelle settled on the booth beside her, Emily's expression darkened.

"You know, it's just sinking in." Emily slapped the flat of her hand against her forehead just like Walt used to do. "I don't believe it!"

"What don't you believe?"

"Am I crazy or paranoid? Is it a coincidence that Chloe got married just days after your lawyer finalized the paper work on her inheritance and everything is settled except the sale of the house?"

"Shame on you," Winna said.

"I mean it. I don't like this. Todd is in line to inherit millions if anything happens to you—like driving off a mountain because your brakes don't work."

"So are you. I can't believe you think I need to worry about this," she said, surprised that she felt hurt.

"Mom," Emily said, looking concerned, "please. I'm sorry. I don't know what's gotten into me. But ever since you found those letters— and told me the story about Whitaker's death on a train—I've had death on my mind."

"Well, darling girl, just get it off your mind—at least where it concerns me."

EMILY'S MINI-VAN headed west on North Avenue and turned left on First Street. First Street was exactly that: the first street running north and south on the west end of town. In her youth, nothing much lay beyond First Street except for a flat alkali encrusted waste-land and the road traveling west to the river and the Utah border. Now the city had spread beyond First Street to include industrial development and a new shopping district.

"What's the number of the house?" Emily asked.

Winna reached for her glasses and the notebook in her lap. "357."

They passed a gas station and a string of small stores and businesses. "Here's 353—and 355—and 359," Winna said, scanning the left side of the street as they passed. "Where's 357?"

"It's gone," Emily said, slowing to a crawl. "It must have been where that construction site we passed was."

As Winna's heart sank, Emily drove to the end of the block and doubled back. She pulled to a stop in front of a vacant lot where shirtless construction workers lolled in the shade of a dump truck. The frame for a new building sat in the burning sun.

"Look at the sign, Mom."

Opening Soon!
Spudnuts
Coffee & Donuts
Western Slope Construction Company

Emily looked confused. "That's John Hodell's company, isn't it?"

"Yes," Winna said, disappointed that the missing house would never add to her growing picture of Adolph Whitaker's life. "John is partners with my friend Kate's husband, Jim Cross."

Emily stared past her mother as the dump truck, loaded with debris, slowly lumbered off the lot onto First Street. "Doesn't Todd work for them?"

They drove home without speaking. Emily had the wisdom to keep her thoughts to herself. Winna knew what she was thinking because she was thinking it too. Trembling inside she began to wonder—it couldn't be true, though, this was real life, not a TV drama. No one had tampered with her brakes.

28

BEFORE THEY REACHED the house on Seventh Street, Isabelle had dissolved into tears and Emily was agitated. Wondering how a strapped-in mother—or grandmother—is supposed to come to the aid of an infant she cannot reach, Winna said, "We didn't have these contraptions when you were little—no seatbelts and no baby seat traps. How in hell are you supposed to get to a kid you can't even see?"

"You are supposed to pay attention to your driving," Emily groaned.

"Honey, if you pull over I'll—"

Emily raised her voice a notch higher and stepped on the gas. "We're almost there." She raced down Seventh Street. After several blocks, she turned on Chipeta, pulled into the drive, and brought her van to a stop by the kitchen door. Winna got out and gathered the weeping Isabelle into her arms. She did her best to nuzzle her into a smile as Emily headed for the door.

"Wait, honey, I locked it," Winna called.

Emily had already turned the knob. The door opened. "You must have forgotten," she said.

"What the hell," Emily cried, stepping into the kitchen. "My God, there's glass all over the floor!" Someone had broken the window in the door, reached in, and turned the knob.

"Emily, get out of that house right now!" Winna yelled.

"No one's here," she called from somewhere beyond the kitchen. "It's a huge mess."

Wailing baby in arms, Winna stepped inside. Every drawer and cupboard in the kitchen had been emptied onto the floor. She could hear Emily calling to her from the front of the house.

"They've searched everything—what a disaster."

Winna headed for the living room arriving in time to see her daughter disappear into the library. The room was a shambles. In the parlor, the sofa was turned upside down with its dust cloth ripped away, drawers had been emptied, and the old rug was thrown back at the corners. It looked like a cyclone had blown through the room.

THE POLICE, JOHN, and Chloe arrived soon after Winna called them. A tour of the whole house revealed that only one room upstairs had been searched—Winna's bedroom. Someone had tried to dig up the cellar floor. The police believed that Winna had not been gone long enough for all the damage to have taken place that morning. They surmised that the basement may have been dug up at any time. Winna hadn't been down there since John looked at the furnace for her, even before she had seen the light in the attic.

At first inventory, a number of things were missing from the house: a small diamond and pearl sunburst, a diamond lavaliere, and a pair of zircon earrings, all from Juliana's jewelry box. A small silk prayer rug was missing from the library, two large Chinese vases and several pieces of sculpture had been removed from the library and parlor. The police stayed for an hour, dusting for prints, making a list of the stolen property, asking questions.

"Mrs. Jessup?" The officer in charge wanted Winna's attention. "According to my information, this is the second break-in this week."

"Yes. Someone searched the attic—when was it? Friday night, I think," Winna admitted, quite aware that she had not told Emily or Chloe about the first break-in. By the looks on their faces, Winna knew that she would soon face their questions.

The officer made notes on his clipboard, then looked up at Winna. "Mrs. Jessup, this house is a magnet for trouble. I'd suggest you install a security system or at the very least deadbolts on all the doors."

As Chloe, Emily, and John wandered around aimlessly in the parlor looking stunned as they tried to restore order, Winna left for the kitchen to get the pitcher of iced tea waiting in the refrigerator. She returned with the tea tray and glasses and put them on the coffee table.

"Let's turn the sofa over so we can sit down," Winna said.

"So, Mom, when were you planning to tell me about the first break-in?" Emily asked, grabbing one leg of the sofa and lifting with John. Have you told John about your brake failure?"

"I didn't want to worry you. I didn't want to worry him."

"What brake failure?" John asked.

"Oh, I had trouble with my brakes on the way home from your house last night."

Chloe was the first to sit down, her expression grim. "You didn't tell me either, Winna." Suddenly, she jumped up from her seat, excited. "I'll bet they're looking for the jewels."

"Chloe, the jewels are a fiction—wish fulfillment for our romantic grandmother," Winna said.

"Whether or not they are," Emily said, "the burglar may think it's a true story."

"No one knows about Gramma's story except the family and John," Winna said, growing tired of all the guessing.

"I told Juno and she said the jewels exist—they are real, Winna."

"What!" Emily shrieked, looking as if she could strangle her aunt.

"No." Chloe said, swift in her attempt to erase a wrong impression. "I didn't mean to imply that Juno told anyone or had anything to do with this. She wouldn't do that—this," she said, indicating the mess.

"I can't believe you told her, Chloe. I know you trust her, but I can't say I do," Winna said.

"Believe it or not, Winna, when I talk to Juno it's like talking to a priest."

John looked at her through narrowing eyes. "What are you talking about?"

"Just that Juno says the jewels aren't in the house anymore."

Long ago, Winna had learned to suspend her judgments when Chloe's sentences began with 'Juno says,' but John looked at Chloe with growing alarm. "Who is Juno?" he asked.

"She's Chloe's astrologer."

"She's psychic too," Chloe added. "She says Dad hid the jewels in Unaweep Canyon—that's why he went there. She says the canyon is both a cursed and blessed place for our family—that we'll find the answer to our spiritual longing there—and we'll find the jewels."

"Have you ever been to Unaweep Canyon?" Winna asked.

"No, but the Stream of Life is gathering there next month, and I'm going," she said in a small voice, kicking off her sandals, tucking her bare feet underneath her.

"Wait till you see it. It's huge. We may find something spiritual there, but we'll never find something as small as jewelry."

Chloe lifted her blonde mane off her neck and looked hard at Winna. "Juno says they belong to us and finding them will break the curse that's been on this family."

"I don't think there's a curse on the family," Winna said. "What makes Juno think our family is cursed?" Winna's anger was obvious. She wanted an answer.

"Anyone with any sensitivity or spiritual awareness would come to that conclusion. Look at how stunted they all were. Dad was a momma's boy, his father was a wimp—his mother was a controlling witch. None of them knew how to love."

"The family wasn't any screwier than anyone else's family," Winna said as a powerful hot flash almost flattened her.

"Of course it was," Chloe insisted.

"Chloe, I suppose you think the last of the screwy people died with your father's generation," Emily jabbed.

"Well, Winna is a bit of an eccentric," Chloe said, trying to make light of it.

"Just Winna?"

Chloe looked like she knew she was in over her head. "We're getting nowhere here. Juno says the curse goes way back to—" She threw up her hands, jumped up from the sofa, and began to pace.

"You don't want to know the truth, Winna, so I'll save it. Juno says we should look under an ancient juniper tree. The jewels were buried under a pile of seven stones—probably very near the place where Dad died. She said we would find them in the last light of the setting sun."

"Facing west," Emily said. "What a pretty story. So all we have to do is comb around every juniper in the last light of the setting sun—near the place where Poppa died?"

Looking self-conscious, Chloe said, "It would take time." She paused, her face colored as she looked her niece in the eye. "I'm feeling very judged by all of you right now. Emily, a closed mind is a very dangerous thing in someone so young. You are just like your mother."

"The trouble with your open mind, auntie dear, is that Juno insists on putting *her* thoughts there," Emily said.

John had been quiet throughout the whole conversation. "Listen," he said. "You all have enough problems without making new ones for yourselves. I'd suggest you put away the pistols."

"Right," Winna said. "Now, how about we all agree that it's okay to disagree and still be friends."

Everyone looked at her like she was a dreamer. Winna left the room.

AFTER CHLOE SAID she felt outnumbered and left, John repaired the broken window. He and Emily insisted that Winna should not stay in the house alone and Winna insisted she should.

"I won't be driven out by some jerk," she said.

John found an iron bolt in the basement and put it on her bedroom door. Everyone seemed satisfied with that. John left and Emily drove her mother to pick up the car. All the way there, Winna fumed about Chloe.

"It upset me that she told Juno about Juliana's story," Emily said.

"Me too, but I should have known because Chloe tells Juno everything. It was her remark about a curse on our family and my closed mind that really angered me. I'm sick of hearing her say that—she's been telling me that since before she was old enough to know what a closed mind is. This business about a family curse—what rubbish. Why is she so eager to believe everything Juno tells her?"

"I think that's obvious," Emily said.

"Not to me. Am I in some kind of denial? Younger generations always find the older odd. Chloe doesn't know how odd she is— jewels hidden in the canyon."

"Someday I hope to be able to take Chloe's side," Emily said, "but not today." She pulled up in front of J & B Auto Repair.

Winna got out. "Thanks, honey, I don't know what I'd do without you."

Emily blew her a kiss. "See you Wednesday morning."

Exhausted, worried, angry, and in a mood to strangle her sister, Winna walked to the auto shop office. After her conversation with Emily that morning and the second break-in at the house, she had questions for the mechanic who had fixed her car.

The young man at the desk greeted her, "Good afternoon, Miss."

Winna bristled at being called "miss" and wished she had the courage to point at her gray hair and say, "Please call me Ma'am." Instead, she said, "I'd like to speak to the mechanic who fixed my brakes this morning."

"What's your name?"

"Edwina Jessup—Mrs. Jessup."

"No problemo, Miss." He looked through some invoices, stepped to the door connected to the garage, and yelled, "Charlie. Front desk."

Obviously finished for the day, Charlie, a man about Winna's age, arrived in his greasy work clothes with a bottle of beer in hand. He was shown the invoice and asked if he remembered the car.

"Yes, Ma'am," he said. "There was a crack in the brake fluid reservoir and the fluid was gone. We replaced the reservoir."

"What caused the crack in the reservoir? Does that happen very often?"

"No—almost never."

Winna assumed the posture of a woman getting down to business. "Could someone have made the crack? What I'm asking is, if someone had wanted my brakes to fail, might they have done it that way?"

The two men looked at one another with raised eyebrows.

Charlie said, "Sure, they could. Look, Mrs. Jessup, if I was you, I'd talk to the police."

29

SLOWLY, WINNA DROVE HOME, cautious at stop signs and the red light on North Avenue. The sun disappeared in roiling black and blue clouds. It looked like a storm was moving in from the northwest. Suddenly, the interior of her car looked shabby: the cracked leather seats, the worn windshield, the dashboard with pale Colorado dust burrowed deep into every crevice. The car had been a gift from Walt one Christmas morning before he began to fade away from her. She felt as if she had just woken up from a dream. Here she was in Colorado, sitting at the wheel of the car she now regarded as an old friend who had betrayed her. She was glad to pull into the drive and park alongside the kitchen door.

Winna unlocked the door and went inside, hurrying past the mess her thief had left behind in the kitchen. Moving quickly down the center hall, she realized that she had no idea where she was headed. She did not want to stay on the first floor. Did she want a bath? To change and go out to dinner? She couldn't cook in that kitchen. It didn't matter, she wasn't hungry.

Frightened, Winna stopped in her tracks. Her eyes moved to all the dark corners of the reception hall. Was she alone? Her feet glued to the floor, she looked past the hall through a wide archway toward the parlor feeling like she had crossed over the threshold into a different world. Scattered streams of sunlight coming through the storm clouds emanated from the old windows, etching everything with an eerie glow. Uncertain about exactly what was happening to her, Winna ran up the front stairs and into her room. She bolted the door and stood in the middle of the floor panting with terror.

WINNA WOKE TO early morning sun coming in through the windows like a spotlight on her face. She turned her head away and opened her eyes to tall windows filled with blue sky. Through the open door down the hall, she heard Isabelle babbling to herself in her crib. Winna knew that soon enough she'd have to get up with the family, but for now she would close her eyes again and try not to think about last night, her flight from the house on Seventh Street, her drive through a violent storm to Emily's house.

Mother and daughter sat up late with a bottle of wine and made plans for Winna's course of action. She would ask Seth to install a new kitchen door—one without a window. First, she'd have to shop for the door, then she was to call a locksmith and have the locks on all the doors changed again. She wasn't to give keys to anyone but Emily—not that she had anyway.

After breakfast outside on the deck with Isabelle and Emily, Winna said goodbye to the view and kissed her daughter and granddaughter. Hugh had left for work and she soon followed him down the mountain.

At Home Depot, she looked for a new door. It was hard. She was picky, but needed to take action. She didn't like the idea of no windows and compromised between a solid wall of door and a paneled door with a narrow light at the top. She would call Seth and have him pick it up. The door wouldn't match the rest of the woodwork. Winna would have to paint the kitchen—no big deal. She wanted to paint it anyway.

On her way back to the house, Winna pulled into the coffee shop where she and Emily had stopped the day before. She sat down in the same booth to collect her thoughts. Ordering coffee, she wondered if it was really only the day before yesterday that she had felt safe and relatively untroubled. The coffee came and she doctored it with cream and sugar. Sipping slowly, she made herself relax. Things looked much better by morning light.

All of a sudden, she felt a hand on her shoulder. Startled, she turned and looked up into Todd's smiling face. "Oh, my goodness," she said. "Where did you come from?"

"The men's room," he said, sliding into the booth.

"What a nice surprise. Have you just come in? Do you want coffee?" Trying to appear welcoming, Winna felt a bit shy, disappointed to have her solitude interrupted. She had never been alone with Todd before. Her sister had always been a buffer between them. Not that she needed a buffer.

Todd smiled again. "The answer is 'yes' and 'you betcha.'"

He ordered, and while his coffee and sweet roll were on their way, he opened the conversation. "Chloe told me about what happened over at the house yesterday. That must have been pretty damn awful—walking into the house and seeing all that. She was really upset last night."

Winna took a sip of coffee and looked into Todd's sympathetic face. "We all were. I spent last night up at Emily's. Today I bought a new door—one without a window to smash."

"Good idea," he said.

"After someone had been in the attic, I was foolish to have that kind installed. All he had to do was break the window, reach in, and turn the damn button."

Todd shook his head, almost as if he was going to scold her. "You should've told me 'bout it. What's a brother for?" He gave her a reassuring smile. "That's what I do—fix things—know what kind of door to put where."

"Thanks, brother," she said, patting the big hand resting on the table. "I've never had a brother before."

"Well, Winnie girl, you got one now."

Todd signaled the server for more coffee. It looked like he wanted to chat some more.

"Look here, big sis, I'm worried about Chloe. She thinks you and the family don't approve of her."

"That's funny." Winna tossed off a laugh. "I think she doesn't approve of me."

"Sure she does," he said. "She looks up to you."

"She sure has a funny way of doing it." Winna leaned back in her seat and sighed. "We are very different and we do appear odd to one another."

"That don't mean you can't be best friends."

"You know, Todd. That's exactly what I would like to happen. We were, once, and I miss that."

AT HOME, WINNA called Seth. He said he would pick up the door and be over around noon. Seth had become one of her favorite people. He came to work almost every day. Lately, he had trimmed the hedges, pruned dead branches from the trees, and cleaned the garage. His truck made dozens of trips to the dump or the Salvation Army, and under her supervision, he had even begun to organize a yard sale.

Though she had not yet admitted it to anyone, she was beginning to make a case for keeping the house, doing things no one would do if they were planning to sell. Just last week she had handed Seth a jar of oil soap and asked him to clean the bookshelves in the library. With reasoning she had since forgotten, she dusted off the books Chloe had already packed into boxes and put them back where they belonged. Then, she called to have the furnace replaced.

Seth talked very little about himself, but through very carefully disguised cross-examination, Winna had learned something about her right-hand man. As it turned out, he was an ex-hippie. The two had laughed about their parallel experiences of protesting the Vietnam War and the civil rights marches they had helped populate. He had fled to Canada to avoid the draft and admitted he had not changed. He said he could tell Winna had turned a bit too conservative for his taste.

He had even opened up to Winna about his first wife—how they and their two children had lived on a commune in Canada. Winna could tell he was not eager to talk about why that marriage had failed, or the fact that he did not see his children. She was surprised to learn that his second marriage to Holly Gordon—a girl Winna had known in high school—had also ended in divorce.

He told her that his mother had died when he was a child. His father had owned a hardware store downtown that Winna vaguely remembered, but the store fell on hard times when Home Depot came to town and, within a very few years, they had to close.

At about noon Winna heard a knock on the door. She peeked through the lace and Seth gave her a wave. She opened the door and let him into the kitchen.

"Hi Seth, have you had lunch?"

He smiled, rubbing the invisible stubble that seemed to make his square jaw itch. "I haven't had breakfast."

"That means you'd like two eggs sunny-side-up and bacon."

"Right on," he said, folding himself onto a kitchen chair. He looked at the empty drawers and cupboards and the debris all over the floor. "Holy shit, this place was trashed."

"That and the door are your assignments for today." Winna peeled off strips of cold bacon. "Some jerk paid me a visit."

"What's missing?" He flipped the chair around and straddled its back between two long jean-clad legs. "Looks like they went through everything."

"We can't be sure." She headed toward the coffee pot. "Would you like some coffee?"

"Sure," he said, dragging himself out of his chair. "I'll make it."

"I hope they got what they were looking for." Winna licked the spot where a piece of bacon spat hot grease on the back of her hand.

"What were they looking for?"

Cautious with her reply, she said, "Actually, we may never know because I haven't made an inventory yet."

"Shouldn't you do that? I'll help you. What does John think about this?"

"John?"

"Your boyfriend," he said, smiling, reaching into the cupboard.

"So now he's my boyfriend?"

Seth laughed. "He's an old flame still flickering—the lucky shit," he said, pouring two cups of coffee.

"Why, Seth Armstrong Taylor, is that a compliment?"

"You know, Winna," he said, changing the subject, "I've been thinking about some of the things I'd like to see you do around here. This place could be restored—back to its heyday."

"Maybe that's a job for the person who buys it," she said, lifting crisp bacon out of the frying pan and patting it dry between paper towels. "This morning I think I hate this place." She poured off the grease and wiped the iron skillet. "What's on your mind? You have no shortage of good taste."

He had returned to his chair and sipped thoughtfully from his cup. Winna knew he wanted a cigarette, but she didn't allow smoking in the house.

"Are there any old plans for the rose garden?"

"I don't know," she said, breaking three eggs into melted butter. "To tell the truth, I don't know half of what's in this house. The whole thing has overwhelmed me—I've moved so god-awful slowly and now this." She pointed the butter knife at the littered floor. "I've been stopped dead in my tracks."

Seth looked at her and nodded, but said nothing.

Trying to pull herself into a better mood, she heaved a sigh. "But I remember the rose garden," she said, buttering his toast. "I spent lots of time there as a child and remember the layout."

"Bet you don't remember which roses your grandma grew."

"No, but I wouldn't put it past her to have saved all the sales slips." She handed him his plate. "That woman kept everything."

"I hope so," Seth said, digging in. "We could recreate it—that would be cool. We should set up an office—for planning—with enough space to organize papers into files."

Winna sat down beside him. "Sounds efficient—none of the papers are organized under any system from what I can make out. As for the rose garden, we could replant using hybrids developed before 1960—I don't think Gramma did much gardening at the end of her life."

He wiped his toast through spilled yolk. "The house is Victorian—so you could use the Victorians' favorite roses."

"It's Edwardian, really," she said. "You know what I really need is a darkroom—a place to work. I've been thinking about turning the old servants' quarters upstairs into an office and darkroom. I'm not ready to go completely digital yet—may never be."

"I was up there poking around the other day," he said. "Those are great rooms. We could block off the window in that large bathroom. You need water in a darkroom, don't you?"

Winna sighed. "But none of that matters unless I decide to stay."

He looked deflated. "Hell, there's lots of folks who hope you'll stay, Winna."

"That's a nice thing to say, Seth." She got up from the table. "I'm just going to ignore these dishes for now. Would you like to see the work our burglar left for you?"

30

AFTER A DAY of hard work, Seth left late that afternoon, the new door in place and the house restored to its former disorder. Fatigued, Winna headed up the stairs to her sanctuary—Juliana's beautiful bathtub. Once, she had thought of the house as belonging to her Gramma, but after living there with all her things and the mysteries surrounding them, Winna had begun to think of the house as belonging to *Juliana*—someone she had never met—a mysterious lady with hidden passions and talents.

On her way to her room, she passed the hall closet and stopped to open the door. She wanted a closer look at the gowns Juliana had been most eager to wear, to save. Winna had kept a number of her mother's gowns and was suddenly overcome with a wish that she had saved her own.

"If only—I'd have a complete collection of twentieth-century dress-up clothes," she said aloud, thinking how much fun it would be to photograph Emily wearing them.

All she had kept was her wedding gown. After Walt left, she found it again in the old cedar chest. As she lifted it for a look, the fullness of the skirt nearly crushed her; the lace and seed pearls mocked her. The sight of the gown she wore as she entered a doomed marriage rubbed out every sweet memory she had experienced in it: walking down the aisle mad with happiness, dancing in her new husband's arms.

She threw the gown across a chair in the light of a window and picked up her camera. Adjusting nothing for this still life, she shot the rest of the roll capturing her sadness, her disappointment in glorious black and white. She loaded the camera with another roll of film, then hung the gown on a hanger from the window frame. Now the gown was a drape through which light filtered. Glowing, it seemed ghostly, lonely, unloved. She kept shooting, hoping that through the tears she was in focus.

The gown was dead to her and she took it down from the window and carried it out of the kitchen door to the row of trashcans. She threw off a lid, rolled the gown into as tight a wad as she could, and buried it.

Looking through Juliana's memory closet, Winna wondered what happy memories these gowns had held for her grandmother. She pulled the chain on the closet light. The top shelf was lined with hatboxes, the floor with shoes and boots. Most of the gowns had long skirts. She removed one made of a golden silk *peau de soie* with a draped bodice and a skirt length that was definitely fifties. Hanging next to it was the black satin gown Juliana had worn to Eisenhower's inaugural ball. Then she found something stunning in brown velvet, the neckline jeweled. She pulled it out for a better look and felt something hard bump against her calf. Hanging the dress back on the rod, she got down on her knees for a better look at the deep hem. Something lay inside the hem. Running her fingers over the velvet, she felt a hard slender object. Immediately, she knew what it was.

Winna called Emily first and then Chloe. She spoke to both, but said nothing about the breathtakingly beautiful diamond and pearl necklace she'd found sewn into the hem of the velvet gown.

"Just get here as quickly as you can—drive safely. I'm fine, but deadly serious. I need you to come."

Both agreed to be there at seven-thirty.

Chloe arrived first, minutes before Emily. Both were eager-eyed and demanded to know what was up.

"This better be good," Chloe said. "Tonight, Todd and I wanted to watch that new show *Who Wants to be a Millionaire?* Have you seen it yet?"

Winna laughed. "You'll know why I'm laughing in a minute." She motioned for them to follow her.

"Stop teasing us," Emily begged as she followed her mother up the stairs. "The suspense is killing me."

"I think I found the jewels," Winna said. "I need you to help me get them."

"Woo hoo!" Chloe cried, as she picked up speed.

"Where?" Emily asked.

"In here." Winna stopped in front of the hall closet door. "First, come in my room and I'll show you what I found. It was sewn into the hem of one of Gramma's gowns."

They entered Juliana's old bedroom where a heap of brown velvet lay on the bed. Beside it lay a long necklace—ropes of pearls clasped at the neck and on both sides with large decorated brooch-like pieces set with diamonds. At the base of the piece was another brooch and from it hung two long tassels made of small pearls like one might see on the rope holding back a Victorian curtain—these were also held by a cluster of diamonds.

"What on earth—" Emily said, lifting the piece. When doubled, it was more than two feet long. "How would you wear this? It's belly button length!"

"It's called a sautoir—I looked it up while I was trying to decide whether or not to call you. I had to talk myself into not running off with it—not leaving you guys in poverty." She smiled at her joke. "Guess what? I found it in Gramma's illustrated jewelry book. Sautoirs were popular early in the century—they looked great hanging on all those long narrow dresses they wore in the nineteen teens and twenties."

Emily reached out to touch it. "There must be a thousand pearls here."

"It's definitely for dress-up," Chloe said, pulling it over her head to ornament her tee. She put her hand on her hip and walked around the room with her nose in the air.

Winna and Emily applauded.

"I felt around and didn't find anything more, but let's keep looking," Winna said. "Just a word of caution, the dresses have a lot of sentimental and maybe some monetary value so go slow. If you have to clip or rip seams, do it gently."

The women headed for the closet, removed hangers full of gowns, and brought them back into Juliana's bedroom where the light was better and they could sit while they worked.

Right away, in a lamb's wool cape, Emily found a vintage aquamarine and amethyst necklace lying innocently in a pocket. She raised it into the light. "The colors—the stones are so large. What's the period, Mom?"

"I don't know," Winna said, taking it into her hands. "Maybe I should go get the book."

"We can study them later. Let's just go mining now," Chloe suggested. "We are assuming these are the real thing, aren't we?"

"Aha!" Emily cried. "The matching earrings are in the other pocket. Yikes, there's something else—" She fished around and came up with a large ring.

"It's huge—diamonds—but what's the stone in the middle?"

"It glows like an opal, but it's blue with green lights," Winna said.

"I want it. Oh, God, it's the most beautiful thing I've ever seen. It looks like the earth from space," Chloe cried as she popped it on her finger. "It fits. It matches my aura. I'm so glad Daddy didn't find these and hide them too."

From then on things went more slowly. The women probed every hem and pocket they could find. Finally, Winna came upon a hard lump under the bodice lining of a beaded gown. Carefully, she removed the hand-sewn stitches and revealed a lapis and gold bracelet.

"This looks Victorian," she said, as Emily and Chloe looked over her shoulder. "Look at all the pearls imbedded in the filigree."

The search continued. Winna found one gown with seven rings sewn inside the waist, then a glowing gold and red amber necklace. Emily pulled coral beads set with gold and pearls from the hem of a coat, then an emerald and diamond necklace sewn inside a fur cape.

"It looks like something Elizabeth Taylor would wear!" she said, holding it up.

"I love it," Chloe said as she searched an elegant silk kimono. "You guys are finding everything." She looked like she felt left out.

"Wait a minute," Chloe said triumphantly. "Here's something." Scissors in hand, she snipped away inside the cuff of a sleeve and pulled out a large piece made of gold. Chloe held it out for all to see. "What was Gramma doing with a rosary?"

"What was she doing with any of this?" Emily said.

"I think this is up your alley, Winna," she said, dropping it into her sister's lap as if it was contagious.

Winna guessed that Chloe was trying to be funny. With a knot in her throat, she retrieved it from her lap and tried her utmost not to cry. She looked at the old rosary set with smooth-cut rubies and sapphires. It was very old, Winna guessed, maybe even medieval. During its long history, it would have meant a great deal to the faithful, but certainly not her grandmother. She wanted to kiss it, to claim it as her own, but knew that would be misunderstood. She put it on the bed with the other jewels.

It was late and they were all tired—worn out with excitement, sated as if they had overeaten at a feast.

"Where am I going to hide these?" Winna asked. "I sure don't want to sew them back into the clothes."

"I know the perfect place," Emily said. "Follow me." She headed toward the front of the house, to the guest room.

BEHIND FOUR LOCKED doors, Winna tried to sleep, but she was too excited. Thoughts of the hidden jewelry versus the rings and things she had found in Juliana's magnificent jewelry box kept her awake. She assumed that the jewelry had been hidden for a reason—but why? Juliana had worn the jewelry in the chest on her dresser—some of it Winna remembered. They were gifts from her husband and parents, things she'd bought herself. Winna thought of the canary diamond and its value. While the things in Juliana's jewelry box were costly and lovely, they could not touch that ring in value—and the jewels they had found that night, especially the ancient rosary which could be of museum quality, dwarfed the yellow diamond ring. Did Gramma have a love affair with a prince? Winna's head spun wondering if she should get a larger safe deposit box.

She could not sleep and padded down to the kitchen for a drink. When she opened the cupboard door where she kept the Johnny Walker, she half expected a hoard of precious jewels to tumble out like a pirate chest emptied on the sand. She splashed some scotch into a glass—about half an inch. Thinking it looked a bit meager, she splashed another half inch and dropped in some ice. She intended to lie in bed with the light on and anesthetize herself.

31

AFTER A LATE BREAKFAST, Winna spent a couple of hours working outside. It wasn't hot, but sunny enough for sunglasses. She looked in the garage for Juliana's old galvanized watering can and couldn't find it, then went back inside. Had she seen it in the basement? Opening the basement door, she flipped on the light and began her descent. One of the stairs seemed to wobble. To steady herself she took hold of the railing.

All of a sudden, Winna felt the railing let go. Instinctively, she reached for the rail on the other side, but too late. She let out a yelp and fell. Already halfway down the stairs, she did not have far to fall, but followed the rail as it broke off to her left, landing on her side among shattered pieces of wood.

She lay there a moment on the cold earthen floor trying to under-stand what had happened. Across the basement lay the two holes hacked by her burglar. Winna rolled over on her hands and knees. The room spun. Deciding she needed to get her bearings before she tried to stand, she sat a while feeling utterly surprised and foolish. One side of her face and her hip hurt and she was shaking. Her sunglasses lay broken and twisted across the floor.

Still afraid to stand, Winna tried to assess her situation. She moved one leg, then the other to see if she could. Nothing seemed broken. Still she felt too weak and dizzy to stand.

She heard the kitchen door open and close. Surprised by her sudden terror, she tried again to get up on her hands and knees. Pain stabbed her shoulder and hip and she fell back to the floor.

"Winna?"

It was a man's voice and she was a wounded animal hiding below, afraid to answer. She heard him walk into the hall, calling her name. The footsteps returned to the kitchen, to the open door at the top of the stairs. "Winna?"

It was Seth. She shuddered and raised one hand to her face—the cheek stung. She felt terrified and embarrassed at the same time.

Seth saw her. "What happened?" He started down the stairs.

Winna could see from the concern on his face that he would not harm her. "Be careful," she called. "One of the steps is loose."

Seth came gingerly the rest of the way. "What happened?"

"I was gardening and needed something down here—I fell. One of the steps—I feel so silly—I can't get up."

He got to his haunches. "Let's see if everything moves." He asked her to move her arms and legs. "Does that hurt?"

"No, but when I roll over and try to stand, I get dizzy."

"You're just shook up. Sit flat on your bum and raise your knees. Now give me both of your hands." He braced his feet against hers and pulled. Winna was on her feet, dizzy, but upright and nothing felt broken.

"Don't let go of me," she begged.

Winna described how she had fallen and Seth slowly helped her up the stairs, testing each step before he stood on it. Once in the kitchen, he stopped to look at her face.

"You scraped your cheek and are going to have a black eye," he said, pulling out a chair at the table and helping her sit down. He packed a kitchen towel with ice and handed it to her. "Here, put this on your left eye."

"Thanks. I think I'd better find a chiropractor for the rest of me."

"You just sit there. I'm going to make you a cup of tea, then I'll take a look at that railing."

"I hurt, Seth. Do you mind getting some aspirin out of that cupboard?" She pointed.

Seth made tea and handed her a glass of water and the pills, then disappeared down the stairs. The tea tasted good. She sipped it slowly, promising herself a second cup, but first she wanted to take the pills and lie down. Carefully, she limped to the parlor and stretched out on the sofa. She slept soundly and woke to the sound of hammering.

Cautiously, Winna got up and made her way toward the sound. "Seth," she called to the figure crouched below on the stairs. "What's going on?"

He stopped working and took a nail out of his mouth. "A number of these stairs are loose. It's a wonder you didn't fall from the first step."

"Come up. I want to talk. I'll make tea."

"How about coffee—and I'll make it," he said, stepping carefully up the stairs.

While Seth puttered around making coffee, he told her that the railing would have to be rebuilt and that several steps near the top of the stairs had stripped nail holes.

"You were lucky. If you'd put your weight down wrong on one of those, the step would've let go."

"Oh, Lord. Maybe you should check all the stairs in the house." Winna thought impatiently of her list of things that still needed doing.

"I'll do that. When did you have that railing worked on?" he asked, handing her a mug of coffee. "It looks like someone touched up the paint recently."

"That can't be. I haven't had any work done down there."

WINNA HAD A gruesome looking black eye. She had received an adjustment on her hip from a young chiropractor who cheerily informed her that falls were the number one reason for accidental deaths in elderly women. She spent the following days taking it easy, feeling stiff, sore, and—elderly.

Chloe and Todd said they would drop by for a visit on Sunday after Winna got home from church. Winna was not looking forward to seeing her sister. She'd had time to think back, to stew over what Chloe had said and done when she found the rosary and was not ready to forgive her. She didn't know why Chloe felt so free to put her down for her faith or why she had tossed Winna so many critical little asides over the years. Winna didn't know how to deflect these comments and when she had tossed them back in the form of a protest or in anger, Chloe would say she was too sensitive—that she took everything personally. Chloe seemed to think that taking things personally was far worse than carelessly saying something hurtful.

When she looked at her own behavior toward her sister, she thought of herself as understanding. She tried not to show her disapproval and was sure that she had hidden her judgments about Chloe's casual approach to motherhood and all the men she'd lived with between marriages. She wondered if the undercurrents of her real feelings showed. Maybe Chloe was psychic—maybe that's why she seemed not to trust her, why she sniped at her?

Now, when they stood face to face, there was a huge gulf between them and Winna did not know how to build a bridge. She wondered what it would take to reconcile, to feel natural together again.

WHEN WINNA OPENED the kitchen door and saw Chloe and Todd standing there, she welcomed her sister warmly. "I'm so glad you guys could stop by." To distract from her lie, she smiled broadly. "What do you think of my beautiful black eye?"

"Good job, Winnie." Todd handed her a bunch of gaily colored supermarket flowers. "So you fell down the basement stairs?"

"How sweet. You brought me flowers." She hugged him.

"Sorry we didn't get here sooner," Chloe said, pushing past Winna. She dropped her handbag on the kitchen table next to a stack of books and sat down. "Are you okay?"

"Yes, as I said on the phone, I'm fine. Just a bit banged up."

Chloe reached for one of the books in the stack beside her. "Gramma's jewelry book. *A Thousand Years of Jewelry*. Have you looked up the ring I want—the big blue and green opal?"

"Actually, I have and it's called a black opal."

"Chloe told me about all the fun you gals had the other night," Todd said, his eyes smiling.

"Let's go see them now—I want to show Todd." Chloe grabbed Winna's hand and pulled her toward the stairs. "Come on, Todd."

Chloe led Todd up the stairs toward the guest room. Winna followed. "They're in here," she said, running into the room, pulling the cushion off the window seat. She lifted the hinged lid and got down on her knees turning her head to look up at her husband. "Wait till you see these."

She reached in and felt around, then stuck her head inside the opening. "My God, Winna, the jewels are gone."

32

"LOOK IN THE TRASH BARREL," the authoritarian male voice boomed in the dream. Winna, hovering in a gray, murky place somewhere below, answered, "But all I'll find is rubbish." She was whimpering like a spoiled child.

"Rubbish of rubbish," said the judge. "Everything they left behind is rubbish. There is no remembrance of former things, nor will any who come after know you."

She woke with a start, certain that something profound had come to her in her sleep. In an effort to reorient herself and make sense of the dream, she sat up and looked around the room.

Lit with early morning light, the stained-glass windows sparkled, sending shafts of violet, aqua, and green onto her pale coverlet. She thought again of her grandmother's magical shade garden and the colors there, then of Juliana sitting here in the light on just such a morning, looking out that same window.

In a moment of clarity, Winna understood the meaning of the dream.

I cannot know them, not really. My search for the real Henry, the real Juliana, the real Edwin is useless. I can't know the past—no more than I can know the truth—and what's worse, when I die, no one will know the real me.

The bedside phone rang and Winna jumped. She let it ring several times, then picked it up. It was John calling to invite her on a picnic. Could she be ready by nine o'clock? She hesitated, thinking of all the work she had to do.

"I can't, John. I'm so behind."

"Look, you've been holed up since your fall and I'll have you home by two. You'll have the rest of the day. Come on, don't spoil this beautiful day with work. I'm taking it off."

Winna hesitated.

"Aw please," John begged.

"Maybe it would do me good," she conceded.

"Put on something cool—sandals, a big hat."

WINNA WAS READY when John picked her up at nine. As she climbed into his white Mercedes convertible, she noticed a wicker picnic basket in the back seat. No amount of pleading on her part got John to reveal their destination. He headed west out of town as she told him about finding jewels sewn into Juliana's old clothes.

"But wait till you hear what happened yesterday."

"It looks like your grandmother hooked up with a rich man and it looks like you hooked up with a fist," he said, referring to her black eye.

"I'd better put on my new sunglasses so you can't see," she said. Their conversation had distracted her from the stunning view. "One last thing, then I don't want to talk about this anymore. I want to be in the here and now."

"When Chloe and Todd came by yesterday, she wanted to show him what we'd found sewn into the gowns. She really upset me the way she pushed her way in. It was so obvious that she had come to see the jewelry, not her poor injured sister. I felt offended or territorial or something wicked like that. She dragged both of us upstairs to the guest room for a look and when she opened up the hiding place, the jewels weren't there."

"The jewels are gone?"

"That's what she thinks. I didn't tell her that I had put them in the safe deposit box. She thinks they were stolen. I still haven't told her."

"That is bad—you are bad. How are you going to get out of this one?"

"I don't know. Do you have any ideas?"

He turned to give her an affectionate smile. "Forget about it and look at the view."

Winna promised to try. "It's been years since I've been up this road."

Built during the Depression by the Civilian Conservation Corps, the drive snaked up Pinyon Mesa around sharp turns with precipitous drops to the canyon floor. Tunnels cut through solid rock in places as the road traveled the very edge of the red sandstone cliffs, an impressive engineering feat, especially for back then.

The breathtaking ascent into the blue cloudless sky was entirely familiar to Winna, like coming home. Twisted junipers and pinyon pines, the dusty green of rabbit brush topped by golden blossoms, tufts of heat-withered grasses, worn remains of long-dead pines gnarled and dry, lay along the side of the road. From that dizzying height, she could see dry creek beds lined with water-seeking junipers, meandering green ribbons at the bottom of the canyons. The faraway valley spread into the distance, fortified to the east by blue Grand Mesa and to the north by the white Book Cliffs.

Suddenly, Winna remembered something she'd forgotten to ask. "Did you know your company tore down Whitaker's boyhood home on First Street?"

John looked puzzled.

"It was on the site where you are building the donut shop."

"No. Are you sure?"

"Yes. I found the address in the newspaper story about his death. Did you see the house—before you tore it down?"

He described the house as a small bungalow. "But you should ask Todd," he said, entering a tunnel carved through the canyon wall. "He ran the crew that took it down."

"Do you know if it stayed in the Whitaker family?" she asked.

"Not many families like you Grummans keep the same house for eighty years," John said.

After several miles of steady climbing, he pulled over and parked at Cold Shivers Point.

"This is where Edwin proposed to Juliana," she said as they got out of the car.

John grabbed his camera and they headed down the path to the canyon rim, Winna still walking with traces of a limp.

"I grew up hearing stories about how Poppa had proposed to Gramma. They came up here in a mule-drawn wagon, with a crowd of their friends."

"Yeah," John said. "Grandma got Grandpa at the very edge of the cliff and threatened to push if he didn't marry her."

She looked out over the spreading table of pink rocks. "There it is." Winna pointed at a series of flat rocks, one balanced at the very brink over the canyon.

"Why don't you walk way out there and I'll take your picture," he said, dragging her toward the cliff by the hand.

"Don't, John," she said as a sudden thrill of fear caught her. "I'm still a little shaky after my fall."

"I did it once," he said, releasing her. John lifted his camera to take her picture with the balanced rock in the background. "Back in high school a bunch of us got liquored up and took turns walking out there. Smile."

"Look," she said, pointing north, as two brave little swifts chased a hawk out of their territory overhead. "See the clouds way off to the west?"

"A storm," John said, leading her back toward the car. "We still have time."

Winna asked if he would put the top up on the car. "It's so hot I'm crisp."

Back on the road, John explained that because of the approaching storm, they would not stop again until they reached the picnic site. Winna assumed he would park at the picnic tables with the view of Independence Monument itself, but he whizzed past the tall sandstone monolith towering alone at the conjunction of two canyons. As they drove off the mountain, he made no move to stop even though she hinted that she was getting hungry.

"It won't be long now," he said. "Another twenty minutes."

Her mind was racing again. "Where did the jewels come from? Certainly not from Dolph. She must have had another lover."

"He'd have to be super rich to afford the jewels you found."

The conversation stopped as John took the car down back roads she had never traveled. He drove past a dry creek bed making its way through flat arid land whose only crop was parched tumble-weeds, past dry pastures sprinkled with cattle and horses, past a grove of spreading cottonwoods in whose gentle shade someone had parked a trailer. Finally, he turned onto north First Street and, almost immediately, onto a little dirt road Winna remembered very well. Slowly, he drove the car across the irrigation canal on a rickety old wooden bridge. He had taken her back to the place where they used to swim. He pulled to a stop alongside the canal.

"This is where we'll picnic."

"Perfect," she said, "but aren't we on some farmer's land?"

"Probably," he said, opening the door. "Damn, it's hot out there— so hot that it feels like it's gotta rain."

"Let's eat in the car with the air conditioner running," she said.

He closed the door and pushed back his seat before reaching around with one hand to lift the lid on the picnic basket. He felt around and pulled out a bottle of chilled white wine. "Can you reach the glasses while I open this?"

"Sure," she said, getting on her knees.

"Look around in there and see what there is to eat." He uncorked the bottle.

"Cold fried chicken, potato salad—this is great. Who packed this for you?"

"The gal at the deli." He handed her a glass of wine.

With plastic forks and paper containers of potato salad, marinated vegetables, and drumsticks, they relaxed into the cool leather seats.

"I can't believe I'm here," she said, sipping wine, watching brown canal water swirl under the old bridge as it headed out to the thirsty fields.

"Remember how we used to swim under that bridge?" John said.

"We had to duck and come up under the bridge for air, then back under the water to the other side. Remember how dark it was and how our hair got tangled in spiders' webs?"

John said nothing. He leaned back in his seat. With the engine idling, they fell into silence as they ate.

The wine tasted chilly and brisk and the food delicious. Winna thought back to summers sitting beside John on the bridge in her one-piece swimsuit, the sun burning her back. One moment John would kiss her, the next, he would hoot like a movie Indian and push her into the muddy water. She would let the current carry her away from the bridge and John. He would dive in and swim to catch her. His strong arms brought him swiftly alongside her floating body. Gently, he would right her, pulling her to the bank into the cattails and rushes where they dug their toes into the mud. Anchored, he would pull the top of her swimsuit down to the waist and cover her with kisses.

John sighed. His head rested against the back of the car seat and he turned to look at her with a smile. "What were you thinking just now?"

A dreamy smile was her only answer.

"Winna, every time I look into those eyes, I see you as you were back then—so lovable, at first so scared to give in to me," he said, putting his hand on her cheek. "You are the most maddening woman I've ever known."

"Back in high school I spent a year kissing you, touching you, trying to get you to give in to me and when you did, I spent another year making love to you every chance I got. I haven't forgotten, Winna."

Saying nothing, she put her glass down and reclined into his kiss.

He turned and, without a word, moved the picnic things onto the back seat. He settled back into his seat and took her into his arms. "You can't go back to New Hampshire, Winna."

"I can't?"

"No, we're in love."

"We are?"

"I am," he said, before he kissed her again. "Still in love."

She closed her eyes and drifted with John back to a hot summer day when they were young, to the canal and the cool water, where clasping him near with both arms and legs was the most urgent business in the world.

Suddenly, he pulled away, put his hands on the wheel, and backed the car down the canal bank and over the bridge. "I'm taking you home," he said.

Winna did not refuse.

A THUNDEROUS SHATTERING of the atmosphere by a bolt of lightning woke Winna and John from their afternoon nap. She shivered from the air conditioning as one bolt after the other lit up the room and gusts of dry wind rattled the wall of windows.

"Where's the rain?" he asked sleepily, as she drew a white blanket over his naked form.

"Mother Nature's going to have a temper tantrum first." Quite aware that her body was no longer the young body he had known, she pulled on her tunic. "Shall I close the drapes?"

"No," he said, taking her hand. "Come here. Let's watch the storm."

He plumped up their pillows and leaned back, tugging her against him. The view from John's bed looked off the mountain. From their vantage point, they watched colossal blue-black storm clouds hovering above the valley as long fiery fingers of lightning streaked the sky with a vengeance.

He sleepily nuzzled her ear. "A fitting conclusion, don't you think?"

She kissed him lightly and whispered, "Definitely worth the forty-year wait."

"Hell—we wasted a lot of time," he said, yawning. "I'm not seventeen anymore. I'm exhausted." He closed his eyes and, with a smile on his lips, drifted off.

She lay a while in his arms feeling his breath against her neck, watching the sky as the storm finally brought the rain. Coming first as splats against the dusty window, the rain built to a crystal deluge washing the window clean. Wishing she were still seventeen, she gently slipped out of his arms and walked barefoot into the kitchen to make a cup of tea.

The thunder had passed and a glint of radiant sunlight lit up the dampened red earth. As a steady gentle rain began to fall, the sun disappeared behind a dark rain cloud. Mercifully wetting everything, rain beaded up on cactus flesh, slid down blades of grass, dripped off twisted branches of pinyon pines, and ran in little rivulets into the thirsty ground. She thought of the creek beds on the mesa, flowing with rainwater, cutting deeper into the floor of the canyons. She wished she were out there with her camera.

The sight from a different kitchen window during a thunderstorm came to mind—Walt running away from her, taking shelter under a spreading maple. How like him to leave in the middle of an argument and put himself in harm's way under the tallest tree in the landscape. She remembered cuddling Emily in the middle of the night after thunder had startled her awake. Winna would take her out to the porch. It was their ritual to snuggle under a blanket on the porch swing. She had made up a story about young robins that watched the storm from their nest in the cherry tree. Emily insisted she tell it every time it stormed.

Winna sat down on one of the tall bar stools with her tea. She closed her eyes and shook her head slowly, smiling at herself. What have I done? She wanted to sing, to dance, to eat, to make love again. Her long suppressed desire for Johnny, the remembrance of their first love brought tears to her eyes and she began to tremble, knowing this was something she no longer wanted to live without.

The rain had stopped and the late afternoon sun lit up the landscape which, washed clean of dust, gleamed like a well-watered garden. She felt a hand on her shoulder and kisses on the back of her neck.

"Are you hungry?" John asked as he leaned to open the refrigerator door.

"Famished," she said, snuggling against his broad back, which filled the white terry cloth bathrobe he wore tied at the waist. She touched the white hair that curled over the back of his collar.

"I love the back of your head," she said, tugging on his sleeve.

With the refrigerator lit up behind him, he turned and flashed a big grin. "Well that's a start."

"John," she said, wrapping her arms around his back as he perused the contents of his well-stocked refrigerator. "I'm going back to New Hampshire to put my house on the market."

33

WINNA DIALED CHLOE'S phone number, but it was Todd, not Chloe, that she wanted to speak with. Adolph Whitaker's boyhood home and Juliana's letters were what she had in mind, or at the very least found papers or objects that had belonged to Dolph, something that might reveal why her grandmother had been in possession of a fortune in jewelry.

Todd answered the telephone and offered to get Chloe.

"No. I called to talk with you. Do you have a minute?" she asked.

"For you, Winnie, I have all night," he said, sounding a little buzzed.

"I just wanted to ask a few questions about that house you guys tore down on First Street—the one where you're building a donut shop."

"Yep, what about it? You ain't going to rip into me for tearing down Grand Junction history are you?"

"No, I'm not—though I'm sure the architecture of the house was more interesting than the donut shop will be. What kind of house was it? Had it been abandoned or had someone lived there?"

"It was old clapboard with a big front porch hanging off it. From the looks of the inside, someone lived there, but they picked up and walked away from it. Don't know how the donut folks got a hold of it."

"Did they leave anything behind?"

"Yep, some old junk and furniture. We bulldozed the whole mess and carried it off. Why?"

"That's the house where Adolph Whitaker grew up."

"The dude who wrote those sissy letters?"

"The very same."

"I'll be damned. Imagine that."

"I'm trying to learn more about him. You didn't find anything did you—like old letters?" Her question came with a nervous chuckle.

"Nope."

"Who else worked with you on that job?"

"Just the usual crew—and Seth Taylor—we signed him on for a couple of days."

"Look, Todd, would you do me a favor and ask the one man you trust the most if he saw anyone carry anything off?"

"Sure enough, Winnie, but that kinda thing ain't allowed—not without my go-ahead. Say, did you talk to the police about the missing jewelry?"

Winna was ready to humble herself, to confess to the fact that she had allowed a misunderstanding about the jewels. "Let me talk to Chloe. Why don't you stay on the line?"

Todd called for Chloe to pick up the other phone and, right away, she heard her sister's voice. "Hello?" She sounded depressed.

"Hi, sis, I wanted to let you know that I've got some good news and some bad news."

"Good news first, please," Chloe sighed.

"Well, the good news is that the jewelry wasn't stolen." A moment of silence followed. "The bad is that I let you guys leave with the wrong impression. All I can say is I'm sorry. I shouldn't have scared you like that."

"Where is it? It sure as hell wasn't where we put it."

"It's in the safe deposit box. I put it there the day after my fall. I'm really sorry. I don't know what got into me yesterday."

"I do. That's when Mercury slipped into retrograde." Chloe sounded exhausted.

ONCE SHE HAD decided to stay in Grand Junction, Winna felt a weight lift from her shoulders and work at the house had new purpose. The pressure to go home was off and she slipped comfortably into what seemed right—being in Grand Junction with her family and bringing life back to the old family home. After her bold announcement to John, she had worried that maybe she was about to make a mistake. The house was, or could be, fabulous, but there were problems: the break-ins and her on-and-off suspicion that someone wished her dead.

She met with Seth a couple of times and they delved into plans for her office and darkroom and the restoration of the house and rose garden. Winna had reassured herself that she wanted to live close enough to be a grandmother to Isabelle and an extra hand for her daughter. She wanted to turn Juliana's old house into her "house beautiful"—and she was in love with John.

Before her life in Grand Junction could begin, Winna had to return to New Hampshire to sell her house and make plans to transfer her business. The morning before her flight to Boston, she looked down on the lawn and out to the street from a window in Edwin's second story bedroom. The lawn was turning brown and she wondered if she should save water and just let it go dormant.

Seth's truck pulled into the drive and parked behind her car. He had promised to come by with the paint Winna had picked out for the kitchen. She wanted to ask him if he would paint the kitchen while she was away.

Hurrying downstairs to let Seth in the door, she heard the phone ring and picked it up in the hall. It was Emily wanting to chat. She'd been invited to speak at the town planning board's August meeting.

Emily had written enough columns and letters to city officials and it had finally paid off. Her voice came to Winna's ear full of enthusiasm. "They want to talk about sustainable landscaping for all the town parks."

"That's just fantastic. If you can convince them, Grand Junction could become a model throughout the Southwest," Winna said, excited for her daughter. "Look, honey, Seth just arrived—I'll call you back, okay?"

Winna went to the kitchen door wondering why Seth hadn't rung the bell or knocked. She opened the door, but no Seth. She looked out at the drive and saw that his truck was still there. Where was he?

Winna stepped down from the stoop and turned to look at the back yard. When she didn't see him there, she walked around the front of her car, startled to see Seth kneeling by her right rear tire. There were tools on the ground. Intent on his work, he didn't see her standing there.

Immediately, she thought of the cracked brake fluid reservoir. Why was Seth fooling around with her tire? She stepped back out of sight and retreated through the open kitchen door. Hardly able to breathe, she quietly closed it. Standing inside, her back to the door, she told herself that she should just go outside and ask him what the hell he was doing. But she was afraid.

From the window, she saw Seth throw his tools in the back of his truck, then lift a box she assumed was the paint. He looked normal— not like he had murder in mind. She pulled away from the window and waited for a knock on the door.

The doorbell rang. She jumped, but her feet were glued to the floor. Should she let him in? The urgency of the second ring came like a command and she opened the door.

"Good morning, Winna. Where do you want me to unload the paint?"

Why is he smiling at me? She opened her mouth to speak but didn't know what she was supposed to say. Had he asked a question? Was that smile the hook she was supposed to swallow? She knew she had better get hold of herself.

"Yes—Seth—I'm sorry—good morning—I was just—uh—"

"Are you okay?" He was chuckling, looking at her like he thought she had just lost her mind. "The paint? Where do you want me to put it?"

"Ah, sure. Why don't you just leave it in the garage?" She looked past him, then at the floor. Suddenly she knew what to say. "I'm on my way out—ah—I have a great idea. While I'm away in New Hampshire, you can enjoy to a two-week vacation from me." She hoped she looked cheerful, unruffled. "We'll paint when I get back," she said, forcing a smile.

Seth looked puzzled, like he sensed something wrong, but he turned and headed for the garage. "By the way," he said, turning to look over his shoulder. "I found your hubcap lying on the ground and did my best to fix it."

"Thanks," she said, doubting him, wishing he would go.

Seth smiled at her. "Well, have a safe trip." His face brightened. "Be sure and take lots of pictures."

Winna got his joke and managed a laugh.

She closed the door and locked it.

THAT EVENING, SHE packed her suitcase, laptop, and photo equipment, hoping two weeks would be long enough to wrap up things at home. She thought back to her afternoon drive to J & B Auto Repair, made after she had convinced herself that Seth had been tampering with her tire.

Charlie was busy, but the young man at the front desk took a look. He removed the hubcap and tire and examined it carefully. She had told him that she had just seen someone fooling around with the tire and that she just wanted to make sure it was not going to fall off on her way up or down a mountain. He found nothing wrong with the tire, but told her that the snap locks on the hubcap looked worn. He suggested she get new hubcaps. Feeling stupid and paranoid, she drove home hoping she hadn't hurt Seth's feelings.

That night, she lay in bed with the moon and stars shining in through her window—a new moon so thin it looked as if it would break. When she closed her eyes, the fear came back—Seth in the driveway working on her tire. She felt guilty for thinking the way she had about Seth and opened her eyes to distract herself from her thoughts. She turned her back to the window and watched the swaying shadows on the wall until her eyes closed and she felt herself fall down the basement stairs. Soon, she was pumping her brakes, her tires screaming around turns.

To distract herself from the instant replay, she decided to lie there and go over her packing list. In the morning, she should pack Juliana's story and some of Whitaker's letters. She wanted to look at them again on the plane. She turned her thoughts to her upcoming trip, her house on a hill with a view of the ocean, and finally welcomed the strange little creatures — the phantasmata — that came to her just before sleep.

BEFORE SHE LEFT for the airport, she searched for the story but could not find it. Winna looked at the clock. The last time she remembered having it was the night she went to dinner at Emily's and figured she had left it in the car. Dragging her suitcase and photo equipment outside, she loaded them into the trunk. Of all her possessions, her state-of-the-art digital camera was the most precious and she did not want to leave it behind. It was getting late. The notebook was not in the car. There was no time to search the house again. *I must have left it at Emily's*, she thought.

Winna's plane touched down in Boston where a rental car waited for her at the airport. On the drive north to Portsmouth and New Castle, she drank in the verdant lushness of the New England forest. After Grand Junction's dry barren alkali flats and boxy adobe houses, its stark red-rock mesas and open blue skies, New England seemed almost too green and gentle. She drove past moist wetlands full of waving cattails, loosestrife, and grasses, tangled woodlands, green meadows sprinkled with midsummer wildflowers, and church steeples set amid the architecture of a civilized past.

Aptly named, Portsmouth lay at the mouth of a seaport — where the Piscataqua River formed the border between New Hampshire and Maine. An old town, it had been settled more than three hundred and seventy-five years ago. Winna had always loved its vibrant river port with fishing boats and ships from afar. Reshaped for shoppers and tourists, the town offered history, good restaurants, and innovative shops.

She had shopped and dined in downtown Portsmouth almost weekly, but her house was to the east on the island of New Castle. Thinking of John, who had agreed to keep an eye on the Seventh Street house while she was gone, she headed out of town, crossing Goat Island Bridge. The road took her through what there was of a little town: the post office, the Congregational church, and the town hall. Driving toward the east coast of the island, she passed a wetland, expensive houses, and a field edged by a stone wall. From there she could see her little white farm house sitting on top of a knoll in the midst of an overgrown lawn. Though surrounded by open space, the nineteenth-century house stood above the lighthouse and the beach on no more land than its own sweeping lawn. The vision brought instantaneous regret. Why didn't I ask John to come? Winna wanted him to see her home, to rest with her on the big porch overlooking the island and out to sea.

Inside, she visited every room—the front parlor with a view of the sea, the dining room with the pumpkin pine floors and the welcoming fireplace, the kitchen where a breakfast nook looked over the neighbor's field at the back of the house—and pulled up the windows to let in the ocean air.

With her half of everything from the divorce, she had purchased the rundown house and it became her haven, the place she retreated to nurse her wounds. Walt kept the house in town where they had raised their daughter.

For a time, Winna had taken refuge there, a veteran of thirty-five years of marriage to a workaholic philanderer. Maybe he was neither. Maybe he just lost interest in me.

Why do I do that—make excuses for him as if I deserved to be tossed away? Where Walt was concerned, questioning her worth was a habit.

She opened the door to her study, painted a soft buttery yellow, a color that warmed her like a pool of sunlight. The yellow paint had been inspired by her favorite rose. In a moment of infatuation, she had taken it to the paint store to have the color matched. Winna had spent the past few years in this room planning workshops, marketing photos, filling orders, building frames, cutting mats, and following up with contacts in Boston and New York where she had clients and exhibitions to fill. Here, she had lived in a world of her own making.

Her photographs made the real world go away—beautiful pictures where nothing hurt—still life, sunrises over the sea, woodlands she had walked through in all seasons. Dark images where she cried and shouted at Walt in a way she could not to his face—her wedding gown glowing in the light of a window, Emily's old doll abandoned on the floor, candles burning on a table set for one, empty chairs, broken windows. She'd done a whole show for a Boston gallery on images of broken glass. It had received critical acclaim.

In that room, she forgot that her husband had left her for a sexy lawyer. Actually, Winna had thought at the time, I don't know how sexy she is, but she is smart and well respected in Portsmouth. I am sure she has to be sexier than me, the wife.

Winna began her photography career right out of college working for a successful Boston photographer—mostly in the darkroom. Sometimes he sent her off on jobs too small for his big talent.

She and Walt moved to Portsmouth when Walt had been invited to join a prominent law firm there. After years of trying not to get pregnant, Emily was conceived soon after they had settled. Everything seemed perfect. While Walt climbed the ladder at Barton Connor and Jessup, Winna stayed home with the baby.

After they moved into their dream house with all the latest appliances and her closet full of beautiful clothes, she did laundry every day and ironed with *The Guiding Light* for company. She made peanut butter sandwiches for Emily, changed sheets once a week, mopped floors, and scrubbed toilets. One day she picked up *The Feminine Mystique* by Betty Friedan.

Winna laughed at the memory and wondered if she still had the book somewhere in her library. The book that blew midcentury womanhood off the map had been like a cold shower for Winna.

What a blow—here she was doing the job her mother had done, but with all this new information. Friedan had dissected the feminine mystique. Generations of women had choked to death on something Winna didn't have to swallow anymore. She didn't have to wonder about her senseless dissatisfaction in the face of all she had or her restlessness or why she had asked herself, is this all there is to life? She didn't have to bury herself because another woman had written that Winna hadn't made up these feelings. She was no longer alone.

She had a talk with Walt—many talks—and he agreed that they could afford some help. She could go back to work part-time. He even pointed out to her that she was the one who had wanted to quit work and stay at home. By the time Emily was five years old and in kindergarten, Winna had held her first exhibition and was landing photography jobs in Boston.

The phone on her desk rang and she answered a call from Emily.

"Perfect timing. I just walked in the door."

"How was your flight?"

"Fine, once I got to Denver and boarded a real plane. Right now I'm standing in my study feeling a little haunted."

"That house can't possibly be as haunted as your grandmother's house. Mom, you never called me back."

"Oh, my goodness, I'm sorry. I must have lost my mind. How did your meeting go?"

"It's next week." Emily chuckled. "I'll let you know."

"Yes, do. I'm excited for you." Winna paused as something came to mind. "By the way, did I leave the notebook with Juliana's story at your house?"

"No, I haven't seen it. Maybe you left it in the car."

"I looked. It must be in the house somewhere."

"Look, Mom, while you are out there you should drive down to Newport and see what you can find."

"Why?"

"Well, you know, that's where Dolph went to make a name for himself. You could check the library for old newspapers. Maybe there's a story about him or his benefactor."

"Do you think he was lying or exaggerating in his letters?"

"All we have is his word for it. What if he was just trying to impress Juliana? On your way back, you could stop in Providence and see where he went to college. I wish I were with you. It would be fun."

"Me too. I'll think about it."

"Whatever you do, do it quick and come home. We miss you already."

"Thanks, honey." Winna kissed the receiver goodbye.

Looking around at her workroom, she felt the urgency of the task at hand. She wanted to leave the house furnished until it sold. Winna had hardly begun to think about what it would be like to work in the West and what that kind of shift would mean in her career. LA and San Francisco didn't rule out New York and Boston. Photographing the West would mean a different life: travel, rising before dawn, stopping before nine o'clock, then out with the camera again from four until dark. It would mean watching the skies, waiting for clouds and storms, camping in the open again. She had never spent a lot of time photographing vast landscapes and this would be her chance. On the plane, she had even envisioned buying a small van in which she could sleep if she had to. She thought of asking Seth to build a platform on top. From the roof, she could set up a tripod and work unencumbered.

Walking back through the house, she visited every room again and made a grocery list. *I think Emily's right. I'll drive down to Newport. I'll eat out tonight and leave in the morning.* She left her grocery list on the counter and grabbed the car keys.

34

SWAMPED WITH TOURIST buses and Sunday drivers, Bellevue Avenue looked elegant as ever to Winna, who had visited Newport a few times over the years. The wide tree-lined avenue's architectural treasures began with an old summer cottage whose design had been perfected by Stanford White. Many of the mansions were built of stone — some of marble — making them look like European manor houses and small palaces. At the far end the boulevard ran into Ocean Avenue, where enormous old summer estates still weathered the storms off the wild Atlantic coastline.

Winna had no idea which of the mansions had belonged to William Ailesbury. She saw no sign for Ailesbury Court, like those trumpeting The Breakers or Marble House, and she didn't remember anything from Dolph's letters that would give her a clue.

She checked into a Bellevue Avenue bed and breakfast and drove to the library.

WITH STACKS OF old histories neatly collected beside her on a long library table, Winna settled in, reading and taking notes. Easily sidetracked, she found herself wandering off to stories on the early congregations of Baptists, Quakers, and Jews who found tolerance in Newport, on shipbuilding, and the trade in Negro slaves. She reminded herself that she was looking in the wrong century and delved into a book on the Gilded Age in Newport. There, she found a description of a typical garden party under a tent on a lawn where the hostess served a traditional English afternoon tea: biscuits, cake, little sandwiches, cold birds, ham, ices, punch, and champagne. The chapter went on to say that sometimes the guests used the lawns for tennis, archery, and croquet. If the hostess had hired musicians, they danced outside on the lawn to the music of a piano and violin.

The wealthy could afford distinguished performers and brought them into their homes to entertain with poetry readings, chamber ensembles of classical and light music, magic lantern shows, storytelling, travel lectures, mesmerism, and psychic phenomena including séances.

With nothing to guide her, Winna had already formed an impression of what Whitaker looked like. Her poet had sandy-colored hair cut at the shoulders and a beard. He was tall and slim—almost too thin for her taste. His hands were graceful with long slender fingers and he had a habit of running them through his long hair, scraping it back off his forehead. His eyes were blue and intense—maybe even a little cold—but his lips were full like Oscar Wilde's. A contradiction. His mouth didn't go with his eyes. Every time she thought of him, this image came to mind.

In a book written in 1920, she found information on the development of Newport as a fashionable resort for the very rich, including details about the construction of the palatial mansions. Another book enlightened her on the summer pleasures of society folk, their clothing and food, the yachts, lawn tennis, galas, balls, and salons. Here, she encountered the first mention of Mrs. William Ailesbury, Dolph's patron saint, Rose. She was real. Dolph did not invent her.

When she realized that she hadn't looked at old newspapers yet, she abandoned her library table and headed to the microfilm room. Her search began with rolls spanning the years 1912-1914, concentrating on the late spring and summer months, when she knew the mansions were in use. She came across numerous stories about weddings, fantastic lawn parties, balls, and famous visitors. Most astonishing were the exceedingly short visits some families made to their luxurious summer homes, staying only a few weeks before sailing off to Europe.

Suddenly, she found herself sympathetic toward the man who might be her real grandfather. What a bewildering world Whitaker had entered. Coming from a small town out West, he had been invited into the seductively beautiful realm of the industrialists and their families. He was in love with Juliana, but what could he offer her? He'd finally seen real wealth and understood at last what Juliana wanted.

Winna pictured the lean poet alone, standing on a lawn that swept down to the cliff above the bay. The mansion shone like a palace at his back. Was he lonely? Did Dolph stand in Mrs. Ailesbury's salon before a room full of notables terrified or confident of his gift? A handsome stranger reciting poetry, painting a world they had never seen. The glitterati present had never heard of Grand Junction. Did his spoken images evoke the raw beauty of the Western landscape, the cruel wilderness, the heedless deserts and mesas? His words must have aroused and amazed his audience. She wanted to find his poems. Had he been published?

Winna left her machine and approached the young librarian behind a desk near the entrance.

"I have the name of a poet from the nineteen-teens. Can you tell me if you have a book of his poems—or if his work might be in an anthology somewhere?"

"Yes, I can," she said, sitting down at a computer. "The name?"

"Adolph Whitaker." The sound of his name as it left her mouth startled her. Like she had just revealed a secret she had promised not to tell.

The young woman's fingers tapped the keyboard. Her eyes darted across the monitor—more clicking keys, more eye movements. Winna waited impatiently.

Finally, the librarian sighed and looked up at her. "There's nothing here—nothing comes up under that name."

Disappointed, Winna returned to the microfilm and her search through old newspapers. Maybe Whitaker had died before he was published. A story written in June of 1914 about a lawn party caught her attention. The hostess delighted her guests with what looked like a fleet of ancient Egyptian vessels floating off shore. The woman had hired a New York set designer to create the scene. Winna laughed at such ridiculous excess, then spotted a story about Mrs. William Ailesbury's Sunday afternoon salon. The names of prominent guests were listed and so was the entertainment—"the promising young poet, Mr. A. Graham Whitaker who read his epic poem *Canyons of the Idols* to the delight of his hostess and all her guests."

Winna wanted to jump to her feet and cheer. Instead, a headline at the top of the next page caught her eye. A short story, discreetly written to protect the victims from publicity, followed.

Bellevue Avenue Robbery

> Newport police filed a report this morning, saying a significant quantity of jewelry was stolen from a Bellevue Avenue residence late Sunday afternoon. According to a police source, the robbery took place during a large gathering of notables and artists. Many guests had come from New York, Boston, and as far away as London, England, and Paris, France. Police would not confirm whether or not they had a suspect or disclose the value of the articles stolen. This is the third such robbery this year.

If her memory served her right, in 1914 Whitaker appeared at numerous soirees given by several Newport hostesses in June and July. Winna's stomach filled up with butterflies. Was Whitaker a thief? Is that where Juliana got the jewels?

She hurried back to the librarian's desk. "I'm sorry. I think I gave you the wrong name. Would you look for A. Graham Whitaker, please? It's getting late. I'll check back with you in a few minutes." She pointed toward the door. "I'm in there looking at microfilm."

With sudden certainty, Winna knew that Whitaker had committed that burglary and possibly others. She looked for more news of housebreaks, scanning page after page of print until the librarian told her she had not found her poet and was ready to lock up for the night.

LONG AGO, BENEFIT Street had been settled on College Hill in Providence. From the historical markers on the eighteenth-century clapboard houses built right at the edge of the sidewalks, Winna deduced that it must have been one of the oldest surviving residential streets in town. On the uphill side of the street, more substantial nineteenth-century houses faced a city view and at their backs lay hidden walled gardens and lawns. All were more sedate, older than anything she had seen in Newport. With the eerie feeling that her feet now walked the same cobblestones traveled by Whitaker, she took a walk with her camera.

Dolph's letters were written from a house on this street. She remembered his description of the neighborhood, of the small room on the third floor where he lived. He wrote of looking through a porthole window at Nightingale House, a mansion of classic proportions and historical significance, which he rapturously described to Juliana.

Her search for the house led her south. The farther she walked, the fewer students she passed on the sidewalk. Wondering what Dolph had worn to school, she felt certain it was not dreadlocks, army pants, and sandals. Near the end of the street, she found a row of three-story houses that looked like they would have been there in 1910 when Dolph set off for college.

She stopped in front of a two-family clapboard with a half porch in front and a second entrance under a small portico to the side. Out of the sidewalk grew an ancient sycamore tree and a gas street lantern, long ago converted to electricity. Up in the third story, she saw a small porthole window which looked down on Benefit Street. Winna turned on her heels and looked across the street. Just a little to the north, on a rise above the sidewalk, sat a colonial mansion. She was looking at Nightingale House. She stood there a moment taking in the exhilaration she felt. I see just what he saw. Could this poet—this thief—have been my grandfather? And why do I have tears in my eyes?

35

WINNA DROVE HOME questioning herself. Why had she jumped to the conclusion that the poetic thief was her grandfather? She'd never been attached to her Poppa Edwin, who worked long hours every day of the week but one. On Sundays, she would find him in the library behind a newspaper or one of his history books. He seemed alone—maybe the loneliest person she had ever known—sitting in the shadows, huddled under his reading lamp, his feet propped up on the footstool, a cloud of cigar smoke circling his head. Though he had a large appetite, he looked like a string bean. He was afraid of everything: cold drafts, not chewing each bite of food twenty times before swallowing, your stomach being eaten away by the Coke you just drank, your features freezing into the ugly face you just made.

When Winna was very small, she would sit on his lap and he'd blow big floaty smoke-rings for her. When she got tired of that, he would wiggle his ears. He taught her how to wiggle hers. She wondered if she still could. Wishing for a mirror, she flexed her ear-wiggling muscles and laughed at herself.

Winna thought back to his long canoe-like feet. He'd ask her to put her own small foot up next to his and they'd laugh at the

difference. When Juliana wasn't looking, she would urge her grandfather to drop his false teeth. If her grandmother caught him doing
that, he'd get a scolding. Besides Cuban cigars, he had a passion for
ice cream and ate a dish of it every night before bed.

She had loved him because he was funny and he was her grandfather and because you are supposed to love the people in your
family, but he had never offered to show her his world, nor asked
to enter hers.

Winna shrugged her shoulders. That's the way men were back
then—none of this diapering babies, pushing strollers around,
giving mom a break from childcare like Hugh does for Emily.

In an attempt to organize her thoughts, she stopped along the
road to make notes. She parked in grass growing alongside the right
lane, so close that the car shook as tractor-trailers barreled past.

On a notepad, she wrote: *Check details in J's story—read between
the lines. Go with evidence not coincidence.* "Chloe says she doesn't
believe in coincidence," she said aloud. "But I do."

Her thoughts turned to the present. Who is searching the
Seventh Street house? She couldn't imagine. Did someone tamper
with my brakes—what about the stair rail? She returned to that
night her brakes had failed: John's kisses, driving down the mountain, sharp curves, hidden precipices, pumping the brakes, the
sound of her tires screaming on the curves. Did someone want her
dead? Who?

Cars and trucks whizzed past, their wakes violently shaking her
car. A driver leaned on his horn as he approached. She clapped her
hands over her ears. Terrified, she restarted her car and moved farther to the right, off the road. She was shaking.

Winna took a deep breath and forced herself to relax. She wanted
to believe that she was suggestible, that the break-ins had threatened her sense of security, that she was imagining that someone had
wanted her to drive off that mountain. Had the stairs been tampered
with—and the rail? No one had suggested it. Did Seth say the rail
had been touched up with paint? She knew it hadn't—at least not
under her direction.

Look into the fall. Make list of break-ins and dates, she wrote. *Where was Todd? Where was Seth? Where was* — she paused, her hands broke out in sweat as she wrote, *John?*

THE HOUSE IN New Castle welcomed her home in a way that it hadn't the other day. She stocked the kitchen with food and settled in. On her way home from the market, she took a detour into town and drove by the old house — Walt's house.

Mornings, Walt and lawyer lady were at work and she would not be seen. She stopped the car and stared at the large gray-shingled house where she had lived for over twenty years, where she had been under the illusion that she was living the good life as a wife and mother. The front door glared at her. Thinking red or a deep forest green too traditional, Winna had the door painted bright yellow. She drove away feeling like a peeping Tom, wondering what was wrong with Walt's new wife, why the door had not been repainted.

Settling in back at home, she called her realtor and made an appointment for him to come see the house. He could come later that day. She called the kid who mowed the lawn and paid some bills. She followed that with business calls. A cup of tea in hand, she rang two old friends. She called Emily to tell her about her find — Adolph Whitaker was a thief — at least she thought so. What did Emily think?

"Sounds pretty obvious to me," she said.

After lunch, she was ready to rest. To help get the house in Grand Junction out of mind, she picked up a book she'd been reading and stretched out on the window seat in the living room with a pillow under her head.

"Sometimes I feel loneliest when I'm with people," the heroine said. "Solitude is different. In solitude I enjoy being with me."

Winna had suffered loneliness after her divorce. She stopped to think what solitude meant to her. Her work required solitude and she thought of it as her friend.

The following words she read aloud: "I've lived with him for years, now there is something in our blood and bones that no change in us can alter."

She read it again thinking of John, not Walt. Something still lingers in our blood and bones that no changes in us have changed. The words hit her hard and her eyes filled up with tears. Was that something the reason her marriage had failed? Why she and Walt had never experienced the intense physical love she had shared with John?

She had hidden her past from Walt. She wanted him to believe she was good, unspoiled, a virgin—someone he could proudly marry. She had never again wanted to hear the ugly words Johnny had spat at her—words and thoughts that were part of the culture then.

She had never been able to let herself go and had always been guarded in her response to Walt in bed. Then it came to her—that long-ago vow she had made when she thought she was pregnant with Johnny's child. She had promised God that she would never want sex again.

Now, she wondered how different things might have been if she had loved him freely. Winna sat up and put her feet on the floor, wiping her tears on the back of her hand. She felt like a door had opened in her mind, like Walt had been wronged, like she could finally see what she had done to the marriage. She wished she could tell him that she now understood why he had sought the love of another woman. Maybe someday she could.

Feeling thankful, like a light had gone on in her mind and heart, she lay down and clasped the book to her breast. Closing her eyes, she let herself rest again. She thought about the house, the one where she lay in a window seat with a view of the ocean. She had lived there nearly three years, not enough time to collect many memories—but one came to mind.

After the separation, Emily had come for a visit. She had stayed half the week with her mother and the rest in town with her father. Emily had always loved the island and its history. Everywhere in the landscape and the architecture one saw traces of the past.

One morning, Winna woke up to the smell of coffee and found Emily making French toast. She no longer remembered why she had burst into tears in front of her daughter, but she thought back to the moment when Emily had embraced her and whispered in her ear, "Mom, you don't really love Dad. I've known that for a long time. Right now you are just jealous because he has someone else."

Winna had felt hurt by her words and wanted to protest, but instead she kissed her daughter and held onto her embrace. Emily was right. The marriage was convenient, not nurturing—not for her, not for him.

After breakfast, Emily cleaned up while Winna toured the garden to see what was left after the frost. She found butternut squash, beets, and cabbages. Chores done, they decided to take a walk in the woods.

Heading across the lawn in the back of the house—over a fence and around an overgrown field full of goldenrod and roseberry bushes—they came to a stone wall built hundreds of years before around a small field. Inside, the field had reforested with trees— oaks for the most part. Animals must have grazed there because the grass was trim. The scene was almost park-like, but an eerie light radiated from the overcast sky through the trees down to the nibbled grass. Emily stopped at the wall and gasped. In that light, the old field seemed enchanted. As if they had come to the edge of a window into the past, they stood there in silence unwilling to move or speak.

From her perch at the window, Winna turned on her side, tucked a second pillow under her head, and looked out at the view. She promised herself that early tomorrow morning she would visit the enchanted field. She wanted to see if her camera could capture the feeling she and Emily had experienced in that place. She would go, knowing that once missed, an image is gone forever.

She fell into a peaceful place and slept for a while. The doorbell woke her. Disoriented, she sat up and looked around at the room and out to the sea. She answered the door, inviting the realtor in.

"I am so sorry," Winna said. "I didn't have time to call to cancel our appointment. I just now realized it—I could never sell this house."

36

ON THE FLIGHT from Boston to Denver, Winna thought hard about the fact that she no longer knew what she wanted. All of a sudden, she had too many choices. Or were they problems? She was obsessed by the past. She had two houses she loved and two men on her mind—one whom she had just forgiven. She had become a wealthy woman, but it had not been enjoyable because she thought someone wished her harm. Questions, fears, and wild suppositions never let up during the whole flight. She wished that while she was in Portsmouth she had gone to talk to her priest about all her fears. She dreaded her return to the town where she was born.

In Denver, she boarded one of the small planes that flew west over the mountains. Even though she knew what to expect, she prayed, trying to make bargains with God. The plane rattled and shook as it flew through crosswinds and down drafts off the mountains. At one point, she looked out the window. The aircraft's wings were shuddering. She held on, wondering if she would survive to find the answers to her questions. By the time the plane bounced onto the runway, Winna was relieved to be back in Grand Junction.

Unsteady as a landlubber just in from the sea, she found her car in the parking lot and drove to the house on Seventh Street. Once inside, she called John.

"I'm home. I'm exhausted and still airsick and, after a bath and a scotch, I'm going straight to bed to nurse my wounds."

"What wounds? Are you all right?" he asked.

"Yes, I just feel damn silly. I flew all that way to sell a house I can't sell."

"Nobody says you have to sell your house, Winna."

He was right. It had been her idea. Winna's mind was too unsettled for any further conversation. They signed off with a promise to talk tomorrow. They had agreed to get together soon—he wanted to cook dinner for her again, up on Little Park Road.

Once she had dragged in her suitcase and camera equipment, she realized that she would not rest until she went over her list. She poured herself a scotch and pulled out the list she had made on her way from Providence to New Castle.

With a quick snap of the mind, it occurred to her that if it meant driving down that road again at night, she did not want to go to dinner at John's. She didn't care how silly he thought she was.

Winna read the through her list. One thing needed immediate attention—to check the details in Juliana's story, making sure to read between the lines. The search was on. She must find the notebook. After looking in every room, every drawer in the library and kitchen, Winna knew it wasn't there. The thief had it.

IN THE MORNING, Winna felt nauseated again, as if she was still on the plane. After a cup of tea and dry toast, she fled the house. She had to get away—get some groceries. Feeling angry, but unable to assign the emotion to anyone or anything specific, she drove to City Market's crowded parking lot where she had to park all the way over in front of Herb's Pet Ranch. On a whim, she wandered in.

There didn't seem to be anyone around. Feeling aimless, Winna browsed for a while through the dog toys, fondling a stuffed chipmunk guaranteed to stand up to dog play. She heard canaries chirruping and followed the call past aquariums full of darting neon lights. Suddenly, she burst into tears, glad that no one was around to see her shudder as she tried to regain her composure. Turning away, she found herself standing in front of a glass enclosure full of puppies in wire crates stacked one on top of the other. She walked along the glass looking at their eager faces; tails wagged, some yelped, others seemed to cry with joy at the sight of her. They were all adorable. Winna wanted one. She looked at the puppies with purpose, as if she was going to make a purchase.

I don't have time to raise a puppy. They are as much work as a baby. Having gotten a grip on reality, she turned and walked toward the exit. As she pushed the door open, she came face to face with a homemade sign advertising two-year-old Pembroke Welsh Corgis, fully pedigreed, fully housebroken, and free to good homes. A phone number was hand-printed on tags across the bottom of the sign. Wondering why the offer was free, Winna tore off a number and slipped it into her pocket. *Here's an alarm system I can love.*

THE MOMENT SHE stepped through the kitchen door with her groceries, Winna's dread returned. She didn't know why. The sky wasn't falling, the world wasn't coming to an end. It made no sense to her. She unpacked her purchases, put everything away, and picked up the phone to call Emily.

"Something's wrong with me," she said. "All of a sudden I feel awful in this house."

"No kidding," her daughter said. "It's about time. You've been blithely walking around on a cloud all this time. It's about time you woke up."

"What would you think if I got a dog?"

Emily said nothing for a moment. "Well, that's a step in the right direction. Dogs bark. They let you know when you are no longer alone on your property."

"I thought of that."

"Look, Mom, you've been through a lot. Get away from the house for a day, even a few hours would help."

"I just got home from a trip."

"Go out for lunch, think seriously about a dog. Go for a long drive. Come up here if you want. You can help me fold laundry."

"So you think what I'm feeling is normal?"

"Yes. Think about it."

"That's a relief."

"Mom, you are a riot. Call me tonight. I'll want to hear how you spent your day and I'll expect it to be good. Hey, it just occurred to me—we're going up to Hanging Lake tomorrow and you're coming with us."

WINNA WALKED TOWARD Main Street, taking in deep breaths of air, just like her mother had when she was out for exercise. Nora would throw her head back, inhale deeply, and command to her daughter: "Breathe, Winna, breathe," as if Winna had never taken a deep breath before. Swinging her arms in time with her long strides, Nora would stir up the dust on the canal road.

Remembering the fabric store where she had seen the tempting drapery material, Winna set off in search of it. She looked across the street at the Cooper Theatre and realized she was only a couple of blocks from the old Grumman's department store.

The impressive three-story edifice still occupied half a block on Main Street. Constructed of red brick and sandstone from the Colorado mountains, Grumman's was still an imposing building. *Grumman's est. 1882* was still proudly carved over the entrance.

She stopped on the sidewalk and looked through the store windows. The first floor of the old department store had been divided up into smaller stores: a weight-loss clinic, a consignment shop full of used clothing, and a senior center which took up the greater portion of the space. Through the windows, she could see what looked like perfectly functional people gathered around craft tables, playing cards and checkers at tables for two and four. Some were clustered in front of a TV set ringed with over-stuffed chairs. The second floor held a furniture outlet where one could rent-to-own a whole living room suite for seventy-nine dollars a month.

Once, these windows featured the latest things people wanted to own. Mr. Dinkins, Grumman's window dresser, had put on the best show in town when he provocatively disrobed mannequins for people watching on the street. No longer did her grandfather's polished sales personnel wait on thickly carpeted floors for customers interested in the latest styles, fine linens, furniture, and rugs. *Very few people can make a living in a place like this anymore, only in big cities like New York,* Winna mused. What had happened to people like Miss Ethel Conrad, head of the women's department, who fit Winna for her first bra, sensitive to both the excitement and trepidation a young girl feels at a time like that? And Mr. G. Percy Hampton who, as far as Winna knew, had traveled the Eastern deserts on camelback buying rugs from weavers. He always had time to read her the stories woven into her grandfather's collection of oriental rugs. And what about Jack Talbot, in the shoe department, who measured her feet, pressing his thumb down at the tip of her toes, and teased, "How many hearts have you broken this week, Winna?"

Now, if you want to make a decent living, you have to go to college and become a rocket scientist. Something significant has been lost, she thought. While she'd watched, the world had changed at the speed of light. She looked at the able-bodied old people playing cards. Why are these people idle? Don't they have vegetable gardens to tend, or grandchildren to chase? Maybe old ladies don't make jam anymore; it's cheaper to buy it. Who is making soup, bread, and heirloom quilts? She knew they didn't sew anymore, neither did she. It's too expensive. *Yes, the world has changed. Price is everything.* She turned away without discovering who occupied the third floor. All of a sudden, Winna knew that, because of her age, she had become a resident of a foreign country.

37

"WHY HAVEN'T I BEEN here before? I didn't even know this paradise existed," Winna said, almost whispering as Emily reached for her hand. She wanted to shout for joy, but could no more disturb the lyrical sounds of falling water than the quiet of a church.

A roundish pool of sparkling emerald water lay unruffled and clear at their feet, reminding her of the smooth round emerald ring she wore on her teenaged finger, the ring she lost and still missed. Winna looked again. No, here the water was topaz and there sapphire and emerald again where trout swam lazily by.

A butterfly fluttered near and settled onto a pillow of soft white blossoms as Emily zeroed in with her camera. Hugh disappeared behind green shrubs with Isabelle strapped to his back. It looked like he was heading toward the cliff wall where water tumbled over the rocks. Winna followed.

Hugh had entered a little cave behind the waterfall. Taking his tiny daughter out of his pack, he held her up where her small hands could catch drops of water coming from above. She was laughing, reaching out, drenching her hands, proud of herself, turning to look at her father's big grin.

Winna's heart ached at the sight. She thought of her father, wondering if he had ever enjoyed a moment like this with her, if he had ever delighted in her like Hugh delighted in Isabelle. She wondered if they had ever made as pretty a picture like this one for others to see: Henry smiling, kissing Winna on the cheek, nuzzling her warm sweet smelling neck—loving her.

Just as Emily appeared with her camera raised, Winna wished she'd brought her own. "Emily, get in here with Hugh and I'll take a picture of you guys," she called.

After she shot some pictures, Winna left the young family to enjoy the waterfall. She worked her way back to the lakeshore, eager to just sit and look up at the towering cliffs, the mossy rocks below the waterfalls. From the green of well-hydrated plants, a busy squirrel darted over the straight gray trunk of a fallen tree, one of many beside the lake, lying like the remains of a tumbled-down wickiup hut. Enclosed inside the rumble of falling water, the lake felt magical, radiant with sunlight and cooling shadows. It did hang there, the water pooled in a bowl resting between the cliffs. She knew she would come back and wondered what the lake looked like in winter with the waterfalls frozen, snow powdering the cliff walls, deer coming to the shore for a drink.

They stopped for a late lunch in Glenwood Springs on Grand Avenue. Planters and pots of petunias, marigolds, and nasturtiums blazed in the sun. Just a few blocks from the roaring Colorado River, they found a table under an awning and sat in the shade looking out on a street where nineteenth-century architecture was still visible in the form of boxy two-story brick buildings. Winna felt happy. She looked at her daughter and son-in-law—who on his day off couldn't be parted from the baby—and knew she had made the right decision. By living at the house on Seventh Street, she would be part of this beautiful family.

Winna picked up Emily's camera and shot a few snapshots of her companions.

"Just ignore me," she prompted, clicking away. She stood up, moving in from different angles, coming in for the shot she wanted.

"Be yourselves. I'm not here," she said as they struck a pose for the camera. The tender glance that had passed between Hugh and Emily had faded to well-practiced smiles, then Isabelle began to squirm and fuss and Emily took her in to be changed.

THE TWO WELSH Corgis had been a Christmas gift for an elderly woman who no longer had the energy to care for two active puppies. She'd tried for a year and was grateful when Winna showed up at her door. Winna had always had dogs. Two summers ago, old blind Foxy had walked down to the road and met up with a truck. Her death, on the heels of the divorce, had left Winna vowing to never again form attachments with man or dog.

Luke and Leia spent their first night on Seventh Street in the upstairs hall outside Winna's bedroom sleeping in their new beds. They ate their first dinner in the kitchen from brand new pet bowls from Herb's Pet Ranch. Soon, Seth would come to supervise the installation of a fence around the back lawn—a play area for the dogs.

Since her return from New Hampshire, Winna had obsessed about the need to visit the family graves, those of her parents and grandparents. She wondered if she could find her great-grandparents—the Smythes and the pioneer Grummans—but she could not make herself get in the car and go. Finding it hard to sleep at night, she had prescribed a drink of scotch for herself every night before bed. The drink put her to sleep, but she would wake up halfway through the night with her mind racing.

Soon, she had recurring nausea and headaches—something she had never experienced before. Emily thought it was stress. Nearly a week after the dogs came home with her, what appeared to be an intestinal flu sent her to bed with both mental confusion and a terrible drowsiness. For three days, Winna had been so sick that she had asked Seth to come by twice a day to walk the dogs and feed them. There was blood in her urine and she decided it was time to see a doctor. Weak, her mind unable to focus, legs trembling, hands numb at the end of arms no longer controlled by her brain, she sought the comfort of her bed. The soft light coverlet and the big squashy pillow swallowed her body as she sank into the featherbed below, promising herself she would call the doctor as soon as she had a little nap.

She heard Luke and Leia bark when Seth arrived later that morning and called out to him, but he did not come to her. She could hear him moving around the kitchen, feeding the dogs, and called again. When no answer came, she succumbed to what felt like a drugged sleep.

WINNA WOULD NOT remember Seth finding her semi-conscious, or his picking up the bedside phone to call an ambulance, or the race through town, siren screaming, to Saint Mary's emergency room. From her hospital bed, she would not remember the anxious faces of her family: Emily and Hugh, Chloe and Todd as they waited for the doctor to talk to them, or John sitting at her bedside holding her hand as she struggled to breathe.

Lab results showed that she had suffered from arsenic poisoning. The police searched the house for obvious sources: rat poison, the tap water, every open bottle in the house, and all the leftovers in the refrigerator. They found arsenic in the bottle of scotch. Someone had poisoned her.

Within hours of her arrival at the hospital, Winna was treated with an antidote and in two days was sitting up in bed, still weak and confused, but missing her dogs. Family and friends came every day to sit with her. Emily brought Isabelle for her to hold, Chloe read to her from *The Hobbit*, John came twice a day, and, at the end of the week, Kate came with her arms full of flowers. Kate's visit happened to coincide with Seth's who brought Luke and Leia. He lifted the dogs up on the bed and Winna received their kisses. She thanked Seth for saving her life. When Kate heard the story, she embraced him and thanked him too.

Todd came with a box of prettily wrapped hard candies and two slightly used magazines: *Cosmopolitan* and *Motor Trend*. He pulled a chair up to her bedside and looked prepared to stay a while.

"Look, Winnie, I really want to give you a hand at the house when you get better."

"But you are so busy and I have Seth," she said, feeling drowsy.

"You have to pay him. I'm free." He grinned looking pleased with himself.

Winna laughed. "I know you are good with a hammer and saw, but what else can you do?"

"I can put up curtain rods—Chloe just had me install some new ones in her living room. She wants to get the house ready to sell. She thinks we need something bigger and better."

"Thanks. I'll remember that Todd knows how to install curtain rods. You'll be sorry," Winna said, closing her eyes for a moment, feeling herself drop into the mattress, her eyes glued shut. "Oh my," she said, fading. "I guess I'm going to nap now." She patted his hand, wishing he'd let her sleep.

AS SOON AS her head was clear enough for her to talk, Detective Lieutenant Matthew Dougherty paid her a call. He stood at the foot of her bed, a young man in a sport coat and tie, his hair redder than his sunburned face. Winna could tell exactly how he looked when he was ten.

"We made a couple visits to your house this summer—break-ins." He looked at the paperwork on his clipboard. "Officers Wilkins and Crawford."

"Yes, there were break-ins and someone is trying to kill me." It had taken lots of talking with family and thinking about what had happened to her for Winna to be able to say "someone is trying to kill me," with certainty and without tears.

Dougherty's eyes narrowed. "Yes, it appears so. Do you have any idea who that might be?"

"No—I can't even imagine. I'm under the illusion that I'm well liked—loved even—but there were two accidents before I drank the poisoned scotch. Both could have been fatal, and I don't know if the accidents are in any way related to the break-ins—whether or not it's the same person behind all of this. Did anyone tell you about my other accidents?"

"No, Mrs. Jessup. I think it's time for you to tell me."

Lieutenant Dougherty listened as Winna described her car's brake failure on Little Park Road, her talk with the mechanic about the brake fluid reservoir, and her fall down the basement stairs. She also informed him that she and her sister were recently made rich by her father's death and that the house was full of valuable antiques and jewelry.

"Who would benefit from your death?" he asked.

Winna looked startled—her face paled. "Everyone—absolutely everyone," she said blankly.

Dougherty looked amused. "Sounds like you're doomed, Mrs. Jessup." They had a laugh.

Though he asked, she was unable to name names—to accuse anyone. "Maybe if I put it to you this way—give me the names of your family and friends and any other close associates. We won't put suspicion on anyone particular. How's that?"

When she had finished her list, Dougherty said, "I'll want to talk with your handyman first." He looked at his notes. "Seth Taylor. He may be able to tell me more about the basement stairs and other things about the house."

"The locks on the doors have been changed and I've given the key to no one but my sister and daughter."

"When you go home on Friday—that's what the doctor told me—I want you to keep your doors locked when you're at home and when you go out. Ask your sister and daughter to return the keys. Do it without notice so that they don't have time to get copies made."

Winna's mind raced. She'd have to ask for the keys? How could she?

"The dogs were a good idea—a great safety alarm," he reassured. "I have one more question. Who do you trust the most?"

She thought a moment and said, "My daughter Emily—and Seth Taylor—and—Chloe—and—I don't distrust anyone."

"Except for your daughter, I don't want you to talk about this or any of your business—especially your movements—when you plan to come and go from the house, with anyone," he said.

"I can't ask my daughter or Chloe for their keys. I just can't."

"Okay, then I want you to call a locksmith and get the locks changed again. Would you like me to do that for you today?"

"Would you?" Winna reached for her handbag, fished for the key, and handed it to him. "Are you sure I can trust you?"

He laughed. "Yes, of course. Now get better and I'll go to work."

WHEN WINNA HAD been home for ten days and was feeling well, she took comfort from her doctor's words. "You have made a remarkable recovery from a mild case of arsenic poisoning," he had said, adding that she was lucky she wasn't a heavy drinker. "I recommend everything in moderation, including arsenic."

John visited her every evening after work and had made dinner for her twice. Emily and Chloe had gotten together to make sure one of them spent time with her every day and Todd had stopped by with more flowers. She and Seth had planned to start working on the house again on Monday.

After the entire family, and John and Seth, had been finger-printed, Detective Dougherty stopped by for a visit. He said that the only prints on the scotch bottle were hers. The kitchen cupboards had been examined for fingerprints. All they found were the prints of family and friends.

"So this is an inside job," Winna said.

Dougherty laughed. "Or someone wearing gloves. Look, Mrs. Jessup, I don't want to alarm you, but we are looking at family and friends—and you should too."

"I'll cry about that after you leave," Winna said, trying to stop the tears that raced to her eyes.

38

JOHN HAD AGREED that Winna could bring the dogs. She could come early for dinner and drive home before dark. He promised not to serve martinis and to show her how to fry trout. After greeting her and the two dogs jumping at his feet, John gave her a kiss.

"What's this about you teaching me how to fry trout?" she asked. "I'm great at trout, you know that."

The dogs sniffed around the corners of the kitchen and John handed her a glass of white wine. "Why don't we let them outside?" he asked. "There aren't any cars up here and they could explore."

"I don't know, they aren't used to playing with coyotes and I'm not sure they'll come when I call them. Aren't they cute?"

He nodded and smiled at her as if she was the cute one. "They look like they belong at Balmoral Castle. I just hope they bark."

"Haven't you heard them?"

Winna went to work making a big salad with romaine, avocado, and fresh grapefruit segments while John put baking powder biscuits in the oven and fried some bacon. He made the trout just like Winna had: dipped in cornmeal and fried in bacon drippings. They took their plates out on the deck. The dogs followed.

"It's awfully quiet over on Seventh Street these days," Winna said, settling herself at the table. "Nobody's stopped by to rob or kill me for almost three weeks."

"Winna, that's not funny," he said, his eyes sparked with anger.

"It's meant to be, John. I have to laugh or I'll go crazy. I'm supposed to suspect someone in the family—or a friend. Can you imagine how it feels knowing that someone I care for wants me dead?"

"Yes, I can imagine, Winna. I don't envy you. I'm terrified for you. I want you to come and stay here with me where I can protect you—or I'll come and stay with you. All you have to say is 'yes,' and I'll pack my bags."

"Oh, John—I don't know. You'd do that?"

"Of course I would. I love you—I'd have you in bed with me every night." He reached for her hand and pulled her up into his arms. "I want you to marry me. Come on," he whispered. "We can eat later."

She laughed. "We aren't seventeen, my darling. We can wait. The bed will still be there. I'm hungry."

"This I must remember," he said. "Winna's stomach comes first."

"Yes—remember that." She looked at him. He looked hurt. "Come on, John, don't make too much of it. Your dinner is getting cold."

John seemed to let go of whatever he was feeling. He smiled at her and they both sat down.

"More wine?" he asked, tipping the bottle over her glass.

"Sure," she said, looking over her shoulder at the dogs sitting side by side near the door with their heads cocked.

"Look at them," she whispered. "They're just sitting there watching us eat."

"They've been trained not to beg," he whispered back.

"I think I love them."

"I'm jealous," he said. "I wasn't kidding about coming to stay with you or you staying here with me. I want to marry you, Winna." He reached out to touch her cheek. "I should have married you in the first place."

Winna shook her head as if she couldn't believe what she was hearing. "You are very sweet, John. I love you too. You know that.

It's something we should think about together. But first, I want to talk about the past—like why you said such awful things to me when we fought as teenagers."

"I don't remember saying worse things to you than what you said to me."

"Well you did—you said no one would marry me because I wasn't a virgin."

"I did? I think you are making that up, but I have to admit that us guys did think things like that back then. Don't you know I'm a feminist now? I'm glad you're not a virgin and that I had the honor of being your first."

Winna laughed. "I guess this isn't going to be a serious conversation—let's forget it." She reached across the table and gave his beard a tug.

After dinner, Winna reminded John that she would be going down the mountain early, before it got too late. They cleaned up the kitchen and he poured her another glass of wine.

"Sorry, I don't want another drink. I'll make some tea," she said. "You get settled and I'll join you in a minute."

John took a seat on the sofa with a view of the mountain. It was dusk and clouds had moved in—the perfect set-up for a spectacular sunset. Soon, Winna joined him. She put her tea mug on the table and leaned into his arms for a kiss. His kiss, his arms around her, made her feel safe and loved, or was it his desire for her that felt so good? She didn't care.

"Stay where you are," she said. "I'll be right back."

"Use mine—it's closer," he said, and she headed toward his bedroom.

On her way to the bathroom, she noticed how nicely he had made the bed and the glow from the impending sunset coming in through the window. She liked that John was tidy in his habits. As she passed his dresser, she saw a small wooden box and stopped to look. It wasn't there after their picnic—not that she'd noticed.

She went to the bathroom and while washing her hands at the sink, she took a look at herself in the mirror. Pleased with what she saw, she realized that, except for the seventies when she'd worn her hair long, she really hadn't changed her basic short style since high school. Now the hair was streaked with silver and waved gently around her face. Her skin was plump and healthy looking without obvious wrinkles. Her large dark eyes stared back at her and she smiled at herself. She was still a pretty woman and her lover was waiting for her in the living room.

On her way back to John, she looked again at the little box on his dresser. It was carved rather crudely as if handmade. She wondered if John had made it. Curious, wondering what kinds of things John kept there, she picked it up. Did he save buttons while they waited to be sewn back on and safety pins? Opening the hinged lid, she saw a collection of old coins and keys and there on top, as if it had been waiting forty-three years for her, was her emerald ring. The ring her grandmother had bought her when she was fifteen. The ring she had lost and had mourned. Her heart beating fast, she picked it up. Tears came as the dark emerald caught the rays of the setting sun.

"Hey, Winna, what's taking so long?" John called from the living room.

Quickly, she put the ring back and closed the box. Why was her ring in this box? Had she somehow dropped it in his car way back then? Had he stolen it from the kitchen or the bathroom counter in her old house? Even as a girl, she never took her rings off except when she did the dishes or was going to clean them.

"I'm coming," she called. Her whole body burning, she decided not to confront John then. Frightened, she wanted to get away.

Hoping she seemed like her normal self, Winna returned to the living room. "I'm sorry, John, but I'm just not feeling well. I must go home. I'm so sorry."

"Me too," he said. "What's the matter?"

"A lot of stomach upset. Maybe I'm not as well as I thought—or maybe it was the way you fry trout." She had to make a joke.

He didn't laugh, but stood up, his expression troubled. Winna called her dogs and grabbed her handbag. He reached for her and she pulled away.

"I may have a bug of some kind and believe me, you don't want it," she said, heading for the door.

John stood in the doorway frowning, watching her go. He looked worried, or was it anger? The dogs jumped into the back seat. Winna hopped inside, turned the key in the ignition, and backed out of the driveway to the dirt road.

THE CHURCH HAD been there since before she was born, but Winna had never been inside. Shafts of colored light from the windows lit the nave. She had not slept well and after breakfast, hoping to clear her head, had gone for a walk. Passing through a little park, she found the church, tried the door, and found that it was open. She moved to the front of the nave and knelt in the shadows near the altar rail.

Why had John kept her ring all this time? She must have told him that she lost it. She remembered looking everywhere, crying because she couldn't find it, hiding her hand from her grandmother until she went away to college.

She'd spent the last night drifting in and out of sleep with John holding her in her dreams—a stranger with a body she knew like her own. When she awoke before sunrise, she got up and sat in the parlor with the dogs. Their warm silky bodies comforted her, their brown eyes gazing openly, honestly. No human being, except for Isabelle, had ever looked at her like that. She made coffee and relived her horrible discovery. What did it mean? Why did it terrify her? She shivered, wondering whom, besides Emily, she could really trust. Then she remembered Dougherty's warning.

Winna sat in silence in the comforting shadows of the nave, her questions holding her for a long time. Kneeling, her hands fell on the back of the pew and she bowed her head. Feeling utterly alone, she waited, taking in the quiet, calming her mind so that she could think. She had already tried to make sense of everything: the break-ins, the accidents, the poison, and now the discovery of her ring. Nothing seemed connected. *This isn't helping*, she thought. She took a deep breath and let it go. *It's too big* for me. In the calm that followed, she knew there was one other person she had to trust.

The sound of the church door opening, followed by footsteps on the terra cotta tiles, informed her that she was no longer alone. She crossed herself and stood to go. As she turned toward the door, she saw Seth slide into a pew and bury his head in his hands. She hoped he hadn't recognized her and left quietly by the side door.

MORNING DAWNED COOL, almost like a fall morning in New Hampshire, with bright sunshine and a cloudless sky. The day after she had called her friend, Winna drove out to Kate's. She'd been invited to go riding. They saddled up and rode north toward the Book Cliffs hoping to visit some of their old haunts. Kate rode like she was part of the horse. Winna tried to remember how to sit in a saddle. She had not been on a horse in years.

"You're going to be sore," Kate warned as they rode side by side.

"I know." Winna grinned at her friend, tipping her hat as they approached a field of ripening cantaloupes.

"Remember? We used to steal these," Kate said, gesturing toward rows of thirsty vines.

"Nothing like a stolen melon ripe and warm from the field," Winna said. "Where are you taking me?"

"The ghost ranch is really old now—everything has leaned or fallen. You have to see it. We'll have lunch there."

"I can't thank you enough—Kate—I—" Suddenly, Winna could not go on without tears. "I'm sorry, but I'm—"

Kate looked concerned. "What's wrong, Winna? Nothing new, I hope."

"I'm just happy to be here with you," she said, regaining her composure.

Kate looked at her friend and smiled. "Same here, honey."

They rode on in silence, stopping now and then for Winna to take pictures of the barren landscape: a dry stream bed's baked mud curls, golden tufts of grass against blue sage, and her friend smiling at her under a Stetson. Finding the mare's spotted rump especially photogenic, she slowed and rode behind Kate's Appaloosa.

The remains of the old corral still stood beside the skeleton of a tree and a dried-up well circled in rocks. The farmhouse, battered by prevailing winds, listed toward the cliffs, its porch rails cracked and broken. At noon, the scene was an abstraction in sunlight and black shadows. Winna swung down off her horse and headed for the house.

"Don't try to go in there," Kate called.

Winna waved her off and poked her head through a broken window. The house looked familiar except that the walls now leaned in divergent angles and the pine board floors looked perfect for a fun house. Winna caught her breath as a stunning image came into view. She looked at the placement of the sun in the sky and called to her friend.

"After lunch I'll need some time and my tripod."

Finding shade against the rear of the house, Winna helped with the picnic things. They ate the lunch Kate had packed and drank chilled water. Kate shared her news: her daughter wanted her to babysit and Kate would be in Denver for a couple of weeks. Briefly, they fell into silence.

"Something's wrong, Winna. Are you going to tell me?"

Kate had opened the faucet and Winna's story poured out. Her words came in a flood filled with attendant emotions. She ended with a question. "What's going on? Is John behind all this?"

"Winna, I'm breaking a confidence by telling you this—but John is in financial trouble."

Winna's heart sank, but she said nothing.

"Thanks to Jim, the company is okay, but John's personal finances are a shambles. As to his obsession with you, that's old news. When he lost you, I guess he couldn't part with the ring—still can't."

"Why are his finances in trouble? Is he gambling?"

Kate looked at her blankly. "I really don't know. Jim won't tell me much, just that he's worried about him—says John's thinking about selling his house."

"He must be in some kind of trouble. Maybe that's why he's asked me to marry him. I'm rather wealthy now, but what does John gain by helping me to my death? I just don't buy it."

Kate gave her friend a questioning look. "Maybe somewhere mixed up with his obsession is rage—maybe he wants revenge because you broke his heart."

Winna shook her head. "That was so long ago—unless he's insane. So you think he would try to poison me?"

Kate shook her head. "No—I can't think that of him."

"It seems to me that if I were plotting this crime, I'd marry the wealthy divorcée, then, once the sex gets boring, arrange an accident."

Kate laughed. "If you keep seeing him, you are nuts."

Feeling a bit more enlightened, though heartbroken and astonished, she sat with Kate in the shade for an hour talking about her decision to keep both houses, her connections in the East, and how she wanted to spend more time with her daughter and grandchild. Kate was pleased to know she'd have her friend close by.

Winna went to collect her tripod. "I promise—it won't take me more than half an hour to get the picture I want."

Returning to the window, she changed lenses and shot, capturing abstract angles in the foreground, on through an open door to an adjoining room and an old rocking chair backlit by the radiant light of a window. As she worked, the tears gathered and she tried to laugh off the thought that the lonely rocking chair could possibly stand as the symbol of her loveless future.

39

CHLOE WAITED IN her garden, a picture of loveliness lounging on the garden bench in the shade with a wild display of black-eyed Susans at her feet. She waved when Winna drove up and walked briskly toward her sister's new car—a bright blue Dodge Durango.

Emily popped out of the passenger seat. "Aunt Chloe, you sit up front with Mom," she called, jumping into the back seat with the dogs.

Chloe gave the car a quick look. "You finally broke down and bought a new car—it's kinda inelegant and rugged for an old lady though."

Winna smiled in recognition of the truth. "If I'm going to compete with Ansel Adams and William Henry Jackson, I'd better be able to get around off road."

"They probably rode mules," Chloe said, fastening her seat belt.

Winna had arranged to meet Lloyd Collins at the entrance to Unaweep Canyon. He was the man who had found her father's body. She had invited Emily and Chloe to come along. Both had said that they wanted to see the place where Henry Grumman had died. Cutting through the desert landscape, she drove south out of town toward Whitewater.

Emily leaned close. "Aunt Chloe, I finally got to meet Todd at the hospital. How's married life?"

"Things are going well. Todd's my favorite husband, so far."

"He's really good looking. When did you meet him?"

"The year before Dad died. It was love at first sight for both of us. Juno says we knew each other in a past life."

"Cool," Emily said. "I've always wondered about that kind of thing. Back there—in the other life—was he a man and you a woman or vice versa?"

"Hell, I don't know, we could have been two butterflies. My sense of it is that he was man and I was woman."

"I agree," Winna said. "You are both so overwhelmingly male and female that I'm sure a few centuries couldn't change that."

"When am I going to spend some time with this overwhelmingly manly man?"

"Soon, Emily, soon. I should cook dinner for all of us—or something—I've been painting like a mad woman. Speaking of mad women—Winna, when are you going to give me a key to the house? You changed the locks—again."

"Yep, I did and I'm not giving out any keys until we know who was breaking in."

"So you suspect me?" Chloe sounded offended.

"No. I'm just following advice."

"Whose?"

"The police."

"Don't worry, Chloe, she hasn't given me a key either," Emily lied.

Whitewater and the mouth of Unaweep Canyon were only fifteen miles south of Grand Junction. Anxious about her sister's feelings—she supposed Chloe was sulking—Winna looked at her watch. They would be on time. She turned right onto State Road 141.

"We're looking for a signpost for 31 4/10 Road. Keep an eye out for Collins. He'll be on the left."

After about a mile, they saw a brown Range Rover waiting for them in the turnoff to a dirt road. Winna pulled up beside him and rolled down her window.

"Hello," she called to the young man she assumed was Lloyd Collins.

"Do you want to ride with me or follow?" he asked.

"I'll follow."

He backed out and turned left on 141, the road that ran through the canyon's green fields where cattle and horses grazed, farmsteads and fences, a rancher's paradise with blue mountain vistas. As they moved south, the canyon walls changed from gray Precambrian rock to sandstone cliffs and mesas. The earth turned red, and green groves of cottonwoods gathered along the streambed.

Winna saw Collins's brake lights go on as he slowed and turned left onto a dirt road. Dust from the Rover poured over Winna's SUV. They put up the windows as the road grew steep and rocky. Winna slowed down and shifted into four-wheel drive.

"Hold on, this is steep!" Winna called out to her passengers as the road narrowed, forcing her to drive very near the edge of a deep ravine. For what seemed a very long time, they bumped along the rutted road wondering if this had been a good idea.

Lloyd Collins's Range Rover stopped. Winna pulled up behind him on the road high above a dry streambed. The women got out of the car in silence and walked to greet their guide.

Following handshakes, he said, "We're on the road where the car was found."

"Right here," Chloe said.

"I don't know. I wasn't here when they found it, but if you look way down there to that streambed, you'll see where we're going. I was hiking down there."

Winna looked at the winding road. "I don't know why he took this road. When he drove me here, the road he took was in much better condition. I'm surprised that Dad was able to get his car up here—it's really steep and rough."

"He had to push it hard to make it this far," Collins said. "That's probably why the engine blew and the car caught on fire."

"What on earth was he thinking?" Emily said.

Chloe knew the answer. "He knew it was time to die and came up here to be in nature."

"Like an old Indian wandering off alone?" Emily looked skeptical.

"Yes. Those really connected with nature—"

Emily interrupted. "Why didn't he just sit here and wait for death to come instead of falling off the cliff?"

Winna was not in the mood for an argument. "We can't know the answers to these questions and never will. So let's not speculate."

Collins asked if they would like to go down to the place where he found Henry Grumman's body. They returned to the cars and continued up before the road turned on itself and went downhill.

After descending for a while through the canyon where the streambed ran, the Range Rover came to a stop and the driver's door swung open. Feeling queasy, Winna pulled up behind and they all got out.

"Follow me," Collins said as he prepared to walk down a slope to the streambed. "Does anyone need a hand?"

"Thanks," Winna said as she took his arm.

Emily, in hiking boots, and Chloe, in flip-flops, scrambled down on their own. He led them across the streambed toward a rock slide.

"He was there," he said, pointing. Coming closer to a large boulder that had fallen and diverted the stream, he stopped. "Behind there."

"How on earth did you see him?" Winna asked.

"Just luck—how much detail do you want?" Collins looked uncomfortable.

"I don't want any detail," Chloe snapped. "This doesn't look right. It's not what Daddy—what he—" She backed off, sobbing, and headed back up to the car.

"Excuse my aunt," Emily said to their guide. "She's not upset with you, Lloyd. How are you doing, Mom?"

"I'm okay," Winna said, looking at Collins. "I do want details. Please tell me."

"Are you sure?" he asked, looking concerned.

"I'm sure."

"I was walking upstream with my dog. He found the body and brought out a bone."

"My God, that must have been terrible for you—finding him," Winna said. "It's why I didn't search. It's like my nightmare, Emily," she said, moving into her daughter's arms.

Collins looked down at his boots. "It's something I can't forget. I'm happy I was able to put an end to your search. It was in the papers so I guessed who he was," he said, his voice wavering.

Winna took his hand. "Thank you, Lloyd. Now, will you two give me just a few moments here alone?"

Collins and Emily withdrew and headed back to the cars. Winna sat down on a nearby stone. "Dad—Daddy, I'm sorry," she whispered. "I don't think you even noticed, but I neglected you." She looked around and, seeing some weathered wood, picked it up. She found tufts of tall grass growing near the streambed and, with that, lashed two small pieces of wood together to make a cross. Placing the cross inside the enclosure where her father's body had lain, Winna prayed for the deliverance of his soul.

40

WINNA THOUGHT BACK to the morning after she had found the ring. John had called to check on her health. Trying to sound normal, truthful, she had said that she was ill. When he asked for details, she led him to believe that she had tried to go out too soon after her release from the hospital. He offered to come for a visit and she had panicked.

"I hate having company when I'm ill—I just want to hibernate. Please understand."

He'd called that night to check on her and again the following afternoon. Winna did her best to sound under the weather. She was self-conscious about going out of the house or into the garden where he might see her. Admitting to herself that she trusted no one, she had told Seth not to come to work. After a couple of days, she concluded that she had painted herself into a corner. She called John.

"I'm much better," she said, "but I haven't been honest with you."

Silence.

"It's hard to explain, but I've hit a wall. I'm unsure."

"About what?"

"Us."

Silence.

"This is hard, John. I'm terribly fond of you, but I'm not ready to accept what you are offering. I—I can't see you anymore."

"This is sudden. What's happened? I can't believe you are dumping me again."

"It's me—not you. My life—all this—has overwhelmed me. I'm sorry, but after all that has happened I hope you will understand."

Following John's attempts to reason and bargain with her, she managed to say goodbye with a finality that she hoped was convincing. She put down the phone and cried. The next day she called Seth and asked if he could show up on Saturday. She needed help with the yard sale they had scheduled for the following weekend.

ON SATURDAY MORNING, Emily arranged for a sitter to watch Isabelle and arrived at the kitchen door before Seth. The dogs barked wildly—music to Winna's ears. Emily hugged her mother and admonished the dogs for leaping on her.

"You should teach them better manners, Mom."

"I should," she said, "but will I?"

Emily handed her an envelope from the drugstore. "Here, I brought you a set of the pictures I took at Hanging Lake. I think I got some great shots and want a pro to have a look at them."

Before Winna had a chance to thank her, the dogs broke into another barking frenzy. Chloe opened the unlocked door and they greeted her with jumps, kisses, and little cries of pleasure.

"What a welcome," she said. "I love it. They are so cute, Winna. They really like me."

"They like everybody," Emily said.

"The muscles will be here soon." Winna was delighted that her workforce had shown up on time. "First, we'll look through boxes and price things. Look what I bought. We get to play store." She held up a handful of string tags and a package of stickers. "We can start with the boxes in the front hall. There are boxes in almost every room. Once they're priced, they'll go out to the garage."

"Price everything low, right?" Emily asked.

"Not too low," Chloe countered.

Luke and Leia loudly announced Seth's arrival at the kitchen door. After greetings, Winna put everyone to work. The women bickered about prices and tagged items for sale, Seth carried old furniture from the attic and boxes into the garage where he had set up temporary shelves and tables for display. In one of the boxes, Winna found the old apple peeler and took it to her kitchen. The dogs followed. Leia had something dangling from her mouth.

"Sit, Leia," she commanded. Leia obeyed, offering up what looked like a rhinestone choker. "Where did you find this? Lord, help me—I hope it's not diamonds." Just in case, she fastened it around her neck.

THAT NIGHT AFTER everyone had gone home, Winna looked at Emily's pictures of Hanging Lake. She smiled at some of the more artful shots of the waterfalls. Emily had captured close-ups of dragonflies and some wonderful shots of Hugh as he struggled up the trail with Isabelle asleep in the backpack. She smiled at the memory, then looked again at all the photos including the ones she took of Emily, Hugh, and the baby at the sidewalk cafe. She hadn't gotten the shot she wanted.

She put the pictures away, checked the doors, and made herself a light supper. Pouring a glass of wine, she picked up her senior class yearbook, which she had finally stumbled upon that day as she was going through boxes for the yard sale. Thumbing through it, she found Maggie's picture first. Her old friend smiled at her over a shoulder, blonde curls tumbling down her back. Winna kissed the image and filled up with tears. She wondered what Maggie's life had been like as John's wife. Was he good to her? Johnny Hodell looked out from the next page, dated by his crew cut. Winna knew that face lit by moonlight, the smile that summoned her into his arms, the churlish twist of his lips as he pushed her away with cruel words. Remembering who they were back then, she shuddered. A few pages back, Winna smiled at her young self, the large eyes exaggerated by her pixie haircut. Her first reaction to that fresh young face was sadness mixed with judgment against a fool. She looked again with the eyes of her heart. *I needed love.*

She flipped through the rest of the yearbook looking at the faces of lower classmen, remembering few. She found Kate, as she looked then, posing without a smile under the neatly trimmed bangs of her pageboy. Near the end of the pages reserved for high school juniors, she came across the name Seth Armstrong Taylor and searched the group picture to see if she could find his face. He was there, the tallest boy in the back row, looking bored. Winna hadn't known him then.

The dogs began to bark and Winna went to the window. It was dark but headlights glared at the end of the driveway. Someone had pulled in. She drew away from the window and checked the lock on the kitchen door, then hurried to the unlit dining room and stood at the window. In the dark, she couldn't identify the car. Whoever it was backed out and drove away in the opposite direction. The driver was simply turning the car around; Winna let out a long sigh of relief.

PEOPLE FROM ALL over town came to look at the venerable old house, the garden, and the Grumman family's castoffs. Winna had planned to hold the sale on both Saturday and Sunday, but so little remained by late Saturday afternoon that she decided she would take the rest to the Salvation Army. Emily, Chloe, Todd, Hugh, and Seth helped — the women with sales and the men with loading large pieces of furniture into shoppers' cars and trucks. While they waited for customers, the guys watched baseball on the TV they had set up in the garage. Winna served sandwiches and cookies to her helpers and kept the lemonade flowing for both workers and shoppers. After lunch, the men broke out the beer.

During breaks between customers, Chloe, Winna, and Emily sat on the verandah.

"What did you think of my pictures, Mom?" Emily said with a proud smile.

"They were great — let me get them. I'll show you my favorites." Winna disappeared into the house and reappeared with the envelope in her hand.

"Pass them down to me," Chloe urged.

Prints in hand, Winna went through her daughter's images, giving praise and some light critique. "You have talent. Would you like to come with me on my next photo shoot? I could even teach you the darkroom."

"Look who's here," Chloe said, pointing toward the driveway.

John Hodell's Mercedes convertible, top down, pulled up the drive and parked. Aware of their breakup, Emily nudged her mother's side with her elbow. Winna put the pictures down.

"Why is he parking there?" Emily said.

"I don't know," she said. "Maybe he feels entitled."

He got out of his car and looked around, as if he were looking for someone, then turned and moved toward the tables loaded with merchandise spread out in the sun. Winna decided it would be civilized to greet him. She walked across the verandah and down the front steps.

"Hello, John," she said, approaching a table full of old games. "Are you looking for anything special?"

He smiled. "I'm looking for you," he said. "I miss you, Winna."

"Now is not the best time to talk," she said, glancing down at her bare feet, surprised to see she had walked off and left her sandals behind.

"When is the best time?" He looked hurt.

"Good question. Maybe we could have lunch sometime," she said, backing away, disappointed with herself. Why had she opened that door?

"If that's what you want." He glanced toward the garage and saw Hugh, Todd, and Seth, then frowned at Winna before he headed off to join them. Looking back over his shoulder, he called, "You'll hear from me."

To Winna, it sounded like a threat.

41

AFTER SOME RESEARCH on the original colors of the walls, Winna ordered paint and hired a man to help Seth with the work. With so many large rooms to paint, Seth estimated they would be at it for at least a month.

Winna was glad her bedroom was finished. She could go there, close the door, open the windows, and not smell paint. Using her memories and the book on garden design Seth had loaned her, she set up a table in her room and began to work on plans for the rose garden. She hoped to start planting by mid-September. Her sister had promised to help her with the selection of roses and perennials.

Chloe was the real gardener in the family, but she had called that morning to say she couldn't come. Todd was away in Denver and a leak had flooded her kitchen. She had to be home when the plumber came. Winna would have to wait for her help.

She walked past the hall table on her way to find Seth and saw the stack of pictures Emily had taken, her favorite one of the waterfall on top. She looked at it again and picked up the phone to call Emily.

"Honey, can you bring the negatives of your pictures? I've got the darkroom up and running and want to print a couple of these shots for you—I love the one of Hugh with the baby on his back and that one of the waterfall—both would look great enlarged and framed."

Emily sounded delighted and said she would bring them by tomorrow on her way to drop off her column at the newspaper.

Winna found Seth in the front hall on a tall ladder. "Chloe can't come by and help me with garden plans today. Can you stay for dinner tonight? I'm going to proceed on my own and should have something to show you."

"Sorry, I'm dining with the mayor."

Winna laughed. "Look. I'm sorry—I make too many demands on your time," she said. "You have a right to say that you just want to go home and watch TV tonight."

"I don't want to go home and watch TV. I'd rather spend my Saturday night having a burger and looking at garden plans with you."

"I can do better than a burger."

OVER STEAKS, BAKED potatoes, salad, and beers in the kitchen, Winna remembered that she had found Seth's picture in the 1956 *Tiger*. She retrieved the yearbook from the counter. "I found you in here—have a look," she said, handing him the book.

With the enthusiasm of a kid on his way to the principal's office, Seth took the book and began to thumb through.

"Let me help you find it," she said, impatiently turning to the marked page. "There you are—with all the rest of the T's."

"I look like a hick," he said. "I'm glad those days are over. I hated school."

"Why?"

He leaned back in his chair and rolled his eyes. "I was smarter than my teachers. At least that's what I thought." He paused and put down his knife and fork. "Look, Winna, there's something I'd like to tell you, but I'm wondering whether or not I should."

"I can keep a secret."

"No, it's not a secret. It's just that I haven't leveled with you—we haven't really talked." He looked troubled. "Hell, I might as well tell you—I was a very good friend of your dad's. The last five years of his life, I spent a lot of time with him."

Winna was astonished. "Really? Why didn't you tell me?" she asked.

"I figured I had," he said, looking a bit sheepish. "We spoke at the funeral and I mentioned it then. Maybe it didn't register."

She tried to remember. "I wasn't myself that day. I don't remember."

"When you never brought it up again, I figured you didn't like the idea, or something." He shook his head. "You probably don't know it, but you Grummans have the rep around this town for being upper crust—not quite approachable by the common man."

"You're kidding me," she said, punching his arm. "I love the idea of you and Daddy being friends. How did you know him?"

"He hired me to do some work around here. I'd be outside clipping the hedge or weeding and he'd come out and follow me around wanting to talk. I figured he was lonely." He smiled fondly at the memory. "I got a kick out of him and his old jokes. As the years passed, I came to like him way better than I liked my own dad. We'd watch sports on TV and go to college games together. Now and then, we'd go fishing. Sometimes he'd get groceries and I'd cook for him. He had me wash and polish his old car every week. I was really sad when he disappeared and volunteered to look for him. No one knew where to begin. They started looking around town, then in the foothills to the Book Cliffs, finally moving on to Pinyon Mesa. I went searching with them every day for as long as they searched and when they gave up, I went searching alone."

"I neglected him terribly," Winna said, ashamed that a perfect stranger—to her at least—had taken on her responsibility. "I appreciate you doing what I should have done. I'll tell you all about it someday."

"I missed him so much that sometimes I'd come over here and work in the garden or just sit on the back porch. I mowed the lawn now and then and even edged the rose beds one day. I love the idea of that garden."

"I wondered who had been working in the rose garden," she said, remembering the day she first arrived.

"I knew he had daughters and I asked him about you girls, but he made excuses for why he didn't see you. He said he hadn't been a good father. He seemed sad about that."

Seth's words came like an apology from the grave and she burst into tears. She did not feel comfortable sobbing in front of Seth. The urge to run and hide propelled her to her feet.

Seth grabbed her hand. "It's okay, Winna. You can cry," he said, standing, pulling her into his arms.

Winna gave in to an embrace that felt like that of a friend or brother. When they parted, she held on just long enough to place a kiss on the back of his hand.

"You don't know what this means," she said, stopping to take hold of her trembling voice. "Please tell me about him. Can you believe—I didn't know him?"

As Seth told his stories, Winna felt her weight lighten. Her questions for Seth and his answers went on for hours. They forgot the garden plan, broke out the tequila and some limes. As the tequila disappeared, their exchange became a wake, a goodbye party with laughter and tears. Henry Grumman finally had a son.

At last, Seth was able to talk with someone about his grief.

And, at last, Winna felt hers.

Seth was too drunk to drive home. Winna led him to bed in Edwin's room upstairs. She went to her room feeling almost giddy with joy. By three, she was asleep.

The next morning was a Sunday, the painter's day off. The dogs insisted on being let out at about ten, but as soon as they had done their business, Winna went back to sleep.

The smell of bacon frying woke her. She put on her robe and went down to the kitchen. Seth was making breakfast, sipping coffee from a large mug. Winna poured herself a cup.

"Good morning," she yawned.

"It's just after noon and breakfast is almost ready."

"We had a party last night," she said, doctoring her coffee with cream and sugar.

"We sure enough did."

Winna suddenly remembered. "Say, I saw you the other morning at the little Catholic church on the other side of the park. Do you go to church?"

"Pretty often. I wasn't good at school, but I'm good at church."

"Me too." Winna remembered something else she had forgotten to ask. "Have the police gotten in touch with you?"

"Yes," he said, turning to look over his shoulder. "Long time ago. I think they've gotten in touch with everyone you know, Winna."

"They made me give them the names of everyone I'm in contact with. Did you get a grilling?"

"I wouldn't call it that. They got my fingerprints. The cops asked questions. I told them I'd been arrested for drunk driving about fifteen years ago."

"I'm sorry, Seth," she said. "I hope it wasn't too awful."

"No, they were doing their job. They also had me show them where I had thrown out what was left of the broken stair rail. They took all that."

"I've heard back about that. According to Lieutenant Dougherty, the stairs and the stair rail had been tampered with. The police have decided that my fall was not an accident."

"When did you hear that?" Seth asked, looking concerned.

"On Friday, I think. The police believe someone wants me dead. So far he has tried twice, maybe three times."

Seth had no time to respond. Someone was at the door. Winna and the barking dogs went to answer.

Emily walked into the kitchen, out of breath, with an envelope in her hand. She looked at her mother in her robe and Seth standing at the stove with a spatula in hand.

"Holy shit!" she said, looking dizzy.

"Emily, it's not what it looks like. Seth and I were—"

"You're both adults," she said, looking like she wanted to run. "I've got the negatives you wanted—"

"Sit down a minute and I'll explain—it's a wonderful story."

42

WHILE ENLARGING SEVERAL pictures for Emily to frame, Winna found the negatives to the shots she had taken at the sidewalk café in Glenwood Springs. Looking closely, she hoped to find one that she could put in a little frame she'd rescued from the attic. She had loved the light and the way her daughter and son-in-law were grouped with the baby. There were several and, in some, the background really interfered with the shot—a large black truck parked across the street showed up in almost every one.

Damning the presence of the truck, she realized that she had seen that truck before—or one like it. She looked again, and among the pedestrians on the street, she saw a tall man coming out of a store. He wore a cowboy hat and what looked like a buckskin coat. She decided to enlarge the image. The man, who looked a lot like Todd, was looking toward the truck and, in another shot, was headed toward it. Winna enlarged the image again, enough to see that the man had just left ABC Pawn Brokers and Jewelers.

If that was Todd, why was he at a pawnshop in Glenwood Springs? If it was Todd, why hadn't he noticed them at the sidewalk café just across the street? The street was wide and Winna admitted that she hadn't noticed him either. That could be a weird coincidence or her imagination was working overtime. She had to force herself not to call Todd and ask if he was in Glenwood Springs last week. Instead, she called Emily, who most emphatically suggested a visit to ABC Pawn Brokers and Jewelers.

IN A STATE of high excitement, Winna, with Emily in the passenger seat, parked her car in downtown Glenwood Springs. They entered the small storefront and immediately found themselves in familiar surroundings: a long narrow room, windowless on both sides, under an embossed tin ceiling painted white, just like so many of the old stores on Main Street in Grand Junction. Shelves with TV sets, VCRs, record players, cameras, sets of china, vases, and musical instruments (mostly guitars) ran along the walls above long glass display cases full of watches, jewelry, and coins. Guns were artfully displayed on racks under the heads of antlered deer and elk. All these things had belonged to people who needed to raise cash. Winna felt as if she was intruding on other people's secret misfortunes. She'd never been in a pawnshop before.

Emily was already at work, scanning the jewelry cases, looking for something familiar. She motioned for her mother to come. "You'd better get to work, Mom. I'm not sure I know what to look for."

Side by side, they came to a shelf full of cameos and brooches. Next, they looked at dozens of rings. Just then, a man, the owner perhaps, approached from behind the counter. "Need some help, ladies?"

"I'm just wild about antique jewelry," Winna blurted, wondering if she sounded as deceitful as she felt.

"We have lots of that. You want a ring or what?"

"Mom," Emily said. "Look at these earrings." She pointed to a pair of antique earrings with pale aqua stones.

Winna gasped. "Those are beautiful." She recognized them as the zircon earrings from Juliana's jewelry box. "These here," she said, pointing for the benefit of the salesman, "what stone are they? It looks like zircons. What are you asking for these?"

"They came in just last week and I'll have to get three hundred for them."

"Ah, that much? You must think they are real. Do you have any diamonds—real ones?"

He took them to a case filled with diamond jewelry and, right away, she spotted the small diamond and pearl sunburst that Juliana used to pin to her suit collars and sometimes her felt hats. She jabbed Emily with one elbow and pointed. "I like that one." She looked up at the man and smiled. "We won't take up any more of your time today. Thanks for the help." She grabbed Emily by the arm and they headed for the door.

"What are you going to do, Mom?"

"We are going to the police station and have them call Lieutenant Dougherty. They need to search Chloe's house. Oh, my God, poor Chloe."

43

THE CRYSTAL CAFÉ would not be crowded on a Tuesday afternoon. Winna had agreed to meet John there at one-thirty following the rush. They sat in a booth at the back. Todd Cody's arrest and arraignment was their opening topic. John expressed his surprise and sadness. He had obviously misjudged one of his foremen.

Winna had been in court that morning, with Chloe at her side. They'd sat in the front row of the gallery behind the prosecution table. Todd stood beside his lawyer dressed in a dark business suit. He looked ominously innocent, his blond curls playing over and under his ears like a child's. He kept his eyes forward. Not once did he turn his head to the right and look at his wife and sister-in-law.

The charge against him read felony burglary. The police had found boxes full of things from the house on Seventh Street in a crawl space at Chloe's house.

When asked about the robbery, Todd pleaded "not guilty." After a brief battle of words between the two lawyers, bail was denied and the defendant was remanded to custody. Chloe sobbed as Todd was led away in handcuffs—so traumatized that Winna cried with her.

Learning that Todd was her thief was not the last surprise. After his arrest, the police had entered his fingerprints into the

FBI fingerprint database and came up with someone named Owen Robert Healey, wanted in Oklahoma City.

"He's been a fugitive for six years," Lieutenant Dougherty had said as Chloe and Winna sat with him in the kitchen at the house on Seventh Street.

"A fugitive from what," Chloe said, dabbing at red eyes with a tissue. She had stayed with Winna ever since Todd had been arrested, sleeping in Poppa Ed's old bedroom.

"He's a suspect in a bank robbery in Oklahoma City—a policeman was killed. His prints were on file from ten years ago, when he was in prison for a string of robberies. He's also been jailed for selling cocaine."

Chloe could contain herself no longer. "I can't believe all this. He was so sweet with me. It's just impossible for me to understand."

Winna took her hand. "For me too—we were all fond of him, honey."

"We are also looking into the possibility that he might have been the one who put the arsenic in your scotch," Dougherty said. "So far the evidence is all circumstantial."

Chloe leapt up from her chair and ran from the room.

"She feels responsible," Winna said. "I feel so bad for her."

He looked away. "It's tough all around, Mrs. Jessup." He stood up, retrieving his briefcase from the kitchen table. "It's going to be a lot harder to prove attempted murder, but we will do our best. I know the DA wants to proceed."

WINNA HAD BEEN nervous about meeting John for lunch but thought it important that she did. Greeting him with reserve, she sympathized with him for not suspecting Todd.

"We were all fooled—especially poor Chloe. She is deeply hurt and deeply pissed. I'm glad they've got him in jail."

"Let's hope he is extradited to Oklahoma. Actually, Chloe is one lucky gal—she was also in danger," John said.

"Chloe's not feeling lucky. I've never seen anyone in so much pain. According to Lieutenant Dougherty, Todd—rather, Owen what's-his-name—has been in prison for selling drugs and burglary charges. His father is in jail and his mother was a prostitute who was murdered some twenty years ago."

John shook his head in disbelief. "A real menace disguised as a good ol' boy."

"A cute good ol' boy. There's more. The police have looked at what was left of the stair rail that caused my fall. Dougherty says it had been tampered with and then repainted. There were two other attempts on my life. But can we prove it was Todd?"

John was silent a moment. "It could be hard—this isn't easy for me to take in."

"He's not the only menace in disguise." Winna shot an accusing look at John.

John shifted his weight. "What's that supposed to mean?"

Staring at her hands, she said nothing for a moment. She looked up. "I found my old emerald ring on your dresser."

John paled, then diverted his eyes. "That last night—up at the house?"

"Yes, when I went through to your bathroom. What's that about, John? My ring—did you steal it?"

"I doubt you'd understand."

"Try me. I can be very understanding."

"It's simple, really." John looked down. "I wanted you. I wanted the baby," he paused and looked her hard in the eye. "How could you do that without even telling me—it was my only child."

Winna winced as if he had struck her.

John was angry. "I stole your ring because I had nothing left of you."

"I couldn't have told you first. My mother didn't tell me why we were going to Denver. What we did was an act of desperation. I know I hurt you terribly. You don't know how long I've grieved over this."

Suddenly out of words, Winna looked down at her hands and shook her head.

"John, we aren't kids anymore. I'd fallen in love with you again. Why didn't you tell me how you felt? Why didn't you return the ring?"

"I probably would have—once it occurred to me. Now it's too late."

"Seeing that ring again made me afraid of you."

"Afraid of me?"

"Yes, someone put arsenic in my scotch."

"I'm sorry. You can't imagine how sorry I am. You found the ring at a bad time—during this nightmare you've been going through."

"There's nothing we can do about that."

"Not now—not yet," he said. "You'll have your ring tomorrow. I'm a patient man, Winna. I love you—always have, always will."

ONCE AGAIN, THE old kitchen on Seventh Street was cluttered with boxes. The police had returned Todd's stash to the house. Anxious to have a look, Winna, Chloe, and Emily gathered in the morning to sort through the boxes. They found the silk rugs, the Chinese vases— much of what had been lost, including Juliana's story.

In one large cardboard box, they discovered a small wooden chest, humbly made and quite old.

"I've never seen this before," Chloe said, lifting it onto the kitchen table.

Inside, they found old photographs, a tiny diary, a pocket lexicon, a soft paperback book, and a stack of yellowed letters surrounded by a collection of small things: a lock of baby hair, a rabbit's foot, marbles, an old matchbook—the kind of things a young boy would collect and keep in a cigar box.

Winna picked up the book. "Here's the Brown chapbook. Finally, we'll get to see Whitaker's poetry." She opened the book to the title page.

"Not now," Chloe said. "I'm not wild about poetry. Look, I found some pictures."

Winna turned to her sister just as a sheet of paper fell out of the book to the floor. She picked it up. "Another poem—a work in progress maybe. It's short—listen, I'll read it."

> Truly, I know, Aladdin's Cave is here,
> In the High Desert. The great Tree of Gems
> Is rooted at this confluence—the stars,

Its fruits, are hanging as from diadems
That crown night-sprites who haunt the upper air.

No Ifrit of Arabia, no Djinn,
Dare trespass in America's free West:
Our sprites are Liberty and the Frontier.

"I think Aladdin's cave was full of treasure," Emily said.

Suddenly interested, Chloe wanted to hear the poem again. Winna read it, this time more slowly.

Chloe looked excited. "He says the cave is here—in the high desert—and he mentions a tree of gems—just like Juno said we'd find in Unaweep Canyon."

"Okay," Emily said, shaking her head in disbelief. "How about we look at the pictures you found, auntie."

Chloe looked at the top photograph on the pile she was holding. "Could this be Dolph?" Yellowed and foxed, the snapshot showed a boy about seven sitting on a swing. He was squinting in the sunshine, wearing knickers and a cap. Another picture showed a smiling young man standing against the wall of a brick building in a gown holding his graduation cap. They appeared to be the same boy at different ages.

"That must have been taken at his high school graduation," Winna said, looking over Chloe's shoulder. "That's how he looked when Gramma loved him."

She'd had it all wrong. Dolph had dark curly hair combed into well-oiled waves and he wasn't tall and thin. He looked to be average height, just the right size man for little Juliana. She could imagine them as perfect dance partners. She looked at his eyes, wishing the picture were in color.

Then it occurred to her. "I think he looks like Daddy."

Both Emily and Chloe wanted to look again and looked over Winna's shoulder.

"Yes, he does," Chloe said.

"Your grandfather was way taller, thinner," Emily said. "Poppa was built more like Whitaker. The plot thickens, but I doubt you'll ever know the truth."

They were silent a moment and, as if she knew she had spoiled the moment, Emily brightened and lifted the stack of letters into the light. "Guess who the letters are from."

"Gramma?" Chloe said.

"Whitaker's keepsakes—where on earth did Todd find this?" Winna asked.

Emily knew. "I'll bet you anything that he found it in the basement of that house he tore down."

Winna made coffee and they all sat around the kitchen table reading their grandmother's letters. They were full of Juliana's hopes and dreams for their future marriage, naïve words—sweet words that surprised the sisters.

"She wasn't always mean," Chloe said, surprised.

"Here's the letter I've been hoping to find," Winna said. She held it up and read it aloud.

Dear Dolph,

I am beside myself with worry. I can't begin to imagine what you are thinking now. As you dashed for the train, you picked up the wrong bag. Mine was so like yours, I might have done the same. I didn't even notice until I got home. The contents of your bag are safe and hiding in a trunk in the attic. Please tell me what you want me to do. These objects mean nothing to me. I cannot use them, nor do I want them. I do not need my bag back, but my things are important to me. Please send them care of Daisy.

Write soon. Tell me if you want me to ship the suitcase to Providence. Until I hear from you, be assured that all are safe with me.

I cannot tell you how sorry I am for this and for
the way I disappointed you. I should have known
better than to think for a moment that I could live
off the fruits of ill-gotten gains. I gave you hope
where there was none, for that, please forgive me.

Farewell, Juliana

Chloe sighed. "Whitaker never read that letter. He died on
the train."

"But now we know how the jewels got into Charlotte Blackleash's
trunk," Emily said, "and that Gramma must have waited to hear
back from him about her suitcase."

"There's no mention of a baby son," Winna said. "That means
Daddy wasn't born yet—doesn't it?"

Her question brought a sudden silence, then Emily said thoughtfully, "Chloe, maybe Juno can tell us?"

Chloe smiled at her niece. "I'm going to take that comment as a
near conversion."

Winna happily watched them hug. "Obviously Todd read the
letter and it confirmed what Gramma wrote—that's why I had all
those break-ins."

"How did the letter end up in this box in the basement of Mrs.
Whitaker's house on First Street?" Chloe asked.

"Think about it. If your son died, wouldn't you send for his things?"

"Of course. The letter arrived and the landlady put it among the
things she sent back to his mother."

"There is no envelope. I assume that means that his mother
opened it and read it," Winna said.

The women agreed that if they put Dolph's letters in sequence
with Juliana's letters, they would get a better picture, but until then,
they had already solved most of the mysteries.

Chloe detailed her version of what had happened. "Juliana
learns her former lover is dead. She grieves, then remembers she's
stuck with stolen property. She can't reveal that without exposing

her adultery, so she sneaks around sewing jewelry into her stash of outdated gowns."

"And who knows where else," Winna said. "You know that rhinestone choker Leia found? I took it down to Page Parsons and they said it's about fifty-five carats of high quality diamonds. We still don't know where the dog found it."

"Will it never end?" Emily said.

Chloe sighed. "I hope not. By the way, you interrupted me as I was making sense of everything. Where was I?"

"You left her sewing jewels into her gowns," Winna said.

"Yes. Then Gramma writes a story using some of the events that really happened. For instance, we never found any of the jewelry described in her story — do you suppose those pieces are in Unaweep Canyon like Juno said?"

"Who knows," Emily said, rolling her eyes.

"Don't get too excited about the jewelry. It doesn't belong to us — it's stolen and belongs to someone else's grandchildren," Winna said.

"Are you kidding?" Chloe cried. "It was meant for us. Gramma would want us to have it all."

"Hey," Emily said, "don't argue about that right now. One thing's for certain. Both of her granddaughters inherited Gramma's knack for falling in love with the wrong man."

Winna and Chloe nodded and rolled their eyes.

Luke and Leia started barking. A knock on the kitchen door followed and Seth came in. He looked like a man on a mission and would not be persuaded to sit down for a cup of coffee.

"I've thought this over carefully," he said. "It's time for me to take you to the attic. I have something to show you."

Seth led them up the front staircase, down the hall, and up the stairs to the attic. Most of the attic's contents had been cleared for the yard sale. Winna was surprised to see that Seth had left the strange bedroom tableau on the braided rug. She said nothing as he led them in that direction.

When she saw the reproduction of her and Winna's childhood bedroom shining in the light from the dormers, Chloe gasped and pulled back as if she were afraid. Winna took her hand and they followed until they stood beside the wicker beds and matching night tables with the little-girl lamps.

Seth spoke first. "I made this little scene."

Chloe was crying. "This furniture came from our house in town—before we moved to the country."

Winna looked confused. "How did you know how things were placed?"

"For some reason, I don't remember, your father and I came up here for something. He saw one of the beds and told me it had belonged to his daughters. He started looking for the rest of the furniture that went with it. He said it would make him happy to see the beds, the dresser, and little rocking chair back together again."

"Yes," Chloe said. "It's our old room." She wiped the tears from her eyes with the back of one hand.

"But the bedspreads and sheets?" Winna said.

"He looked for them," Seth said. "Did he get the right ones?"

"I don't exactly remember, but they look pretty close."

"Well, he went around looking in old chests and boxes—I could tell he was on a mission, like he was on a treasure hunt—until he found these. I helped him make the beds."

Winna sighed and shook her head. "I can't believe he did this. I found it not long after I came back. I didn't mention it to you, Chloe, because it had really upset me."

"At the time—as we were putting it all together—" Seth said, "I thought your father was kind of memorializing your childhood. He seemed earnest and single-minded as we worked. At the time, I thought he was missing you."

"He must have cared about us," Winna said.

"Maybe he cared about you. He disinherited me," Chloe said.

Seth looked at Chloe. "The last few years he was forgetful. I really think he forgot that he'd left you out of the will. The man I knew wouldn't have let that will stand. Besides, he described you to me lovingly. He didn't say, 'I love one daughter and I disinherited the other.'"

Chloe sat down on the faded pink satin bedspread. She picked up the baby doll Winna had dropped. "I remember you." She looked up at Winna and said, "Remember baby Jennie?"

"Of course," Winna said. "We all laughed at you because you loved her so much that you rejected the new doll Santa brought that Christmas. You broke that doll's shiny new heart."

"Shouldn't we dismantle this little scene?" Emily looked troubled.

"No!" Chloe tucked her doll in under the coverlet. "Let's keep it. Daddy wanted it this way."

Epilogue

1915

THE YOUNG MAN had lost count. Just the same, he wanted another Manhattan and waited eagerly for the dining car attendant to return to his table. Having passed through the miracle of Glenwood Canyon where tracks cut a narrow swath above the Colorado River, he had been on the train for several hours speeding through miles of majestic mountain scenery. The train had entered the granite walls of the Royal Gorge, narrow as a tunnel at its base, widening to a few hundred feet at its top some thousand feet above the Arkansas River.

Over the past five years, Adolph Whitaker had taken the train once a year from his university in the East to Grand Junction and back. Nature's magnificence and man's engineering wonders had always delighted him—but today his mind traveled elsewhere.

The dusky evening light masked the mountains. He could see his image reflected in the window glass. The face mustached, dark wavy hair cropped close, a grave expression he could not hide even behind his spectacles.

He had grown used to the sound of the rails and, though the train rocked side to side, he no longer heard them. The bell clanged a warning as they passed through a small town. He took out his pocket watch and flipped it open. They would be in Denver in less than two hours. Motioning the waiter to his table, he ordered another drink.

Earlier, the porter had wanted to make up his bed for the night. Whitaker had picked up the smaller of his two bags and gone to the club car. He drank alone, speaking to no one. When a couple of dandies had threatened to intrude on his solitude, he left for the dining car.

Entering the long narrow space—one aisle with tables seating four crowded to the right—he headed for a table for two on the other side. He tucked his bag under the table and pulled out the chair. Though he was not hungry, he had ordered the trout. When his waiter presented it to him with a flourish, he could not eat. The fish, with one eye fixed on him, had lain there untouched, growing cold among the peas and Denver potatoes.

Confused, tragically lost, he could not believe what had happened. The cruel disappointment from the only woman he had ever loved. Her goodbye had been a betrayal. After all he had worked for, all he had abandoned and then risked for her, she had, in one sudden breathless sentence, sent him away from her forever. She had literally fled.

The waiter appeared with a tray. He placed a white coaster on the tablecloth where he centered the Manhattan. His black hands reached to light the candle lamp and return the red rose in a silver plated budvase to its place against the window.

The cold sweaty glass already in hand, Whitaker thanked the waiter with a coin and was glad when he was gone. He sipped his drink slowly, letting its dark sweetness burn his tongue as it rolled away to his throat. He cast his eyes around the dining car, at the people seated near: a young woman alone with her back to him—her hair bobbed—a table of four that looked like a family—mother, father, and two daughters, the youngest with an absurdly large white bow at the back of her head. He could feel the liquor in his fingertips now and the white bow seemed to dance on and off the girl's head.

He downed the last few drops and absently took the cherry into his mouth. The sweetness made his stomach turn. Suddenly, alert to the feeling that someone watched, he looked behind him. Seeing nothing but diners and waiters—no faces he knew—he reached under the table for his bag and stood up to go.

The bones in his legs seemed to melt. He straightened his back and inhaled a deep breath as he carefully navigated toward the front. He wanted to return to the Pullman car and his bunk—to sleep. Nauseated and thinking a breath of fresh air would do him good, he redirected himself toward the back of the train and the observation car.

Choked with smoke and jovial travelers—mostly men and a few girls with skirts above their ankles—he moved through the crowded car bumping shoulders. Singing boisterously, everyone appeared to be in their cups.

"Pack up your troubles in your old kit-bag, and smile, smile, smile."

Avoiding eye contact, he plowed his way through.

"What's the use of worrying? It never was worthwhile, so pack up your troubles in your old kit-bag, and smile, smile, smile."

At the very end of the train, he opened the door to the observation deck and stepped out into the warm night air. Abruptly assaulted by the violent roar of steel wheels on steel tracks, he looked back through the window in the door. No one looked his way. His whole body could feel the speed, the great power of the train as it raced toward the city.

The small deck was empty. He put down his bag and, alone with his thoughts, reached for the railing to brace himself. He tried to focus on the dark landscape. Silhouettes of pines and mountain ridges edged in moonlight came into view as the train withdrew from the mountains.

The things I've done for her. He could feel the precious bag full of jewels leaning against his feet and wanted to open it. Tears wet his cheeks. The chances I've taken. What now? He thought of his future alone. After what I've done, I will have to get away—to hide in Mexico, or Europe perhaps. My crimes have made me rich, but what good is it without her? There will be no comfort for me. Sobbing, absorbed in the debacle he had made of his once promising life, he raised one hand to remove a handkerchief from his pocket. It wasn't there. *Someone might come and see me shedding tears like a woman.*

Someone had.

Unnoticed, a tall man wearing a lightweight coat had appeared just outside the door. The rush of the wind and the grinding of the train against the tracks had provided cover for his entrance. Standing in the shadows, against the back of the car, he waited.

His nose dripping, his cheeks wet with tears, Adolph Whitaker searched again for his handkerchief. The car lurched to the left. He reached out for support. The car shuddered, then lurched again as if it wanted to shake him loose—as if a hand had reached out to throw him off balance.

The railing slipped from his hand. He stumbled. Just then, two strong arms took hold from behind. He turned and glimpsed the face of a man he knew. With chilling certainty, Whitaker realized he was going to die. He knew the arms that grabbed him would push him over the side of the speeding train.

It happened so fast he had only the brief sensation of disaster, then falling, his tears suddenly stopped by the sound of his own last cry.

Edwin Grumman picked up the small black suitcase, threw it over the side, and disappeared into the crowd of happy travelers.

KAREN VORBECK WILLIAMS is the author of *My Enemy's Tears: The Witch of Northampton*, a historical novel based on the life of her eleventh great–grandmother, who was accused of witchcraft in 1675. She is a prize-winning photographer and Master Gardener living in Rumford, Rhode Island. Learn more at http://www.karenvorbeckwilliams.com/.

MORE GREAT READS
FROM BOOKTROPE

One Day in Lubbock by **Daniel Lance Wright** (Fiction) William Dillinger despises how he spent his life and has one day to find out if rekindling love can change it.

Spirit Warriors: The Concealing by **D.E.L. Connor** (Fiction) Suspenseful, romantic, and awash in Native American magic, Spirit Warriors captures the tragic enchantment of the American West—and confirms the power of friendship.

The Dead Boy's Legacy by **Cassius Shuman** (Fiction) 9-year-old Tommy McCarthy is abducted while riding his bike home from a little league game. This psychological family drama explores his family's grief while also looking at the background and motivations of his abductor.

The Long Walk Home by **Will North** (Fiction) Forty-four year-old Fiona Edwards answers her door to a tall, middle-aged man shouldering a hulking backpack—unshaven, sweat-soaked and arrestingly handsome. What neither of them knows is that their lives are about to change forever.

The Paragraph Ranch by **Kay Ellington and Barbara Brannon** (Fiction) A motley group of writers and a cast of small-town Texas characters prove that maybe you can go home again, and find love in the unlikeliest of places.

Discover more books and learn about our
new approach to publishing at **www.booktrope.com.**

Made in the USA
Middletown, DE
11 August 2015